THE ENCHANTED GARDEN

'My father doesn't seem interested. He just expects me to stay at home and carry out social duties for him. Do you think that's why he doesn't like me, Julian? Because I'm not a very good substitute for my mother? I do try to do my best, but I'm not much good at entertaining strangers. I never know what to say to them. And, somehow, Father always gives me an inferiority complex. Sometimes I think he hates me,' she said quietly.

Julian was silent for a few moments. He was too fond of Fiona and had too much respect for her intelligence to comfort her with false platitudes, and there were times when he, too, believed that her father was hostile to her. It was delicate ground and there were undercurrents which Fiona knew nothing of and about which he had no right to enlighten her. She looked very childish and defenceless as she sat beside him, gazing out across the the garden to the dark mass of the North Downs against the sky-line. His face was a little grim as he thought of his uncle. Fiona was such a tender, gentle person. How she had remained so with a home life like hers, he didn't know, but nothing had changed that quality in her which the French called *douceur* and for which he could not find the exact English equivalent. Only her increasing shyness and elusiveness spoke of a need for defences.

**Also by the same author,
and available in Coronet Books:**

The Tangled Wood
Alex And The Raynhams
A Sheltering Tree
Encounter at Alpenrose
The Gay Intruder
Rosevean
Rough Weather
An April Girl
Challenge of Spring
The Young Romantic
The New Owner
The Broken Bough
A House Without Love

The Enchanted Garden

Iris Bromige

CORONET BOOKS
Hodder and Stoughton

Copyright 1956 Iris Bromige

First published in Great Britain by
Hodder and Stoughton Limited 1956

Coronet Edition 1958
Third Impression 1976

---

*The characters and situations in this book are
entirely imaginary and bear no relation to any real
person or actual happening*

This book is sold subject to the condition that
it shall not, by way of trade or otherwise, be
lent, re-sold, hired out or otherwise circulated
without the publisher's prior consent in any
form of binding or cover other than that in
which this is published and without a similar
condition including this condition being
imposed on the subsequent purchaser.

Printed and bound in Great Britain for
Coronet Books, Hodder and Stoughton, London
By Richard Clay (The Chaucer Press), Ltd.,
Bungay, Suffolk

ISBN 0 340 198761

BOOK I
LIME AVENUE

CHAPTER ONE

THE path across the wheat field was hard and cracked under the August sun, and the golden ears stretching away each side were still and silent as though they were painted there. Fiona liked it best when a breeze rippled the wheat and evoked its gentle rustling voice to accompany her on her way. There were splashes of poppies among the gold, and at the edge of the path their gaudy intrusion was repeated in miniature by the scarlet pimpernels.

She sat down to remove a collection of small stones from her sandals, and stayed there for a few minutes, her thin arms clasped round her knees, seeing the wheat field as a forest of slender, pale gold trunks. What an attractive world for field mice and voles to live in, she thought. A world of peace and plenty, of gentle music, and the illusion of sunshine even on a cloudy day. Until the reaper came. She turned her mind from this thought, unwilling to mar the mood of that golden afternoon. Julian would say that cruelty was part of the pattern of nature and must be accepted, but she could never accept it without an inner wincing and protesting. She picked an ear of the wheat and rubbed it between her hands. Wheat and poppies. Food and dreams. The two most important factors in human life. Fiona chewed the wheat kernels reflectively and felt immobilised by the heat.

The fact that Fiona Goring, at eighteen, should rank dreams as high in importance as food would surprise nobody with a discerning eye, for the curve of her lips, the flaring nostrils of her straight, narrow-bridged nose, the widely spaced eyes, all suggested a sensitive imagination, a too sensitive imagination a realist might think. It was an uncommon face, brushed just then by an unconscious wistfulness as she gazed across the field. Her light brown hair was silky and fine and straight, curving closely to the shape of her head, a fine fringe half concealing the wide forehead. The hazel eyes were her best feature, large and long-lashed. The high cheek-bones were well defined above a firm jaw line which curved in to a rather pointed chin. A face difficult to classify: not pretty; not good-looking; something elusive and poignant about it; its charm as mobile and insubstantial as reflections in a stream. She was slender to the point of thinness and her long legs gave her a coltish look when she stood up.

She walked on, climbed the stile at the end of the footpath and began to cross the meadow towards the partly concealed grey stone house which was her destination. She loved this view of Alanbridge behind the larch trees which bounded it on the meadow side: the tiled roof weathered by time to a soft medley of colours, with lichen and moss adding yellow and green to the pattern; the mullioned windows; the Elizabethan chimney pots. She could just see the top sprays of the climbing rose which reached nearly to the roof of the gable of the short wing. Mermaid. It was her uncle's favourite rose and its large single yellow flowers adorned the wall in profusion from July until late into the autumn. It was only one of the many delights which the garden of Alanbridge had to offer, and to Fiona, the garden, the house and its occupants made up a corner of Paradise in her lonely, often frightening, world. In her heart the word Alanbridge spelt warmth and kindness and beauty, and she loved it with the passionate devotion of a child starved of these qualities in her home life. And the core of her devotion was her cousin, Julian, who had admitted her to the world of Alanbridge.

The parcel in her hand was for Julian. Today was his thirtieth birthday. Thirty sounded quite old, but she had known Julian for so long that to her he was ageless. The close companion of her mind and heart, the only close companion she had ever known, there had never been any barrier of age between them since that day eight years ago when his kindness had broken down the wall of shyness which constricted her and had lit a candle in her life which had never dimmed.

She had telephoned him that morning to wish him many happy returns of the day and had asked if she might bring her present over that afternoon. She was pretty certain to find him in the garden on a day like this, she thought, as the shade of the larch trees welcomed her. The grounds of Alanbridge had been laid out in the form of several gardens, however, all established for many years so that the trees and hedges had grown tall and one might search for a long time before tracking down one's victim. She sauntered along the winding path through the shrub garden which led her to an archway in a yew hedge and thence to the rose garden. Here she found Leo, the marmalade cat, asleep in the sun, but no other sign of life. Leo opened his amber eyes and purred lazily as she rubbed his back by way of greeting, but he did not stir. His fur was hot to her fingers and an aura of sun-baked contentment surrounded him.

Beyond the rose garden was the long walk between wide herbaceous borders, at their most brilliant just then with sunflowers, Canterbury bells, marigolds, lavender and hollyhocks standing out from the grouped masses of plants. Halfway down the path was an Italian fountain which had charmed Fiona ever since she had been a small child unable to see over the rim beyond the carved dolphins. She dabbled her fingers in the spray as she lingered for a moment, entranced by the cool tinkle of the water. It was a gentle fountain and it sparkled in the sunshine with a mesmerising beauty. As she stood there, Joe Bramble appeared at the end of the walk trundling a wheelbarrow, and Fiona called to him before he could disappear round the hedge.

'Joe. Do you know where Mr. Falconer is? Mr. Julian.'

He put the wheelbarrow down and straightened himself slowly. Everything Joe Bramble did was slow and deliberate. He was a dark, ruddy faced man of about forty and had been gardener here ever since Fiona could remember.

'Mr. Julian. I reckon you'll find him in the heather garden, miss. Leastways, that's where I last saw him.'

'Thank you, Joe. This garden is heaven on a day like this.'

'Maybe. But there are plenty of enemies lurking. More like a battlefield, I'd say.'

He grinned and moved on. Fiona skirted the paved court behind the house and crossed the lawn to a flight of half a dozen shallow stone steps which led her into the shade of the pergola. The long, covered walk looked like a green tunnel with the sunshine waiting again at the end. Here and there the sun splintered through the arch of climbing roses and wistaria, the latter so old that the branches writhing round the stone pillars were as thick as tree-trunks. In May, when the wistaria was in bloom, it was so lovely that Fiona felt that she could never feast her eyes long enough upon it. When she emerged at the far end, the sun fell on her like a blow. And half-way down the slope on which the heather garden had been made sat the object of her search, leaning against a boulder, smoking his pipe.

'Hi, Julian. What a lovely day for your birthday,' she said as she came up, smiling.

'M'm. You've caught me out. I came here filled with good intentions about weeding. How's life?'

'So so.' She handed him the parcel a little shyly. 'I hope you'll find this useful. And I hope you have many more happy birthdays, and happiness all the other days, too.'

He squinted at her lazily.

'Thank you, poppet. That's a very generous wish. I shall be lucky if it comes true. This looks interesting. Sit down and be lazy with me.'

He drew out of the wrappings a stiff-covered book on which was printed *Catalogue of Gramophone Records*. The first letter of each word emerged from a delicate scroll-like design which on close examination proved to be formed of staves of music. The cover was framed in a half-inch border of the same delicate lined drawings depicting musical instruments linked by notes on curving staves of music. The work had been done in Indian ink with a very fine nib and was beautifully executed.

'My dear, this is lovely! You must have spent hours on it.'

'I enjoyed doing it. Look inside.'

At the top of each page was the name of a composer, printed in the same style as the words on the cover.

'I thought it would be best to put the records under their composers,' said Fiona a little anxiously. 'It seemed to be the quickest way for finding them. They're in alphabetical order.'

'But when did you get them all listed?'

'When you were staying in London at Easter. Uncle John let me come over every day until I'd finished. I was so afraid you'd start on the job yourself before your birthday, because you're always saying you must get your records listed.'

'And never do it. Just get furious every time I hunt along those racks for a particular record and wonder whether that elaborate system of numbering each division is such a bright idea, after all. Fiona, you're a darling girl. This is quite the nicest birthday present I've ever had, and I shall cherish it always. You know, you're very clever at this kind of drawing. Persuaded your father to let you go to a decent art school yet?'

She shook her head.

'No. He says I'm too young to go to London, and that I can go to evening classes in Elton if I'm that keen.'

'Oh. What are his plans for you, then, now that you've left school?'

'That's the trouble. He hasn't any. He doesn't seem interested. He just expects me to stay at home and carry out social duties for him. Do you think that's why he doesn't like me, Julian? Because I'm not a very good substitute for my mother? I do try to do my best, but I'm not much good at entertaining strangers. I never know what to say to them. And, somehow, Father always gives me an inferiority complex. Sometimes I think he hates me,' she said quietly.

Julian was silent for a few moments. He was too fond of Fiona and had too much respect for her intelligence to comfort her with false platitudes, and there were times when he, too, believed that her father was hostile to her. It was delicate ground and there were undercurrents which Fiona knew nothing of and about which he had no right to enlighten her. She looked very childish and defenceless as she sat beside him, gazing out across the garden to the dark mass of the North Downs against the sky-line. His face was a little grim as he thought of his uncle. Fiona was such a tender, gentle person. How she had remained so with a home life like hers, he didn't know, but nothing had changed that quality in her which the French called *douceur* and for which he could not find the exact English equivalent. Only her increasing shyness and elusiveness spoke of a need for defences.

'I think your father has a grudge against life, Fiona, and you're handy to focus it on.'

'But why? He's head of a successful business, he has

good health. I know Mother died when I was a baby, but could that give him a grudge all his life?'

'I'm not a psychiatrist, my dear. The complexities of human nature take a lot of understanding.'

'I wonder if they were happy together. Mother and Father. I can't imagine him happy. He never mentions her, and he hasn't kept up any contact with her family. I suppose he doesn't want any reminders.'

'Probably. You're not to have any sort of career, then?'

'No. Father's not interested, it seems, except in a negative way. But we haven't really discussed it. I keep meaning to, but . . . Julian, it sounds awfully feeble and silly, but I'm frightened of him. I try to pretend I'm not, but I know I am.'

'He's not unkind to you, is he?'

'No. He's not unkind and he's not kind. He's just inhuman. I mean, he doesn't seem to have any feeling. Cold and critical. But let's not talk about it. It's such a lovely day and your birthday. I do think Alanbridge is the loveliest place in the world. Your grandfather must have been a very great man to have made this wonderful garden.'

'He was a great horticulturist. Plant collectors used to send him specimens from all parts of the world, and he was always entertaining gardeners and botanists of all nationalities. You'd have liked him. He was a nice old boy and so kind-hearted that I think he even felt sorry for the greenfly he waged war on.'

'All the Falconers are kind. I hope there will always be Falconers at Alanbridge.'

'Let's hope they can always afford to keep the place going. Fortunately the house is a reasonable size, but the upkeep of the garden isn't a small matter.'

'But such a wonderful achievement that it would be worth any sacrifice.'

He smiled at her vehemence.

'Taxation and death duties take no account of sentiment, I'm afraid. It'll probably be a job for the National Trust in the end.'

'Oh, no. It's such a personal garden,' protested Fiona, her eyes wide with distress.

'Well, let's not worry about posterity. There's a bumble bee crawling up you. Can his sight and smell be so poor that he mistakes those flowers on your dress for the real thing?'

'Isn't he lovely? So furry.'

'That's a pretty dress. I haven't seen it before, have I?'

'No. It's new.'

'Your father doesn't keep you short of money, anyway. Or does he?' he added, as she said nothing.

'He gives me anything I ask for, but I always have to ask. I have nothing unless I ask. That's why I want to find a job and earn some money. Then I won't have to go to him.'

'It's foolish to mind asking, my dear.'

'It's because he likes me to have to beg. I know he does. It took me weeks to pluck up courage to ask him if I could go to an art school. I'd rather go without than ask for anything more.'

That was why Julian's present was not more costly, she thought. She would have liked to give him the sun and the stars and the moon, but all she was able to give was a cheap book embellished with loving care.

Julian frowned as he knocked out his pipe.

'Do you think your father would look favourably on a suggestion that you should join the staff of my school of music?'

Fiona's face quivered with eagerness.

'But . . . would I be any use?'

'You could help Miss Lesley in the office. She needs an assistant.'

'Oh, I'd love to, if you think I'd be able to do the work.'

'Why not? You're intelligent, you've had a good education and you know enough about music to be able to order it without mis-spelling the names of composers. Then you could go to art classes in the evening and find out if there are any possibilities for you in that direction after a year or two.'

'I wonder if Father would agree. After all, we are relatives and it would be in the family, so to speak. Miss Lesley's the tall, fair person who was talking to you after the end-of-term concert, isn't she?'

'That's right. She's a pleasant soul.'

'Yes, she looked it. Not a person to be scared of.'

'You'll have to cure yourself of this habit of being scared of people, poppet. Shall I ask your father, or will you?'

She hesitated, and he knew that she would prefer him to

broach it, but he was anxious to get her to stand on her own feet, so he said casually:

'You raise it with him first, and then if he's sticky, I'll have a go. You've left school now, you know. He'll have to realise that you're a young woman with a future to think about. O.K.?'

'Yes. I'll do it. What would my work consist of? He might want to know more about it.'

'Well, Miss Lesley keeps the books, renders accounts, orders music, keeps records of examination results, and generally copes with most of the administrative side of the school. You would assist her, in a junior capacity, of course. Will that satisfy him?'

'I hope so. And thank you, Julian. I have so much to thank you for, I'll never be able to repay you.'

He pulled her hair.

'You're a nice child. I'm rather fond of you. We haven't mentioned pay. Do you think your father will be interested in that?'

'No. He won't think I'm worth much, and I shan't be. That doesn't matter.... In fact,' she went on earnestly, 'I think I should only be paid enough to cover my lunches at first, until you see if I'm any use. Or I could come home to lunch, of course, though I'd rather have it in Elton.'

'We can talk about all that later. Best see what the parental attitude is first. Lord, I feel lazy. I believe the smell of this heather's drugging me.'

He shifted himself away from the boulder until he could lie full length on the grassy slope and closed his eyes. Fiona looked down at him. Viewed with detachment, it was not a handsome face; too long and thin, and the nose was slightly crooked. He had crisp black hair and his dark skin was tanned. But she could never be afraid of the dark brown eyes, now hidden from her, or wince at any words from that wide, firm mouth which so often wore a humorous twist when he was with her. The open neck of his white shirt and the rolled-up sleeves revealed a smooth, pale brown skin. He was over six feet tall, and it was seldom that Fiona saw this six feet and one inch in such an inert state, for Julian was a very active person and moved always with the swift litheness of a man who is physically hard and fit. She twisted her head round to see the watch on his wrist. Nearly four o'clock.

He had the strong hands of a skilled pianist. He could have been a celebrity, she supposed, if he had chosen to become a concert pianist. Instead, he had turned to teaching and composing. She removed an ant from his shirt, and he opened his eyes.

'I'm just wondering whether it's too hot to go and look for tea.'

'Would you like me to go and fetch you a cup?'

'Angel child, I was hoping you'd suggest that. Mrs. Blakeney brews at four o'clock.'

'Anything to eat?'

'No, thanks, Don't let me put you off your gargantuan appetite, though. I know you've a weakness for Mrs. B's cakes.'

He closed his eyes again, and Fiona went off towards the house. Mrs. Blakeney was just bringing a tray of tea out to Julian's father on the terrace.

'Hullo, Uncle John,' said Fiona, smiling. 'How nice and cool you look.'

'Hullo, my dear. Glad to see you. Are you going to join me for tea?'

'I've been sent to fetch a cup for Julian. He's in the heather garden, too lazy to move.'

'Well, we don't get many days suitable for lazing in this country. We must make the most of them. How's your father?'

'Well, thank you.'

Fiona hid a little smile as she followed Mrs. Blakeney to the kitchen. As long as she could remember, the formula had always been the same. The only reference to her father was this polite enquiry about his health, and that disposed of, her father was never referred to again by Uncle John. Mrs. Blakeney made another pot of tea and loaded the tray with cakes, for she believed that Fiona was half starved at home, which was not to be wondered at with a housekeeper like Mrs. Ware in sole charge. Mrs. Blakeney was a person who formed rapid opinions about people, and never changed them. Because she had once seen Mrs. Ware purchase two fillets of plaice, so dainty as to be almost ethereal, in an Elton fish shop, presumably for dinner that night, Mrs. Blakeney had condemned her as parsimonious, and nothing would now redeem her.

'There you are, my dear. Can you manage?'

'Yes, thank you. Your cakes are super, Mrs. Blakeney.'

Her arms ached by the time she had carried the tray to the heather garden. She thought Julian was asleep, but he sat up at the first chink of china and said:

'Good girl. I hope this will revive me sufficiently to make the prospect of climbing into a boiled shirt tonight less distasteful.'

'Are you going out?'

'Yes. I am committed to driving Miss Coachford to a very smart roadhouse to dine and dance. An appalling programme for a hot August night.'

'Why did you suggest it, then?'

'I didn't. By an odd coincidence, Norah Coachford and I were born on the same day of the same year. She thinks the coincidence should be jointly celebrated, and this was her choice of celebration.'

Fiona chose a cake and appeared to be giving it her close attention. She could never make up her mind what sort of relationship existed between Julian and Norah Coachford. Norah was a member of his staff at the school of music, and taught singing. During the past year or two, the business relationship had slipped into friendship and Norah was a fairly frequent visitor to Alanbridge, but Julian maintained a very casual air about her and it would have needed a considerably more mature and experienced person than Fiona to gauge what was involved. She only knew that she was conscious of a little chill in her heart at the mention of Norah's name, which was very foolish, she thought, because she had no right to judge Julian's friends. He would be bound to marry some day, and he would never think of her in that way. She was his cousin, for one thing, and he only thought of her as a child. But if she could not contemplate Julian marrying without feeling mangled, the thought that Norah Coachford was destined to be the future mistress of Alanbridge hurt beyond endurance, because Fiona was sure she wouldn't make Julian happy. And how Julian would laugh if he heard her say that. Rightly, perhaps. At eighteen, just out of school, why should he think that she knew anything about his prospects of happiness with a woman? She had no experience. Only an instinct where he was concerned. An instinct based on her own deep love for him.

'I expect you'll enjoy it when you get there,' she said politely.

'I dare say. Afraid I can't idle here any longer with you, ducky. One or two things to see to before I change. You carry on with the cakes. Let me know what your father says about our proposition.'

'Yes, I will. I do hope he says yes. You've forgotten your present, Julian.'

She held the catalogue up to him, and he rubbed her head as he took it.

'Thank you, dear. So long.'

'So long.'

Fiona watched his long, lean figure stroll up the slope and disappear behind the pergola. She no longer felt hungry and fed the last of her cake to a robin. As she carried the tray back to the house, she tried to work out the best approach to her father.

CHAPTER TWO

LIME AVENUE was the last residential outpost of the town of Elton before the country prevailed again. It was a wide, tree-lined road with large red brick Victorian houses at regular intervals along it. Number ten was distinguished by a monkey-puzzle tree in its front garden and to Fiona this tree was the symbol of the bleak, warped life lived in this house which was her home. She never went through the front door without feeling chilled, as though the dark angular shadows which the tree threw across the house clouded her heart, too.

She had made up her mind to tell her father about Julian's proposition after dinner, over their coffee. The large Elton store owned by her father closed at five-thirty and he arrived home about six o'clock. They dined at seven, usually alone, and these dinners were the greatest ordeal of the day to Fiona. She saw little of her father apart from that. She dressed with care that evening, knowing that he had a critical eye for her appearance. Unfortunately, she had only to meet his gaze to be convinced that she was the plain, odd creature he thought her.

He greeted her with his usual preoccupied air, and they sat opposite each other, eating silently. The dining-room was large and lofty, as were all the rooms in that house. In winter as cold as a tomb, in the present heat it was pleasantly cool. The windows were large, but the dark tree outside and the heavy mahogany furniture inside combined to give an atmosphere of gloom, particularly marked on that bright day. So different from Alanbridge, thought Fiona, which was always so light and sunny, with views of the garden coming into every room. Her father leaned back in his chair and finished reading the *Daily Telegraph* while Mrs. Ware took their plates and returned with the sweet course, which she placed in front of Fiona. Stewed fruit and blancmange. Her father continued reading as he ate and Fiona rehearsed her opening speech, wishing that for once he could appear more approachable.

As long as Fiona could remember, her father had never looked any different. He had never looked young, and now, just on sixty, he did not look old. He was a sparely built man of medium height who gave an impression of great self-control. His hair was grey, his face pale, his eyes grey and cold. His features were good and he dressed with meticulous neatness, but the overall effect was of something dried up and bloodless, like a mummy. It was this which Fiona found frightening.

Mrs. Ware brought in the coffee, but Mr. Goring's attention was still turned to the financial page of the *Daily Telegraph*. Fiona spoke as soon as he put the paper down.

'Father, would you object if I went to work in Julian's school of music?'

He looked at her then, and raised his eyebrows as he stirred his coffee.

'I wasn't aware that you had qualifications for teaching any branch of music, Fiona. Enlighten me.'

His voice was dry, like dead leaves, and Fiona clasped her hands under the table-cloth.

'Not teaching. In the office. He needs an assistant for the secretary.'

'Really? You surprise me. I shouldn't have thought it necessary.'

'Julian says that Miss Lesley, that's the secretary, could do with an assistant, and he asked me if I'd like the job.'

'And you rushed in with your usual enthusiastic response to any suggestion from that quarter, no doubt.'

'Well, I did like the idea. Now I've finished with school, it's time I thought of some occupation.'

'It's not necessary for you to earn your living, Fiona. I am a moderately wealthy man. You would only be taking money that somebody else could do with. If you want to fill up your time, you can do some sort of voluntary work, although I should have thought running this house and making it a little more comfortable would have given you plenty to do.'

'But Mrs. Ware runs it.'

'She sees to the bare essentials. A lot more could be done. And I'd like to do more entertaining now that you've left school and can take on the duties of hostess. You're not a child now, and instead of running wild about the country or haunting your cousin, you might assume a few responsibilities in your home.'

'But other girls have jobs and earn money.'

'Because they are not in your fortunate position. You can have anything you like in the way of money from me. You have only to ask. I'm a well-known figure in Elton, and I don't choose to have my daughter in some twopenny-halfpenny job. You've probably wheedled Julian into manufacturing it for you, anyway, and we don't need to accept any patronage from that branch of the family.'

'But he is my cousin. I don't see why you should think I'd be losing face by helping in his school of music. As a councillor, you support any cultural movement in Elton.'

Fiona's voice was always soft and low, but it had an unusually firm note in it now, and her father put down his paper, to which he had turned again as he dismissed Julian's patronage, and gave her his full attention.

'I'm not discussing this absurd idea any further, Fiona. As a councillor, as the head of a large business, I require a certain background which I think my daughter should be willing to provide. You have lacked for nothing. You have had everything that money could buy. Unfortunately, I have not had the support that a wife can give to the building of a successful position. Nevertheless, I have built up a position of some importance in Elton, and I think I have every right to expect my daughter to take over some of the social responsibilities which a wife would normally undertake.'

'But I'm not good at entertaining.'

'That I have observed, but most things in this life, Fiona, can be achieved with willpower and perseverance. You have had a good education, you have been taught dancing and music, you move and speak well, and when you take trouble with your appearance, you are pleasant enough to look at. Also you are not nearly so unintelligent as your frequent dumbness in my presence would suggest. All you need is experience and a desire to please.'

'But entertaining your friends is still not going to fill my days, Father.'

'I don't think you quite grasp my meaning. I'm not asking you merely to say good evening, politely, when we have guests. I am asking you to take your place as the daughter of this house. That means studying people's tastes and comfort, making the house look less of a museum, accompanying me to local dinners and other functions, remembering people's names and their interests so that when you meet them you can talk to them. In other words, grooming yourself for assuming social responsibilities which I have a right to expect you to shoulder. That's your job, Fiona, and I'd be glad if you'd get down to it in earnest. If you do it properly, it will take up quite a lot of your time. I should be quite happy, if you still find that you have time to spare, to see you take up a little local voluntary work. In fact, I think it would be a good thing for my daughter to show interest in local affairs and charities. You may not realise it, but I shall probably be Mayor of Elton within the next few years. Had that occurred to you?'

'No. It hadn't.'

'You have your head too much in the clouds, my dear. In discharging my duties, I should expect your help. It would mean a very busy social life. It's with that in mind that I ask you to start preparing yourself. Schooldays are over, Fiona. The next few years should prove an enjoyable and valuable experience for you, but they'll be busy ones, so don't think any more of this silly suggestion of Julian's. You have a more important function to fulfil and you might tell Julian so.'

'Would you like any more coffee, Father?'

She hoped that he would refuse and that she could escape, for his programme for her future filled her with such alarm and dismay that she wanted to get away from his eyes, out of the house, to the comfort of the country and her own thoughts. Uncannily, he seemed to sense her panic, for it was most unusual for him to have a second cup of coffee.

'Thank you, I will. A little more milk this time, please. Do you like the idea of your father being Mayor of this town, Fiona? You didn't seem to register much pleasure at the prospect.'

'It was a surprise. I'm afraid I haven't really had time to take it in. Of course, it will be . . .'

But what it would be was beyond Fiona's powers of expression just then and her voice tailed off into silence. She felt the colour stealing into her cheeks as she avoided his scrutiny.

'And what will it be?' he asked gently.

'An honour, of course,' she said in a strangled voice.

'I would like to feel that my position in Elton gives you some pride and pleasure. Should a father expect that of his daughter? Or is it asking too much?'

When he turned to gentle sarcasm, Fiona was finally defeated, and she handed him his coffee, with a hand which shook.

'Apparently it is,' he observed.

She swallowed hard.

'No, of course it isn't, Father. I know you're a prominent person in local affairs, and I wish I felt I was more suited to play the part you wish me to play in helping you. I'm afraid I haven't enough self-confidence to be much of an asset.'

'That will come with experience. You're young. A certain modesty is becoming, and if you will take trouble and try, I think you'll do quite well. You need guidance, though. I'll have to see if I can find somebody to give you a lead. We're holding the store annual dinner and dance on the first of October. I think we might make that the start to your social education, my dear. It's time my daughter put in a public appearance. August is a dead month, but we'll see about opening up this house a bit in the autumn. However, I can't discuss it any further just now. I'm expecting Mr. Masterson and Mrs. Crayshaw this evening. Think over what I've been saying, Fiona, will you?'

'Yes, Father.'

'On second thoughts, I think I'd like you to be here when Masterson and Mrs. Crayshaw come. It will be a good opportunity to introduce you to local affairs. You know Mrs. Crayshaw, don't you?'

'No. At least, I saw her open a fête last year.'

'She might be the very person to help you. She's an active member of the Women's Institute, she's on several committees and takes a leading part in all local activities. She could be useful.'

Fiona remembered Mrs. Crayshaw as a commanding woman with practical efficiency written all over her.

'Mr. Masterson,' went on her father, 'is the head of the Woodside Children's Home. They are coming to see me tonight about the fund for buying and equipping a playing field. Mrs. Crayshaw has organised several sales and dances in aid of the fund and I think they're not far short of their target. I am thinking of making up whatever sum they still need. Are you listening, Fiona?'

'Yes, Father.'

'Then I wish you wouldn't look out of the window while I'm talking to you. I'm telling you this so that you can appear reasonably intelligent this evening. And interested, I hope. They'll be here about eight-thirty, so don't disappear.'

He left her, and she went up to her room and sat on the window-seat, her heart sick with dismay and apprehension. Although always aware of the atmosphere cast by her father while she was in the house, she did not actually spend much time with him, apart from the dreaded meals. Now, it seemed, she was to be his companion on many occasions. Shy by nature, she enjoyed only the friendliest social occasions, and the thought of formal functions under the critical eye of her father, where she was expected to pay a creditable part, filled her with dread. In his presence, she never felt natural. Years of cold criticism from him had destroyed all her confidence when she was with him. She twisted her hands unhappily, the contrast between Julian's proposition and the prospect now before her so great that she felt overwhelmed. If her father had ever shown her any kindness, had tried to get to know her, had invited her affection, she would willingly have embraced the role he demanded of her. But it was her duty, she thought, to try to take her mother's place now. Perhaps they would become closer. He had spoken a few words of praise that evening, after all, and that was so rare as to be remarkable. She sat there feeling lost and lonely, wishing passionately that she could talk to Julian about it and remembering that he was on the way to the roadhouse with Norah Coachford by now. Without the excuses of a child or the defences of a grown up, Fiona felt only a sense of helplessness and strangeness.

The evening with her father's visitors passed off more easily than she had anticipated, for Mrs. Crayshaw monopolised the conversation to such an extent that even if Fiona had been talkative, she would have had little opportunity to use her tongue. But for all her loud voice and assertive manner, Mrs. Crayshaw was a cheerful person with a breezy kindness about her that softened the edge of Fiona's apprehension. Mr. Masterson was a tall, thin man with watery eyes and a sad face who said very little. But what struck Fiona most about that evening was the new light in which her father appeared. She knew him only as a self-contained, cold man of few words, but that evening he showed a more expansive social side to his personality. He would never exude charm, but a certain dry humour, a careful attentiveness to what other people were saying, and a pithiness in his own remarks, brought home to Fiona the fact that to the world he presented a far more agreeable face than she knew. She realised, too, that he made his mark. No matter how much Mrs. Crayshaw talked and Mr. Masterson nodded, it was her father who kept the conversation on the lines he desired and it was to her father they deferred when a decision was sought. He could control people. That was why he was successful, she thought. And she would have bartered all his success for a little warmth of feeling.

At the end of the evening, after brushing aside Mr. Masterson's thanks for his generosity, Mr. Goring brought up the subject of his daughter.

'I want to launch her out on our social life, Mrs. Crayshaw, and as she hasn't a mother's guidance, I wonder if Fiona might come to you for advice when she needs it. You're a leading light in local affairs and I'd like Fiona to learn to play her part as a good citizen of our community. The trouble is, she's just out of school, rather raw and shy.

I know she'd be grateful for any introductions you could give her.'

'Of course,' said Mrs. Crayshaw, beaming. 'We can do with some young blood. And she's charming. Where have you been hiding her all this time, Mr. Goring? Shame on you.'

'Well, it's a job to realise that she's grown up, you know. We intend to open up our house more now that Fiona's of an age to take over. I wish we had somebody to lead her, though. Even our housekeeper is no help. A decent body, but with very little idea of how a house should be run.'

'Now that gives me an idea. Mrs. Marchant. If you would consider employing another person here, I think she's the answer to your problems.'

'Go on, Mrs. Crayshaw. I might have known you would have a solution.'

'Mrs. Marchant is a widow. Her husband was something important in the city and they had a beautiful house in London, entertained lavishly, travelled a good deal in connection with his business and really led a very full social life. Then things went wrong. I don't know exactly what happened, the poor dear never talks of it, but her husband went bankrupt and died a year ago leaving her penniless. She came here to live with her sister and has applied for one or two jobs, but of course there's nothing suitable for a woman of her type. She's in her fifties and has never worked for her living in her life. And I'm afraid sharing her sister's home is not a success. Well,' added Mrs. Crayshaw, lifting the palms of her hands heavenwards, 'we all know that Miss Mowburton is a little difficult. Now I think that if she knew that she was coming to a nice family and wouldn't be treated as a servant, Mrs. Marchant would be very happy to come here as a housekeeper, companion, or what you will. Of course, I don't know whether that would upset Mrs. Ware.'

'Mrs. Ware will accept it. We can do with extra staff here, anyway. And you think she would be a help to my daughter?'

'A great help. Such style. Of course, Mrs. Marchant was used to a far grander social life than we enjoy here in Elton. But I do know that she is herself a fine cook—she undertook that for her sister, although I doubt whether Miss Mowburton knows the difference between butter and margarine. So depressing to a connoisseur of good food. She could advise Fiona on dress, show her how to put on a good dinner party, help her in a hundred ways. It's so hard for a young girl to be without a mother at this half-hatched stage of her life,' concluded Mrs. Crayshaw, smiling kindly at Fiona, who smiled back, feeling rather like an unpromising duckling whose chances of becoming a good table bird were doubtful.

'Well, I'd certainly like to see Mrs. Marchant and have a chat with her,' said Mr. Goring. 'It sounds as though she's just the person we want. Now isn't it about time we offered our friends some refreshment, Fiona?'

Her father seemed in a good humour after he had seen his visitors off that night.

'Well, that was a useful evening's work, although I'm a hundred pounds the poorer. If this Mrs. Marchant's all she's cracked up to be, I think we can expect our life here to be a good deal less limited than it's been in the past. You must learn to show more interest, Fiona. Make a positive contribution.'

'Yes, I'll try. I think I'll go up to bed now. I'm rather tired.'

Her fine hair shone like silk under the hall light and the shadows under the high cheek-bones emphasised the haunting, wistful quality of her face.

'You look very much like your mother, standing there,' said her father, and it was so unexpected that she turned quickly, her eyes wide and startled.

'Do I? I wish we had a photograph of her. I've no idea what she looked like.'

Her father stopped, one hand on the sitting-room door, to say:

'By the way, you haven't asked me for any money lately. There's no need to be so careful in your expenditure, you know. I'm not a poor man.'

'I was wondering . . .' She hesitated, then took the plunge. 'Now that I've left school, and you don't want me to earn any money, couldn't I have a small fixed allowance? It would save me having to bother you at odd times.'

'It's no bother. Are you short now?'

'I have exactly five-pence.'

'Well, I wish you wouldn't run yourself out like that.'

He took out his wallet. 'Here you are. Five pounds. That should keep you going for a bit. The only bill I've had in for your clothes was an item of a few pounds for a pair of shoes some months ago. You'll have to keep a decent wardrobe now, you know. You're an odd child. Not many girls of your age would be so unwilling to benefit from their father's pocket.'

'You won't let me have an allowance of my own, then?'

'I prefer you to come to me when you want it, Fiona. I've never refused, as far as I can remember.'

'No. It's just that it makes me feel that I'm still a child, having to ask for pocket money.'

'When you show an understanding of your responsibilities, I shall know that you are no longer a child and we'll talk about it again. In the meantime, I prefer you to ask for what you want and to have some idea of how you spend it. Good-night.'

'Good-night.'

Her face burned as she ran upstairs. She knew that nothing gave her father more satisfaction than to have her ask humbly, like a beggar, for money; to make her acknowledge her dependence on him. It had been so all her life, and each year that went by made it more difficult for her to approach him in humility. And now it would go on, since he refused her the right to earn any money herself.

It was still hot in her bedroom under the tiled roof, and a full moon cast a pale light into the room. She sat by the window looking out on what was, perhaps, the most beautiful summer night of the year. How lovely the garden at Alanbridge would look in the moonlight, she thought. The houses in Lime Avenue had small, rectangular gardens, backing on to grazing land. The garden of number ten was neatly laid out in the form of a rectangular lawn with a border of rather uninteresting shrubs round it. A gardener came in for one day a week and kept it trim. Trim and soulless, thought Fiona, who was in a pessimistic mood. A black cat stalked silently across the lawn and disappeared through the laurels. Beyond the grazing land and Linney Farm lay a belt of woodland. Beyond that, out of sight, was Alanbridge. For a long time she sat there in that dim room, looking out across the country like a prisoner gazing at freedom, her thoughts wandering in the garden at Alanbridge, seeing the little fountain in the moonlight, dreaming that she had spent the evening there with Julian. In dreams she could always escape.

CHAPTER THREE

THE introduction of Mrs. Marchant to the household of number ten, Lime Avenue, brought considerable change to the life within those red brick walls. At first, Fiona thought the change was all for the better, for Mrs. Marchant rapidly took charge of the domestic side with great benefit to the catering and comfort of the house. Within a matter of weeks, she subdued and reorganised Mrs. Ware, persuaded Mr. Goring to install a central-heating system, took on a woman one day a week to do what Mrs. Ware termed 'the rough', a favour for which Mrs. Ware had asked in vain for years, and succeeded in obtaining the small room at the back of the house, hitherto known as Mr. Goring's study, for her own private sitting-room. And this had all been achieved with a smiling graciousness which filled Fiona with admiration.

Her attitude to Fiona was kind and affable in the extreme, and apart from the rather grim ordeal of meals, which Fiona still took alone with her father, life at Lime Avenue seemed to be a good deal brighter and Fiona felt that she had a potential friend in Mrs. Marchant. This happy expectation, however, began to fade after the talk which her father had with Mrs. Marchant about his daughter. It took place on a day which was memorable to Fiona because she had spent it with Julian and they had walked for miles across the Surrey hills together, lunching in the garden of a little country inn where some scarlet dahlias made her long for paint and canvas. They had started in morning mist, but the sun had broken through soon after, turning every dewdrop into a jewel and spangling every spider's web. Julian had inherited his father's interest in botany, and his knowledge was wide, so that walks with him had an added spice. With September in its last days, the trees were beginning to turn colour and the countryside looked warm and glowing. At ease with Julian, as she was with nobody else in the world, the day was one of rare happiness for her, and she returned to Lime Avenue in the dusk of the evening still wrapped in its joy.

She met Mrs. Marchant in the hall, who gave her a smile and said:

'Hullo, Fiona. Have you had a nice day?'

'Heavenly, thank you.'

'I wonder if you would like to come along to my sitting-room some time this evening and have a little chat. Your father has been discussing a few things with me and I think you and I will have to make some plans. Any time that suits you.'

'I'll just have a wash and tidy up, then I'll join you,' said Fiona, feeling some of the glory of the day retreating.

Mrs. Marchant had furnished her sitting-room with her own furniture, and Fiona thought how pretty it looked with its chintz-covered chairs and little Queen Anne table.

'This room looks so much nicer than it used to look as Father's study, Mrs. Marchant.'

'Thank you, dear. I've always been sensitive to the atmosphere of rooms and I do like to live with nice things around me. This house is far too gloomy.'

'I know. The furniture is so heavy and dark.'

'Bright curtains and carpets could do a lot. And that brings me to one of the things your father was discussing with me. He says you have never shown much interest in your home and he would like me to encourage you to take more interest now that you're no longer a schoolgirl. I must say I think that's a good idea. You'll be getting married one day, and training in homemaking seems sadly lacking for girls these days. It's all careers. Long training, more often than not at the country's expense, for everything under the sun except the one career most important to a woman—homemaking.'

'Yes, but I expect most girls soon learn, once they are married and have a home of their own.'

'In a fashion. But there's a great deal in running a home successfully and being a help to your husband. Early training is invaluable and I think your father is very wise to emphasise its importance for you now.'

Fiona sensed a subtle change of attitude here. Until now, Mrs. Marchant had in some measure deferred to her, had treated her as the daughter of the house with whom she wished to stand well. Now there was something more autocratic in her manner. The wind had changed, and was decidedly chillier.

Fiona's eyes studied Mrs. Marchant gravely as she waited for her to go on. She was a very well-preserved woman and looked less than her fifty-three years. Tall, with a well-controlled figure, she dressed plainly but with a good taste which even Fiona's inexperienced eye could appreciate. Her dark hair, brushed up from her face, showed few signs of greying, and a discreet make-up partially offset the squareness of the face and sallowness of skin. Her eyes were dark and small, but her other features were good and she smiled more than anybody Fiona had ever met. She always wore matching ear-rings and necklace, and the rings on her well-kept hands looked very valuable.

'First of all, dear, we must have you at home more. If I'm to bring you out, so to speak, and teach you how to be a good hostess and run a home for your father, I must have you here more often. I know you like running wild about the country and enjoy being with your cousin, but this is your home, you know, and your father has a right to expect you to show some interest in it.'

'But my interests are out of doors. I can't bear being cooped up.'

'That's an exaggeration, my dear. Nobody is suggesting that you should be cooped up. However, I can quite understand that, without a mother, you have been thrown on your own resources and have had nobody to guide you in a woman's sphere. Your good father has done his best, of course, but no father can make up for a mother's care. It's been a sad gap in your life. I have a daughter. We were always very close. So I know just how much you've missed, dear.'

'I didn't know you had a daughter. How old is she?'

'Valerie? She's twenty-eight. Unfortunately for me, she married an Australian we met on our travels, and she lives in Queensland now. She married when she was not much older than you. I must confess I was a little disappointed that I lost her so soon.'

Fiona, who had a sensitive ear, detected a certain edge to Mrs. Marchant's usually well-modulated voice.

'Yes. You must miss her very much.'

'Well, when my husband was alive, of course, we led such

a full life that I hadn't much time to miss my girl. But things have changed a lot since then.'

'Have you been to Australia to see your daughter since she married?'

'Not yet. I keep promising to, but, well I must confess the journey has put me off, and Australia is not a country that attracts me. So uncivilised in many ways. And a terrible climate where Valerie is. I could never stand the heat. However, I shall enjoy taking you under my wing instead, Fiona. I'm sure we shall make a very good team.'

Fiona, a little taken aback at being moved down in status to being Mrs. Marchant's charge, and knowing that she had her father to thank for this, smiled faintly and said:

'I hope so.'

'Now to get down to facts. It is your father's store dinner next week and you'll need a new dress for it. I think we'd better have a day in London, shopping. I've suggested to your father that we open an account for you at a London store that I always used to deal with. That has several advantages over shopping locally. At the end of the month, your father's sixtieth birthday will make a good opportunity to have a supper party here. Your father wants to do more entertaining, as he should, in his position. Then I thought you might like to run a stall at the bazaar Mrs. Crayshaw is organising at the beginning of November for the Elton Community Association. I expect she can find you one, although she always has plenty of volunteers, I know.'

'I don't think I'd be any good at running a stall,' said Fiona firmly. 'And I can't see the point of doing it if I don't enjoy it and Mrs. Crayshaw can get people who do.'

Mrs. Marchant smiled.

'But there is a point to it, dear. An important point. If you can get known as a public-spirited girl willing and able to take a leading part in local affairs, that will be a great help to your father as a councillor and possible future mayor. You have to look ahead, Fiona. The first thing I have to teach you is the importance of knowing the right people, of being seen with the right people. Elton is not a very large town, but it has its own social importance and your father is a leading citizen of it. He needs your support. You're too young to realise it now, but women have an important part to play in the background of men's public lives. My husband never tired of saying how much of his success he owed to me. Moreover,' added Mrs. Marchant brightly, observing that Fiona showed little enthusiasm for the important role she was to fill, 'it will improve your chances of finding a suitable husband. The more people you meet, the better your chance of making a good match. And don't tell me you're not interested in that, because I shan't believe you.'

As Mrs. Marchant's voice rolled musically on, it became apparent to Fiona that nothing was more important in Mrs. Marchant's opinion than worldly success, which was for her the crown of life waiting for those who were the ablest strategists and fighters in the contest. And Mrs. Marchant, it was clear, had always fought with the greatest determination and ardour.

When Fiona finally escaped to her room, it was with the depressing thought that she and Mrs. Marchant did not speak the same language. Her sense of values did not seem to belong to the same world as Mrs. Marchant's. If she told Mrs. Marchant that she would barter all her father's money and position for a little humour and affection from him; that contact with the country, with flowers, with music, appealed to her far more than contact with socially desirable people; that she would rather eat sandwiches alone in a field than attend the most sumptuous dinner: if she said any of this, she would be laughed at as a foolish girl who needed educating in the art of civilised living. But to Fiona, Mrs. Marchant's idea of a civilised life seemed little better than a camouflaged jungle where every step needed planning with guile. And if she told Mrs. Marchant that she loved Julian and could never imagine wanting to marry another man, Mrs. Marchant would dismiss this as an adolescent obsession which made it all the more desirable for Fiona to enlarge her social life.

She had taken up her favourite perch by the window, and was allowing her thoughts to wander back over the day when a knock at the door startled her.

'Fiona, are you there?' asked Mrs. Marchant.

'Yes.'

She opened the door.

'Don't bury yourself alone up here, dear. I'm just making a pot of tea for your father. Come down and share it with him, will you? He hasn't seen you all day.'

Fiona went down and joined her father in the sitting-room. He put down his paper as she came in.

'Nearly ten o'clock, and the first time I've set eyes on you today. There's no need to ask where you've been, of course.'

Fiona's heart sank. He was in one of his bad moods. The pattern of his behaviour towards her varied little. He displayed either indifference, dry tolerance or criticism. But on rare occasions he seemed to be seized with a malicious wish to goad her with a cruel sarcasm which left her raw and wincing. Meeting his grey eyes, cold as stone, she felt his malice extending to her now.

'I've been out walking all day with Julian. It was such a lovely day. And I went back to Alanbridge for dinner. I told Mrs. Marchant this morning.'

'I hope you don't make a nuisance of yourself, Fiona. You seem to favour Alanbridge with a great deal of your presence. It is possible to overdo your welcome, you know.'

Fiona's eyes were wide as she faced him, but he could not shake her on this ground.

'I don't make a nuisance of myself. Julian would tell me if I did.'

'Well, hardship though it is, apparently, for you to stay in your own home, I must ask you to do so a little more now. Mrs. Marchant has kindly undertaken to help you assume the responsibilities about which you seem to be so vague. So when she wants you, see that you're available. I don't like all this sneaking off to Alanbridge. I don't consider the Falconers a very good influence, anyway, and if Julian has nothing better to do in the week than idle his time away, you have.'

'Julian works very hard. He happened to have no pupils today, and he's been working furiously lately on a new composition which he's just finished.'

'I don't call that working. However, I know that in the eyes of my brother-in-law and his artistic son, I am a common tradesman who cannot be expected to appreciate the value of their efforts. Work. They don't know the meaning of the word, and they're far too precious to want to find out.'

Fiona knew that she would only be playing into her father's hands by arguing with him. He wanted to goad her and he knew that attacking the Falconers was as good a way as any.

She poured out a second cup of tea and passed it to him without a word.

'Oh, well,' he went on dryly, 'it's very pleasant to be born with money and be able to play about growing flowers and making up tunes on a piano, instead of having to work for a living as less fortunate people do. However, that sort of dilettante existence is dying out now. Taxation takes care of that, and a very good thing, too. I started with nothing, but I think I'll finish up in a much stronger position than our elegant relatives. They're on the way out. Before I've done, the name of Falconer won't mean as much as the name of Goring in these parts.'

'I don't think they'll mind,' said Fiona quietly. 'Uncle John likes a retiring, peaceful life, and Julian avoids publicity like the plague.'

'They'll mind not having the money to lead their pretty little lives.'

'I don't know anything about that.'

'No. You've always had that sublime disregard of money which only those who have had everything showered on them can afford. But it doesn't drop out of the sky, you know. It has to be worked for.'

'I would be very willing to earn my living if you would let me, Father. I want to.'

'You can earn it here by helping me.'

'I'll try,' said Fiona, pressing her hands together to hide their trembling.

'Good. How do you like Mrs. Marchant?'

'I think she's a very clever person.'

'Very competent. I like competent people. She'll be better for you than any expensive finishing school. She knows the world, that woman. She can teach you far more about life than you'll learn at Alanbridge, so spend more time here with her, please, and less with the Falconers. You understand?'

'Yes, Father.'

'I think perhaps we might invite our superior relatives to our first supper party. Show them that we don't live like savages and have a few refined tastes. It may be beneath their dignity to accept, of course.'

It was impossible to think of any two people less socially conscious and pretentious than her Uncle John and Julian, thought Fiona, but they might refuse on other grounds, for although Uncle John was scrupulously polite always in his references to her father, she knew that they had nothing in common, and Julian never hesitated to turn down invitations which sprang from expediency rather than friendship, for, being a fine pianist, such invitations were not uncommon. She said nothing, however, for there were no words which could breach the wall between her father and herself and she only bruised herself if she tried. Her passivity seemed to irritate him still further, for he said curtly:

'If you've nothing to say, you might as well take the tray out and go to bed. I hope to goodness Mrs. Marchant will be able to teach you how to use your tongue, otherwise you're going to be the reverse of a social asset.'

Why, she wondered, did he hate her so much? She could feel it always, like cold steel between them. As far as she knew, she had done nothing to earn his dislike. She had never been defiant, had never caused him anxiety or trouble. Now she felt imprisoned by forces which were too strong for her, and saw her life being strangled between her father and Mrs. Marchant while they tried to fashion her into a social asset, whatever that might be.

The following days were largely taken up with shopping and what Mrs. Marchant called 'grooming' in preparation for Fiona's appearance with her father at the store dinner. On the day before her ordeal, she came out of the hairdresser's in Elton in time to post herself outside Julian's school of music. She knew he had a lesson that afternoon and that he usually left about tea-time on Thursdays. He gave only three days a week to the school, spending the rest of his time at Alanbridge, helping to maintain the garden when he was not composing or arranging music. She had not seen him for a week and she ached for the comfort of his presence, even if only for a few minutes. She looked in the windows of the shop which sold music and gramophone records and over which were the school studios. Julian had put Mr. Cheney in charge of the shop after a road accident had damaged his hand so that his career as a violinist was finished. Fiona could see his beaky profile behind the counter, and thought how lovely it would be to work behind the counter with him or help in the office. She had studied all the music displayed, and now turned her attention to the lists of gramophone records. It was a grey day and there was a chilly wind. She hoped Julian would not be long.

She waited twenty minutes before his long figure strode through the swing door. He stopped short as he saw her.

'Hullo, Fiona. What brings you to the portals of this noble academy?'

'I had to come to the hairdresser's, and I wondered if I might catch you.'

'You look cold. You should have come in.'

'I didn't want to interrupt you. Are you going back to Alanbridge for tea?'

'We-ell, I might let a certain young person persuade me to patronise a café in Elton for tea. What about it?'

'Yes, please,' said Fiona, smiling happily as he took her arm and they walked towards the High Street.

They turned off the High Street just short of the imposing façade of her father's store, which dominated the shopping centre of the town, and found a corner table in a small café nearby.

'You look different,' said Julian, after he had ordered tea and cakes.

'It's my fringe. Gone. Mrs. Marchant said it was too childish.'

'Dear me. I can't see much under that beret, but I trust they haven't curled you up like a little lamb.'

'No. Only shaped it. I had to have my hands manicured, too. I didn't like it. All that fiddling about just because I haven't got half-moons. I refused to have red finger-nails. I expect Mrs. Marchant will disapprove.'

'Let her. If you have red finger-nails, I shall insist on your wearing gloves whenever you're with me. Revolting fashion. Only suitable for murderous ladies like Lady Macbeth. Show me what they've done.'

Fiona spread out her hands obediently.

'That's all right. What fragile looking hands you've got. Not meant for manual work, that's evident. They'd be nice to draw.'

Fiona flushed with pleasure as she said:

'They're not much good for the piano, though.'

'M'm, you need more strength than that in your hands. Still, all music doesn't call for strong hands, you know. I've never heard you play.'

'You'd squirm if I did.'

'How many years did you have at it when you were at school?'

'Two. Father thought it would be a waste of money to go on any longer, and I guess he was right. I can play well enough to amuse myself; that's all. Father wanted me to be brilliant, like you, and then he could show me off. I'm not at all a satisfactory daughter, I'm afraid. I don't shine at anything.'

'I think you have a real talent for drawing and painting. It's a pity he wouldn't let you go to London to study.'

'I've just started evening classes. I think I'm going to enjoy them. I've got to have something,' she added a little despairingly.

'What have you been doing with yourself this week? I was counting on you to help me design a striking poster to advertise a recital by one of our pupils.'

'I'd have loved to do that. But I've been told to spend more time at home now. Home is my finishing school, and Mrs. Marchant my teacher,' said Fiona with an attempt at lightness which didn't come off under Julian's dark eyes.

'Tell me more,' he said, passing her the cakes.

She told him of her father's social programme and of Mrs. Marchant's change of attitude.

'Between them, I don't feel I have much chance,' she concluded unhappily.

'H'm. So the hermit really is opening up his private life, is he? Well, in some respects it will be a good thing to let a little light into number ten, my dear. You'll soon get over your shyness with strangers.'

'Not with Father's eye on me, looking for faults. They're trying to make me into something that I'm not, Julian. Their world and mine aren't the same. What they seem to find important seems to me to be just silly showing off for the benefit of people who don't mean a thing to you. Anyway, I can't think that any of my father's acquaintances will care two hoots whether I've got half-moons on my fingers. And nothing,' she added defiantly, 'will get me into corsets.'

Her back-to-the-wall expression caused Julian to choke over his tea, and it was some moments before he recovered and was able to say:

'Shouldn't have thought there was enough of you to prop up.'

'They can always find something. According to the woman in the shop, I shall be like a sack of flour in five years' time if I don't do anything about it now. I said I'd wait until I was. Mrs. Marchant was annoyed, but there are limits. Fancy having to walk round all day encased like a mummy, with whale-bone digging into you every time you stoop.'

'Shocking. Your Mrs. Marchant sounds like the answer to every advertiser's prayer.'

Fiona sighed.

'I don't think we shall ever understand each other. All the things that matter so much to me don't seem to enter into her life at all.'

'Such as . . .'

'You know. I don't have to tell you. Are those cakes with the nuts on nice?'

'Not very. But then I don't like marshmallow.'

'Nor do I. Perhaps I'd better not have any more.'

'I'd still like to hear about those things that matter to you. Besides cakes.'

'Well, there are so many things that make me happy, but Mrs. Marchant never seems to have come across them. There's the country and everything alive and growing in it. There's music, poetry, all the lovely things like the sky at night, and the wind in the trees, and just looking at beautiful shapes and colours. Oh, I can't make a list of them, but they're all to be found at Alanbridge, and you've shown me the way to so many of them. But Mrs. Marchant thinks I should like dinners and parties and dressing up and drinking sherry, only dry sherry, and impressing the right people and attracting the right husband.'

'Dear me. What is known as a worldly woman.'

'And all the things I like she thinks of as adolescent mooniness. It's time I learned the realities of life, she says. As though those things aren't real and all this acting I'm supposed to do is. It's like Alice in Wonderland. All topsy-turvy.'

'There is no end to the oddness of people's sense of values, my dear. What is worth while, and what is not: if life teaches you anything, it must surely teach you that. And yet how many people go through life without ever seeming to appreciate the difference between pleasure and happiness, between the real and the synthetic, the trivial and the fundamental. You should feel sorry for the Mrs. Marchants. They miss so much. She thinks she is a realist, but she has no reality within herself at all. Stick to the reality inside you, Fiona. It's all that matters, and pays rich dividends. The Mrs. Marchants of this world are second-handers—be sorry for them but don't let them obscure your own clear vision. Not that I think you will. You have the kind of simplicity which sees truth through the wrappings.'

'Yes, but if I'm forced to live according to their ideas, that's not much help.'

'Cheer up. You won't be a child for ever, and you'll find a way to independence. Meanwhile, you can skate along the surface of Mrs. Marchant's pattern. After all, having the corners rubbed down and learning to mix with all kinds of people is useful experience, and you may find you get quite a spot of enjoyment out of it.'

'I don't think enjoyment and Father go together. Anyway, strangers seem to paralyse me. Do you like parties and dinners, Julian?'

'Formal ones, seldom. Small talk bores me. I like something more intimate. A few friends and a good dinner make up a pleasant evening, I think.'

'There's a lot of difference between duty dinners and friendship dinners,' said Fiona mournfully. 'I don't suppose you would want to come to a party Father is giving at home at the end of the month. It's his sixtieth birthday. He said he would invite you and Uncle John.'

'Great Scott! It's years since we've put a foot across your threshold.'

'I know. We've never done any entertaining before. I suppose being a widower made it difficult for Father. Now I've got to step in. I don't expect you and Uncle John would enjoy it very much, but . . .' she hesitated.

'You'd like me to come?'

'Of course. You would make anything bearable. And perhaps it might help to make things a little easier between our two families. I'm so afraid he'll try to stop me from coming to Alanbridge. If he knows anything means a lot to me, he's apt to use that as a weapon. I try to hide how much

I love being at Alanbridge with you and Uncle John, but I think he knows. So if you accept his invitation, it might help a little, though I don't want to force a miserable evening on you.'

'If honoured with an invitation, I will come. I can't answer for Dad, though.'

'Oh, thank you, Julian. That *is* noble of you. I can promise you good food and drink. Mrs. Marchant is awfully clever at that side of things.'

'Enough said. I'll be there. Now I'm going to drive you home. I've got a lot of work to do this evening.'

But to his father that evening, Julian expressed himself more forcibly.

'You can imagine what it will be like, can't you? All the civic busybodies and anybody who might be useful. The whole evening a crashing bore. You won't come, I take it?'

'No. I've reached the age when I please myself, and can always shelter behind the excuse of my poor health. You have always been precociously emancipated in such matters, though. I'm surprised at your acceptance.'

'I'm only doing it for Fiona's sake. It wouldn't take much to make Uncle Graham sever all connection with us, and that would make things even more difficult for Fiona. She's a nice kid. I hope they don't spoil her and turn her into a conventional little doll. It's a bad atmosphere for any young person.'

'I think Fiona has enough integrity to keep herself intact.'

'I'm sure she has, but I don't like her having to live with all this opportunism, and be used as a stooge in her father's pursuit of power. He's already the wealthiest man in Elton. What more does he want?'

'Social importance. You're very fond of Fiona, aren't you?'

'Yes. She has a rare quality about her. And she's as responsive to beauty as plants are to light.'

'You've taken a lot of trouble with her.'

'That's the teaching urge in me,' said Julian, grinning. 'If I see young raw material as promising as that, I have to get my hands on it. I wish one or two of my pupils had half of her responsiveness.'

'I thought you only took the promising ones and shoved the others off on the rest of the staff.'

'So I do. I find I have less patience with obtuseness as I get older, and what's the good of running a school if you can't pick your pupils?'

'I suppose you're aware of the fact that Fiona worships the ground you walk on and that everything you say has the authority of Jove?'

'Oh, she's at the hero-worshipping stage. She'll grow out of that,' said Julian casually. 'I hope I'll be able to keep an eye on the kid, though, until she's secure on her own feet. You're looking tired, Dad. Been overdoing it?'

'I helped Joe clear up the leaves today.'

'You know what the doctor said about taking things easily.'

'I know. If I go about in a wheel-chair I may live an indefinite number of years, but who wants to live an indefinite number of years in a wheel-chair? I shall go on working as best I can in the garden, Julian. It's my greatest joy and achievement. Would you choose otherwise?'

'No. But it doesn't make me very cheerful to contemplate Alanbridge without you.'

'I wish you'd get married, my boy, and bring young life here again. At thirty, it's time you thought about it.'

Julian moved restlessly in his chair and then got up to throw a log on the fire.

'Afraid I've only met one person I'd like to settle with and she, unfortunately, doesn't want to settle.'

'Ah, that's it, is it? I wondered. It isn't always musical matters that keep you in London so often, then?'

'Not entirely.'

Julian leaned against the marble mantelpiece and began to fill his pipe with a preoccupied air. John Falconer looked at the dark, sensitive face of his son with affection and pride in his eyes, and a hint of anxiety, too. The boy had a hungry look about him lately, and was restless. He had suspected that some woman might be leading him a dance. He was very eligible: gifted, personable, with a good background. Not unattractive to women, his father thought, but himself very fastidious in that direction. He knew nothing of this woman, and, close as he and his son were in understanding, he would never have dreamed of questioning him. It was one of John Falconer's virtues that he could respect another person's private ground, however close that person was to him. He had only sensed that his son was not at peace with himself of late. His son and Alanbridge: all that his heart held now. He looked on Alanbridge as a trust from his father and grandfather, and had maintained the garden, which was so well known in the horticultural world, with all the zeal and love of his ancestors. At first, he had thought that music would claim all of Julian's devotion, but his son had inherited enough love of horticulture and pride in Alanbridge to ensure its survival as a place of beauty. Now it needed only a wife who could share Julian's interests and give him a happy home and children to carry on the Falconer tradition here at Alanbridge, to fulfil all that John Falconer still hoped from this world. He would like to see that before he died.

Julian said no more on the subject, and after he had finished his pipe he went up to the music room, leaving his father alone by the fire with his thoughts, which so often went back into the past these days. The cat on the hearthrug at his feet suddenly began to purr with a far-away look in his eyes as though he, too, were enjoying the recollection of things past.

CHAPTER FOUR

FIONA survived the ordeal of the store dinner and dance without bringing any fire of criticism down on her head afterwards, but when she took off the very elegant white brocade evening dress which Mrs. Marchant had chosen and kicked off the high-heeled silver kid slippers, she was conscious of a kind of dead weariness which she had never experienced before. She supposed it was the strain of acting a part under her father's eyes for several hours, during which the tension within her never relaxed. Most of the people to whom she had been introduced were elderly or middle-aged and somehow their deference and obvious efforts to please her had made it all the more difficult to relax and feel natural. The whole evening had possessed an atmosphere of unreality for her, and now she sat down on the bed thoroughly exhausted.

She was to be conscious of this strange dead tiredness after every social function which she attended with her father in the months that followed. His birthday party was the first occasion on which Fiona assumed the responsibilities of hostess, and although she hid her trepidation under a solemn little air of dignity which was not without its charm, the strain beneath the surface was apparent to Julian when he came up behind her and laid a hand on her arm to feel her jump like a startled fawn and turn frightened eyes to him until recognition brought a relieved smile to her face.

'Oh, it's you, Julian. I thought you were enmeshed with Mr. Gilbert and his stocks and shares for at least an hour.'

'I'm adept at the graceful fade-out,' he said. 'You look cold.'

'Yes, I feel shivery. This dress is like cold water on my skin. Don't look at me, Julian. I don't feel a bit nice in it. It was Mrs. Marchant's choice, and I know it doesn't suit me at all.'

'You're too young to wear black,' he said, thinking how incongruous her tender young face looked above the tight black frock with its plunging neckline and long tapering sleeves.

'I wish we could escape, but Mrs. Marchant would be bound to notice.'

'She's quite impressive, isn't she,' said Julian softly, his eyes dwelling on Mrs. Marchant, who was laughing at something their host was saying. She was wearing a beautifully cut grey dress and her ear-rings glittered as she moved. 'And one of the family already.'

'Yes. She joins us now for everything. In a way, I'm glad because it does mean I don't have to endure those awful silent meals alone with Father any more. Mrs. Marchant can always talk.'

Fiona stopped and tensed suddenly as her father came up.

'You're neglecting your guests, Fiona. We thought of making up a few tables for bridge, Julian. You'll join in, won't you?'

'Well, I'm not much of a bridge player, but I'll make a fourth if needed. What about you, Fiona?'

'Bridge isn't one of Fiona's accomplishments,' said her father in his dry voice. 'Neither Mrs. Fisher nor Mrs. Renwick play, either, so you might see if you can entertain them with your lively prattle, my dear.'

Fiona's cheeks flamed at his sarcasm, and Julian clenched the hand in his pocket.

'I'll help Mrs. Marchant set up the tables first,' she murmured and moved swiftly away.

She was not alone with Julian again until the end of the evening, when she slipped into a coat and walked with him to the gate.

'I'm afraid this hasn't been the sort of party you enjoy, Julian. I know you don't like cards.'

'All experience, my dear. Come over to Alanbridge whenever you can. We're always glad to see you about the place. You fit in, somehow.'

She suddenly picked up his hand and laid it against her cheek.

'I don't know what I should do without you and Alanbridge.'

'Good-night, poppet.'

He rubbed her head affectionately and climbed into his car. She stood on the pavement watching until the tail light disappeared....

As the weeks of that autumn passed, Fiona's efforts to mould herself to the pattern desired by her father and Mrs. Marchant brought no easing of the situation. Her temperament and nature were so alien to the role they forced on her that she could never resolve the conflict within her, and the strain of playing an artificial part began to tell on her.

Looking out of the dining-room window at the boughs of the monkey-puzzle tree one Saturday afternoon in December, she thought that they were like the bars of a prison cell, and she suddenly felt an overwhelming need to escape from the house. Mrs. Marchant had informed her that morning that they would be going to a jumble sale after lunch. Her father had gone to a south coast town to inspect some shop premises which were for sale and was not expected back until late. She turned as Mrs. Marchant came into the room.

'I feel a craving for fresh air and exercise, Mrs. Marchant. I don't think I'll come to the jumble sale, if you don't mind.'

'I think you should. It's for a good cause.'

'Yes, but I don't want to be shut up today. This is the first fine afternoon for ages. I shall go for a walk and call in at Uncle John's for tea.'

Mrs. Marchant's smile was frosty. She had come to take it

for granted that Fiona would acquiesce in her plans, and was deceived by the girl's gentle manner into thinking that her domination was secure.

'I don't think your father would approve. He likes you to be seen at local functions for charity.'

'I'm sorry,' said Fiona quietly, and walked out of the room before Mrs. Marchant could say any more.

It would be reported to her father, Fiona knew, for the past weeks had revealed that Mrs. Marchant was not averse to presenting Fiona in a poor light. It was done with subtlety, more in sorrow than in anger, even sometimes with an indulgent smile, but Fiona's perceptions had become very acute during the years she had lived at Lime Avenue, and she knew that Mrs. Marchant was no longer for her. Too young to understand motives, she concluded that Mrs. Marchant did not like her and wondered in her more disconsolate moments whether there was something wrong with her since neither her father nor Mrs. Marchant could feel any affection for her. From the morbidity of these moments, however, the kindness and warmth which welcomed her at Alanbridge rescued her, and as she set out that afternoon her spirits lifted with all the resilience of youth.

It was a sunny, frosty day, and she swung along happily, her hands in the pockets of her comfortable tweed coat, her feet happy in her walking shoes, a beret perched jauntily on her head. The ground was still iron hard, and frost trimmed every blade of grass as she crossed the field at the end of Lime Avenue. The trees stood out against a pale blue sky, beautiful in their bare silhouettes. The elms were loveliest, she thought. Or perhaps the silver birches with their delicacy of line. She had drawn such trees many times, never tiring of the beautiful clarity of form which winter revealed. There was ice on the puddle at the foot of the stile and it cracked as she jumped down on to it.

She hoped Julian would be home. He had been in London the last time she had escaped to Alanbridge, and it was nearly a month since she had seen him. She began to sing Greensleeves as she crossed the meadow towards the larch trees and Alanbridge.

Approaching the house through the garden at the back, she did not see the car parked in the drive in front of the house, and her first intimation that there were visitors at Alanbridge came when Julian emerged from the sitting-room into the hall, saying over his shoulder:

'Cigarettes on the radiogram, Laurie. Help yourself.' He stopped as he saw Fiona, and his heart-warming smile reassured her. 'Hullo, Fiona. You're a refreshing sight. Just in time for tea.'

'You've got visitors, Julian. I won't disturb you. I only looked in to ... to ...' She tried desperately to improvise some reason for a hail-and-farewell visit, but failed, and Julian regarded her with his head on one side and a quizzical look in his eyes.

'You'll never be a good fibber, ducky. Even polite fibs fox you. Come along in and meet two very good friends of mine. You've heard me talk about them. Now you can meet them.'

'Oh, no, Julian. I don't want to butt in. I'll come again tomorrow.'

She had backed to the door before Julian took her firmly by the shoulders.

'They won't eat you, and I'd like you to meet them. Let me take your hat and coat.'

Reluctantly, she allowed him to take them. All the training she had received at Mrs. Marchant's hands had not succeeded in banishing an instinctive shrinking from strangers. If anything, it had increased her self-consciousness. She looked down at herself nervously.

Julian eyed her with some amusement. In her red sweater and fawn skirt, with her soft hair a little ruffled and her eyes bright and apprehensive, she reminded him of a robin. He took her arm and said in a dramatic whisper:

'They're terribly important people. If you say the wrong thing or create a bad impression, my whole career will be ruined, and I shall never have a chance to compose that soap opera for American broadcasting.'

Fiona's cheeks dimpled.

'You're pulling my leg.'

'Could be,' he said, grinning as he put an arm round her shoulders and propelled her through the sitting-room door.

A tall dark man rose from the settee as Fiona went in. He was rather handsome in a brooding sort of way: clean-shaven, with heavy black eyebrows over dark eyes, a square jaw, and black hair showing a sprinkling of grey at the sides.

To Fiona he appeared a little forbidding, but the young woman sitting in the corner of the settee looked a much friendlier proposition and gave Fiona such a warm smile as they shook hands that her fears melted like frost in the sun. Fiona had heard Julian mention them often: Dr. Deverel, head of the Research Station at Marchwood, and Celia, his wife.

'I'll just go and tell Mrs. Blakeney we're ready for tea,' said Julian.

Celia turned to Fiona with a smile.

'I'm so glad you came while we're here. I've heard so much about Julian's young cousin, and just before you arrived, I was admiring that little drawing over the book-case, which Julian tells me is yours.'

'Yes. The Italian fountain in the garden here,' said Fiona shyly.

'It's delightful.'

'The garden is so lovely that I could spend my life drawing here and never run out of subjects.'

'Not just a garden, but several gardens, and all enchanting. Laurie and I are green with envy. Ours just isn't in the same class, though we do our best.'

'Generations of fine horticulturists have achieved this, my dear,' said her husband. 'To compare our garden with this is like comparing the local amateur operatic society with Covent Garden.'

'Have you much ground?' asked Fiona.

'Only a third of an acre. It's quite a pleasant plot, though. Do you know Marchwood?' asked Dr. Deverel.

'Not very well. Only the part round the cricket green and the War Memorial. It's a very pretty place, I think.'

'My wife thinks there's no place in the world like it,' he said with an odd little smile that dispelled the air of rather austere authority which Fiona had found faintly chilling.

Julian came back, closely followed by Mrs. Blakeney with the tea-trolley, and over the tea-cups the Deverels and Julian became immersed in a discussion of a modern opera which they had all recently seen in London. Fiona listened, her wide eyes dwelling gravely in turn on the speakers. They could all express their opinions with a clarity and firmness which she envied. Celia Deverel's spirited manner and impetuous tongue contrasted strongly with her husband's calm, objective views. She was very attractive, thought Fiona, with that auburn hair and the dark grey eyes in a face brimming with vitality. Julian, with greater knowledge than either of his friends, pointed out with good humour several merits in the opera which he thought they had overlooked, and shook his head at them with a twinkle in his eye as he added:

'I didn't expect Laurie would like it. He's too conservative for words. But I thought your mind was more open to new roads in music, Celia.'

'But such uncomfortable, bumpy roads. Still, I expect greater familiarity would reveal a few consolations. I'm not prepared to go further than that.'

'And I,' said Deverel firmly, 'shall stick to Verdi.'

'Not Wagner, darling?' asked his wife mischievously. 'I always think you're the Wagnerian type.'

'And you, my dear, belong in spirit to Mozart. Quite irrepressible. No wonder I find it difficult to instil some sense of discipline into the boys with your blood in their veins.'

'And yours, dear,' said Celia sweetly. 'Their strong wills are pure Deverel. I wish I had a gentle little girl to leaven the loaf.'

'Well, you'll have to see what you can do,' said Julian, grinning. 'And if Laurie's aura is Wagnerian, and yours Mozartian, don't you agree that Fiona is pure Debussy?'

'Bang on, Julian,' said Celia, thinking that she would never again hear 'L'Après-midi d'un Faune' without seeing this girl's wistful, unworldly face. There was a sensitive, dreamy quality about it which attracted her strongly and she determined to get to know this cousin of Julian's.

Fiona found herself relaxed and happy that evening. Julian played to them, and Celia, herself a fair pianist, added her contribution. Fiona curled up on a cushion on the hearthrug and listened, enrapt. Half-way through the concert, Dr. Deverel moved his armchair forward and eased Fiona's back against the arm with such a friendly smile as she screwed her head round to him that she wondered how she could ever have thought him forbidding. Why were her father's friends never like this, she wondered. But then, they were not friends, but acquaintances or business associates cultivated for their usefulness. She did not think her father could boast one real friend.

She was startled when she heard the clock strike ten, and reluctantly decided that she must go. She had not intended to stay so long, for her father would be back by now and enquiring about her. In spite of her protests, Julian insisted on driving her home.

'It won't take more than five minutes in the car, and it's a lonely walk at this time of night. There's no bus for half an hour.'

'But you don't want to leave your friends, Julian.'

'They'll be quite happy without me, I assure you. Now don't argue.'

The night was bitterly cold, and frost sparkled in the moonlight with a glitter that outdid the starry sky.

'I have enjoyed this evening, Julian. Thank you so much for making me stay. They're nice, the Deverels, aren't they?'

'Yes. I thought you'd like them.'

'Have they been married long?'

'Let me see, it must be eight years. Young Peter's seven. I'm his godfather, and a livelier handful has never come my way.'

'What about his brother? There are two, aren't there?'

'Yes. Philip's five. He looks a cherub, but in his subtle way he's just as big a menace. A good thing they've a firm father. Laurie doesn't stand any nonsense.'

'I shall be meeting them. While you were getting the car, Celia asked me to go over and spend an afternoon with her next week.'

'Splendid. You could do with a friend of your own sex, my dear, and Celia Deverel will be very good for you. Here we are. How are things at home, by the way?'

'Oh, much as usual. Did you enjoy your few days in London?'

'Very much, in patches. So long, ducky. Take care of yourself.'

Fiona went in with some trepidation about her father's reception, but she found him in an unusually pleasant mood drinking coffee with Mrs. Marchant in the sitting-room and she went to bed with no more exchange between them than an affable sentence or two, and 'Good-night'.

* * *

The village of Marchwood was little more than half an hour's bus ride from Elton, and Fiona had no difficulty in finding Wingate Lodge, the Deverels' home. It was a friendly looking house, its bricks mellowed to a warm russet colour, and its oak door bore a heavy iron knocker in the shape of a lion's head.

Celia opened the door with a welcoming smile, and in a few minutes Fiona was toasting her toes before a roaring fire and admiring the bowls of bronze chrysanthemums which glowed warmly in a room which defied the grey wintry sky outside. All the colours of autumn were in the room: the capacious armchairs and settee were upholstered in a rich bronze material, the shade of fallen beech leaves; the carpet was moss green and the velvet curtains which framed the large windows were the same pale gold as poplar leaves before they fell.

'The children are going straight from school to a tea-party, so we shall have a nice peaceful afternoon. Nan has gone off to meet them when they come out of school and see them to their friend's home. Otherwise, Peter's quite likely to take it into his head to go off on his own, and where Peter leads, Philip follows. He did that once before. When Nan went to collect them from a tea-party they weren't there. Peter had explained to his class-mate and would-be host that he didn't feel like a party, and he and Philip had got on a bus to Elton to go and see the market instead. They arrived home about half-past six, just after an almost incoherent Nan had telephoned me from the friend's house.'

'A young man of independent mind, evidently. That's him with Philip on the book-case, I suppose?'

'Yes.' Celia fetched the photograph for her. 'They're like Laurie, both of them.'

Fiona studied the photograph of the two sturdy little boys. Peter, with his dark hair tumbling on his forehead, certainly looked a most determined character. The little boy sitting on the wall next to him looked like a fair cherub, however, and Fiona could see no resemblance there to either of his parents.

'I don't think Philip is like either of you.'

'He's like Laurie when he smiles. That's not very good of him. He's posing. He always has been able to put on that guileless innocent air when expedient. But I mustn't bore you with my children. I fear you'll see and hear them all too soon. They're a lot better when Laurie's around, and as he'll be home before them this evening, you'll probably find them quite bearable. Tell me about yourself, Fiona. Don't you find it lonely at home without any brothers or sisters?'

'Sometimes. But I'm not so conscious of being lonely on my own as when I'm with people I don't understand. On my own, I can enjoy the country or music or sketching, and I'm perfectly happy. And, of course, I've always had Julian and Alanbridge. Anyway, lately I've become involved in so many local social affairs that I don't have an awful lot of time alone.'

They chatted on as the light began to fade and the flames of the fire sent shadows flickering up the walls and across the ceiling. There was something in Celia's warm personality that dispelled all Fiona's natural shyness and drew her out, so that she found herself discussing all sorts of things which were normally kept close to her heart. Perhaps it was because Celia, although so much older, treated Fiona as an adult that she felt she could respond without reserve. For even Julian, dear as he was, in many ways still treated her as a child. They had been talking of his musical talent when Celia said:

'I hope he gets married. He has so much to hand on. But I sometimes wonder whether he will. Laurie says that music is his mistress and Alanbridge his wife, and that they fill all his life.'

'Yes. He has a very full and satisfying life, of course. You don't think that Norah Coachford? . . .'

'No. She'd like the chance, but she's far too managing and bossy for Julian. Handy on his staff, but the last type to appeal to him in any other capacity, I'd say. I'm not so sure about Gillian Courtney, though.'

'Gillian Courtney? The actress?'

'Yes. Didn't you know that she was a friend of Julian's?'

'No. But then, of course, he seldom talks about his friends to me. She's a jolly good actress. I saw her play Rosalind in *As You Like It* when I went with a school party. And she's lovely, too. I wonder why Julian didn't tell me they were friends. She's such a well-known person and he knows I admire her.'

'Well, maybe there's nothing in it. We met them in a Soho restaurant together one night, and Julian had to introduce her. But he's quite a clam about it. We're very fond of Julian, Laurie and I. And not just because he can work miracles with our children. They're just like putty in his hands. It never ceases to amaze me.'

'I think Julian has a way with all young things. He must be an awfully good teacher, though he doesn't do so much of it nowadays. I know I owe him a lot.'

'The telephone. If that's Laurie saying he'll be late I shall sue for a divorce. It'll be the third time this week. Excuse me.'

Celia ran out to the hall and Fiona picked up a magazine from the little table beside her. In it, there were some photographs from Gillian Courtney's new play. She was certainly lovely, thought Fiona, as she studied a photograph which showed Miss Courtney, in evening dress, facing two men at what appeared to be a dramatic moment in the play. She was tall and slender, and her head was beautifully carried in that picture of proud defiance. There was a lot of character in her face, so that one's first thought was not how beautiful, but how interesting. An intelligent, alive face. A good match for Julian, thought Fiona, feeling suddenly depressed. Any man would be proud to have such a gifted, attractive person for his wife.

Celia came back with a tea-tray in her hands.

'Sorry to leave you, but I guessed you were ready for this. Laurie will be late. He told us not to wait dinner for him. He'll just have sandwiches and coffee when he gets in. And if there's anything more infuriating to a cook than that, I don't know it. Never marry a man who is wrapped up in his work, Fiona, unless you're content to be like a box of chocolates lying around until he has time to sample you.'

Celia spoke lightly, but her eyes sparkled angrily, and Fiona glimpsed a fiery streak in her new friend.

'Scientific research must be absorbing.'

'Yes,' said Celia dryly. 'I suppose if I were the kind of wife who's glad to see the back of her husband each day, I wouldn't mind. However, I married a clever scientist, and must accept the consequences. I sometimes wish I had equally absorbing work, and then I wouldn't miss him so much.'

'The children?'

'They're absorbing, but not in the way I meant. They

absorb my time and a good deal of my energy, and I love them dearly. But sometimes my mind feels starved and lonely for other adult minds. In particular, for my husband's.'

Fiona could understand this, knowing how hungry she sometimes felt for the presence of Julian's lively intelligence.

'Men are lucky, aren't they?' she said slowly. 'Having work which fills their lives so completely.'

'They are if they happen to be doing work they like. I don't think they realise how limiting home life can be to a woman's mind. At least, Laurie doesn't. He has a very Victorian outlook about women in the home.'

'And yet, you have so much, Celia,' said Fiona, thinking that even if Julian came home late every day and was immersed in music to the point of forgetting her, she would still be in heaven if their lives were joined, and if she could minister to his happiness in any way.

'I know,' said Celia, smiling. 'And I do appreciate it, believe me. If I weren't so happy with Laurie, I wouldn't mind how little I saw him. Pay no heed to me, Fiona. I fly off the handle rather easily, you know, and I felt just now as though Laurie was addressing the housekeeper. Probably had someone with him and had to be formal.'

They spent a tempestuous half-hour with the children that evening before their bed-time restored tranquillity, and after dinner they listened to a Beethoven concert on the wireless. It was nearly ten and Fiona was about to leave to catch her bus when Dr. Deverel arrived home. He looked tired, but greeted Fiona with a friendly smile and an apology for his absence. Celia was so polite to him that Fiona guessed she was labouring under considerable strain.

'I've cut some sandwiches, Laurie, and the coffee's only just been made. I'll bring it in for you, and then see Fiona to the bus.'

'I'll run her along in the car, dear.'

'No,' broke in Fiona, 'I shouldn't dream of troubling you. It's only a few minutes' walk and you must be tired.'

'We'll walk, Laurie,' said Celia firmly. 'I could do with some fresh air.'

The air was indeed very fresh, but they had to run the last few yards to catch the bus, and as Fiona waved good-bye from the platform, she felt warm and glowing both inside and out, happy in the knowledge that a warm frank friendship had been offered to her that day, lighting a second candle in her life. She hoped that the dash for the bus might have released some of her friend's high tension. Somehow, she didn't think that Dr. Deverel would be an easy man to cross swords with. Had she seen Dr. Deverel's expression when he greeted his wife on her return, however, she would have felt reassured, for he crouched down on the settee and held a cushion up before his face in pretended fear as he said meekly, but with a twinkle in his eye:

'Don't be too hard on me. I really couldn't help it.'

Celia looked at him sternly.

'You can always help everything you do, Laurie. You're that sort of person, so it's no use trying to act a victim of circumstances. It was too bad of you. You've known all the week that tonight Fiona was going to be here. The only night I had arranged anything.'

'But I'm sure you two girls enjoyed yourselves all the more on your own. Young Fiona is half scared of me, I believe.'

'You're apt to have that effect on the tenderer members of our sex.'

'But never on you, sweetheart.'

'Never. But then my fibres are as tough as a door-mat.'

'I wouldn't say that. Resilient, perhaps, like this settee.'

His face was solemn, but a suspicion of a smile caught the corner of his mouth and his eyes teased her. She felt her anger dissolve and knew that she was beaten. As she looked at him, she was aware of a mixture of exasperation and affection. How sure of himself he was, and always had been. She felt annoyed that her love for him should give his male arrogance so many victories when her pride revolted. But always he had beaten her, even in their single days when her pride had been so much stronger and her heart less deeply his.

'I can accept having to play second fiddle to your work, Laurie, as long as it is second fiddle and I'm not just regarded as the music-stand. You sounded as though you were giving orders to the cook when you spoke to me this afternoon.'

'Did I, my dear? That was very discourteous of me. I apologise.'

'Did you have someone with you?'

'No. I was digesting some rather unexpected results

we'd had from an experiment, and I'm afraid my mind was mainly on that.'

'I don't think that's any excuse. You could have removed your mind for the space of two minutes while you were talking to me.'

'I know. But I have a terribly one-track mind. Don't stand over there like a lecturer, sweetheart. Come and sit down here and fight it out at close quarters. So much cosier.'

He held out his hand and she allowed herself to be drawn down beside him.

'I like your young friend. Those large, gentle eyes of hers remind me of a doe. She looks as though she'd bound away, too, at the least hint of violence. Perhaps she'll help to fill Margaret's place.'

And take my mind off missing you so much, thought Celia shrewdly. So that's what you think, my lord. Well, it was true that since her friend, Margaret, had married a South African a year ago and had gone to live in Johannesburg, Celia had been more aware of the loneliness of the long days when Laurie worked late. But the last role she wanted to play was the possessive wife, jealous even of her husband's work, and she smiled as she said:

'Perhaps. Sorry if I was a bit fierce, Laurie. I should be used to the claims of the Research Station by now.'

He put an arm round her shoulder.

'My fault. Like to go up to London for dinner and a show tomorrow? I can get away early now that this experiment's concluded.'

'Yes, I'd love to.'

'Right. You decide what you want to see, and we'll make a night of it. Boys in good form today?'

'Yes. They enjoyed their party. I promised you'd look in and say good-night, however late you were. They'll be fast asleep, of course, but a promise is a promise.'

'So it is. I'm far too comfortable to move at the moment, though. For a music-stand, you're uncommonly yielding, I must say.'

Celia smiled and said nothing. As long as she knew that underneath the work that absorbed so much of his life his love for her was still alive, nothing else mattered. As though reading her thoughts, he added:

'As a matter of fact, you're not second fiddle, either. You're one of the strings of my instrument, and it wouldn't be much good without you.'

CHAPTER FIVE

DRIVING home from a Conservative Party dinner with her father one January night of driving wind and rain, Fiona was conscious of his cold displeasure before he said anything. The windscreen wiper ticked monotonously, the wheels swished along the wet road and the rain slanted across the beam of their headlights like fine steel rods.

'I must say you made a nice fool of yourself with Colonel Shipley tonight, Fiona. A fine impression he'll have of my daughter.'

'In what way?'

'Taking up that childish, absurd attitude to hunting and shooting. You know Colonel Shipley's one of the finest shots in the county and that he hunts regularly. Have you no idea of tact after all the schooling Mrs. Marchant's given you?'

'He asked me my opinion. I saw no reason to lie. I do think hunting and shooting are cruel and I can't understand anybody getting pleasure out of it.'

'Fiddlesticks. You're a silly, sentimental child and nobody is interested in your opinions. You could have made some non-committal answer that wouldn't have been offensive. Upon my soul, I never knew a more hopeless social proposition than you. Either you're completely dumb, or else you say the wrong thing. Colonel Shipley is a very influential member of the ratepayers' group and I'm expecting them to put me forward as their nominee for Mayor at the next meeting of the General Purposes Committee. I can't say you've been any help to me.'

'I'm sorry, Father.'

'You're just a silly little fool, and I suppose I can't expect anything better from you. No worldly sense whatever. You live in some cloud cuckoo land that doesn't exist outside of your imagination. However, I shan't have to call upon your doubtful aid much longer. I might as well tell you now. I'm going to marry Mrs. Marchant, Fiona.'

'Marry Mrs. Marchant?'

Fiona sounded amazed. Such a thought had never crossed her mind, perhaps because her father had never seemed human to her and she could not credit him with affection for anybody, or imagine anybody wanting to marry him.

'Is it so surprising? Lena has transformed our home since she came. I need a partner. Someone to run my home and entertain my friends. Lena fits the role admirably.'

'I hope you'll be very happy,' said Fiona, feeling that some such comment was called for.

'Thank you,' replied her father dryly. 'I have no doubt that it will be a very convenient arrangement for all concerned.'

'When will it be?'

'We've arranged it for the last Friday in February. No fuss, of course. I hope you'll do your part to make Lena feel that she is a welcome addition to the family.'

Sleep eluded Fiona that night, tired though she was. Wondering how the new development would affect her life, she was conscious of a sense of relief that her father would not now need her in his social life, that she could take a back seat. Perhaps this marriage would make him happier, although she found this difficult to imagine. In a way, she supposed there would not be much difference in their life, for Mrs. Marchant had already assumed many responsibilities of a wife. She found herself wondering about her mother, about her father when he was young. But it was difficult to imagine her father as young. Restlessly, she tossed and turned, aware of a feeling of distaste at the thought of this marriage and yet knowing that for her father it was a convenient and sensible solution to his home problems. She wondered what Julian would think of it.

Julian, in fact, said very little, and she had the impression that he was not surprised.

'Well, well. How are you going to like your stepmother?' he asked.

'We don't understand each other at all, and she does have an itch to manage everybody, but we don't get on too badly,

I suppose. Perhaps now that she will be taking over my place as Father's right hand, she won't have to badger me into good social shape. She'll make an awfully good Mayoress, won't she?' added Fiona, with a twinkle.

'Excellent. Graciousness personified.'

'I'm thankful I can hand over these social functions to her. I was in trouble with Dad again because I told Colonel Shipley I thought hunting and shooting were cruel.'

Julian grinned.

'That old fire-eater? Good for you. I can just see his face,' said Julian, chuckling.

'Well, I do think it's cruel, and I couldn't say anything else. Mrs. Marchant's going to be much better at social life than I am. I can't think why she wants to marry my father, though.'

Julian filled his pipe and looked at her reflectively. She was adding some records to his catalogue and her head was bent over her task as she lovingly printed the titles. It had simply not occurred to her that her father's wealth was the attraction and that Mrs. Marchant had considerably diminished Fiona's prospects of inheriting it by this marriage. He smiled and rubbed her head as he went to fetch some matches, causing her to spoil the perfection of one of her letters.

'People marry for lots of different reasons, ducky.'

'I think there's only one good one.'

'At eighteen, you know all about it, of course.'

He was teasing her, and she flashed him a reproachful look.

'Nearly nineteen. You were saying the other day that young people often have clearer eyes than older people.'

'So they do, in a way. Before the contagion of the world's slow stain has caught them. Ideals clear, compromise unthought of, the lures of Mammon unfelt. Bless your clear young eyes, you shall pronounce on the subject of marriage and I will listen in all humility.'

'No. You're teasing.'

'Not really. But your formula of love-marriage-bliss, although charming in theory, is nothing like so simple or inevitable in practice. And with all due respect, I think you are a little young to appreciate that.'

'Go on.'

'Haven't time. I've a pupil coming here in a few minutes.'

'Here?'

'Yes. He's got an exam next week and I wanted to fit in extra time for him, but the studios at the school are all booked up today, so we're having a session here. He's a brilliant boy. I think he has a great future.'

'I'll just finish this, and then I'll go.'

'There's no need to. We like having you about the place. Wait and have tea with us.'

'Will you expound your views on marriage?'

He shook his head, smiling.

'Far be it from me to cloud what you see so clearly. When you marry some nice young man for love, I shall be at your wedding to give you my blessing and tell the young man he is unusually lucky.'

It was strange, thought Fiona as the door closed behind him, that although he understood her so well and they were so close, he had no idea how those words hurt her. She went on printing her titles to the sound of the piano from the music room at the back of the house.

Fiona's main feeling at her father's wedding was one of unreality. She felt that she was witnessing the union of two strangers. The ceremony was held in Elton Church and there were only half a dozen people present: Julian, Mrs. Crayshaw, two fellow councillors, Mrs. Marchant's sister and Fiona. Mrs. Marchant had been radiating good spirits for weeks past but Fiona, conscious all the time that beneath this smiling exterior lay a purposeful stranger, had no clue to the inner feelings of her stepmother. Now, as she watched them being married, she knew that she was completely shut out from the thoughts and understanding of these two people. Her father's hostility would not be changed by his new wife's influence, she knew. Starved of their confidence, of their affection, she was a stranger in her own home, and once again she found herself wondering if things would have been different if her mother had lived, and wished that she could remember her. She turned to Julian's profile for comfort. Life, she thought, would be unendurable without him. Number ten, Lime Avenue, seemed to cast such a long shadow over her life and she could not see how or when it could be lifted.

But barely three months later, the pattern of her life was changed completely with a suddenness which stunned her, for her father had a stroke while at work one morning, and was taken to Elton hospital, where he lingered half paralysed for a week, and died in the early hours of a sunny May morning. When Julian came round to Lime Avenue on the evening of his uncle's death to see if he could do anything to help, the second Mrs. Goring accepted his offer gladly, displaying a dignified and restrained grief which made Julian's task easier. Fiona looked white and shaken, and said little. When she left them to make some coffee, Julian followed her and found her crying over the gas stove. He sat on a corner of the kitchen table, a little puzzled at her deep distress.

'What is it, dear?'

'Every day I went to the hospital, he refused to see me. Last night he was too ill to refuse, but when I took his hand, he turned his head away from me and closed his eyes. He didn't say a word. I felt it was terrible to inspire such dislike that even when he was dying . . .' Her voice trailed away, choked.

'He may not have been conscious.'

'He was. He talked to . . . my stepmother. What is there wrong about me, Julian? Why did he hate me?'

He took her in his arms and stroked her head gently.

'There's nothing wrong with you, dear. There was a lot wrong with him. He was a very hard and embittered man, and it wouldn't have mattered what kind of a person you were, he would have felt the same. The pity of it was that you were so gentle and kind that he could maul you. He deserved some tough brat who could have stood up to him.'

'But why, Julian? Why? It's so unnatural. I feel I must have been wrong, somehow. You can't dislike a person for so long, right to the end, without reason.'

'There is a reason, and I think you should be told, but not now. You're tired out and suffering from the shock of it all. Here, take my handkerchief and dry your eyes. All right? Now listen to me. Take a couple of aspirins, go to bed and try to put all this out of your mind. Come over to Alanbridge tomorrow afternoon and have a talk with Dad. I've some things still to discuss with your stepmother. You buzz off to bed. There's no reason for you to be present and you've had enough. I'll see to the coffee.'

'You're so kind to me, Julian. Thank you. I'm sorry to give you all this trouble when you're so busy.'

'Don't be silly. Going to take some hot milk with you?'

'Yes, I think I will. I feel so cold.'

'There's nothing to worry about. Go and get some sleep. You haven't had much this week, by the look of you.'

When she had gone, Julian took the tray of coffee into the sitting-room and briskly disposed of the matters outstanding. He drove home in an unusually grim mood and released some of his anger on his father.

'When I think of the way that cold-blooded devil has blighted that child's life, I feel like murder. To take it out of somebody as helpless and sensitive as Fiona for all these years —what sort of a man was he, for heaven's sake?'

'Cankered.'

'She'll have to be told, Dad.'

'Isn't it best to let sleeping dogs lie, Julian? I don't know that it will serve any good purpose to tell the child now.'

'I think she'd rather know the truth. She's tormenting herself with some weird idea that she's to blame, now. Anyway, it's out of our hands whether she knows or not, because Mrs. Goring—or should I call her Auntie?—is going to tell her if we don't. Her late husband told her to. I'd rather Fiona heard it from you, since you're the only person with first hand knowledge of what happened.'

'And what of the future? Has he left Fiona provided for?'

'According to Mrs. Goring, and I have no reason to doubt her, Uncle Graham made a new will just after they married, leaving everything to her, apart from a few bequests to local charities. Charity! If anybody was ignorant of the meaning of the word, he was.'

'So Fiona has nothing?'

'Nothing. And it was his wish that his widow should not pass anything on to Fiona. He considered that his responsibilities were discharged,' concluded Julian dryly.

'It's incredible. To let pride and hatred get hold of you like that. Your mother used to say that even as a small boy, Graham had a terrible cold implacability about him, but I must confess that this last evidence has shocked me.'

'Not only will Fiona be penniless, but she'll have no home. Our merry widow is going to sell number ten and go to live in London, her spiritual home. I'd like Fiona to come here, Dad. What do you think?'

'Of course, my boy. It would be better for her, though, if your mother were alive. This is very much a man's world here at Alanbridge.'

'I was thinking as I drove home—what about Aunt Lou? Do you think she'd give up her cronies in that boarding house and come and live here for a year or two, until Fiona's able to decide what she wants to do with her life? She's only a kid now, and in a shockingly nervy state. The long strain of life at Lime Avenue has taken its toll, I guess. Aunt Lou's a breezy, kind soul. She'd be good for Fiona, and we both get on well with her. What do you think?'

'A good idea, if you can wean her away from *her* spiritual home. You know how united those three women are at The Towers.'

'We could bribe her with the paddock for a rest home for old horses. She's been nagging me about that for ages, and I don't suppose we shall want to use it now. Our days for enlarging the garden are over, I guess.'

'Yes,' said John Falconer slowly. 'That's quite an idea. I'm very fond of old Lou. She'll probably do it for you. And she'll be near enough to her pals to keep her from fretting. As long as she doesn't lecture me on anti-vivisection all day. I'm too old to be drawn into crusades, however worthy. I never imagined I'd see Graham out, though. I can't remember him having a day's illness.'

'Creaking doors hang on the longest. You'll see a good many years yet. You're quite happy about my suggestions?'

'Quite, my boy. You go ahead, and I'll think out what to say to Fiona. Don't want to shock the child.'

'You won't do that. She has a very simple and direct approach to life.'

'Well, you'd better be in on it, too. You sanctify anything in Fiona's eyes. I suppose it is better coming from us than her stepmother?' he added doubtfully.

'Of course. Fiona would hate to hear it from her. Anyway, she's a stranger to the family. Played her cards pretty shrewdly, I must say. Everything planned out, even to knowing what she wants to keep and what she's going to sell.

I don't think I've ever met a woman so calculating in her materialism.'

'The female of the species can be very deadly. I'm off to bed, Julian. After our little talk tomorrow, I shall take Fiona off to the greenhouses with me to help me do some potting-on. She's got a deft touch and it'll be a nice soothing occupation for her after all this upheaval. She can leave all the letter-writing to her stepmother. The sooner the child is out of the atmosphere of number ten, Lime Avenue, the better. Mausoleum of a place. Always was.'

When Fiona arrived at Alanbridge the next afternoon, she looked pale but composed. She found her uncle and Julian on the terrace about to have tea, and while she poured out for them, they talked of the garden. Julian's dark eyes rested on his father with amused affection. He knew that he did not relish his task, and Julian wondered whether he ought, perhaps, to have tackled it himself. His father, always a reticent man where emotions were concerned, was now so far removed from the passions and follies of youth that he found it hard to conjure them up in words. But, unexpectedly, Fiona herself broached the subject after she had made a pretence of eating.

'I think I know what you have to tell me, Uncle John, about my father. I've been helping sort out papers at home this morning. There was a bureau in the spare bedroom that was always kept locked. We couldn't find a key, but we forced the lock. Inside there were some letters and a photograph and a few snapshots. The letters were signed by someone called Robin, and were written to my mother before she was married. At least, one was in an envelope addressed to Miss Barbara Greenlaw, the rest weren't in envelopes but they were all written about the same time. I read two of them, but I couldn't read any more. It seemed . . . wrong to intrude. I don't know. I can only guess. But I've been thinking about it all the morning, and about my father's attitude to me, and I've a feeling now that he wasn't my father. Is that what you have to tell me?'

'Yes, my dear. How much did those letters convey to you?'

'Only that Robin—I don't know his other name—was deeply in love with my mother and that they were engaged to be married. Do you know what happened, Uncle John?'

'Yes, I know, my dear, because your mother was a very close friend of your Aunt Olive's although she was a lot younger. They had no secrets from each other, and I think my wife was the only person besides your father who knew the truth about you. And she didn't even tell me all of it until after your mother died. I'm not happy about raking it up again now for you, but Julian says that your father instructed your stepmother to tell you about it in order to explain his reasons for disposing of his estate as he has. Have you been told about his will?'

'No. My stepmother is getting it from the solicitors this afternoon. I would like to know the truth, anyway, Uncle. And you're the only person who can speak for my mother.'

'That's very true, my dear. She was a most lovable, warm-hearted person, your mother. We were very fond of Ba, as we always called her. She was in her early twenties at the time we first knew her, and she had two suitors. One was Olive's brother, Graham, who was not far short of twenty years her senior, and the other was young Robin Menmuir whom she met when she was on holiday in Edinburgh, where he lived. I only saw him two or three times. Elton and Edinburgh were separated by too many miles to enable them to be together as often as they would have liked. Graham was never in the picture. Ba liked him as a friend, but there was a huge gap in their ages. He was serious and rather quiet in those days. But he was determined to win your mother. My wife never got on well with her brother and she was relieved when Ba told her that she was going to marry Robin. The wedding had to be postponed twice. Once because Robin's mother was seriously ill, and, in fact, she died on what was to have been their wedding day. The next time, Ba went down with measles, of all things. They began to feel there was a hoodoo working. They fixed the date for the third time, and two days before the wedding, Robin was killed in an accident. He was an architect and was surveying a site for an aerodrome when an aircraft crashed in the same field, and Robin was hit by some part of the machinery as the aeroplane blew up.

'Your mother went nearly out of her mind. She had no family to turn to, and Aunt Olive and I did what we could, but it was Graham who came forward and took your mother in hand. A few weeks later, she told my wife that you were on the way, that Graham had asked her to marry him and let him give both her and Robin's child a home and security, and she had accepted. Graham had just been offered the job of assistant manager at another branch of the chain-store business for which he then worked, so that he and Ba were able to get married quietly there a few weeks after he moved, and they didn't come back to Elton until two years later. Not long after their return, your mother died of pleurisy.'

'So that was what happened,' said Fiona slowly. 'Poor mother. And that was why he didn't like me. I suppose he could never forget that I was another man's child.'

'I'm afraid his marriage was not a success, my dear. Your mother married him to give you a home and a name. Graham married her because he was violently and possessively in love with her and you were a strong weapon in his attempts to win her, but she never loved him, and he knew that Robin and Robin's child were all she really cared about. I used to feel sorry for him, in a way. He was insanely jealous of Robin, even though he was dead. If there had been any children of his own, things might have been better. As it was, he lost his wife and was left with you as a reminder of Robin Menmuir. He promised your mother to look after you until you came of age, but when your mother was dying, she asked my wife to do what she could to help you because she was afraid that Graham had little love for you. That's the whole, sad story, my dear, and now I think we should let it rest in peace. You are in our care now, as your mother wished, since your father, your legal father, is dead.'

'I'm not really any relation to you, then, Uncle John?'

'There is no blood relationship, but legally you are my niece by marriage, and morally your mother bequeathed you to us, and very glad we are to have such a legacy. Has your stepmother talked to you about the future at all?'

'No. Except to say that she intends to leave Elton and go back to London to live. I expect Father has left everything to her, don't you?'

'Yes,' said Julian, who had been watching her closely. 'He has, according to the lady in question. We want you to come and live here at Alanbridge, Fiona. We feel that you belong here. At least, until you want to make a life of your own. Will you?'

She gave him an odd little smile.

'Oh, Julian, what a question to ask! Only . . . how can I say thank you? It's too big to say.'

'Then don't try,' said Julian, grinning. 'We're already making a list of all the chores we can sling on to you, and Dad's jumping in with potting right now. You wait until you've been at Alanbridge for a few weeks. You'll find out that it's not all flowers and tea on the terrace.'

And Fiona, who would gladly have weeded beds or scrubbed floors for them all day, could only smile with trembling lips, her heart too full to speak.

She spent the next hour potting-on batches of young chrysanthemum plants. The potting shed and greenhouses were cut off from the rest of the garden by a hedge of holly, above which two laburnum trees lifted a shower of gold which made even the sunshine seem pale. Her uncle said little as he worked beside her with patient, skilful hands, and Fiona was glad to be left to her thoughts, for that afternoon had brought such a change into her life that she could scarcely realise all that it meant.

The garden was full of scent and colour as she strolled back to the house in the early evening. In the paved garden a small bed of lilies of the valley spread their fragrance over the groups of flags and rare irises which hung banners round the central pool. In the rose garden, it was an early flowering musk rose which had outstripped the tea roses, still only in bud, and filled the air with its faint, sweet scent. Fiona paused under the carved archway, over which a pale blue clematis twined, to look down the long walk between the herbaceous borders, now brilliant with colour. Her eyes lingered on the silver spray from the Italian fountain and then were drawn to the mullioned windows and mellow bricks of the house at the far end. Whenever she thought of Alanbridge, it was this view which she saw. She paid her tribute to the fountain as she passed it, and hung her hand out to dry as she made a detour round the house to see the pergola, smothered now in the lavender coloured wistaria which would soon be yielding to the roses already breaking into flower here and there.

When she had finished her pilgrimage, she collected her bag from the terrace and went into the house to remove the traces of her recent toil. She could hear the piano, and she wondered whether to disturb Julian to say good-bye, or not.

If he was composing, he wouldn't want to be disturbed, and from the odd phrases, punctuated by short pauses, she imagined that he was in the throes. Then, suddenly, he crashed down on a chord, sketched rapid arpeggios up and down the piano, and silence followed. Inspiration had failed, she thought, and she poked a cautious head round the door,

'Can I?'

He turned round and nodded.

'Come in, my child. Genius is not burning brightly in this quarter today.'

'What are you on?'

'Music for a film. Background music.' He swung round to face her. 'Dad's told you about Aunt Lou?'

'Yes. You know, I can't help feeling I'm causing a certain upheaval in your comfortable bachelor lives.'

'Do us good to have a few females about the place. You'll get on well with Aunt Lou, I think. She's one of the crazier Falconers, but a darned good sort.'

'Yes. I ran into her a few weeks ago at a church sale. She was distributing pamphlets on anti-vivisection, and she nailed my stepmother and harangued her for about quarter of an hour. I loved every minute of it. I think she's a dear.'

Fiona eyed the sheets of manuscript scattered over the piano and said, 'You're busy. I only came to say goodbye.'

'But you're hovering over it, ducky. What is it?'

'I wondered whether you would like to see this photograph of my father,' she said tentatively, as she drew it from her handbag.

'I would. I never saw him. I was away at school at the time of these goings on and it all went over my head. So that was Robin Menmuir.'

Julian looked at the photograph in silence for a few moments. It was a conventional head-and-shoulders study of a fair man with square jaw and a look of determination. Across the back was written in ink which had turned brown, 'You asked for it, my darling.'

'I think I should have liked Menmuir,' said Julian, smiling. 'You've got his nose.'

She passed him two snapshots, one of her mother arm in arm with Robin, and another of Robin indulging in a tug of war with a bull terrier. In both of these he was laughing

64

and looked much younger than in the studio portrait. A tall, broad-shouldered man, he dwarfed the slender figure of Fiona's mother.

'I remember Aunt Ba quite well, of course. She was always very gay in the early days, but after she came back to Elton with you and your father, she was dimmed. Even though I was only a kid, I remember thinking how much she'd changed. She wasn't fun any more. Quiet and withdrawn.'

'I wish I'd known her.'

'You're not upset at knowing the truth?'

Her eyes met his candidly.

'I'm glad I was born of two people who loved each other.'

'Yes. It was a tragic business for all of you, including your late father, poor devil. Still, you're young, my dear. You haven't had the happy home-life you should have had, but it hasn't spoiled your life. You've everything in front of you, and you can build on the past.'

'I owe so much to you, Julian. You've always been so kind to me. I can never repay you and Uncle John.'

'Nonsense. We feel you're one of the family, and I'm not nearly so altruistic as you think. You'll be horribly disillusioned when you've lived here for a bit, you see.'

'How silly. I know you as well as I know myself.'

Her confident tone brought a smile to his lips.

'Dear me. That could be disconcerting. I still think the pedestal on which you're inclined to put me will wobble a bit when you live here. Perhaps it's as well that it should,' he added thoughtfully.

'Well, I do think that's a silly thing to say,' said Fiona frankly, 'after all the years we've known each other. We talk the same language. We always have. There's no question of pedestals. Has anybody been getting at you?'

He grinned, surprised at her perspicacity.

'It has been suggested to me by somebody who shall be nameless that you feed my sense of vanity and that is why I like you around.'

'I think that's a horrid remark and so untrue that it could only have been said by someone who doesn't really know you at all. Who was it?'

'It doesn't matter. Nobody under this roof. Our motives

are often deeply hidden, though. A lot of philanthropists would be amazed and shocked if they realised the true motives behind their philanthropy.'

'I don't know about that, but there was never a person with less vanity than you, Julian. I don't believe you care one scrap what the world thinks of you. You go your own way and are not interested in what sort of picture other people have of you. I wish I was as independent as you.'

'You've been handicapped, my dear. You've not known the taste of freedom until now. I've been fortunate in that respect. But there'll be no ties here, Fiona. You'll be free to lead your own life.'

She was sitting on the window-seat looking out into the garden, and he saw an odd little smile flit across her face, but she said nothing, and he wondered what was in her mind just then. He thought again of Norah Coachford's words that morning when he had told her of their plans for Fiona. He knew that his motives were based on real affection for the girl and that Norah's accusation of vanity was wide of the mark. Norah's own motives, he thought, could do with a little honest examination. But he was not blind to the fact that Fiona had enthroned him and crowned him king of her world. Sometimes this element in a very real and close friendship made him uneasy until he laughed himself out of it with the reminder that Fiona, for all her sensitive intelligence, was no more than a schoolgirl and still subject to the adolescent's urge for hero-worshipping. It happened to be him. It could as easily have been the games mistress or the art master. It was something which maturity would deal with, leaving the solid foundation of friendship intact. Coming to live at Alanbridge would help to speed up the process. There was nothing like the rub of daily life to remove the veils of illusion. She was a grand kid. As honest as the day. He was glad that it had been in his power to lead her life into happier channels. How she had survived that home atmosphere, with its undercurrents of resentment and hate and frustration, its shadow of a past which Graham Goring could never bury, without damage to a nature far more sensitive than most, he didn't know. Perhaps the Celtic blood in her had helped. That Scot looked pretty resilient. Small wonder that in the circumstances she had found Alanbridge a King Arthur's castle and himself a Galahad. Starved of affection at home, she had found an outlet here for the deep longing of youth to belong, to feel wanted. With a secure background, her affections and interests would spread, and his own eminence in her world be challenged. In a few years, her outlook would be very different.

'Julian . . .'

'Yes?'

'This has been such a wonderful and remarkable day. Would you round it off by playing to me before I go? Just for a little while.'

'Righto. Anything special?'

'Just one thing. The "Moonlight Sonata".'

'I might have guessed.'

She was looking out of the window, seeing, he guessed, a future bathed in the rosy light of music, garden, Sir Galahad and all. And who was he to break into her dreams? Man didn't live by bread alone. He lifted his hands for the first tranquil notes of Beethoven's 'Moonlight Sonata'.

BOOK II
ALANBRIDGE

CHAPTER ONE

FIONA stood back and surveyed her canvas with a critical eye. She was painting, in oils, the flight of shallow stone steps up to the first arch of the pergola, and was not satisfied with the colour of the stone. She had not captured its warmth of tone. And she hadn't succeeded very well, either, with the shadowy green walk receding from the arch into the background. That was a tricky bit to catch in colour: the tremulous, evanescent light cast by the sun through a thick canopy of twisting leaves and branches. Colour was not her strong point; she was best at the delicate lined drawings which gave her eye for fine detail full scope. But, encouraged by the teacher of art at the evening classes which she still attended, she had found a market for paintings with a firm of Christmas card and calendar publishers, for whom this particular painting was destined.

She glanced at her watch and decided that it was all she could do to it today. She had promised to put a fresh dressing on the galled back of Aunt Lou's latest acquisition in the paddock, to help her uncle water the plants in the greenhouse, and to cycle into Elton to fetch a score which Julian had left at the school and post it off to him in London by the evening post. And already it was two o'clock. She had skipped lunch, making do with a sandwich and a glass of milk. It was one of the many joys of life at Alanbridge that such decisions caused no concern or fuss. At Lime Avenue meals had been sacred and no leave of absence granted without a long inquest and good reasons. Her reasons had seldom been good enough. Remembering those long, silent, painful meals with her father was like looking back into a dark tunnel from a great distance. Those days seemed so far away and unreal that she could scarcely credit that little more than a year had elapsed since she had left Lime Avenue. She felt that the girl who had endured those long bleak years of criticism and cold hostility was a shadowy ghost in a dream world. A bad dream. But when she thought of her father now, and it was seldom, a feeling of pity for him replaced the old baffled fear. To love somebody who didn't love you was hard enough, but to have a constant reminder of his wife's love for somebody else would put a strain on any man's nature. He had made a big gesture in offering a home and a name to his rival's child, but he hadn't been big enough to live up to it. Fiona wished she had known the truth while he was alive.

She packed up her easel, collected her things together and made for the house. She would go down to the school first and make sure of catching the post, since Julian had been so emphatic about it on the telephone that morning.

There was only one trouble about life at Alanbridge, she thought. There was never enough time to do all the things she wanted to do. Julian had been right about life there not being like a garden party, and Fiona had been drawn into the whirlpool of the Falconer activities from the word 'go'. Both Julian and his father were deeply, almost passionately, absorbed in their work, which was their life, and they were both glad to use any help Fiona could contribute. With Aunt Lou adding another enthusiast to the Falconer household, and one equally unscrupulous in using Fiona's willing hands for her cause, it was sometimes difficult for Fiona to find time to pursue her own modest career. But she loved every bit of it, and threw herself into all these spheres with the greatest zest. If only, she thought, there were more hours in the day.

She cycled along the lanes to Elton, and propped her bicycle by the kerb outside the Elton School of Music. In the shop, Mr. Cheney was playing a record of a Chopin nocturne for a customer, and Fiona had to linger by the music counter to hear it. At first she had been sorry that Julian hadn't brought up again the suggestion that she should work here at the school, but she realised now that she was of more use at Alanbridge and that his advice that she should try to do something with her own talents was proving sound. All the same, it would have been nice to see more of him. When the record was finished, she ran up the stairs to Miss Lesley's office on the first floor.

Miss Lesley looked up from her typewriter and greeted Fiona with a pleasant smile.

'Mr. Falconer left a score here last night, Miss Lesley, and he wants me to post it to him. Is his studio being used now, do you know?'

'No. Mr. Jameson has a pupil due at three. You know the room?'

'Yes.'

'Did our esteemed Principal happen to mention to you what time on Thursday he would be returning to his little hive?'

'Lunch-time. He's driving from London in the morning and coming straight here. Didn't he tell you?'

'He dashed out last night flinging something over his shoulder which I didn't quite catch, although I did hear the word "Thursday". He went like a rocket, and if he drove up to London in the same mood, he'll be lucky if he hasn't collected a summons for speeding.'

Fiona walked up two more flights of stairs, passing doors from behind which came various strains of music, evoked by, in turn, a violin, a piano, a clarinet and a human contralto voice. The effect was decidedly odd. On the top floor, there was only the one studio, and here all was silence. The room was a large one and contained a piano, stool, two chairs, a desk and, in solitary glory on the mantelpiece, a metronome.

Fiona was taking the score from the top drawer of the desk when Norah Coachford came in.

'Oh, it's you, Fiona. I heard someone come up and wondered whether Julian had returned unexpectedly.'

'No. He asked me to collect this score and post it to him. He forgot it last night.'

'I'm not surprised, from the way he tore off. He must have had a very important date,' she concluded dryly, coming across to look at the score. 'What does he want that for?'

'I don't know,' said Fiona, who was often irritated by Norah Coachford's inquisitiveness.

'Where are you posting it to?'

Fiona's face took on a rare poker expression as she looked at the tall, dark young woman who faced her across the desk. Norah would have been quite attractive if her eyes were not so small and close together, but they gave her face a shrewd, hard expression which marred it. Fiona thought her bossy and interfering, and although Julian said she was an excellent teacher of singing, Fiona had long since decided that if she had a voice worth training, Miss Coachford was the last person she would want to train it.

'To Julian's club. He always stays there when he goes to London.'

'That's what he tells us,' said Norah, pretending to joke, but the pretence seemed a little thin. 'I guess Miss Courtney's flat is his headquarters.'

'I know nothing about that.'

'No. He's quite an oyster in some respects, isn't he? Well, I've a lesson to take. So long.'

Fiona went back to Miss Lesley's office to pack up the score and then hurried off to the post office. Cycling back to Alanbridge, she was still bristling over Norah Coachford's innuendoes. Julian's private affairs were no concern of hers and such remarks were in very bad taste, to say the least of it, but Fiona could not help wondering how much truth there was in them. Julian never mentioned Gillian Courtney's name, but the Deverels and Norah Coachford knew of their friendship. She had felt sometimes lately that Julian was not altogether happy. He seemed more than usually restless and preoccupied. If the friendship were a casual one, he would surely mention it. It was only feelings which ran very deep which you kept sealed up inside you, thought Fiona. In any case, he wouldn't have much time to spend with Gillian Courtney during these two days in London, for he had an appointment to keep with his music publishers, he was attending the rehearsal and the performance of one of his own compositions in a concert at the Wigmore Hall, and he was dining with his old Professor of music one evening. Since Gillian Courtney was then appearing in a play in London, they would have little time to spend together. In any case, it was none of Norah Coachford's business, or of hers, thought Fiona, sternly trying to discipline her thoughts and conjectures. But Julian was so close to her heart, that everything that touched Julian touched her.

As she neared Alanbridge, she caught up a sturdy figure plodding up the land with feet well turned out and head thrust forward. Fiona rang her bell and slid off her bicycle.

'Hullo, Aunt Lou. You're back early.'

'I was in the chair, and I cut the cackle. Want to get the accounts written up before dinner. You know, I think I shall have to learn to ride your bicycle. I had to wait nearly quarter of an hour for the bus.'

Fiona smiled at a mental picture of Aunt Lou sailing into Elton on a bicycle.

'You'd have to wear smaller hats, and you'd hate that,' said Fiona, for Aunt Lou's passion for ornate and large hats was a family joke.

'That's the worst of this fashion for short hair. When I was a girl you could skewer your hat on as firmly as a rock with a couple of hat pins. Did your work go well today, dear?'

'So-so. I've just sent off Julian's score, and now I'm going to tackle Sam's back.'

'I wonder if I could screw any money out of Colonel Shipley if I sent him some pamphlets? I met him this morning, and although he doesn't approve of me, I think I earned a good mark by my attention to that old spaniel of his.'

'He's a keen hunting and shooting man.'

'Ah, but such people always maintain that they're fond of animals and they usually worship gun dogs, hounds and horses. People aren't logical, my dear. Not in this country, anyway. The French, perhaps, but not the English. The colonel's very sentimental over that dog. I shall send him our pamphlet dealing with vivisection on dogs. That should fetch him. You look pretty in that dress, dear, but it's not warm enough without a coat.'

Fiona, accustomed by now to Aunt Lou's grasshopper manner of conversation, agreed that she could have done with a coat and added that Colonel Shipley was, in her opinion, proof against attack on his pocket by Aunt Lou.

'We'll see. I'd dearly like to get him to contribute towards the welfare of the world in which he slaughters. It might make his account with the Almighty a little less black. Men. Creatures of destruction.'

'Not all of them.'

'No, there are a few who create. What's wrong with Julian?'

'You've noticed it, then?'

'Can't help noticing it when he's as restless as a squib. Not sleeping well, either. He looks hag-ridden, but then these thin, dark Falconers soon look like that.' She shot a quick glance at Fiona. 'You've no idea if he's worried about anything?'

'Nothing definite that I know of. It could be Uncle John. His health is failing, and Julian's very fond of his father. Or it could be . . . Well, your guess is as good as mine.'

'Precisely. A woman. Oh, well, that's one advantage of being my age. Done with all that tiresome, complicated business.'

Fiona's eyes twinkled as she looked at Aunt Lou. It was difficult to imagine how she had looked when she was young, but there was no doubt about the fact that there was a good deal of the grotesque about her now. She was a tall, well-built woman with a large, weather-beaten face and straight grey hair. She had very fine dark blue eyes beneath shaggy eyebrows, a prominent beaky nose above a tiny cupid's bow mouth, and a long chin that seemed to precede her everywhere. Coupled with the fact that Aunt Lou scorned all make-up, and combined a purely functional attitude to clothes with a bizarre taste in hats, her appearance was unusual, to say the least of it. Beneath her odd exterior, however, was a warm and generous heart and a shrewd intelligence. Fiona had grown very fond of her. But Aunt Lou in love? It was hard to imagine, for it would be an all-conquering spirit indeed which could win and tame Aunt Lou's independent, crusading temperament to his service, Aunt Lou's opinion of men being the reverse of high.

Busy as she was during Julian's absence, Fiona could not keep her mind from straying to him and wondering what was wrong. When he arrived back at Alanbridge on Thursday evening, he looked a little tired but assured her that he had enjoyed his two days in London.

'Shall I put the car away for you, Julian?' she asked, as he dumped his case in the hall.

'Thanks, ducky. My brief-case is in the back. Bring it in, will you?'

Fiona drove the car into the garage. Julian had taught her to drive, and she was able to relieve him of a good deal of fetching and carrying, for Uncle John no longer felt able to drive and Aunt Lou had no inclination to do so, for she regarded cars as an enemy of peace and frequently deplored the invention of the internal combustion engine. When Fiona came back, Julian was running a bath.

She watched him at dinner that night with anxious eyes. His tongue was as lively as ever. In fact, it was too lively.

She felt that he was covering up. He took his coffee off to the music room, but no sound came from it when Fiona passed the door. She hesitated, then went out to the rose garden to finish cutting off the dead roses. Now, at the end of June, this was a lengthy task, and it was nearly dark when she wheeled the barrow full of rose blooms, as gay and varied as Joseph's coat, towards the compost heap. She loved the hour of dusk in the summer, with the light changing every minute and the gaudiest flowers giving way to the white blooms which stood out in the gathering darkness with pale, breath-taking loveliness. She stopped to smell a group of tall Madonna lilies, waxy and still, and as she straightened up she saw Julian's head above the hedge. He didn't see her but walked on towards the heather garden, stooping to light his pipe before he disappeared.

When she had stowed away the barrow and secateurs, she went after him, but there was no sign of him in the heather garden. Since few gardens were as well suited to a game of hide and seek as Alanbridge, it took her some time to track him down and it was only the flare of a match in the gathering darkness which led her to the seat in an alcove of the yew hedge round the paved garden. Even then, she hesitated to join him. He was leaning forward, nursing his pipe, and something in the attitude told her that he was miles away in a desolate world. Then from some shadowed part of the garden nearby, a cat let out an unearthly moan and Julian looked up and saw her.

'Hullo. How long have you been hovering there like a moth?'

'I've only just come. It's taken me nearly all the evening to cut off the dead roses. They made such a lovely canopy on the compost heap.'

'You're a very busy bee in the garden these days, aren't you?'

'I like it. And Joe has an awful lot to cope with now that young Ben's gone into the army.'

'Yes. Couldn't have gone at a worse time. Hope we'll get a replacement soon, but our advertisement doesn't seem to have brought any rush. I ought to find more time for it now that Dad's getting past it. Not that he'll admit it. He'll go on until he drops.'

'Is that what is making you unhappy, Julian?' asked Fiona a little timidly.

'What makes you think I'm unhappy, ducky?'

'I just feel it.'

'Well, life isn't all jam and we can't have everything we want. Man's a greedy animal. However much he has, he always wants a bit more. I'm just feeling baulked and a bit weary of responsibilities tonight. Pay no attention. Probably had too much wine last night. I'd better put in some hard work in the garden tomorrow morning to sweeten my liver. Dad hasn't had another of his turns while I've been away, has he?'

'No. But he does look . . . so fragile, Julian.'

'I know. He's done better than the doctor anticipated, though. He was given a few years if he led the life of an invalid, and a few months if he didn't. Well, he hasn't and he's kept going for a year since the doctor's verdict. We've got to face the facts, though.'

'Couldn't you persuade him to stop work in the garden?'

'He wouldn't listen if I did, and I don't think I would, anyway. This garden is his life, as it was his father's. Take it away from him, and he's left with a meaningless existence.'

'But he has it all round him to enjoy.'

'He can't see it as a playground, my dear. He's a horticulturist and this is his work. You couldn't keep him from it any more than you could keep an artist from his brush, or me from the piano, for that matter. Anyway, it's the quality of life that matters, not the quantity, and I wouldn't want to see him kept alive by the medical profession as an inert body to be washed and fed. He'd sooner die on the job, and so would I.'

They fell silent. He wasn't going to tell her what was gnawing at him. She hadn't expected that he would, but she cherished the hope that one day he would stop thinking of her as a child. She wanted so much to help him, to comfort him, but he would never come to her for help. She was Fiona, a dear child, to be looked after and helped, and he knew nothing of the ache in her heart to give instead of take, to be looked on as an equal, a woman, not a child. She shivered, for the night air was chilly, and wished Leo would stop making such unearthly moans for his love.

'Another unsatisfied soul,' said Julian. 'Think I'll stroll round the garden and then take myself to bed. Don't worry your little head about me, my dear.'

He went off, leaving Fiona cold and forlorn on the seat.

It was the first time she had ever felt that her presence wasn't welcome to him. Everybody needed to be alone with their thoughts sometimes, but she wished she hadn't intruded and forced him to close the door in her face.

Oh, Leo, she thought, exasperated as another moan rent the air and destroyed the peace of the night. She went in search of the perpetrator and found two pairs of glowing eyes in the grass below the holly hedge. Fiona, who normally might have felt some sympathy for these rites, found that tonight the desolate sounds echoed painfully in her own heart and she clapped her hands and shooed them off with some vigour. One pair of eyes disappeared through the hedge, another vanished round the corner of the greenhouse. And silence fell once more over the garden as she walked slowly towards the house.

Whether Julian, fearing that he was revealing more than he chose, purposely avoided them all that week, Fiona did not know, but the fact remained that he was in the house only for his breakfast and his bed. On Sunday, too, he took the car out immediately after breakfast and said he would not be back to lunch. It was a cheerless, grey day and Fiona felt unusually depressed, so that when she drifted to the piano in the music room that afternoon, she chose to play a nocturne of Chopin's which was in keeping with her mood. She was not a good pianist and in this house she seldom played, and never when Julian was in. Now and again, however, she would doodle over one or two of the simpler pieces of her favourite composers, enjoying the beautiful tone of Julian's Bechstein piano even under her inexpert fingers.

'B flat,' said a voice behind her, making her jump. 'B flat in that left-hand chord.'

'Hullo, Julian. I didn't expect you back until this evening.'

'Didn't you? I had no set plans.'

'Just driving?'

'Just driving. I rather like it, you know.'

She looked down at her hands, aware again of that shut door.

'Let me hear you play that.'

'Oh, no. I was only browsing. I can't play it properly.'

'It didn't sound too bad. Very soulful, anyway. Go on.'

He had drawn up a chair beside her, and reluctantly she

went back to the beginning of the nocturne. Some bars, she knew, were quite beyond her, and when she browsed she usually skipped the trills and the difficult run near the end.

'*Legato*. Make it smooth,' said Julian, and as she faltered, he picked up the melody an octave higher and played it with her so that she followed his rhythm and gained confidence from his right-hand accompaniment. But when she came to the run, she gave up and let him complete it, rejoining him for the last few bars.

'It's no good,' she said despairingly. 'There are some people with fingers that just seem to ooze music, and notes and accidentals and those horrible leger lines don't seem to have anything to do with it. It flows naturally. What's the good of talking to me about *legato* when I'm counting leger lines to find the right note?'

Julian smiled.

'There's no short cut, and it only looks easy because hard work has made it so.'

'Well I do think somebody might have invented an easier system of notation. If only the notes were the same in both hands, it would be a lot simpler.'

'You're not the first person to think that. Would you like to study again?'

'No, I don't think so, Julian. I haven't really the time to spare and quite honestly I don't think I've got any gift for it. I'm too fond of music to want to murder it and I'd never have the patience to work at scales and arpeggios for hours. I've endless patience with my drawing and painting, but I shouldn't have with the piano. I should want to play like you straight away. So I suppose that means it's really not my line.'

'Perhaps you're right. Best be single-minded. I met Kirk in Elton yesterday. He seems to think you're not at all a bad artist in spite of being mainly self-taught.'

'That's very modest of him. What does he think he's been doing all this time? I've learned a lot at his classes.'

'You could have gone to London to study. We would gladly have financed it.'

'I know. And I appreciated your offer, Julian. But we went into all that before, and I still feel the same. I'm happy tackling it this way, and I should hate to live in digs and only see Alanbridge at week-ends.'

'Well, it's your life, and Alanbridge certainly seems to inspire you. You're not an ambitious person, Fiona, are you?'

'I've never thought about it. No, I suppose I'm not. I'm so happy here with you and Uncle John. Success couldn't mean much compared with that.'

He smiled and pulled her ear gently.

'I'm glad you're happy here, my dear. Happiness isn't all that common, but you have the kind of blessed simplicity of heart that finds it more easily than most, I guess. And ambition can be a cruel jade. So you're not going to play to me any more?'

'No. It might mean the end of a beautiful friendship,' said Fiona solemnly.

'I doubt it.'

'I suppose you don't feel like playing now?'

'Why not? There's a composer to suit every mood.'

'And what mood are you in now?'

'The mood for Bach, at his most intellectual.'

'What a pity. I was in a nostalgic mood myself, and that's why I was mangling the Chopin nocturne.'

'I'll snap you out of that. Not good to indulge the emotions too much. Let's have a little mental discipline.'

Fiona relaxed in a chair to listen, glad that he had returned from that far country which had made strangers of them all. Bach was Julian's favourite composer, but she could not share his passion although she knew enough of music to appreciate that in contrapuntal music, Bach was supreme. Her approach to music was far more from the heart and less from the mind than Julian's, and Bach could never reach and move her as the romantic composers did. Julian, she knew, could follow each thread of the melodies which weaved in and out of Bach's compositions, and be ravished by them as she was by Chopin's simple lyrical line, but her ear was not sensitive enough to pick them up and the result was pleasant but not stirring, which was why, when he started playing one of the preludes, her mind was free to think about him instead of being drowned in the music.

Whatever it was that had been haunting him that week, he had had it out with himself that day, she felt, and had come to terms. He would never tell her. It did not occur to him that his unhappiness made her unhappy, too. Living under the same roof as Julian had in no way lessened her love for him; it had grown, and in growing, had changed its face a little, that was all. He was the same kind, honest, good friend to her that he had always been, and proximity had done nothing to diminish him in her eyes. The evidence of human fallibility which daily life revealed only served to make her attachment less of a dream, to send its roots deeper into reality. But there had come a change in one respect, she thought, and daily she became increasingly aware of it. She was hungry for more, and Julian had no more to give. In his eyes she feared she would always be a nice child and although at one time his friendship had been the sun in her life, and the thought of living at Alanbridge represented Utopia itself, now that she was no longer a child, the ache for more had crept in, a small shadow in the sunshine at first, but lengthening with a rapidity which startled her. And Bach had no answer for her.

CHAPTER TWO

The music school closed at the end of July for the summer vacation, and after a week in London, Julian took the car to the Continent for a tour, taking in Salzburg for the music festival, at which a friend of his was conducting. He did not return to Alanbridge until a few days before the beginning of the autumn term, and to Fiona his absence seemed interminable, although she was very busy at the time on a picture for the Elton Art Group exhibition to be held at the end of September. This was a modest affair, organised by Mr. Kirk for the benefit of artists and students in the district.

Julian arrived home looking brown and fit, and seemingly in good spirits. Fiona, overwhelmed by the rush of feeling when she first saw him unloading the car, found it difficult to say anything until his own cheery, unselfconscious greeting restored her equilibrium, and she set about helping him unload the jumble of oddments in the back of the car.

'You had a job to get through the Customs with all this, didn't you?' asked Fiona, as she followed him into the house with the last consignment.

'No. I must have an honest face. I'm the world's worst packer, and I do seem to have acquired a lot of bits and pieces this time. Somewhere here there's a package for you. Let me see. I know. I put it in my raincoat pocket. Sling it over, ducky.'

He rummaged in the pocket and produced a small flat parcel.

'A present from Rome to tie round your neck.'

Inside the wrappings was a flame-coloured silk sweater scarf, as soft as a robin's breast. It was the first time he had ever bought her a present outside of Christmas and birthday exchanges, and her delight was mirrored in her face.

'Oh, Julian, it's lovely!' She tied it round her throat, knotting it at the side, and turned to face him. 'Isn't it?'

'Definitely fetching. Been a good girl while I've been away?'

'How old do you think I am, Julian?'

'Let me see. Can it be twenty-one next March?'

'It can.'

'Dear me. Hardly credible. A very mature age.'

For once, she found his teasing unwelcome.

'You sound as though you're my grandfather. You're not so very much older than I am.'

'Twelve years, my child, is quite a gap, though not, I agree, a grandfatherly gap. What's biting you? Should I call you Miss Goring and treat you with respect?'

His dark eyes were laughing at her although his face was grave, and Fiona gave up.

'It doesn't matter. You shall tie a pinafore on me if you wish, my lord.'

Any hope that her words might leave some faint impression on his mind faded a few evenings later. The Deverels had invited them to a dinner and dance in Elton to celebrate Celia's birthday. It was the first time Fiona had ever gone to a social function with Julian as her escort, and she dressed for the occasion with the greatest care. A dress bought just before her father's death, and never worn, now suited the occasion perfectly. It was made of grey tulle over a pink foundation, with a bodice cut low at the back and a halter neck. At the time, she had felt it too sophisticated and revealing but had bowed to the enthusiasm of her stepmother and the sales girl. Now, she could appreciate its grace and subtle charm, and she welcomed the opportunity of appearing before Julian in a dress which was undoubtedly not girlish. On the previous day she had bought a pair of glistening drop ear-rings for the occasion, and she felt confidence flooding into her as she looked in the long mirror. Although her shoulders were a little on the thin side, her skin was white and smooth and the line of neck and shoulder pleased her artistic eye. She wasn't sure about the ear-rings. If they made her look a day older, she would wear them for that reason alone. She looked at herself with her head on one side like an enquiring bird. Yes, they did give her dignity. Julian just couldn't pull her ear, ruffle her hair or slap her backside, all of which he was prone to do at odd times, if she looked as dignified as this. Whether they suited her odd-shaped face or not, the ear-rings should stay.

One of the many architectural charms of Alanbridge was its lovely wide curved staircase. If Julian were waiting in the hall for her, she could make a fine entry. One of her more romantic and blush-making dreams consisted of the vision of herself descending that staircase in her bridal gown, and this sometimes gave way to a vision of their daughter coming down the stairs on Julian's arm on her wedding day, but such sentimental dreams were carefully hidden, with a rueful smile at her foolishness. This evening, however, and for the first time in her life, she was out to make an impression on Julian. Somehow, she'd got to break through this kid sister attitude of his.

There was a tattoo on her door.

'Ready, Fiona?'

'I'll be down in two shakes.'

She heard him go downstairs, then draped her velvet coat carelessly over one arm, picked up gloves and embroidered bag, and descended the stairs with what she hoped was a poised, mature grace. But Julian had gone to fetch the car, and she descended to an empty hall. He came in a few minutes later, knotting his white scarf and buttoning up his coat.

'This is a bit of a bore, glad rags, isn't it?'

'I don't think so. It's rather fun.'

'I thought you loathed social functions and dolling up.'

'That was when I went with Father for business purposes and didn't know anybody. It's different with friends.'

'Well, I still think a boiled shirt's a bore. You'll want your coat on. It's quite chilly tonight.'

Fiona put on her coat, and made another effort.

'Do you think ear-rings suit me, Julian?'

He studied her for a moment, and then said:

'Don't think you're really the type, but I guess you feel out of it if you don't wear them these days.'

'Why aren't I the type?' persisted Fiona.

'Don't ask me, ducky. You're just not. But all you youngsters like to be in the fashion, I guess.'

He sounded just like an indulgent uncle, thought Fiona, exasperated.

'Well, I'll take them off if you don't like them.'

'You don't have to pay any attention to me. You look quite nice as you are. Very suitably dressed for the occasion.'

She looked at him closely. She had a suspicion that he must be stringing her along. He couldn't unconsciously be so provoking. Quite nice. Anything would have been better than those two words.

'There is such a thing as damning with faint praise,' she observed.

But Julian appeared not to have heard, and merely said, as he stood by the door waiting for her to precede him:

'I hope it's a good dinner tonight. Dancing doesn't thrill me.'

Fiona swept past him before the urge to throttle him with his white scarf became too strong for her.

It was a good dinner and the men lingered over it long after Fiona's feet were tapping the floor in time to the music which came from the other end of the room. There were a few couples dancing but neither Laurie nor Julian appeared interested. Celia, looking a little pale but very striking in black velvet, wore a beautiful pendant necklace clasped round her throat. It was Laurie's birthday present, and even to Fiona's inexpert eye, it looked very valuable.

'That is beautiful, Celia,' said Fiona, echoing her earlier admiration as the stones flashed fire when Celia turned.

'Yes, isn't it? Laurie kept it very dark. I'd no idea until I opened the box beside my plate at breakfast this morning.'

'That's not bad after how many years of married life, Celia? Eight or nine?' asked Julian.

'It will be our tenth anniversary next June. It's hard to believe. Harder still to believe that I've managed to get

Laurie to a dance. He thinks it's a foolish pastime, although he's not a bad performer at all.'

'I share his sentiments,' said Julian. 'And I wish that saxophone would play in tune. It's murder.'

'Well, you're neither of you going to get out of it tonight,' said Celia firmly. 'And it's no use waiting until the floor's full so that you won't be noticed, because there aren't enough people to fill it even if they all danced.'

'I have no objection to being noticed, my dear,' said her husband. 'May I have the pleasure?'

'Certainly, Dr. Deverel,' replied Celia, a gleam in her eyes. 'I am being indulged today, aren't I?'

'It's your birthday.'

Julian leaned back in his chair and asked Fiona to pour out another cup of coffee for him.

'It will be cold now, Julian.'

He felt the pot and signed to the waiter. Fiona stifled a little sigh and turned to watch the dancers.

'Celia's seemed a bit on edge lately. Anything wrong, do you think?' asked Julian, when he had ordered more coffee.

'She told me that she's been feeling very restless and wished she had an absorbing job to give her mind something to bite on.'

'Should have thought the boys kept her busy.'

'I think it's adult companionship she needs. Laurie works such long hours and Celia says she seems to spend most of her life waiting for him to come home. Of course, she adores the boys but they're both at school, and Celia's not the type to live only through her children.'

'No. She has a lively mind and an independent nature. She and Laurie are alike in some ways. No wonder the sparks fly occasionally.'

'Celia says Laurie should have married a tractable domestically-minded woman who would bow to him as the breadwinner and master of the house and be happy in seeing that nothing disturbed him, not even herself.'

Julian grinned.

'There is a streak of the Victorian in our Dr. Deverel, I admit. I guess they're good for each other, for all that. No harm in being kept on one's toes.'

But Fiona wasn't so sure, and lately had been a little worried about Celia. For all her joking references to Laurie, and she never voiced serious criticism, Fiona had the impression that her friend was not altogether happy.

She poured out Julian's coffee and decided that she might as well have another cup herself as he was obviously not going to dance yet awhile. Her attempt to impress him had fallen completely flat, and she decided mournfully that she might as well give up the idea before disappointment spoiled the very real and happy friendship that existed between them. The trouble was that once you had travelled beyond that, it was difficult to get back. With every nerve in her body clamouring to feel him take her in his arms, with the rhythm of the waltz intensifying her longing, it was difficult to keep up a casual manner. She was conscious of every movement he made although she kept her eyes on the dancers.

Before she could discover whether Julian intended to ask her for the next dance, another partner had claimed her. He was one of the art students, a short, stocky young man who took Life and Art very seriously. He was not a very good dancer, but would have been better if he had not talked all through the dance about the Art Group exhibition which opened the next day. He was showing two water colours.

'I didn't think dancing was in your line, Eric,' said Fiona, as they began the encore.

'It's not. My sister bullied me into coming because she couldn't get a partner. Now she's found a group of buddies she was thick with about a year ago, and she's joined them. Shockers.'

'In what way?'

'Oh, all hearty and old mannish and cracking silly jokes at the girls. They're not exactly kids, but talk about callow! Not one intelligent word seems to pass their lips. I sometimes wonder what's wrong with our education system to turn out such morons.'

Eric, who was all of twenty-two years, looked disapprovingly at a girl who waved to him as she passed by in a series of intricate steps with a willowy young man who bent over her like a protective stork.

'My sister,' said Eric darkly, and then turned the conversation to Julian.

'I'd like to meet Mr. Falconer. A fine musician.'

Fiona, wishing that he didn't invest everything with such solemnity, could do no less than invite him to their table to meet Julian and the Deverels, whereat Eric promptly attached himself to them for the rest of the evening, encouraged, a little wickedly, Fiona thought, by Julian, who listened gravely to all that Eric had to say on Art. Eric, it was true, did once suggest half-heartedly that he didn't want to butt in, but Laurie politely waved this notion aside and Julian, ignoring Fiona's appealing eye, backed Laurie up with:

'Of course we're glad to welcome any friend of Fiona's,' which finished it.

In the cloakroom with Celia towards the end of the evening Fiona expressed her thoughts with unusual indignation.

'Aren't they the limit? Julian and Laurie. They just hand me over to that boy and you to your friend Bill Rusper, and then sit back and talk about nuclear fission or chemical fertilisers or the economics of concerts as though their duty to us is done. I'm sorry, Celia. I've no right to criticise Laurie, but he's really not much better than Julian, and it *is* your birthday celebration.'

'Men are adept at finding excellent reasons for suiting themselves. Laurie is doubtless telling himself that it's nice for me to have run into Bill Rusper, an old friend of mine whom I haven't seen for a long time, and Julian is telling himself that a young man of your art circle is much better company for you than he is and he's certainly not going to cramp your style.'

'And really they're both relieved at not having to dance. It's rather humiliating, isn't it?'

Celia smiled a little wanly.

'Yes, it is. Not something one can very well complain about, though. At least, I can't. Pride won't let me. Anyway, I should be used to it by now. A cushion in the background, to be used when there's time for me.'

'Oh, no,' protested Fiona. 'It's just thoughtlessness, I'm sure. That present was a token of what is really there.'

'Could be conscience money, dear, and I'd rather not be bought off.'

There was a dry detachment about Celia which Fiona had never seen before. Celia was warm and impetuous by nature. She flared up and the flare was soon over. This coolness was so alien that it seemed to indicate that there was something seriously wrong. Fiona felt distressed for she was very fond of Celia and liked Laurie, in spite of the autocratic streak in his nature which all his charm could not conceal.

They came out of the cloakroom into the hotel lounge, and Celia said:

'I'm thirsty, and it's nice and quiet in here. Shall we stop and have a drink before inflicting ourselves on the men again?'

'Yes, let's. I'd like a lime juice.'

Celia ordered a lime juice for Fiona and a gin and tonic for herself, and they took themselves to a couple of armchairs at a small corner table. Fiona studied her glass thoughtfully, trying to find the right words.

'It's awfully easy,' she said gently, 'to take people for granted, but it doesn't mean that the basic feeling for them has changed. It just gets overlaid, but it's there. If you suggest that you'd like to have a corner of the carpet up sometimes to see it, I'm sure the suggestion would be met.'

Celia's smile warmed her face and took away the years.

'How nice you are, Fiona. But I haven't nearly such a sweet disposition as you. If a man shows by his actions that he doesn't want me, that he's lost interest in me, I'm afraid my pride won't let me go down on my knees and ask for a few favours. You can't ask for love. It's either there, or it's not. I had it once. For longer than most wives, perhaps. I'm probably crying for the moon in expecting it to survive years of daily married life without degenerating into mere convenience and habit. I must just get used to it, that's all. But that's enough about me. What about your sinner?'

'Julian? Oh, I guess his sins aren't very serious, and I've been a bit silly, anyway. I seem to have been in rather a silly mood all day,' added Fiona reflectively.

'In what way?' asked Celia, smiling.

'Trying to turn a glass of milk into champagne.'

'Dear me. Would you like to be more enlightening?'

'Trying to glamourise myself and being rather absurd about it. Not the glamorous type.'

'Nothing so synthetic, my dear,' said Celia, thinking how much more interesting Fiona's face was than any conventional type of beauty or glamour. There was a piquant charm about that boyish head with the short silky hair curving closely to its contours. More than most, it was an expressive face. In repose, it had an appealing wistfulness, an other-worldness which made one curious to follow her thoughts; and it could light up with mischief so vividly that Celia was often reminded of her elder son. Fiona had gained a lot in confidence, she thought, since living at Alanbridge, and no longer shrank from people although she would never project herself with any force. Her charm was elusive and delicate, but behind it there lived a quiet strength of mind and spirit which had several times surprised Celia in the early days of their friendship. Julian's influence had obviously been the greatest in her life, and Celia had to admit now that it was a very good one, in spite of the very strong feeling against the male sex which gripped her that evening.

'Julian's defections are forgiven, then?'

'Yes. He hasn't any that aren't easily forgivable, anyway.'

'I wonder what Julian would have to do before you condemned him? Half a dozen murders? It's risky to expect too much from any man, Fiona. They're not made in a selfless mould, any of them.'

'I've never had an unkind word from Julian, and he's completely selfless where I'm concerned. I don't know why he should be so kind and good to me. Except, of course, that he has a very kind heart. I can never repay him.'

'Yes, he is kind. But why shouldn't he be good to you, dear? You devote yourself to him and to Alanbridge in every way open to you. Don't be so modest. You pay him back in many ways. And your paragon isn't above making you fetch and carry for him like a lackey. Beware. He'll take it all for granted if you're not careful.'

I can't be careful with people I love, thought Fiona, and I wouldn't want to be, but all she said was:

'I would still be in his debt.'

'Bless your heart, don't let me infect you with my jaundice. I'm feeling my age today. The forties are looming very near, and meeting Bill Rusper has made me acutely conscious of it. We grew up together and now he looks a middle-aged man to the last thinning hair.'

'How long is it since you saw him?'

'Five years. He went to Australia just after Philip was born, I remember. He's put on weight and gone to seed, somehow, but he's the same good-natured soul as ever. Before the war, it was thought by our respective families that

Bill and I might make a match of it, but we weren't the same boy and girl after the war.'

'How did you meet Laurie?'

'He succeeded my father as head of the Research Station, and I worked there as librarian. We fought like cat and dog for about a year, and then he was too much for me. Now we have reached the calm, indifferent waters of a well-established marriage, and we don't squabble any more. We are automatically polite, and quite encased in habit, like wax fruit under glass. Shall we return to our partners? I don't suppose they've missed us.'

'I hope Eric's joined his sister again.'

Julian and Laurie, deep in conversation, rose politely when Celia and Fiona joined them. Eric and Bill had both disappeared.

'You've lost your partners, girls. This is the last waltz and they gave you up for lost,' announced Julian.

'Then,' said Fiona sweetly, for pride was not going to prevent her from asking, 'you can take me.'

'I was going to suggest it. I'm not good at reversing, so I hope you don't get giddy.'

In fact, he danced very well, with a long stride which suited Fiona, and the only trouble was the briefness of the dance.

'What a pity it's over. That was lovely,' said Fiona. 'You were a coward, leaving me to Eric all the evening, Julian.'

'I thought he might be your heart-throb, and why should I be a spoil sport?'

'Does Eric seem the sportive type to you?'

'We-ell, not on first acquaintance, but you never can tell what lurks underneath these sober exteriors.'

'You know all right. You just took advantage of Eric's arrival to dodge your social duty.'

'Them's hard words, girlie. Why should I be vain enough to imagine that you would prefer dancing with me, an indifferent performer, when a nice young man like Eric turns up? If for no other reason, he's a pleasant change for you.'

'You're wriggling, but we won't go on with it,' said Fiona, who could hardly tell him that she would rather dance with him, even if he couldn't tell a fox-trot from a quickstep, than with anybody else in the world.

When they came out of the hall they found that it had been raining, although the sky was now clear and pricked with stars. Water was running fast down the gutters, and the lamps threw glistening reflections across the wet road. The air smelt sweet and fresh, and Fiona sniffed appreciatively as she lifted her skirt to cross the pavement and step into the car beside Julian. The Deverels were already away, their tail light vanishing as Julian pressed the starter.

'Must have had a lot of rain,' he observed.

Fiona said nothing, content to sit there and watch his hands on the wheel, to be close to him in the privacy of the car. She wondered, a little mournfully, how he would behave if it were Gillian Courtney sitting beside him in the darkness, and wished that he could see her with those eyes. The ironic humour of that evening was not yet exhausted, however.

It happened when Julian, taking a short cut up a narrow, rutted lane, was forced into the hedge by a high-powered car which shot past them at high speed. Had Julian not been a skilful and cool driver, they must have collided, but as it was, they escaped with a scraped wing, the sight of which caused Julian to smother a word not suitable for Fiona's ears.

'Raving lunatic. Probably had too much to drink,' he said when he could trust his tongue. 'Wish we'd got his number.'

Fiona was leaning out of the window on the off-side while Julian investigated the rear with the aid of a torch.

'No more damage?' asked Fiona.

'Don't think so. It's not going to be easy getting out of here, either,' said Julian, eyeing the shallow ditch in which the two near-side wheels were resting. 'Too much mud there for my liking.'

His pessimism was justified, for in spite of his efforts, the wheels spun round in the mud and the car would not budge. Julian was happily not a man who allowed trying circumstances to excite him or gnaw at his temper. He switched off the engine, lit a cigarette and proceeded to discuss the problem with Fiona.

'I've an old piece of sacking in the boot. Might try to get that under one of the wheels. Then, I'm afraid, my child, I shall have to go gathering bracken in that field.'

'And try ramming it under the wheels?'

'That's the idea.'

'And if that doesn't work?'

'A half-hour's walk home, ducky, and a tractor in the morning. We're not likely to get a lift.'

Julian got out and rummaged in the boot for the sacking.

'I'd better come and help you,' said Fiona, emerging from the car in a billow of tulle.

'Not exactly dressed for the part,' said Julian. 'You'd better leave your frock in the car and put my coat on.'

'Then you'll ruin your suit. Wait a minute. That looks like your raincoat on the back seat. Can I have that?'

'Sure. I forgot I'd left it there. I'll get over that gate and collect the bracken. If you'll stand this side and take it from me, it'll save acrobatic feats over the gate each time. It's padlocked and not particularly well balanced.'

Fiona left her velvet coat and tulle dress in the back of the car, tied the raincoat tightly round her waist and rolled up the sleeves which covered her hands. It nearly reached her feet and the effect above high-heeled silver sandals was decidedly quaint. Fate had certainly decided that for her, glamour was out that evening.

She carried armfuls of bracken to the car, and they pushed it under the wheels as far as they could. Fiona armed herself with a long stick to ram the bracken home as Julian started the car. At the second attempt it moved, and Fiona, pushing valiantly on the boot, almost fell as the car lurched up on to the crown of the lane again.

'Well done,' said Julian, as his helper climbed in beside him.

Fiona shivered. The raincoat wasn't very warm and her feet in the mud-stained sandals felt damp.

As they drove up the lane and the gables of Alanbridge came into view darkly against the sky, Julian said:

'Don't know about you, Fiona, but I've a raging thirst and a longing for large quantities of tea. That's the worst of wine.'

'I'll make a pot. Doesn't Alanbridge look lovely at night? It has such a pleasing silhouette, and always looks welcoming, somehow,' she added as they came into the light of the lamps which flanked the wide oak door.

'What an odd child you are. Instead of falling in love with young men, you fall in love with a house.'

'But you love Alanbridge, too.'

'Yes. Love it, and perhaps hate it a little, too, sometimes. It puts chains of responsibility on me.'

'But it's worth it. And everything has to be paid for. Would you really have preferred not to have such a lovely inheritance?'

'It would have been better, perhaps, if there had been more of us to inherit it. I love the place, but I wish I were a younger son, and didn't have the sole responsibility. There's always a conflict inside me between the man of property and the musician, and I don't think I'll ever resolve it to my satisfaction.'

'I don't think you would be happy without Alanbridge, and I suppose to strike a balance between the things that matter most to us is a problem that besets most people. The awful thing would be to have a life in which nothing seemed of much importance.'

'You know, you've turned out to be far too good a pupil. I'm left with no arguments, and can only suggest that you buzz out and get that pot of tea ready. I'll bring in the finery.'

When he joined her in the kitchen, she was pouring the water into the pot.

'I've put your coat and dress on the chest in the hall. Sorry the evening's had such an inglorious end. You've got some mud on your nose. Here.'

She stood in front of him while he removed the mud with his handkerchief, and the ache to feel his arms round her was almost more than she could bear. He had taken his coat off, and his dress suit had emerged unscathed from his forays for the bracken. Fiona, standing there in a raincoat which hung on her like a dun-coloured shroud, her hair wind-blown, her shoes stained, felt half-way between tears and laughter. The contrast between the picture she had hoped to create coming down the stairs that evening and the spectacle she must present now was so ludicrous that she felt her control slipping.

'That's better,' said Julian in his more practical voice, returning his handkerchief to his pocket. 'Afraid you've lost an ear-ring, my dear. The one on the right has gone.'

And that finished it. To Julian's astonishment, Fiona broke into peals of laughter and became quite helpless for a few moments.

'Don't get it,' said Julian, when she borrowed his handkerchief again to wipe her eyes.

'It doesn't matter. I can't explain. Let's have that tea.'

'Are they valuable? Those ear-rings? Shall I go and have a look in the car?' asked Julian, still puzzled.

'No. Drink your tea. They weren't valuable and I don't think ear-rings are meant for me, anyway.'

Her lips were still quivering as she sat on the table holding her cup of tea. Julian lowered himself into the old rocking chair with a sigh of relief.

'One thing you can always be relied on for, Fiona: a good cup of tea,' he observed.

'Well, that's something,' she replied, her eyes still dancing, although the smile that curved her lips as she watched him drinking his tea held a wistful tenderness that must have set him wondering had he seen it.

CHAPTER THREE

FIONA was showing three pictures at the art exhibition; two drawings and a water colour. The exhibition was held in the British Legion hall in Elton and lasted for a week. When Fiona paid a final visit on the last day, she was delighted to see the little red tabs which denoted a sale affixed to all three of her pictures. She found that the Deverels had bought her drawing of a hedgerow in June, Aunt Lou's friend Thea had bought the other drawing of the reed-fringed pool on the heath, while the water colour of daffodils in the woodland garden at Alanbridge had gone to a buyer unknown to her.

Aunt Lou was there, beaming with pride under a hat trimmed with cherries which would itself have made a fascinating still life study, with her two friends in attendance. Julian irreverently referred to these two ladies as Moth and Mustard-seed, although it would need a very large stretch of the imagination to associate Aunt Lou with Titania, the only apparent link being a liking for animals. Perhaps in a grotesque way, though, Aunt Lou did suggest fairyland, thought Fiona, watching her conduct her friends round. She certainly ruled the other two like a queen. Thea Moffington and Janet Motherley were cousins who owned a shop in Elton which specialised in art needlework and knitting materials. They were spinsters in their fifties and had made a success of their business in spite of their extremely unbusinesslike manner. Creating an impression of gentility and refinement, they would have looked more at home behind a silver tea-pot in a Victorian drawing-room than behind a shop counter. Thea was tall and willowy, with thin features and soft grey hair waved neatly to her head; Janet was small, with a round face and china blue eyes beneath cloudy, mouse-coloured hair. Both had soft, cultured voices and a ready smile, Janet's a shade deprecating and over-anxious to please. And both shared Aunt Lou's passionate devotion to animals and worked unsparingly in their cause. They lived at The Towers Guest House in Elton, and since two young assistants now took the brunt of the shop work from them, they had ample time to spare for their voluntary work with Aunt Lou, whose word was evidently law to them. It had only recently begun to dawn on Fiona that the removal of Aunt Lou to Alanbridge must have been a blow to all of them, although Aunt Lou was still a very frequent visitor to The Towers.

'Where's Julian?' asked Aunt Lou, as they rejoined Fiona. 'Wasn't he coming along this evening?'

'Yes. He was teasing me about having to buy my pictures to save my face. Now we can make him eat his words. He's late though. He said he'd be here by six. He was helping Uncle John in one of the greenhouses when I left.'

'Well, we're due at a Committee Meeting, so we'll have to leave you now, dear. I'll be home about ten, I expect.'

'Good-bye, Fiona. We've enjoyed this exhibition so much. Elton is really getting art-conscious at last, isn't it? Such a desirable trend, for Elton, culturally, has always been a little backward, don't you think? Except musically, of course, and there it's Mr. Falconer who carries the torch,' said Janet Motherley reverently.

'Yes, I agree. We only need a good theatre now,' said Fiona.

'Come along, girls,' said Aunt Lou firmly. 'We mustn't set a bad example by being late.'

'And we're so thrilled with your picture, Fiona,' said Thea over her shoulder as they followed Aunt Lou. 'Such delicate detail . . . delightful . . .'

Her voice faded away as they fluttered after Aunt Lou like two gulls in the wake of a tramp steamer and disappeared through the door.

Fiona stayed on for a while, talking to Mr. Kirk, and was just wondering whether to give up waiting for Julian and take the bus home when he came in, and she knew immediately that something was wrong. He stood just inside the door and waited for her to join him.

'Fiona . . .' He took her hand. 'I've bad news. Dad. He collapsed in the greenhouse this afternoon. He was dead before I could reach him.'

'Oh, Julian! No.'

'It was all over in a minute. He couldn't have known much about it. It was the kind of end he'd hoped for. The kind we would all hope for.'

Driving home with him, there was little she could say. They had known for a long time that this must come, but the shock bit deeply, for all that. Death was so frighteningly final, thought Fiona, and the sudden blotting out of a loved personality was no easier to realise and accept because of a doctor's warning.

She did what she could to help Julian in the days that followed. He attended to all the formalities with a practical calmness which she knew hid a deep grief, and it was not until the night after the funeral that he let the mask drop, and then only because he thought he was alone.

Fiona had gone to Joe Bramble's cottage with a message from Julian, and had stayed to have a cup of tea with him and listen to his reminiscences of John Falconer. Joe's father had been head gardener at Alanbridge when Julian's father was young, and it was in his time that much of the best creative work of the garden was achieved. Old Tom, Fiona gathered, had been something of a dictator and his underlings, including his son, had had no easy time of it. She lingered longer than she had intended, and took the short cut home across the paddock and through the garden. It was a dark night, and as she approached the back of the house, she could see Julian standing by the long windows which led out on to the terrace. The light shone across the stone paving, outlining him sharply as he stood there, quite still, his hands clasped behind him, gazing out into the darkness. Fiona stopped by a holly bush below the terrace, out of range of the light, and watched him with an aching heart. There was something desolate about that immobile figure, and she longed to comfort him. What was he seeing as he looked out at the dark shape of the garden? A burden that he now had to carry alone? She could sympathise with the dilemma of the creative artist saddled with practical responsibilities. But Alanbridge itself was to her such a creation of beauty that it justified any sacrifices it demanded. If only Julian had a wife who could lift much of the responsibility from his shoulders, leave part of his life clear and undistracted for the composing which was his true work, and give him a background of love and understanding, he could bestride Alanbridge and his music, and enjoy both his worlds. He deserved to. And she would gladly spend her last drop of blood in doing this for him. But Julian, who had given her so much, had no need of anything she could give him. And the ache of that grew harder to bear every week.

She moved into the light and he saw her and opened the window.

'I gave Joe your message, Julian, and he says he'll see to it first thing in the morning.'

'Righto. Thanks, Fiona. Air feels a bit sharp tonight. I think I'll go and check the temperatures in the greenhouses.'

'Can I do it for you? You look so tired.'

'Well, it's not with the work I've done today. I've achieved precious little. Can't bring my mind to bear, somehow.'

'He meant a lot to you, Julian, didn't he?'

'Yes. It leaves a big gap.'

'I'm so sorry. I wish I could help.'

'Bless you, pet, you do. Don't encourage me to feel sorry for myself. Frightfully bad for the morale. I'll just check those temperatures.'

'Shall I come with you?'

'No. You buzz off to bed. Aunt Lou says I've run you off your feet today, and I guess she's right. I feel like a stroll round. Good-night, my dear.'

'Good-night, Julian.'

She watched him go out into the darkness with eyes that blurred suddenly with tears.

Whatever Julian's feelings, he tackled his new responsibilities with vigour that autumn. A young assistant was found for Joe Bramble, and Julian took over the reins. He gave just as much time to the school and to his own work at the piano, but his visits to London practically ceased and he stayed at Alanbridge for Christmas instead of going abroad, as he usually did in the school holiday periods.

They spent Christmas Day quietly at Alanbridge, Aunt Lou's friends joining them in the evening. On Boxing Day, Fiona and Julian went to a party at the Deverels. It was a few days after this that Celia caught a chill, developed pneumonia, and was seriously ill for several weeks. Fiona spent a lot of time with her during her convalescence, which was slow, and she was thinking about her friend with some anxiety as she jogged back on the bus from Marchwood one sunny February morning. She had taken some books and had found Celia up for the first time, but curiously listless, as though life had lost all interest for her. Perhaps, with the cold grey weather which had lasted since Christmas now breaking at last to reveal signs of spring, she would take heart. Already the catkins on the hazel trees were turning gold and Fiona had seen the first silver buds of the pussy willow shining by the pond on Marchwood green that morning. And there were drifts of snowdrops in flower in the woodland garden at Alanbridge.

When she arrived home, she found a car standing in the drive which she had never seen before. It was a smart grey coupé. As she closed the front door behind her, Mrs. Blakeney came into the hall carrying a bottle of wine with reverent care.

'Hullo, Mrs. Blakeney. Raiding the cellar?'

'Yes, Miss Fiona. We've an unexpected guest to lunch. A very important one. Mr. Julian asked me to fetch this wine. A special vintage. And if I shake it up, he'll have my blood.'

'Dear me. Let me open the door for you. Who is this august personage?'

Fiona opened the dining-room door, and Mrs. Blakeney whispered softly as she passed her:

'Miss Courtney. Gillian Courtney, the actress.'

Fiona had the impression, during the lunch which followed, of being caught up in a warm and vibrant stream and carried swiftly along in a state of dazzled delight through a strange country: such was the impact of Gillian Courtney's personality. If her features were analysed, she was not beautiful, and yet she created an impression of beauty. Dark hair, a creamy skin, and deep blue eyes; a tall slender figure which moved beautifully; and a deep musical voice: these were the main points, but it was the indefinable quality of personality which irradiated Gillian Courtney and made Fiona think her the most beautiful woman she had ever seen. And to all this was added the power to put people at ease, to appear sympathetic and interested in them so that Fiona, far from being awed by this dazzling stranger, felt drawn to her in warm friendliness and talked happily and freely with her. It was not until Julian took Gillian round the garden that Fiona felt as though the sun had gone in and faced for the first time the hopelessness of her own desires. How inevitable that Julian should love her, and how well matched they would be. A gracious and lovely mistress of a gracious and lovely home. And artistic gifts to match his, so that there would be a common ground of understanding. Could any man look elsewhere with Gillian Courtney shining in his sky?

She went out to the greenhouse to test the pots for dryness, and spray and water where necessary. This was a part of the work in the garden which Fiona had taken over, after several weeks of instruction from Joe Bramble on detecting the particular ring of a pot which was too dry and assessing the amount of moisture needed. She loved the warm earthy atmosphere of the greenhouses, especially the one which housed the freesias with their lovely scent. There were African violets and rare lilies in this house, too, and she was lingering over one magnificent red-trumpeted lily when Julian and Gillian Courtney stopped outside the house. Fiona, hidden from them by the green foliage of some ferns, could not help hearing part of their conversation, for the warm sunshine that afternoon had prompted Joe to open some of the lights for ventilation and their voices carried on the still air.

'This is a lovely place, Julian. Even lovelier than I'd imagined from your descriptions of it. You could never be free of its hold on you. You're enmeshed for life, but what a beautiful web to be caught in.'

'I knew you'd love it if you saw it. I wish you'd come before, when Dad was alive.'

'I think I was afraid of its spell.' She was facing Julian with a little smile, and Fiona saw her take the lobes of his ears in her hands and shake them gently as she said, 'I was right, dear, wasn't I?'

'Yes, Gillie, you were right,' said Julian, putting an arm round her shoulder as they moved on.

It was only a small exchange, but their easy manner with each other, the unforced intimacy of their gestures, brought home to Fiona far more forcibly than any words of love the fact that these two people were very close to each other.

Gillian left shortly afterwards, for she was appearing in London that night in the last performance of a play that had been running for nearly a year. As she shook hands with Fiona, she gave her a warm smile and said:

'I'm so glad to have had the chance of meeting you, Fiona. Julian has often spoken of you, but I'd not gathered an accurate impression from him at all. I thought his young cousin was still a schoolgirl.'

'Well, so she is,' said Julian, pulling Fiona's hair gently. 'Unlike most of the young generation these days, Fiona is blessedly free from sophistication and has the wide-eyed simplicity of eternal youth.'

'A Peter Pan. You have just the right face for the part. If I were casting the play, I'd simply have to have you for my Peter. Don't you agree, Julian? Pure Barrie.'

'Yes. Star dust and all.'

And then Gillian had gone, leaving a chilly gap.

'What a lovely person, Julian,' said Fiona when he came back into the room.

'Gillie? Yes.'

'Were you expecting her today?'

'No. She telephoned just after you left this morning.'

'I've seen her on the stage, but she's every bit as fascinating off it. And so natural and unaffected. I like her tremendously.'

'Good.' He filled his pipe with a preoccupied air, then said suddenly, 'Now what about your twenty-first birthday, ducky? How would you like to celebrate it? I feel that such an auspicious occasion should be marked.'

'I hadn't really thought about it.'

'It's a fortnight on Wednesday, isn't it?'

'Correct.'

'Would you like a party, or would you prefer a show in London?'

'Oh, I think a little dinner here with Celia and Laurie would be a happy way of marking the day.'

'No friends from the art class?'

'I think I'd prefer just the four of us, and Aunt Lou.'

'Very modest.'

'My world's a small one,' said Fiona, smiling. 'And will you play for us that night?'

'My dear child, I'll play for you any night. You know that.'

'Yes. But that's why I just want Celia and Laurie, because they'll enjoy that kind of evening as much as I shall.'

'Very well, my dear. I'll leave you to fix it.'

He went up to the music room and Fiona decided to gather some snowdrops for a flower drawing. Gillian Courtney's visit had filled her with a sense of her own inadequacy. What had she to offer Julian in comparison with Gillian? She was not beautiful, not particularly gifted; she had no money and no background. She hadn't really any right to her name, and would be homeless were it not for the Falconers' kindness. She was only just beginning to earn enough by her work to feel a small measure of independence, but she felt that she was in truth a Cinderella with nothing to offer but her love. And sitting there among the snowdrops in the woodland garden, she acknowledged finally the hopelessness of her love. Friendship and affection she would always have from Julian; no more.

She gathered some ivy leaves to arrange with the snowdrops, and even in this mood of despondency, the fragile beauty of the flowers against the shining dark leaves of the ivy lifted her spirits. In her hands she held a beauty of shape and texture that moved her to wonder. If all else failed, this birthright of beauty was hers, as it was that of every living soul with eyes to see. Comforted, she went back to the house to try to portray a little of that beauty. . . .

As long as she lived, Fiona remembered her twenty-first birthday. It started off happily enough with a present of a beautiful little wrist-watch from Julian, and several unexpected presents and cards conveying good wishes. The sun shone from early morning until evening, a dazzling day of spring, with the crocuses in the grass spreading a pageant of glowing colour when she walked round the gardens with Julian after breakfast. The almond trees were in bloom, and the daffodil buds had turned down and were showing yellow tips. The garden was full of birdsong that morning, with nesting activities very evident. One sparrow gathered up a tuft of the cat's hair only a yard from their feet and flew off with it triumphantly. The hawthorn hedge showed its first faint veil of green, and Fiona imagined that she could feel the sap rising everywhere. It was a morning of such lovely promise that what came afterwards struck with all the more cruelty, so that she never saw the first heart-stirring signs of spring again without thinking of that early frost.

They had an unexpected guest to dinner in the shape of Norah Coachford, who arrived with a message for Julian just as they were about to sit down, and perforce was invited to join them.

'I didn't mean to butt in,' she said, after she had congratulated Fiona, 'but I felt I ought to talk to you about it straight away, Julian, because I shall have to telephone Frank Carstairs tonight if we don't want him to accompany Joyce. After all, he is an important man, and won't want to be messed about.'

'I'll ring him after dinner. I know him pretty well. He'll understand. But why Joyce didn't decide that she wanted me to accompany her in the first place, I don't know.'

'I'm afraid I put her off. I told her you were very busy these days, and, after all, Frank Carstairs' name does count for something at a recital.'

'One of our pupils is giving her first recital at the Wigmore Hall shortly,' explained Julian to the Deverels. 'She's suffering badly from nerves at the prospect, and seems to think my face over the piano will have a calming effect on her.'

'I think she has a great future,' said Norah. 'The best mezzo-soprano I've ever had through my hands. I do hope she doesn't let nerves spoil her performance.'

'Julian will give her confidence, I'm sure,' said Fiona, who thought that Norah's intense attitude would foster nerves in anybody who wasn't made of steel.

'Well, she's a silly girl. She has all the talent and the technique, and yet she's behaving as though she's a novice and seems to be petrified at the thought of critics.'

'It must be something of an ordeal,' said Celia. 'With so much at stake, it's difficult to forget oneself.'

'She'll be all right on the night,' said Julian. 'I'll drive her up and keep her happy. Celia, my love, you're looking very willowy still. A dim wraith of yourself. How are you feeling?'

'Oh, much better, thanks. Never behaved with such appalling weakness before.'

'That brings me to a proposal I have to make,' said Laurie. 'Celia isn't really fit yet, and I want her to go away for a couple of months. A friend of mine has a chalet in a village in the Savoy Alps, not far from Chamonix, and he's offered to rent it to me, complete with the couple who look after it for him, while he's away in America. He's a writer and he's off to Hollywood shortly on a script-writing commission. I want Celia to have a couple of months there. Nothing like that mountain air to put you on your feet.'

'Sounds an excellent scheme,' said Julian. 'Appeal to you, Celia?'

'Well, I don't really think I ought to be away from the boys all that time.'

'My dear girl, that's nonsense,' said her husband firmly. 'They're at school all day, they have a perfectly competent nannie, and Aunt Bea is quite willing to come and take over the reins while you're away. She's very good with the boys, and they adore her. And you need a break from them. You're not strong enough yet to cope with those two dynamos.'

'Well, if Laurie's got it planned, I guess I'll be going,' said Celia with a faint smile.

'It would do you a lot of good to get away from your responsibilities for a spell, Celia,' said Aunt Lou. 'Responsibilities weigh heavy when you're not fit.'

'I agree,' said Fiona. 'You're not yourself by a long way, dear.'

'We're wondering, Fiona whether you'd care to go with Celia,' said Laurie. 'I don't want her to be alone too much. She'll only brood over the boys. She'd love to have you with her, and I'd be relieved to know that she had a companion to keep an eye on her. Could you, do you think?'

Fiona looked startled.

'Oh, I'm afraid I couldn't, Laurie. Not for all that time. It's nice of you to want me, but . . .'

Her voice trailed away. It wasn't easy to explain that the idea of being away from Julian for two months was impossible to contemplate.

'Well, I think it's a wonderful chance for you to travel, dear,' said Aunt Lou. 'Don't you agree, Julian?'

'I do. You've never seen anything of the world, Fiona. In fact, you've seen precious little outside of this neighbourhood. And there's no lovelier introduction to the Continent than the Savoy country. You'd love it.'

'I shouldn't want asking twice,' said Norah emphatically.

'It's very kind of you, Laurie, and I do appreciate it, but I think . . .'

'Don't decide now,' said Laurie kindly, for Fiona looked embarrassed. 'Think it over.'

'Do just as you like, Fiona,' said Celia. 'Don't be badgered into it. After all, it's not easy to throw up everything for two months and go off to another country as though you're just moving down the road. You'd be the first to appreciate how difficult it is to break off the routine of your daily life like that, Laurie, I'm sure,' said Celia, with a faint smile.

Laurie's eyebrows went up at this gentle dig, but he said quietly:

'Of course.'

'And I shall be able to look after myself and benefit from the rest quite happily on my own, Fiona, although I'd love to have you with me if you could spare the time. Give me a ring tomorrow and let me know, and don't let anybody else decide for you.'

To Fiona's relief, Aunt Lou then took charge of the conversation with a spirited account of the feud now raging between her and Coloney Shipley.

Julian played to them that evening, and Norah stayed on. Listening to him playing all her favourite pieces of music, Fiona felt that she could not go away from Alanbridge and not see him for two whole months. Her heart cried out against it. He was part of the fabric of her life and she could not tear him out of it for the sight of the loveliest place on earth. His absences abroad were hard enough to bear, and they seldom lasted for more than two or three weeks. To banish herself from him wittingly would be like cutting her heart in half. Celia would understand.

But some of the happiness of the evening had somehow evaporated. Perhaps it was Norah's presence that had broken the harmony. She had such an aggressive personality, thought Fiona. It made itself felt like a draught in the room. It was as though she always carried a chip on her shoulder.

The Deverels offered to drop Norah in Elton on their way home as she had missed the last bus, a suggestion which Fiona fancied was not altogether welcome as she would doubtless have preferred Julian to offer this service. Fiona went upstairs with her to collect her coat, and watched her gravely as she stood in front of the mirror adjusting her hat. It was a particularly ugly one, Fiona thought, with an artificial bird's head on the brim, its sharp bill projecting above Norah's right eye in a most unfriendly manner. And the dull purple colour of her coat was not at all becoming to her dark complexion.

'You don't give Julian much of a break, do you?' asked Norah, pushing a piece of hair back beneath the hat.

It was so unexpected that Fiona could only stare for a few moments and then stammer:

'I don't understand.'

'Then it's time you did, and if Julian's too kind-hearted to tell you, I will. Do you really think he wants Alanbridge to be saddled with you and that eccentric old harridan for ever? Don't you think he's a right to a life of his own? To marry and have a family, if he wants one?'

'But I'm not stopping him.'

'Do you think any woman would agree to take on you and Aunt Lou with Julian? Who would want a home with another young woman in it who hangs round her husband's neck all day? Use your imagination, for heaven's sake.'

'Julian would tell me if he didn't want me here. If he proposed getting married.'

'Would he? Julian's fond of you and he's always been sorry for you. He wouldn't want to hurt your feelings. He offered you a temporary home when you were in a jam, and now that you've assumed it's yours for good, he wouldn't want to hurt your feelings by having to tell you something that your own sensibilities should have told you long before this. I think it's a pretty poor way of repaying his kindness.'

Fiona had gone as white as a ghost, and Norah said in a softer voice:

'I'm sorry to have to say this. You don't mean to be a brake on Julian, I'm sure. You probably just haven't thought. You've known Julian ever since you were a child and I suppose when your uncle died you didn't realise that Julian had a right to his inheritance unencumbered. But you're not a child now, my dear, and I do think it's rough on poor old Julian to be saddled with a situation which makes it very difficult for him to embark on any life of his own.'

'Has he told you that he wants to marry?'

'Julian doesn't talk much about his personal affairs, but I do know he hasn't been too happy this past year or two. I don't know whether it's Gillian Courtney, or who it is, but can't you see how unfair to him this situation is? Would you want to marry a man with half of his relations living in the house at the same time? Particularly someone so glued to him as you are. And when you have a chance to give him a break, and he welcomes it, you turn it down.'

'I would be the last person in the world to want to hamper Julian in any way. I can't believe that he wouldn't have told me if he wanted me to go. We've always been perfectly honest with each other, and I'd have understood.'

'Would you? Well, you've been pretty blind so far. Aunt Lou was only brought in on your account. She'd far rather be back at that hotel with her old pals, and I don't suppose Julian particularly wants her here. She's as mad as a hatter, if you ask me. All that obsession over animals.'

'I think you've said enough about Aunt Lou, Norah. She is a very kind, generous-hearted person, and you have no right to say such things about her. You take too much on yourself. I may have been a bit blind, but that's all I want to hear from you on the subject. Shall we go down?'

Norah shrugged her shoulders and preceded Fiona down the stairs. When the car had driven off, Julian turned to Fiona.

'You look very pale, ducky. Feel all right?'

'Yes, thank you. A little tired.'

'It's all the excitement,' said Aunt Lou. 'You shall have your breakfast in bed tomorrow morning. I'm going to take some hot milk to bed with me. Will you have a glass, dear?'

'No, thank you, Aunt Lou.'

'Do you good. Put some fat on you,' said Aunt Lou, going off to the kitchen.

'Not worried about that suggestion of Laurie's, are you?' asked Julian. 'No need to accept. Old Laurie's a past master at ordering everybody around, but Celia will understand if you'd rather not go. Perhaps you are a bit young to appreciate the joys of travel just yet.'

'Oh, no, Julian. Now I've had time to think about it, I've decided I will accept. It will be a new experience for me, and a nice change for you not to have me around,' she concluded lightly.

He rubbed her hair.

'Noodle. I think you'll enjoy it, once you've stepped outside your cosy little world into the vast unknown. A bit scared of the idea at first, weren't you?'

It was easy to let him think so, and she managed a smile as she said:

'Perhaps.'

'It'll be an education for you, dear, and one you'll enjoy. Magnificent country. It's not good to live in too small a world. You can write me reams about it and I shall be green with envy. Now you'd better run along to bed. You look all eyes. Very nice ones they are, too.'

'Good-night, Julian. Thank you for today. And thank you for all the happy days you've given me.'

She had picked up his hand and laid her cheek against it in a sudden caress, then she slipped away and ran up the stairs leaving him staring after her with an odd little smile about his lips.

CHAPTER FOUR

FIONA and Celia were leaving at the end of April, and when Fiona took her last walk round the gardens on the day before their departure, she was conscious of a leaden tiredness that partially numbed her unhappiness. The strain of acting a part for the past few weeks was beginning to tell, and in an odd way it was a relief to be at the end of it now. It was so hard to act to Julian, with whom she had always been on such close and honest terms. She had never hidden anything from him, and their minds were so perfectly attuned that she felt he must see through her acting. Last night he had asked her again if she was quite sure that she wanted to go, and his eyes had searched hers uncomfortably as she replied.

She had spent hours thinking over Norah's words, discounting those activated by malice, for Fiona had known for a long time that Norah was jealous of Julian's affection for her. She had telephoned the next morning in something of a panic, asking Fiona whether she had mentioned their conversation to Julian, and extracting a promise from her that she would never tell him about her part in it. Not that she retracted a word, she explained, but Julian was her employer and he would resent her interference in his private affairs if he knew. And she did not want to lose her job. Fiona had reassured her with a gentle irony quite lost on Norah. But when she had put aside the malice, Fiona had to recognise a large residue of truth. She had been blind. She had seen the situation through her own eyes, and never through Julian's. She remembered now that he had offered her a home until she wanted to make a life of her own. He had not foreseen that she would never want a life of her own, away from him. When her uncle died and Julian became master of Alanbridge, she should have realised that it was time she left the haven they had offered her. Blinded by her love for him, she had hindered him from achieving the happiness he deserved, for she was sure now that she was the reason why the long-standing relationship between Julian and Gillian Courtney had not culminated in an announcement of their engagement. And the feeling of mangled pain that she should have done this to Julian, who had been so kind to her, was scarcely less than the pain of leaving him now. She had overstayed her welcome, assumed rights here at Alanbridge to which she was not entitled. Some day, she would ask Julian to forgive her. Now, she could only get out of his way.

She walked slowly round the whole area of the gardens, saying good-bye to it all. The cherry trees were in bloom, and she thought of Housman's lovely lines. Even if she were an avid traveller, she would never choose to be out of England in April, she thought. The scent of wallflowers was everywhere, and bees were busy about them. She walked back down the rose and wistaria walk, and wondered how many times Gillian and Julian would walk that way. There could be no lovelier home for any bride to come to than Alanbridge.

Back in the house, she went in search of Aunt Lou, and ran her to earth in the study addressing envelopes.

'Are you busy, Aunt Lou?'

'Just sending out a few pamphlets to possible sympathisers, dear. I've nearly finished now.'

'I wanted to have a little talk with you. I shan't have much opportunity later, because I've not started packing yet, and I'm going up to the Wigmore Hall tonight to hear Joyce Dell's recital.'

'We shall miss you, my dear. You don't seem awfully excited about your first trip abroad, but you wait until you see the Alps.'

'Aunt Lou, will you tell me something?'

'Fire ahead.'

'Would you rather live at The Towers than at Alanbridge?'

'What a question to shoot out of the dark! In some ways, dear. I have so many meetings and connections in Elton that it would be more convenient and save me a lot of exasperation at waiting for buses if I lived on the spot.'

'And you've missed the daily companionship of your two friends, haven't you?'

'A little. You see, we're of an age, and that counts. But bless my soul, I like Alanbridge and you're a dear girl. I have nothing to grumble about.'

'Did you expect you were going to stay here permanently when Uncle John asked you to come and keep an eye on me?'

'Well, there was nothing definite said about it. I was willing to come for as long as I was wanted. Now what is the meaning of this inquisition, young woman? Don't I suit?'

'You've been wonderfully kind and good to me, Aunt Lou. I'm only just beginning to realise what sacrifices other people have made for me. But what I wanted to tell you was this. I shan't be coming back to live at Alanbridge.'

Aunt Lou pushed her chair back, startled, but found Fiona's face calm and resolute.

'Go on, my dear. There's more to this.'

'Well, I think Julian wants to marry, and I've been a completely blind idiot not to realise that I'm the stumbling block. Julian and Uncle John offered me a haven when Father died and I was left with no home and no money. And I've repaid them by sticking like a burr. Of course Julian expected me to stand on my own feet some time, but he's too kind to drop any hints.'

'Now before you go any farther, let me say this, Fiona. Julian is devoted to you and your presence here has given him great satisfaction and happiness.'

'I know. I'm not doubting Julian's affection. I could as soon doubt the existence of the sun. To Julian, I'm a dear child. But I can be an embarrassing child when it comes to explaining me to his future wife. Can't you see the difficulty I create? I just don't know how I could have been so blind, especially as I knew about Julian and Gillian Courtney and wondered why nothing was announced.'

'You think it's serious, then?'

'I know it is. It's lasted for a good many years, and seeing them together the other day, I knew I was looking at two people who were very close in every way. So it's high time for me to retire from the scene, Aunt Lou. This trip abroad will help me to make the break. But I wanted to tell you before I went, so that you could go back to the hotel and your friends. But please don't tell Julian that I'm not coming back. I shall write and tell him in my own way when I feel the time is ripe. But if you just say that you'll go back to the hotel for the time being until he wants you back, that will be reasonable without actually telling any fibs.'

'Well, you have sprung a surprise on me. That's what has been on your mind these past weeks, then. You're not happy about it, Fiona, are you?'

'How could I be? I love Alanbridge, and Julian is . . . Julian. He's always been the king of my world. But it's time I grew up, I guess. I've been lucky to have had these past two years here. They've been like a lovely dream, in a way. An enchanted garden, king and all. But my father always said I was a silly little romantic dreamer, and I suppose I am. Otherwise I should have seen all this sooner. But I accepted it all like Cinderella, and now I can't forgive myself for making difficulties for Julian. Still, it's not too late.

There is obviously no quarrel between him and Gillian. I hope he'll be writing me about his engagement some day soon. He needs a wife. Alanbridge is a lovely inheritance and should be handed on to Julian's children. Uncle John was desperately anxious for Julian to marry. He told me so once.'

'Yes. I always think it's a pity when people of talent don't have children. So many morons do, and heaven knows we can do with a leavening of artists to help our sense of values.' She shot a keen look at Fiona. 'He'll miss you, though, Fiona, even if he does want to marry Miss Courtney. You're a very comfortable habit with him now.'

Fiona smiled a little wanly.

'I've outgrown my role, Aunt Lou. Julian doesn't realise it, but I do, now. He'll always see me as the nice kid he took under his wing and eventually rescued from Lime Avenue. And I shall never be able to repay him for all he's done for me. Only, things don't stand still. I can't play child parts any longer. You do see that I'm right, don't you?'

'Yes, dear, I do. And I think you're brave and wise to tackle the situation before it deteriorates, before it spoils what has gone before. Have you any idea what you'll do after this holiday with the Deverels?'

'I haven't thought that out yet. This will be a breathing space for me. I shall write to Julian about it as soon as I see my way clear.'

'Will you come back to Elton?'

'I just don't know. I need time to think.'

'Well, if you want any help, don't hesitate to write to me, dear. And you can always come and stay at our hotel. It's very comfortable. Good cooking. Pleasant people. And not unduly expensive.'

'I'll see.'

'What about money, Fiona? Let me help you there.'

'No, thank you, Aunt Lou. It's really time I stood on my own feet, you know. I've earned a modest amount this past year and not spent much. I've enough to see me over a few months, and I shall have plenty of material in Savoy for more pictures, from the sound of it. A complete change of subject will be good for me. Now I simply must pack. Thank you for all you've done, Aunt Lou. If ever I'm rich, I shall bequeath large sums to your animal welfare work.'

'I'll keep you to that. Bless you, my dear. And the best of luck to you. I shall expect losts of cards from you, and I'll let you know all the local news, including Julian's.'

Fiona packed most of her things, leaving her pictures and books and a few articles of clothing so that the room did not have a stripped appearance, for she felt quite unable to tell Julian the truth before she went. She needed time and she would prefer to write to him, for she was afraid that in his presence she would not be able to hide her love from him, and that could only embarrass him and cause him pain. He would hate to hurt her. She knew that. Now she tried hard to pretend that she was not leaving for good, that she was just going off for a holiday, concentrating on the immediate future with a desperate effort of will.

She hoped Laurie would not think she had too much luggage. He was driving them across France to their destination and was going to stay a couple of days while they settled in. He proposed to come and fetch them at the end of June or early in July, whenever he could fit it in. They were starting at six-thirty the next morning, for they had to be alongside the Dover Ferry by nine o'clock, so that there would not be time for lingering farewells in the morning. Tonight Julian would be intent on calming Joyce Dell's nerves and nursing her up to give of her best at her recital, so that it shouldn't be too difficult to get through these last few hours.

And this proved to be the case. Only at one stage in the evening's proceedings did Fiona's composure threaten to break, and that was when Joyce finished the first half of her recital, which had contained some difficult singing, on a simpler level with 'Fair House of Joy', a song which she evidently loved, for it came over with a moving beauty which blurred Fiona's eyes.

Whatever nervous qualms Joyce may have suffered, she showed no signs of nervousness that evening. Her rich easily-produced voice filled the hall and there was an attractive warmth about her personality which came across well. She was a tall, dark girl and she wore a very becoming sea green evening dress. Norah and Julian must be feeling very proud of this pupil, thought Fiona, for the girl obviously had a good future in front of her. But for most of that evening, Fiona's eyes were on Julian's dark face at the piano, on the hands which accompanied the singer with so much skill and sympathy. Much of the credit for Joyce's confident performance that evening would be due to him, she thought. He was very good with young, nervous people. She remembered how gently in the early days he had broken down the timidity and shyness which had always handicapped her. He had such a sensitive way of handling people that they blossomed without ever realising that they had been handled at all. Any child brought up under his care would be a most fortunate child, she thought, remembering her own unhappy upbringing at Lime Avenue.

At the end of the evening, Fiona, who had avoided Norah Coachford until then, went up to her and congratulated her on her pupil's triumph.

'Yes, she did very well. Better than I expected. A good attendance, too. You never know at these affairs. You pester everybody you know to buy tickets, and give away a good many, but you can never be sure whether the poor performer will have to face lots of empty rows. I hope she gets a good press.'

'I'm sure she will. I thought she sang beautifully, and has such a rich voice.'

'Yes. But your ear probably isn't as acute as a professional critic's. Excuse me, there's someone over there I must have a word with. See you later. Julian's taking us to supper, I believe.'

And Fiona, dismissed as an amateur, walked across the hall to Joyce, who had just appeared carrying one of the several bouquets of flowers which she had received. She acknowledged Fiona's congratulations with a tremulous smile.

'Thank you. It's kind of you to say such nice things. I feel rather weak at the knees now it's all over.'

'You looked wonderfully composed and sure of yourself.'

'I felt a bit hollow when Mr. Falconer led me on, but once I started singing, I was all right. Mr. Falconer was marvellous. He seemed to send radiations of confidence out to me and I picked them up.'

Julian came up behind her.

'I don't know about you, Joyce,' he said, as he laid a hand on her shoulder, 'but I'm starving. Or are dreams of the fame that is about to burst upon you in the press tomorrow food enough for you?'

'I'm not counting on the fame. And I am hungry.'

'Good. Did you enjoy it, Fiona?'

'Very much. I think your pupil is a great credit to your school, Julian.'

'Well, we had good material to work on, you know. But Norah's done her job well. Wouldn't it be more convenient to put those flowers in the car with the others, Joyce?'

'I suppose it would, but I haven't thanked you for them, yet. They're lovely, and I shall always keep the card you put in with them to inspire me when I'm struggling to get auditions and thinking I'll have to turn to crooning to earn a crust.'

'If you do, I shall come and strangle your vocal cords myself. Ah, here's Miss Coachford. Come along, Norah. We're all feeling faint from lack of food.'

'My breathing in that last bit of Mozart wasn't quite perfect. Did you notice, Miss Coachford? Mr. Falconer saved me there, I fancy.'

'Yes. I think, after all, it might have been better to snatch a quick breath in the middle of that phrase. It's a difficult one. But your control just lasted out, although the last note was a little thin. You did very well, Joyce. Can't rest on your laurels, though. There'll be a lot more hard work.'

They walked to a restaurant close by, and three members of that quartet enjoyed with the utmost zest the supper that followed. Julian ordered champagne, and by the time they were nearing the finish, Joyce was bubbling with as much vivacity as the wine that had come out of the bottle, and even Norah displayed a gaiety which Fiona had never seen in her before.

'We mustn't forget in this riot of triumph that Fiona, here, is embarking on her travels in the morning. The first time she's braved foreign lands. Let's drink to a very happy first holiday abroad,' said Julian, lifting his glass.

'Hear, hear,' echoed Norah.

Fiona, feeling that the smile on her face was now beginning to hurt her, thanked them and drank with them. Unfortunately, champagne didn't seem to have the same enlivening effect on her that it did on others. If she could have drowned the leaden lump inside her, she would have asked Julian to order another bottle, but since two glasses had merely made her head ache, she didn't think it would help to go on. Julian himself drank sparingly, for he was driving them home, but he was in high spirits and it was obvious that Fiona's impending absence was not weighing on him.

In the car, it was Norah who sat with Julian and Fiona joined Joyce in the back until they reached Elton, when Norah and Joyce were dropped and Fiona took the seat beside Julian. They were at Alanbridge in a few minutes, however, and Fiona said, as the car drew up:

'Don't tell me. You want a cup of tea.'

'Right first time. Don't know what I'm going to do without you to read my thoughts and pander to my wants for the next two months. Make it strong, ducky.'

She carried the tray into the sitting-room. Julian was lounging back in an armchair, looking very distinguished, as he always did in evening dress. The light fell on him so that half of his long, thin face was in shadow, emphasising the cheek-bone and jaw-line of the other half. The black hair, which all the brilliantine in the world would not flatten, grew far back on his temples, making his face seem even longer. In that light, he looked older than his thirty-two years, she thought.

'Penny for them,' he said, as she handed him his tea.

'I was wondering why your nose is crooked.'

'Probably came like that, or perhaps it was pushed out of true when I fell off the staging in one of the greenhouses when my age was a mere matter of months. At least, I'm told that happened when my father put me down in an absent-minded manner in order to inspect a plant that had unexpectedly wilted. Horticulture always came first in our home life,' he added, grinning.

'I rather like it. It adds a certain piquancy to your appearance.'

'If you can't be handsome, be interesting. If we're going to be personal, you're looking washed out, ducky. Not cold feet?'

'Not cold feet. Are you a good correspondent, Julian? I shall want to know what goes on at Alanbridge.'

'You shall. Now, you're sure you're all right for funds?'

It might have been a father seeing his child off to school at the beginning of a new term, she thought, feeling that something inside her was being mangled.

'Of course. I'm rich. The result of frugal living and a Christmas card eye.'

'Botanically, you're going to be in Savoy just at the right time, when the snows melt and the spring flowers emerge. We haven't got an alpine garden here. It's one of the things I'd rather like to develop.' He stifled a yawn and added, 'It's nearly one o'clock, my dear, and you've an early start in the morning.'

'Yes.' Every minute with him had become precious and agonising at the same time, and yet she was bereft of words. At some levels of feeling, words were no use, she thought. She wanted to hold him close and never be parted from him. But what she said was, 'Good-night, then, Julian. I'm glad the recital went off so well. Are you going to share my six o'clock coffee in the morning?'

'Do my best. You're having breakfast on the road, aren't you?'

'Yes. Laurie knows an hotel on the way where we can get a good breakfast.'

'Can't fault Laurie on organisation. Well, don't let excitement keep you awake. You've a long day in front of you. Laurie intends to get well into France tomorrow. Aiming at Fontainebleau for the night. That's going to make quite a day of it.'

But Fiona found it difficult to sleep. Even now, she could not realise that this was the last night she would sleep in that room, the end of the daily contact with Julian which had brought her such happiness. Only the reminder that it was Julian's happiness that she must think of, kept her resolution firm. She had no doubts about the rightness of her course. Even if there were no Gillian Courtney, there would be somebody one day, and since it had been made abundantly clear to her that the somebody would never be her, she must leave Julian free and stand on her own feet. She had realised that night, too, that she could not go on living under the same roof as Julian, acting the part of dear child. It was not as a child that she loved him, and she would not be able to hide that from him. The situation had become impossible. If only, she thought as she turned restlessly, the ending of it didn't feel like suicide.

She heard the clock in the hall strike four before she fell into an uneasy sleep, and then failed to hear her alarm-clock in the morning and woke to find six o'clock striking. It was as well, perhaps, that she then had no time to think of anything but the necessity of being ready when Laurie and Celia arrived at six-thirty. Laurie wouldn't be a minute late, she was sure, and he would frown on any delay. She knocked at Julian's door, flew into and out of a bath, said good-bye to Aunt Lou and somehow managed to be ready and drinking a scalding cup of coffee with Julian in the kitchen when Laurie arrived. She left half her coffee, gave Julian a blind hug, heard him say from what seemed a great distance, 'Have a good time, ducky, and take care of yourself,' and then was looking back through the car window to wave to him as he stood on the steps of Alanbridge, his hand raised in a final salute. The figure blurred but she remained leaning out of the window, waving, until the car turned out of the drive into the lane, and Alanbridge was lost behind its trees.

BOOK III

THE VILLAGE IN THE ALPS

CHAPTER ONE

FIONA'S impressions of the first two days of that journey which took her away from Julian were confused. The eager curiosity with which she would normally have welcomed such an experience was dimmed by the private unhappiness which seemed to spin a web across her eyes, and the speed with which Laurie drove them on to their destination tended to create a kaleidoscopic picture of a choppy channel crossing, long straight roads across flat agricultural country which spun past them to the throb of the car engine for what seemed hours on end, and stiff stumblings from the car in search of food. It was not until the third day, when the Alps reared up ahead of them and they approached the lovely province of Savoy, that Fiona felt herself coming to life again, and her first sight of snowy peaks brought her clear of the tangled web of unhappiness which had bound her.

The last stage of their journey took them off the first-class road surface which had enabled Laurie to travel at such speed, on to a narrow, winding, climbing road with a bad surface which enforced a leisurely pace for which Fiona was thankful, for the scenery was too beautiful to be rushed through. On one side of them a mountain stream was tumbling down its rocky bed, its waters swollen by the melting snows from the mountains which now towered before them, gleaming in the brilliant sunshine against a blue and cloudless sky. Now and again the road bridged the river so that it was first on their right and then on their left, as Laurie nosed his car along with careful consideration for its springs.

'I'm glad your first encounter with the Alps has been in sunshine, Fiona,' said Celia. 'The peaks were shrouded in mists and rain on my first visit and I never saw them for three days. In fact, I couldn't believe they were there.'

'How much farther, Celia?' asked Laurie.

Celia studied the wriggling line on the map and calculated

that the next bend after this short straight section should reveal the village which was their destination. The gorge up which they had been travelling had begun to flatten out into a wide valley, and they found that the village, a collection of wooden chalets and a few small hotels, spread itself on both sides of the river on a meadow which stretched to the wooded lower slopes of the mountains. Snow still reached down to the tree-line but Celia described how it would be retreating every day, revealing high meadows as richly coloured with spring flowers as the floor of the valley before them, until only the peaks remained in their eternal snow and ice. Fiona, feasting her eyes on the crocuses and little blue anemones which had only recently emerged from the snow, was enchanted by this new world of beauty, and was already choosing the words which should describe it to Julian.

The chalet they were seeking was on the fringe of the village, close to a little stone bridge across the river, and there they were welcomed by Armand and Grace Orlais, who had prepared a sumptuous cold supper for them, to be preceded by Armand's famous onion soup.

Celia looked white and tired after the long days of travelling, and she went to bed soon after supper.

'I shan't be long myself, dear,' said Laurie, and Fiona thought he looked a little worried as he turned to her after his wife had gone.

'I hope this holiday will put Celia on her feet and bring back her old pep. It should. The air here is marvellous.'

'I'm sure it will. I think she stood the journey very well.'

'Yes. But she's always been such a superbly fit person. I can't understand why she's taking so long to pick up. She eats and sleeps pretty well. Just doesn't seem to have any vitality.'

'A few weeks away from responsibilities and the demands of the children will work wonders,' said Fiona. 'Getting away from it all can restore one's sense of proportion, too. It's so easy not to be able to see the wood for the trees when they're too close to you.'

Laurie looked at her sharply.

'She hasn't anything to worry about.'

A faint smile touched Fiona's lips at this blithe masculine assertion, but she merely said:

'We can all find something to worry about when we're run

down,' then wondered whether that statement wasn't putting the cart before the horse.

'Too true. I think you'll both be comfortable here. The Orlais couple seem very pleasant and capable people, and Armand is a fine cook, according to Malcolm.'

'He was telling me that he was chef in a Soho restaurant when he met Grace, who worked in an office nearby.'

'What made him come here, I wonder?'

'It was simple. Your friend, Mr. Colton, used to lunch at the restaurant. Armand had a row with the owner. Mr. Colton had heard about this chalet when he was on holiday here and decided he would like to make it his headquarters. Armand, who was engaged to Grace then, married her and accepted Mr. Colton's suggestion that they should come and keep house for him.'

'You've soon found out all about it. You know, there's something about you, Fiona, that makes people confide in you. You don't say much and I don't know exactly what your secret is. Perhaps it's because you look so unbrushed by this world that people sense sympathy and no harsh judgment. You help them to preserve their rosy image of themselves.'

She smiled but said nothing. She sometimes found Laurie too direct for comfort when he was being personal. It was not to the strong, autocratic Laurence Deverels of this world that Fiona could open her heart.

'You must be tired, Laurie, after all that driving.'

'I like it. But I must confess I'm ready for my bed now.'

'What a pity you can't stay for a little while. Must you go back the day after tomorrow?'

'Afraid so. I shouldn't really be away from the Station now, but I wanted to see you two safely stowed away.'

'Well, that's a fine way of regarding us,' said Fiona, laughing. 'Left Luggage Department. I don't think I'd better repeat that to Celia.'

'Well, you know, in a way I'd rather like to see her fly off the handle. It's this docility that is so unnatural in her and worries me. Still, my choice of words then was not happy. I apologise. I wanted to see you two happily settled in a place where I was satisfied that you'd be well looked after. Better?'

'Much.'

All the same, Fiona wondered whether his first choice wasn't a more accurate expression of his thoughts. She looked at his dark, square-jawed face: middle age had not added any surplus flesh to his build, and he was as handsome and impressive now, Fiona guessed, as he had been when Celia first met him. A man of driving force, indivisible from his work, strong-willed and apparently invulnerable. If she had given her heart to this man, as Celia had, how would she have fared with him? He would be too strong for her, she thought. If she truly loved him, she supposed she would accept the crumbs he gave her and hope that time would bring her more. Perhaps that was what Celia had decided. At all events, it was obvious that she had stopped fighting.

When Laurie left her, Fiona fetched her coat and walked out to the bridge across the river. It was dark, and the sky was spangled with stars. The moon had not yet risen, but a soft opalescence that seemed to hang over the rounded peak of the mountain which closed the end of the valley heralded its appearance. The water below her gleamed palely as it cantered over boulders on its downward flight from the mountains, and she felt a touch of the coldness of ice in the air as she leaned on the bridge. If only, she thought, Julian were here beside her, knocking out his pipe, talking to her as nobody else ever talked to her, in a companionship as close and natural as this river with its bed. Without him, she was conscious of a terrifying loneliness; here she stood on a bridge, a tiny speck in this world of towering mountains, itself a speck in the universe which glittered millions of light years away. It was strangely beautiful and frightening. It was love's greatest feat, she thought, that it could banish the essential loneliness of the human soul. So urgent was her need, then, for some contact with Julian, that she decided not to wait for the moon and went straight up to her room, rummaged in her luggage for a writing pad, and began a letter to him. She tore up the first attempt after she had covered a page, as she felt it was too revealing. A light touch was needed, and her heart must be put away on a shelf. She thought a moment, then began:

DEAR JULIAN,
We arrived here today after being driven across France as though devils were at our heels. Inevitable, of course, as Laurie has to be back by Monday, but I am left with an odd medley of impressions and haven't really got my

breath yet. The most leisurely part was the channel crossing, which was boisterous and good fun, but you've crossed the channel so many times that you know all about that. For the rest: I remember cobbled streets and tree-lined boulevards, much loud hooting from cars, tables outside restaurants where people watched the world go by (including us—a very fleeting impression), window boxes and bright shutters to windows, no hedges and immense flat views with lots of sky, and then the mountains looming up, and so to this lovely Savoy country which you know so well.

This chalet is very picturesque—I will sketch it for you some time—the couple in charge are pleasant and friendly, and the village is even lovelier than I'd anticipated. I hadn't expected so many flowers, and snowy peaks against a blue sky are even more thrilling than I'd imagined.

I wish Laurie could spend more than a day with us, but he has promised to spend at least a week here when he comes to fetch Celia, and by then I hope she will be really fit. The air here smells so clean and sharp that it seems to add wings to your feet. If it weren't dark, I would go exploring tonight, for I don't feel a bit tired. I think Laurie would consider this a little unwise, however! If you were here, you would feel the same and be out under the stars with me, I guess. The country has a different mood and personality at night—often so lovely. I hope, when I'm middle-aged, the magic won't have evaporated. I shouldn't like to live in a world which held no wonder for me. I feel that Laurie has everything, *just everything*, taped.

How is Alanbridge? I know I only left it a few days ago, but it seems an age. I hope Joyce had good press notices—I'm sure she deserved them.

Please write when you have time and tell me all your news. I am not a very good letter writer, I'm afraid, but I'll add one or two sketches when I write which may 'set the scene' a little better.

Ever yours,
FIONA.

At the bottom of the last page, she drew a sketch of a car streaking down a tree-lined boulevard, a dog fleeing away from it on one side, a waiter bearing a tray of glasses gazing after it on the other, and behind the waiter some shadowy figures grouped round tables in various leisurely attitudes. She surveyed this for a moment, her head on one side, then took another sheet of paper and added a quick drawing of Laurie striding up to the chalet, a female form under each arm, with the caption 'We are safely delivered'.

When she had sealed this epistle, she felt better. Drawing was always a pleasure to her, releasing tension, providing an escape, and writing to Julian had brought him closer so that the pit of loneliness was bridged over, and she could look forward to exploring this stimulating new world with Celia.

Never having been abroad before, it was through the fresh wondering eyes of a child that Fiona saw the Savoy country unfold to her on her tireless explorations in the weeks that followed. The weather was changeable during that first month, offering golden days of sunshine and grey days of mist and rain in quick succession, but June came in with a perfect day when it seemed impossible that it could ever rain again, and on that day Celia for the first time embarked on a whole day's climb with Fiona. Hitherto, when Fiona proposed to climb, Celia had usually accompanied her for short distances and then dropped out, lazing about waiting for Fiona's return if the weather was good or making her way down to the valley again. There were few walks in that neighbourhood which did not involve climbing, and those they had explored thoroughly.

'I'm getting to that snow-line today, if it kills me,' said Celia, as they set off for the track which led up through the pine woods.

'You're certainly not,' said Fiona. 'I'm pledged to restore you in good health to your husband at the end of this month. I must say you're looking heaps fitter now than when you came.'

'I feel as fit as a fiddle, and although I carry so many more years than you, young woman, you're not getting the better of me today. I used to do a bit of climbing with Laurie when we were first married. We came here for a holiday and went to Switzerland, too. But that stopped after the children arrived. Laurie was an expert.'

Celia spoke nostalgically, and Fiona said:

'Well, you can start again when Laurie comes. He looks pretty fit.'

'He is. He's always been the lean, hard type. I wonder if we could recapture the old fun together.'

'I'm sure you could. A holiday from responsibilities will have the same effect on Laurie as on you. I wish he could see you now.'

And indeed, Celia, in a bright yellow jumper over a grey flannel skirt, a yellow cardigan tied loosely by the sleeves round her neck, auburn hair blowing in the breeze, looked little more than a girl again. Her pale skin had a faint tan and there was a dusting of freckles on her forehead. But more reassuring even than the physical evidence of her return to health was the old vitality which was beginning to blaze again.

'Wouldn't the boys love this? Perhaps they're a bit young. But we must bring them here one summer when they're a little older. According to Aunt Bea, they're behaving like little angels. I hope they won't shed their wings as the novelty of Aunt Bea's presence wears off.'

'From Peter's last letter to you, I gather that Laurie's put them on their honour to behave well while you're away.'

'I know. But it's awfully difficult to be good for two whole months when you're a small boy bursting with energy. Aunt Bea's very sensible and good with them, though. She had quite a lot to do with Laurie when he was a small boy, so she understands the Deverel temperament. And if the weather's good, they'll both be out of doors a lot, birds' nesting, I'm afraid. I've tried to make them see how cruel it is to rob nests, and I think Peter realises it, but young Philip!' Celia sighed. 'He can always find such good excuses for doing what he wants to do. Last year he came back from an expedition with a blackbird's egg in his pocket, but he hastily explained that he'd only borrowed it to show me the colour and he would return it the next morning. And with those heavenly blue eyes looking up so guilelessly into yours, what are you to believe? Laurie always says, the worst.'

'I adore Philip. I think the world will always yield him what he wants. Peter will probably get it by determination and hard work, but Philip will just smile and open his hands, and the plums will fall in. Some sort of magnetism, I guess. I'm no match for him, anyway.'

'Laurie thinks that public school life will do them both

good. He's a great believer in getting the boys away from soft feminine influence,' said Celia dryly, and then added, 'As a matter of fact, where my two offspring are concerned, he may be right. He often is.'

'He's a good correspondent, anyway.'

'Yes. His letters are brief and to the point, but regular. And in the last one I detected a slight intimation that he'd realised that it was Aunt Bea who was dishing out his vegetables and not me. For the first few weeks, I don't expect he noticed. So there's hope,' concluded Celia mischievously.

They were climbing steadily through the shady woods, their track winding in hair-pin bends. The ground was soft with pine needles, and large brightly coloured grasshoppers were chirruping around them. When they came out of the wood, the sunshine hit them with dazzling force, and there before them was a meadow covered with white narcissi and purple spotted orchids, so that Fiona caught her breath and could only gaze with an almost reverent rapture while Celia exclaimed at its beauty. Such a spot could not be passed by quickly, and they sat down by a rocky outcrop to feast their eyes, and soon decided to stay and have lunch there before moving on.

After lunch, Celia, drugged by the sun, lay flat on her back, her head propped on the haversack, and dozed off. Fiona wandered off to examine the saxifrages and mosses which were abundant in every rocky outcrop, and was rewarded by coming unexpectedly on a patch of gentians of such an intense blue that the colour seemed to bore into her eyes. There were many plants which she did not recognise and she collected a few flowers to press and send to Julian for classification. His botanical knowledge was far greater than hers and he had studied alpine flora on many of his holiday expeditions. Celia was still sleeping when she returned and she pulled Julian's last letter out of her pocket to read it again.

The last page she read twice.

I miss your bright presence about the place and keep expecting you to pop out from behind a bush at any moment. Deserted by Aunt Lou and you, I have bought a young labrador for feminine company—an ingratiating animal, gold with mournful brown eyes. Bought her from a friend of Laurie's because she was gun shy and no use to him. Leo is outraged.

Laurie and I consoled ourselves for our solitary state by dining together in Elton last night. His lordship is bearing up well and glad to get such favourable reports about Celia.

No, my dear, I have no personal news of any importance. Have a new pupil who promises to be something exceptional —a girl of twelve who has been allowed to develop some bad habits but who can already play Bach with a musician's understanding. I wish I'd had her earlier.

No composing at the moment—my creative powers seem to have bogged themselves down in the mud. Or perhaps I'm drugged by the scent of the lilacs—never known them so heavy with bloom as they are this year, and Mrs. Blakeney has filled the house with it. She hasn't your artistic touch, though.

We can't keep up with the work in the garden at this time of the year, so adios. And keep on enjoying yourself and writing me your raptures—they make me forget my advancing years.

JULIAN.

No mention of Gillian, no suggestion that his solitary state was likely to be changed. Fiona wondered why he kept that aspect of his life so hidden; why such a close relationship should seem so abortive. Perhaps he talked about Gillian to other people and not to her, but nobody seemed to have any clearer conception than she of this shadowy affair. It was like a hovering ghost. And always the tone of an affectionate uncle to a favourite niece.

'Why so pensive? Homesick?' asked Celia, sitting up.

Fiona smiled and turned this off with:

'Who was going to get to the snow-line?'

Celia looked at her watch and gasped.

'Oh, heavens! We shan't do it now.'

'Why worry? This is heavenly.'

'We might go a bit farther, because over that next hump there's a little lake, I believe. At least, that's what Ben told me last night while you were writing your letter. I think he wanted me to invite him to join us, but three's an awkward number and I didn't know whether you wanted him making sheep's eyes at you all day.'

'At me?'

'Yes, my innocent. The young man is smitten. Didn't you know?'

'Of course he's not. I scarcely know him.'

'So young,' said Celia shaking her head. 'Doesn't it strike you that he shows uncommon interest, coming round every night? It's quite a rough ride up here from Chamonix on a motor-bike.'

'Well, I expect he's lonely. He's only been working at the Chamonix tourist office for a short time, and probably hasn't got to know many people yet.'

'He's a nice lad, but diffidence is not one of his characteristics, pet. That young man probably knows half Chamonix by now, and he wasn't exactly backward in coming to your rescue the other day.'

'Well, it was just outside the café where he was having his *apéritif* that I fell down and spilt apples and tomatoes round him.'

'And the diffident young man leapt up, collected the produce, insisted on buying you a drink to offset the shock and then conveyed you home on the back of his motor-bike.'

'Because I'd just missed the bus. And how I tripped up like that, I just don't know.'

'He probably stuck his foot out, my dear. However, I'm not complaining. I like him, and shall be quite happy if you want to include him on any of our jaunts. He'd jump at the opportunity, I assure you.'

'Of course not. I'm not interested. I think myself that he comes up here because the *pension* he lives in is so dim. It's full of mangy cats and noisy children, he says. He's looking for a new billet.'

They strolled on, stopping now and again to inspect a particular plant that caught Fiona's eye, and soon reached the little lake nestling in a hollow before the next steep rise up over the shoulder of the mountain, which would have taken them to the moraine of its glacier, and above that to the snow-fields which culminated in the smooth dome-shaped peak. But they had lingered too long, and time was their enemy, so that they left the lake and retraced their steps with their goal unattained.

CHAPTER TWO

Quite how it came about, Fiona never knew, but it became a regular part of their programme in the weeks that followed to embark on any major climbs in the company of Ben Dawlish and a French mountain guide, Bertrand, who was a friend of Ben's. They made one or two of these excursions every week, leaving Bertrand to choose routes which were moderately easy and called for no special climbing prowess.

It was Celia who was bitten with the climbing bug, for Fiona was perfectly happy exploring the higher alpine meadows below the snow-line for flowers, stopping to sketch anything that appealed to her, or just sitting and feasting her eyes on the snowy peaks and domes around her. The world above the snow-line, although often infinitely beautiful and strange, was to Fiona still a dead world which would never appeal to her like the world of growing things. But to Celia the peaks were an ever-present challenge, and Fiona's fear was that her friend might over-tax her new-found strength in meeting it. Celia, however, was obviously very fit, and Fiona, after a confidential talk with Bertrand, was content to leave the choice and extent of their climbs to that very sensible Frenchman. Fiona and Ben often elected to drop behind and leave the others to bag their peak, joining them again on the return journey, a reversal of the order of their first expeditions which underlined the benefit which Celia had obtained from the mountain air.

'I've never seen such a transformation,' said Fiona to Ben on one such occasion as they sat eating their sandwiches, comfortably propped against a boulder, watching the figures of Celia and Bertrand receding across the glacier above them, and already difficult to pick out against the grey moraine.

'It's good air, right enough, but the country's too strenuous for my liking. You won't die of bugs—only of a strained heart,' concluded Ben laconically.

He was a large, loosely built young man with a fair skin, reddened now by the sun, and a pair of friendly blue eyes which appeared to accept the world before them with lazy amusement. He was an easy, pleasant companion, but not, Fiona thought, quite as guileless as he appeared, for he had brought about this quartet without any co-operation or keen desire on the part of Fiona or Celia, although they found it a pleasant enough arrangement.

'Well, you're not straining yours at the moment,' she said, foraging in the rucksack. 'Apple?'

'Will you peel and quarter it for me? I've never seen anybody present an apple more appealingly than you. You make quite a work of art out of it.'

Fiona peeled the apple carefully while he watched her.

'You seem to be able to have a lot of time off from your office,' she observed, finding his gaze rather disturbing.

'Two days a week? Don't call that much. Afraid it'll only be Sundays after this month, though. The rush starts at the beginning of July. Still, you'll keep Sundays free for me, won't you?'

'Mrs. Deverel is returning at the end of June. I thought you knew that.'

'M'm. But you're not.'

Fiona looked up from her task, startled.

'How do you know?'

'Madame Orlais told me you'd asked her what prospects there were here for a job.'

'Oh, she promised she wouldn't tell anybody.'

'Why the secret?'

'Because I haven't decided definitely yet what I'm going to do, and until I have, I'm not telling Mrs. Deverel or anybody else. Please don't say anything about it, Ben. I shall explain to Celia as soon as I've decided.'

'Silent as the grave. I'm delighted at the news, of course. You like it here, I gather.'

'I wouldn't mind staying on for a few months. I'd like to get some more drawings and paintings done before I go, but I'll have to find a bread-and-butter job if I'm to stay.'

'What about your esteemed cousin or guardian or whatever he is? Won't he stump up?'

'I don't really think it's your business, Ben,' said Fiona seriously as she handed him the four quarters of his apple.

'Crushed. I apologise. But I do hope you stay on.'

'We'll see, but I intend to spend most of my time working. I haven't done much yet because I thought it would be rather dull for Mrs. Deverel if I were glued to a sketchbook or easel, but I shall get down to it seriously if I stay on.'

'Warning me off?'

'No. Just making the position clear.'

'I could carry the easel and paraphernalia for you.'

'I wonder what that pinky-mauve flower is over there?'

Fiona went across to the patch of colour in a little hollow, and returned with a couple of flowers and a leaf. These she put inside a small tobacco tin.

'What are you going to do with them?' asked Ben, smiling.

'Press them and send them home for identification. I think it's some sort of primula.'

'You know, you're a most unusual girl,' said Ben slowly. 'You intrigue me. I've never come across anyone like you. I can't pin you down at all.'

'I should hate to be pinned down,' said Fiona, half smiling.

'Sometimes I think you're with me, and then I find you've escaped into another world. And you're shockingly unconventional. What normal girl would find a wild flower more interesting than a young man's offer to be her most humble and devoted servant?'

'What is a normal girl?'

'One who is interested in the opposite sex.'

'There are other interesting things.'

'Not at your age. It's a rule of nature.'

'You'd better write me off as an exception.'

'There are no exceptions to nature's rules. You could be like the sleeping beauty, but I don't think you are. I think somebody's wakened you. What is it, Fiona? Unrequited love, a secret passion for someone out of reach? Tell your Uncle Ben and he will console you with words of wisdom.'

'Did you know that someone once said that every time we put our thoughts and feelings into words, a little of the truth is lost?'

'Meaning?'

'That words make clumsy bridges.'

'But there are no other ways of communication.'

'There are. If you'll keep quiet and relax, we can fill our eyes with this meadow, feel the sun sink into our skin, listen to the grasshoppers, and be in perfect communication with this little bit of the world.'

'They're not grasshoppers; they're cicadas.'

'What you call them makes no difference to the chorus they make. Only your voice drowns it. That's what I was meaning.'

She was leaning on her elbow, half turned from him, looking dreamily across the meadow sloping away from them, its flowers and grasses moving gently in the wind. Already she was miles away from him, he thought, teased, as he had been ever since he first saw her, by that gentle elusiveness which seemed to draw him like a will-o'-the-wisp. Was it the fact that she was so different that attracted him? Was it the novelty of pursuing when he had always hitherto been either pursued or met half-way? The shy, retiring type had never appealed to him before, but there was some quality in this girl which both baffled and drew him. And exasperated him, he added to himself, as he noted the boyish curve of the head and the clean-cut profile which might have been a head on a coin for all its awareness of him. She wore a plain pale green skirt and matching cotton jumper, with a flame-coloured silk scarf tied closely at the throat. She obviously spent little on dress, but her clothes seemed to him to express her personality so well that they might have grown on her. She was slender without being angular, and as his eye traced the soft lines presented to him, he was filled with such a strong impulse to force this girl into an awareness of him that he had pulled her into his arms and kissed her almost before he realised his own intention. She did not struggle against his urgent lips and hands, but when he released her she moved away from him and said gently:

'I wish you hadn't done that.'

'Why?'

'I don't belong to you, Ben.'

'Then who do you belong to?' he asked angrily.

'Myself.'

'Oh, don't be such a prig. No, I take that back. You're not a prig. But come down to earth, Fiona. Let's have a bit of fun. Be human.'

'But I want to choose who to have that sort of fun with, Ben.'

'How can you choose if you never make a start? Why not give me a chance?'

'We hardly know each other.'

'That's what I'm saying. I want to know you better,

and there's one sure way of getting to know each other better. I'm sorry if I was a bit rough just now, but it's because you run away from me. Provokes my hunting instincts,' he added, grinning, his natural good humour restored. 'But if you'll stop running, or could even bring yourself to take one step towards me, I promise I'll be good and make the rest of the journey very gently. We could have such fun, and more than fun. I could teach you a lot about this earthly world which you haven't yet learned to enjoy. And maybe you could give me a few hints of the joys that appear to inhabit your unearthly world. What about it?'

He was very appealing as he smiled at her and put a friendly arm round her waist and Fiona knew then that she would have to tell him.

'I'm very sorry, Ben. If I were free, I might take that step, but I'm not. I love somebody else. I shall never be free.'

'Oh. So that premonition I had was right, after all.' He was silent for a few moments, then added:

'Can I know who it is?'

'No. Nobody knows about it, and it's quite hopeless, because somebody else made the same choice as I did and he loves her. I'm not in the running.'

'Well, for heaven's sake, you're not going to spend your life chastely dreaming about what might have been, are you? You might do that at forty, but not at twenty-one. It's ludicrous.'

'No, I'm not going to do that. I know I've got to make my life without him, but I haven't had much time to get used to the idea yet, Ben, and he's still too close to me to allow anybody else in. I'm sorry. That's how it is.'

'That's why you're staying out here?'

'Yes.'

'You're young to have such a deep attachment. To be so sure. I think you'll find time will change your tune sooner than you think.'

She smiled, but said nothing. How explain that Julian was so alive in her heart, so close to her, that he was just as much her constant companion now as when he was physically present. She carried him in her heart always. She could not foresee a time when he would be absent. And although she could not say so to Ben, the close and long-standing companionship of a man like Julian, so much older and more mature than she, had made the kind of fun which lively young men like Ben indulged in seem callow and silly. Somehow, because of Julian, she had missed that adolescent stage of development, and although she could sympathise with Ben's attitude and in no sense disapproved of it, she was not interested in that playground. Ben, she thought, would do a lot of experimenting before he became seriously involved and grew up. In years, he was two years her senior, but she felt that he was a lot younger. His life had been an easy and a happy one, she guessed. He was very likeable and had probably been spoilt at home, for he was the only son in a bevy of girls.

'Well,' he went on cheerfully, 'I'm certainly not being turned off for any wraith. I've known feminine hearts to mend with amazing rapidity, and my healing powers are considerable.'

'Is Chamonix devoid of patients?'

He smiled at this gentle dig.

'You're a break in the usual pattern. I find you a more interesting case.'

'It's no good, Ben. You must look elsewhere.'

'Oh, no. My professional pride is roused. And don't think you can hide from me, because I shall winkle you out.'

Fiona, however, was not alarmed at this threat. Her home life at Lime Avenue had trained her in the art of eluding capture. It had been a hard school, but she could fade out as skilfully as any Indian if she wished, and she did not think that Ben would be a very patient pursuer.

'That looks like our two climbers,' she said. 'I think I'll go up a little way to meet them.'

Ben reluctantly hoisted himself to his feet, and they set off over grass and rough moraine rubble until they came to the glacier across which Celia and Bertrand were now picking their way, roped up. The glacier was jaggedly toothed, and dark blue shadows indicated several crevasses. The end and sides of the glacier consisted of grey dirty-looking moraine, with lines of water snaking down bare rock, but the main body of it was a glistening blue and white mass, sometimes wrinkled and broken, seldom smooth, and carrying with it, Fiona thought, a threatening, merciless quality as it ground its slow inexorable way down, so that the dazzling smooth snow-fields above seemed like a serene promised land by comparison. Celia waved as they drew near. She still wore a skirt and a sports shirt for her climbing activities, with a heavy sweater tied by the arms round her waist, but she had added a pair of climbing boots, a floppy linen hat and a pair of sun-glasses to her attire. The latter she took off as they came up and unroped.

'Hullo, you two lotus-eaters,' she said. 'You look as refreshing as a nice crisp lettuce, Fiona. I could eat you.'

'Did you get to the top?'

'Yes. It was wonderful But we weren't the only ones there, which rather spoilt it. Just as I was feeling that we owned the world, a party of six arrived, including an elderly gent, which made me stop feeling as though I'd conquered Everest. Have you anything left in the rucksack? I'm hungry and thirsty.'

'One apple and a packet of raisins,' said Ben, handing them over.

Celia had the apple and Bertrand took the raisins. He was a stockily built, clean-shaven man of about thirty, with a leathery textured, tanned face which creased deeply when he displayed his dazzling white teeth in a wide grin, which he did frequently.

'She goes better every time,' he announced, regarding Celia with approval, 'but no lingering now. Otherwise you will stiffen and lose the rhythm. Go down steadily—not fast, not like a grasshopper—that is the way to finish a day's climb.'

And steadily, therefore, they went down, Fiona and Celia ahead, the two men following.

'These boots have made all the difference,' declared Celia. 'I could tackle slopes without a tremor. They bite in beautifully. I never thought I'd be raking these out of store, although I'd always cherished them and looked after them. Laurie gave them to me. They're beauties. Do you know, he almost refused to send them. He was too gallant to say that I was too old to go climbing again, but he begged me not to be reckless and to remember what happened once in the Lake District.'

'Go on. What did happen?'

'Oh, I fell down an almost vertical drop on to a little ledge. I'd lost myself in a thick mist. It was all loose scree and a bit nasty to climb up. Soon after I'd scrambled back to terra firma, leaving lumps of skin and clothing on the way, Laurie arrived on the scene in a bit of a state, lectured me fot attempting climbs when I'd had no experience, and then proposed to me. I was too shaken to do anything but weakly accept,' concluded Celia, smiling.

'You can't wait to get him out here, can you?'

'What a discerning child you are. Is it so obvious? I've enjoyed this holiday here with you immensely.'

'I know. And so have I. But lately, I don't think a day's gone by without your mentioning Laurie at least three times.'

'That man Deverel's difficult to slough off. But I've been doing a lot of thinking while I've been away,' went on Celia more seriously. 'Climbing again here has brought back the days of our engagement so clearly. Laurie's a good climber, or was. He taught me. Anyway, I've been thinking about our marriage. You know that lately it's . . . not been going too well.'

'Yes. You were unhappy about it long before we came away, I know.'

'I felt Laurie had lost interest in me as a person, that I just fulfilled the functions of housekeeper and mother to his children and that he wanted no more from me than that. Well, I still think that's true, but I knew when he asked me to marry him just what kind of person Laurie was. That he didn't approach women as his equals, and therefore wouldn't see marriage as the close partnership that I thought it should be. In a way, he's got the old Victorian attitude —you protect your wife, you provide her with as much comfort as you can afford, you buy her handsome presents occasionally. In return you expect your home smoothly run, your children well brought up, and your wife soothing and willing to suit herself to your every mood. But you never let her interfere with your man's world, with your work, with the serious business of life. I knew Laurie had that attitude towards women, and I knew he was a strong enough character not to be easily weaned from such an outlook. But I agreed to marry him. At first, we were so much in love that we couldn't have been closer. But when the years rubbed that gloss away, the old Laurie was there, and I started to feel aggrieved. Now, I think I was wrong. I took a chance on our love being strong enough to bring about the full relationship which is my idea of a true marriage. Well, it didn't come off. Perhaps it never would come off. People's natures don't change after maturity. And perhaps familiarity nearly always ends in indifference, and I've been crying for the moon.'

Celia was talking more to herself than to Fiona, finding it a help to clarify her thoughts, and Fiona said quietly:

'I think you underrate Laurie's devotion to you. His letters have proved how anxious he has been about you.'

'Oh, I'm a useful possession as a wife. I know he appreciates that. But I suppose it all boils down to the fact that I want to have his love, to know I have it, and I don't. If I did have it, I don't think he could be so engrossed in his work that he doesn't even know I'm there during the few hours we do have together. He answers politely if he hears. Often he doesn't hear what I'm saying. But his thoughts are never with me. That, to me, seems to spell indifference, or, at best, tolerance. Once or twice in his letters lately, though, I have felt the old spark alight again, but I don't want to count on it too much in case I'm disappointed.'

'I don't think you will be. I think it's a pity Laurie isn't more articulate,' said Fiona gravely, and at that Celia chuckled.

'He can be very articulate if he wishes, I assure you. But come what may, spark or no spark, I'm going to stop feeling hurt and accept what I have, which is a great deal. An injured woman is an abomination, and I want the boys to have a happy home life. So I'm just going to accept with a good grace the limited role Laurie assigns to me. Otherwise, the whole thing will deteriorate and our marriage break down completely. We're neither of us very patient people, Fiona. I'm afraid of what I might say in anger. Some things Laurie would never forgive, and he could be ruthless. So I must try to behave sensibly. My father used to know how to damp down my fiery impulses. I've never stopped missing his good advice.'

'He died soon after your marriage, didn't he?'

'Yes. I've been trying to think what counsel he would give me now. I think he'd say, expend your energy on some cause which will make you forget yourself and fill in the space that Laurie leaves. Anyway, when the boys go away to school, I shall do that—look for some kind of social work, perhaps. Laurie would never agree to my taking a job and earning money—the Victorian again. But there are a lot of social causes that I could investigate and get my teeth into. I'm so afraid of an empty life, Fiona, and with the boys away and Laurie wedded to his work and oblivious of me, I feel my middle years are going to bring a vacuum unless I do something about it.'

'Well, you'd better consult Aunt Lou. She will be able to suggest plenty of banners worth carrying. I think you're right about that. Any kind of creative or constructive work can make you forget your own troubled ego.'

'Creative more than anything, but I have no creative gifts, unfortunately. I envy people like Julian and you, who have your escapes so readily to hand. However, I must find my release in the constructive, once the boys are off my hands.' Celia stooped to tie up the lace of one of her boots, and observed as she straightened up, 'My knees are beginning to feel a bit wobbly, but I must finish in good style with Bertrand's critical eyes on me.'

They swung on down through the pine woods without faltering, and then back to the chalet where Ben had left his motor-bike. With Bertrand on the pillion, Ben roared off down to Chamonix, and Celia went in to run her bath. Fiona lingered in the meadow behind the chalet to give George, the sad-faced cart-horse, his piece of sugar. This had become a morning and evening ritual, and now, as soon as George saw her, he ambled up, his shaggy hair half screening his large, liquid eyes, his soft lips moving before they reached the outstretched palm. He was an old horse and spent more time in the meadow than between the shafts. He had the patient, kind expression of most of his breed and Fiona was very fond of him. As she fondled him, he butted her gently.

'Aren't you a lovely colour in the setting sun? The same colour as Celia's hair. I shall make a drawing of your dear old face and send it to Julian. Will you be a good model and stand still for me?'

George blew thoughtfully through his nostrils and Fiona gave him a last pat and left him, knowing that his dark eyes followed her until she disappeared.

Madame Orlais appeared as she stepped into the cool shady hall, and beckoned her into the kitchen.

'We can be private in here,' she said. 'Armand is out. I heard of a little job that might suit you, Miss Goring, although it is not exactly what you are used to, and I hope you won't feel offended at all by the suggestion.'

'I'm sure I shan't. I'm willing to try anything.'

'Well, you know the little *pension* Chez Vincent? It's the one by the bus stop with the window boxes you were admiring the other week.'

'I know. With pale blue shutters.'

'That's it. Well, Madame Vincent is a friend of ours and I met her this afternoon and heard that her daughter has just accepted a job in a *pâtisserie* in Chamonix and refuses to work any longer in her mother's *pension*. Madame Vincent is shocked at this behaviour, but, after all, Yvonne is young and there is not much fun for a young girl in this little place, and I pointed out to Madame Vincent that times have changed. Children go their own way now. Of course, the French family spirit is much stricter in many ways than at home, and that's why Madame Vincent is so put out.'

'You still think of England as home, then?'

'Of course. I don't want to go back, except for a holiday, perhaps, but I always think of it as home. To come to the point, however, Madame Vincent is in a bit of a fix without Yvonne, and with the busiest time of the season coming on. If she could get somebody for a few hours in the morning to clear off breakfast and tidy the rooms, and leave her free to cook and shop, she could manage. She has a woman who comes every Saturday and cleans the place through. Now I mentioned you, and explained that you were an art student. That is right, isn't it?'

'Near enough,' said Fiona, smiling.

'And I told her that you wanted to stay on here a little while and do some painting if you could earn a few francs and your keep. I didn't commit myself at all, but she said she would be very happy to see you if you think you can come to some arrangement with her. She suggested your keep and a small wage in exchange for your help in the mornings. It may not suit you at all, of course, but I thought I'd mention it. Madame Vincent is a nice person. She would treat you properly. But, as I explained, you are a young lady with a very good background who might well refuse to contemplate such work, although students these days have to turn their hands to all sorts of jobs, I believe, in their holidays.'

Fiona had opened her mouth to speak, but Grace Orlais in full spate was difficult to stop, and she went on, with scarcely a breath:

'Of course, you may prefer to see what that young Mr. Dawlish can fix up. I didn't think you'd mind me mentioning it to him, because in his job he meets a lot of people and there's so much more scope in Chamonix than in this little village.'

'Oh, no,' broke in Fiona. 'I don't want to work in Chamonix. I want to stay here. I'll go and see Madame Vincent tomorrow morning, and I'm glad you suggested it.'

Another ten minutes went by while Fiona listened to the history of the Vincent family, and it was only the return of Armand that enabled her to escape.

The next morning, she presented herself at the little *pension* with the pale blue shutters. Madame Vincent led her into a small sitting-room at the back of the chalet, which was similar in design to the other chalets in the village but about twice the size of most of them.

'You will have a glass of wine, or perhaps you prefer coffee?' said Madame Vincent, who spoke good English, the fruits of her convent education.

Fiona accepted the wine, which was already on the table. Her hostess was a woman in her middle forties. Thin, dark skinned, with a prominent nose, she seemed at first a little forbidding, but she unbent rapidly, and a shrewd twinkle came into her black eyes as she said to Fiona, when the formalities had been dispensed with:

'My friend, Grace Orlais, misled me. I was expecting a haughty young English lady who wanted to earn money without soiling her hands. I had no hopes. Now I find a pleasing young girl with no pretensions, and I have hopes. Let us see what we can fix.'

She explained her position to Fiona, took her over the establishment, showed her the little dormer-room which Fiona might have for her bed-sitting-room and outlined the help she needed.

'I have usually about twelve guests. Often they take picnic lunches and are out all day. If you can clear away breakfast and tidy up the rooms in the morning, that will leave me free for everything else, and I can manage. Saturdays you would be free. I think you know how to be useful in a home, *n'est-ce-pas?*'

'Yes. I had to be. My mother died when I was a baby.'

'How sad. But when I saw you I knew that you were not the type that expects to be waited on all her life. It is good. I have no patience with young women who know nothing about running a home until they get married. To my shame, I have to admit that my Yvonne will make a very poor wife, and the good Lord knows that I have done my best with her. However, I must not burden you with the failings of my daughter. I think we will fit in with each other very well. You will have afternoons for your art, I will have an extra pair of hands in the mornings. Now for terms.'

Madame Vincent pitched her terms on the low side, expecting this to be the basis of a little gentle haggling, and was surprised when Fiona accepted her offer without demur.

'All your meals, of course, you will have here, and I am a good cook. And any friends you may care to invite will be welcome,' added Madame Vincent as a sop to her conscience.

Fiona thanked her, arranged to move in and start her duties on the first of July, and took her leave feeling a little scared now that she had burned her boats. But the really difficult part lay ahead: writing to Julian and telling him that she would not be returning with the Deverels. And it wasn't going to be easy explaining to Celia. Until now, she had managed to push the actual fact of her parting from Julian into the background. Now, it stared her in the face with all its harsh reality. For a moment the longing to run back and cancel the arrangements with Madame Vincent, to return to Alanbridge with Laurie and Celia was so strong that she had to stop and lean on the stone parapet of the bridge, gripping the rough surface so that it hurt her, before she could summon up her resolution and go on.

CHAPTER THREE

Two days passed before Fiona could summon up the courage to tell Celia of her decision, and then it was a letter from

Laurie which forced her hand. Celia had seized on it eagerly on their return from a morning stroll and her face lit up as she read it.

'Laurie says he'll arrive here to lunch on the twentieth. And he'll be able to stay ten whole days. Isn't that grand? I hadn't expected more than a week. There'll be time to take him on all our favourite climbs.'

'Splendid. You'll be able to have a second honeymoon, and I shall make myself very scarce.'

'Noodle,' said Celia, smiling, but Fiona knew that she was tremendously pleased and excited at the prospect of her husband's arrival. 'As a matter of fact,' went on Celia, 'this will be our first holiday without the children for a good many years. It'll be good to be with Laurie as a wife and not a mum for a short time. The twentieth is our wedding anniversary—I wonder if he chose it because of that. Sounds a bit too romantic for my husband, but absence makes the heart grow fonder, they say.'

'Of course he chose it specially. It couldn't be coincidence.'

'We might stop at Paris for a night on our way home. I think you ought to see Paris before you leave France, Fiona.'

And this, thought Fiona, was the moment of truth.

'Celia, I've a surprise for you. I've decided to stay on here for a little while. I've accepted a part-time job at a *pension* at the other end of the village, and I'm going to do some more drawings and paintings of this part of the world.'

'What job?' asked Celia, after a moment's silence.

Fiona explained, and Celia looked at her thoughtfully.

'When will you return to Alanbridge, then?'

'I don't know. This job will last for July, August and the beginning of September. I'll decide then.'

'Have you told Julian?'

'Not yet. I'm going to write to him today.'

'It all sounds very plausible, my dear, but you're not telling me everything, are you? Julian and Alanbridge are your world.'

'It's all rather complicated.' Fiona stopped and could not bridge the silence. Then Celia said gently:

'Your life is your own, dear. You don't have to account for it to me or anybody. Only, I feel that Julian sent you abroad for the first time in our care, and I don't think I'm going to like leaving you here on your own, not fully understanding your reasons.'

'I've got to stand on my own feet, Celia. Julian thinks of me still as a child, but I'm not. He has his own life to live. He won't always want to be saddled with me. He'll marry some time. And I've my life to live, and I must start getting used to it without Julian's protection. I've stayed at Alanbridge too long. I should have left when Uncle John died. I owed it to Julian. Only I didn't realise then.... Anyway, that's the real reason, Celia. And I do like this lovely country, so it seems sensible to stay put for a little while here until I can see a bit farther ahead.'

'Julian's not going to like it, you know,' said Celia slowly.

'It will be a bit of a shock at first, but he'll welcome his freedom when he's had time to take it in. I was very much of a habit with Julian. It's always strange and a little bit unpleasant breaking a habit, even if it's to your ultimate advantage. This holiday of mine will have begun the break already.'

'He's very fond of you, Fiona.'

'I know. Who knows better? I owe him more than anybody else in the world. It's because I owe him so much that I can't go on being a responsibility to him. Don't you see, Celia? If it hadn't been for me, I think Julian would have married before this. What position do I hold in his house now that I'm a child no longer? That's what Julian hasn't realised, or if he has, he's been too kind to tell me. I'm not finishing our ... friendship. I couldn't. But I'm not going to choke him with it. That could destroy it—nothing else could.'

'Yes, I see what you mean.'

'I'm glad you understand. I was so afraid you wouldn't. It's a difficult situation to explain.'

'I still think, dear, that it might have been better to have told Julian, talked it over with him before leaving Alanbridge.'

'I couldn't,' said Fiona slowly. 'Not without distressing him. He's so kind. I don't want him to feel guilty. Heaven knows there's no reason why he should. If I write, I can write brightly and he can't see my face. It's the most sensible way. Best for both of us. And then when we've got used to our freedom from each other, we can meet quite happily again. After all, it's much the same as you'll feel when the boys go away to school. And whatever happens, I shall come back after Julian's wedding.'

'You seem to have that very much in mind. Any clue as to the bride?'

'Gillian Courtney.'

'Could be. I've never fully understood that affair. Julian's been as silent as the grave about it.'

'I've an idea I might unwittingly have been the cause of that stalemate. I'm a little difficult to explain away and rather old for a stepchild,' concluded Fiona a little dryly.

'I wonder. Well, I'm very fond of both you and Julian, and I hope you sort yourselves out happily, my dear. There is one snag that comes to my mind regarding the immediate future. Dr. Laurence Deverel. He'll never go back without you unless he personally has Julian's agreement. I can assure you of that.'

'But I'm not a child, Celia. I'm twenty-one. Laurie has no jurisdiction over me.'

'My dear Fiona, I can see you have not yet plumbed the autocratic depths of my esteemed husband. He will hold himself responsible for your safe return to Alanbridge. That was the arrangement with Julian, and he'll carry it out if he has to tie you on with the luggage. So you'd better get Julian to O.K. your defection. If you write today, Julian will have time to see Laurie before he leaves.'

'Righto. I'll do that. I'll get it off this afternoon.'

'Think I'll go into Chamonix after lunch and see if I can find a suitable wedding anniversary present for Laurie. I'd like to buy him the moon and the stars for remembering it and writing such a warm letter. I do believe he's looking forward to doing a little research with his wife for a change.'

Fiona smiled and had her hand on the door when Celia added:

'I suppose young Ben hasn't had any influence on your decision to say here?'

'None. I must wash my hands before lunch. George has been slobbering over them.'

Alone in her room that afternoon, Fiona gazed out of the window at the green meadows and the snow-fields which ruled over them, listened to the sound of the river and the mellow notes of cow-bells from the high pastures, but gained no inspiration to help her fill the blank sheet of paper in front of her. She could not tell Julian the whole truth without hurting him; her love she must keep hidden, and since that was the core of the matter, how could she explain her decision not to return to Alanbridge? There was one simple explanation which would seem natural and which he would accept: Ben. But it would not be the true one, and she could not tell him deliberate lies even if she had to conceal some of the truth. In the end, and it took her nearly two hours, she wrote:

DEAR JULIAN,

You know I told you a couple of days ago that I hadn't done much work here—well, I've decided that I would like to make a collection of water-colours, and have accepted a part-time job in a little hotel here in return for my keep and a small wage, so that I can stay on for the rest of the summer. I might even have an exhibition of my own when I return!

Would you explain to Laurie before he leaves, as Celia thinks his lordship won't agree to leaving me behind unless he has your authority. My twenty-one years go for nothing, it seems.

I can't spare any more time now as I want to catch the post so that you can catch Laurie, but I know you will do the necessary as you don't, thank heaven, share Laurie's managing instincts!

Bless you. I expect Alanbridge is looking its loveliest now. I have my nostalgic moments!

Ever yours,
FIONA.

She had shirked the real issue and had only bought time, but it was all she could do at present. Perhaps by the end of the summer, Julian would be married or would have announced his engagement and that would pave the way.

But Julian's reply ruled out the possibility of this solution.

MY DEAR FIONA,

Of course you can stay on if you want to—I'm glad you like Savoy so much. You'll let me know if the finances are strained, won't you? I'd like to hear more about this job when you write next—wait until you've time to be discursive, as I enjoy your chattering and your enlightening sketches, and was a little flattened by this brief factual appeal, though I appreciate the urgency. Have informed Lord Deverel that you have my permission to stay on for the rest of the summer. I don't think he approves—you're too young. I even feel a few little niggles of uneasiness myself, so keep on writing at length so that I can keep these objectionable managing instincts under control.

I miss you here. Somehow, the garden doesn't seem complete without you. I feel that you're as much part of it as the Italian fountain, but when I expressed similar sentiments to Aunt Lou the other day, she replied rather tartly that it was time I stopped thinking of you as part of the fixtures and fittings. Quite shook me.

By the way, when you have decided on the date for your return, will you let me know, as I shall be coming to the Continent for a tour this summer—Salzburg again—and will arrange the dates so that I can pick you up and bring you home. The train journey across the Continent can be a bore and I know flying doesn't appeal to you. Also, I'd like to see your hide-out. No hurry, but give me a few weeks' notice if you can.

Shall we hire a gallery in Bond Street for you?

JULIAN.

And that, thought Fiona desperately, helped her not one bit. She was still the child in his care. His casual suggestion for fetching her, his bland request for detailed letters, confirmed that only too well. And he was forcing her to come out into the open about not returning to Alanbridge. His letter arrived the day before Laurie was due, and she decided to postpone answering it for a few days.

Celia made no attempt to hide her excitement as the time for her husband's arrival drew near.

'Tomorrow, we'll not plan anything. I expect Laurie will be a bit tired after so much driving, and we'll just stroll up the river a little way in the afternoon and get up to date with family news. Then I thought we might try some gentle climbing for the next few days, weather permitting, and on Monday I've booked Bertrand to do the Chasseur. It's not too difficult, but I think we'll need a guide because Laurie's rusty and he doesn't know that particular peak.'

'As it's your wedding anniversary tomorrow, I think we

ought to get Armand to make a special occasion of the dinner and lay on champagne. I'll have a word with him,' said Fiona.

'Good idea. Would you like Ben to make a foursome at dinner?'

'Not particularly. I think it should be a two-some, really, but I'll make a pretty little speech and fade out with the coffee.'

'You'll do no such thing. We've been married ten years, my dear, not ten days. I hope Laurie will like that tie-pin. I'm beginning to wonder if it's a bit too doggy for his rather austere taste.'

'I like it. A good memento of your holiday together here. When are you going to give it to him?'

'I'll put it on the dinner-table.'

Celia went into Chamonix early the next morning to pay a visit to the hairdresser, and the telegram arrived just after she had gone. Fiona eyed it with misgiving, hoping that it was not from Laurie postponing his arrival; then she reassured herself with the idea that it was a message of congratulation intended for his wife at the start of their anniversary day. She walked to the bus stop to meet Celia with it, and as the light died out of Celia's eager face, she knew that her first misgivings were justified.

'Laurie's held up. He won't be here until Monday,' she said flatly, and handing the wire to Fiona, she walked on ahead without another word. Fiona read it.

'Unavoidably delayed. With you same time Monday. Laurie.'

Fiona wondered what she could say to soften that stark message, but when she caught up with Celia and saw her stony face, she knew that nothing she could say would help.

'I expect there'll be a letter in a day or two,' she ventured.

'I doubt it. This says all there is to be said. I expect some interesting experiment in the labs is not yet concluded,' said Celia bitterly, and that was the last word she expressed on the subject.

But the rest of that week, Fiona was conscious that Celia was banking down a fiery anger with difficulty. Fiona could sympathise with her. There had been no letter from Laurie. No recognition of their anniversary. To plan so eagerly for the holiday that was to bring them together and then to be so baldly disappointed would rouse the anger of far less fiery temperaments than Celia's. Fiona had the impression that this was the last straw after the past unsatisfactory year of their marriage, and she felt worried and afraid of the effect of Celia's anger on a dangerous situation.

Feeding George on Sunday morning and faced with the knowledge that she could not long postpone her next letter to Julian, Fiona felt overwhelmed by the complexities of personal relationships. Men, she thought, could be very difficult. Even her own dear Julian, the kindest and best of men, demanded the inmost secrets of her heart to be made known to him while keeping his own heart securely shuttered. Not a word about Gillian, who was obviously in behind those shutters. She would just have to knock at them, and risk being rebuffed. He probably didn't think she was old enough to have the right to knock, she thought unhappily. That was the root of the whole trouble: the different planes of approach. If only Julian would realise that she was an adult, as he was, he would see that her presence at Alanbridge had become untenable. Would, perhaps, have told her about Gillian. Would certainly concede her right to make her own decisions without his supervision, for he was not a domineering or possessive man and valued and respected the freedom of the individual. But he could never see her as other than the motherless child who had been the victim of a harsh father; the child who, for family reasons as well as his own affection for her, was in his care now.

She looked up as Celia joined her.

'Ben's here. Says you're going up the river to paint this morning and he's going to be porter.'

'I told him I was going to work. There was no suggestion of needing his help.'

'Well, you've got it, my dear.'

'Come along with us, Celia.'

'Sorry, but I must write a letter to Aunt Bea and to the boys. The last one before I see them.'

'Will you be going back next Friday, or do you think Laurie might have wangled a few more days as he's been delayed in starting his holiday?'

'He'll keep to the original date for returning, I'm sure. There's some conference or other he wants to attend early in the following week,' said Celia briskly.

'We'd better suggest a cold lunch tomorrow, I suppose, in case he's a bit late.'

'Might as well. I shan't be in. I'm doing the Chasseur climb with Bertrand.'

Fiona's eyes opened wide.

'You won't be here to meet him?'

'No. Tomorrow is the only day Bertrand has free, and I do want to get that climb in before I go home. You can tell Laurie I'll be back about half-past six,' concluded Celia in a matter-of-fact tone.

Fiona whistled a little tune as she stroked George's nose. Storm clouds were certainly rolling up thick and fast, and she wished now that she had accepted Celia's original invitation to join the Chasseur climbing expedition. Even chipping her way up an ice-fall would be more comfortable than lunching alone with Laurie the next day. However, the expression on Celia's face made any expostulation impossible, and she walked off to write her letters leaving Fiona still whistling softly to herself. For a moment she couldn't think what it was she was whistling, then realised that it was the opening movement of Beethoven's fifth symphony. Heaven grant you wisdom in your handling of this situation, Dr. Deverel, she thought as she walked slowly back to the chalet and the waiting Ben.

It was difficult to be angry with his cheerful face, and Fiona merely said:

'You know I'm going to work. You'll be awfully bored, Ben.'

'Not I. Often wondered how paintings get done. Now I'll see. Don't tell me you have to take all that,' he added, looking at the array on the hall table.

'It all packs up quite neatly. The brushes, bottle of water and jam jar go in the haversack.'

'What's in that tobacco tin? Or do you smoke a pipe while you're working?'

'Tubes of paint. This portfolio holds the board and paper. That just leaves the easel.'

'A good thing you've got me for a donkey. Do you usually manage all that outfit yourself?'

'Of course. The haversack goes on my back, and then I've two hands for the easel and portfolio. I don't usually travel far, you know.'

'Should think not. Here, I'll take the haversack and the easel. You take the rest of the outfit.'

Fiona's destination was a bend of the river where a rough bridge of boulders and an overhanging tree had caught her eye a few days earlier. The granite boulders at the edge of the water seemed to be growing from a bed of ferns and she had wanted to capture the contrast of the delicate scrolled fronds against the granite, and the play of sunshine and shadow on the water rushing by.

'Don't see why we had to carry that bottle of water with all this around us,' observed Ben, watching Fiona set up her easel.

'I thought the river might be a bit gritty.'

'What are you wetting the paper for?'

'So that it dries taut when I've fastened it to the board.'

While Fiona drew her subject lightly in with a soft pencil, Ben inspected the tubes of paint in the tin.

'What odd names. Rose Madder, Cadmium Yellow, Burnt Umber. When I was a kid, I remember my paint-box containing something called Crimson Lake. I used to wonder why a lake should be described as crimson and thought that maybe somewhere there was such a lake, and wished I could see it, all gory and lurid.'

Ben exhibited all the candid curiosity of a child that morning, and it became more of a lesson in water-colour painting than anything else, for even Fiona's absorption in her work was not proof against his lively tongue and inquisitive fingers. He insisted on squeezing out the colours on the palette, changed the water for her at most inopportune moments and stood behind her watching every movement with unflagging interest.

'Water's a tricky thing to control,' he observed at one stage, as Fiona quickly wiped out her last wash of paint with a soft rag. 'Think I'd prefer oils—they'd stick better. What are we waiting for?'

'That wash has to dry before I can put another one over it to deepen the colour. The river's not right. It looks too opaque.'

'The ferns are lovely.'

Fiona surveyed her work with a critical eye. It wasn't good. She couldn't concentrate with Ben chattering away.

'Think I'll leave it, Ben. I'm not seeing it very well, somehow.'

'Can I have a go?'

The morning ended with Ben wielding brushes with glorious abandon across a clean piece of cartridge paper, and achieving on that sunny day a remarkably sultry representation of boulders and grass which might have served for the blasted heath of Macbeth's witches.

'You know, this is getting me. Think I must take it up. Do I show any signs of talent?'

'As a matter of fact, it's not bad. You've plenty of boldness in your approach, anyway, and that's half the battle. I'm not good at broad effects. I'm better at a filigree style of drawing—it's fine detail and line that fascinates me. But the colour here is so beautiful that I feel I must try some landscape paintings, and I thought this small composition would be a start.'

'Wouldn't oils be better for the vivid colouring of this country?'

'Yes. Technique's more difficult, though, and I'm not that good.'

'Much money in this line?'

'No. Only for a very few of the most gifted.'

'Pity. Rather a nice life, coasting round painting places.'

'There's a good deal of hard work and concentration as well, you know. But it's great fun, and you can forget the rest of the world completely. I'll wipe those brushes before they go away. Have to take care of them—they're expensive.'

'Well, what do I get for my assistance?'

'You've had a free lesson, and that's more than you deserve. Might just as well try to work with a kitten swarming over you.'

'If you're suggesting that I'm kittenish, I regard that as a deadly insult to my masculinity and shall avenge myself.'

Fiona retreated before him, eyeing the jam jar of dirty water in his hand with some apprehension.

'No horse play, Ben. Be a dear and help me pack up.'

He turned aside as though complying, then caught her arm as she came within reach.

'I shall pour this down your neck unless you apologise and kiss me as a reward for my morning's help.'

Fiona's belief that this was an idle threat was unhappily

disproved, for at her refusal, Ben, without a moment's hesitation, tilted the rim of the jam jar inside the neck of her blouse and poured the contents down. Fiona sprang away from him with a high-pitched yelp as the cold water hit her middle regions and ran down her legs.

'Ben Dawlish, you horrible wretch! Fancy playing a schoolboy trick like that. Now I'm soaked.'

He grinned as he said:

'Want me to dry you?'

'No. And I don't think it's at all funny. Just adolescent and silly.'

He caught her to him, still smiling. Then kissed her.

'We could have fun, you know,' he murmured into her hair.

Why, thought Fiona, letting her face rest against his rough tweed jacket for a few moments, why are things so contrary? It's like a jig-saw puzzle that won't go together. Why can't Julian and Ben and Laurie go where they're needed? Why must they be so perverse? She gave Ben's ear a gentle pull to show that she bore no ill will before she drew away.

'I know, Ben, dear, but I'm not free. Let's get packed up. I'm going to be late for lunch.'

'Come down to Chamonix and have tea with me this afternoon.'

'No, Ben. It's no use,' said Fiona firmly, as she mopped her legs with a clean rag.

'I know where you can get a really good pot of tea, believe it or not, and the most delectable *pâtisseries*. And we can remain in the public eye all the time and I promise to be very good.'

'But you'll begin to think I'm changing my mind if I agree, and I'm not, Ben. Really and truly—I'm not free.'

'I'll accept that—for the moment. I just hate Sunday afternoon on my own. We'll go up on the *téléphérique* after tea and sun ourselves on the terrace at Planpraz and gaze across at Mont Blanc and be frightfully adult and sensible. You've no idea how old and sensible I can be if I really try. I'll be as courteous and platonic as though you were my Aunt Agnes, only please don't condemn me to a solitary Sunday afternoon.'

'All right,' said Fiona, thinking that Ben would, at least, distract her mind from the storms which threatened.

CHAPTER FOUR

THE sun streamed into Fiona's bedroom the next morning, lighting up the drawing of the garden at Alanbridge which stood on the chest of drawers. It was a good drawing, one of her best, but she had never been able to capture the enchantment of that garden, although one could hardly expect to be able to draw enchantment. She lay there looking at it: the steps, the beautiful curved stone urns with their trailing plants which stood at each corner of the shallow flight, the gnarled and sinuous coils of the wistaria climbing round the stone pillars of the pergola, the pattern of the light and shade receding down the walk. How cool it was, walking down it on a hot day; how fiercely and splendidly the sun fell on you when you emerged.

When she had studied music at school, she had learned a piece called 'The Enchanted Garden'. She had never been able to play it really well, but somehow the music held for her the grace of the Alanbridge garden, and when she listened to Julian playing it for her, she was there, in the garden, and the moonlight was glittering in the gentle spray of the Italian fountain. Her father had once overheard her describing a part of the garden to Mrs. Marchant and had scoffed at her romanticising, sentimental outlook. But she had worked in that garden, knew all about weeds, insect pests, blights and killing frosts. It wasn't just a pretty picture on a card, it was a working reality. But for her a grace of spirit walked in that garden which she never experienced elsewhere. Perhaps it was because she had found her first real happiness there, perhaps because the garden and Julian were inextricably mixed in her childhood days so that it had come to represent all the beauty he had opened her eyes to, all the affection he had shown her. It epitomised a way of life which contrasted so strongly with her father's desert of materialism that she could not but think it a place of spiritual grace and enchantment.

And now she felt overwhelmed by a longing to return to it and to Julian. Why not go back and wait until Julian's marriage forced her out? I think it's a pretty poor way of repaying his kindness. That was what Norah had said. And she not only wanted Julian and Alanbridge, she wanted his love. And she would only hamper his own chance of a full and happy family life and destroy the real friendship that existed between them if she went back hungering for what he could not give her. She had been over it time and time again, and knew her decision was the right one. Somehow, she must find the resolution to stick to it.

She turned restlessly, and endeavoured to fix her mind on the immediate future. She had half hoped that the weather might have prevented Celia from embarking on this climb, but the day looked exceptionally promising and she could hear Celia already about in her room on the floor above her. The day, she felt, was going to be a long one. She would, perhaps, try to draw George's head that morning, hoping that his kind, forbearing expression would help to soothe her uneasiness.

Whatever Celia might be feeling, it was not uneasiness, decided Fiona as they breakfasted. Resolute, full of enthusiasm for the climb, it might have been an ordinary day of the holiday. Perhaps an extra restlessness hinted at pent up feelings, but it would be difficult to gather that anything but the climb was in her mind. Her husband was not mentioned until Bertrand arrived and they were just leaving. Then Celia smiled at Fiona and said:

'*Au revoir*, dear. I hope Laurie doesn't hold up your lunch today. I shouldn't wait if I were you.'

And that odd little smile seemed to Fiona like the harmless-looking little plume of smoke from a volcano. Hell hath no fury like a woman scorned, she thought, and wished that Laurie was a more tolerant man. She was beginning to feel like a small canoe between the fire of two battleships.

Laurie drove up with a loud hooting of his horn a few minutes before one o'clock. On Fiona, hovering in the dining-room of the chalet, that cheerful fanfare had a similar effect to the dentist's cheerful welcome. She put on a smile as she went out to the car.

Laurie slammed the door and turned to her triumphantly.

'Bang on time, and I had a hundred and twenty miles to do this morning. Not bad going. And how are you, Fiona? Looking fine, anyway.'

'It's good to see you, Laurie. Yes, we're both as fit as fiddles. You won't know Celia. She doesn't look the same person as the one you brought here.'

Laurie took his case out of the boot and followed Fiona into the hall.

'And where is this wife I shan't know? Hi there,' he called blithely up the stairs.

Fiona took a deep breath.

'Celia's out climbing. She'd booked a guide for today to do the Chasseur climb with you, and felt she couldn't call it off because it was the only day Bertrand was free this week.'

For a split second before the polite mask was clamped on, Fiona saw incredulity give way to anger in that dark face, then it blanked out and he said calmly:

'She's been well and truly bitten by this climbing bug, hasn't she?'

'Yes. I'll pour you a sherry, Laurie. I expect you can do with a drink and lunch.'

'Thanks, my dear. I'll just go upstairs and clean up. Ah, *bon jour*, Madame Orlais,' added Laurie with a smile as Grace emerged from the kitchen with Armand at her heels.

Fiona left them exchanging greetings and went into the dining-room, thankful that the worst moment was over. She could now rely on Laurie to behave like the perfect English gentleman and ignore the matter of his wife's absence. Nothing, she knew, would induce him to discuss his wife with her or anybody else. They would both behave as though it was the most natural thing in the world for his wife not to be there to welcome him after two months' separation.

And they did. Laurie answered Fiona's polite enquiries about the boys, and gave her all the news of Julian which he had. Fiona told him of their life in this village and her plans for the future. Then they embarked on a discussion of climbing, about which Laurie knew far more than she did. After lunch they went for a walk along the river valley, with the Chasseur's rounded white dome standing out among the peaks that enclosed the valley and mocking them all the way. Fiona felt as though they were acting in some crazy kind of farce and she was running out of her words. It was a very long afternoon and she was reminded of social functions which she had attended with her father and over which had hung the same glazed, drawn-out atmosphere.

She spent as long as she could over changing for dinner

that evening to give Laurie and Celia the chance of being alone when they met, but this scheme was foiled by Celia's late arrival, for at seven o'clock she had still not arrived and when Fiona went down to the dining-room she found Laurie staring moodily out of the window. He turned as she came in.

'What time did Celia say she'd be back?'

'She said half-past six, Laurie, but of course anything can happen to set you back on a climb, and she was determined to get to the summit today.'

'Well, let's have a drink while we're waiting.'

It was Fiona, standing by the window, who saw Celia first.

'Here she comes. Heavens, she looks tired!'

Laurie stayed where he was, glass in hand, and Celia came in a moment later, looking extraordinarily neat and trim in her grey skirt and matching wind-cheater, inside which she had tucked a green scarf. Fiona guessed that she had stopped to repair the ravages of the day's climb before she met Laurie's eye, and the tiredness which Fiona had noticed as Celia walked along the road had been shaken off for Laurie's benefit, for she was very erect as she moved easily across the room to him and said with a calm smile:

'Hullo, Laurie. Have a good journey?'

'Very, thanks.'

He stooped and kissed the cheek she offered, then said steadily:

'No need to ask you how you are. Obviously a hundred per cent fit. Did you bag your peak?'

'Yes. My best achievement to date. Sorry you weren't able to get here to do it, Laurie. Too bad.'

'Yes, indeed. But it couldn't be helped.'

'Of course not. Well, if you'll excuse me, I'll hop into a bath presto, or I'll be keeping you waiting for dinner. All's well at home, I gather, Laurie?'

'Very well. The boys sent their love. So did Aunt Bea.'

'I'll hear all the news later. So long.'

As the door closed behind her, Laurie held his glass up to the light and appeared to be lost in contemplation of its amber depths. Fiona could feel her scalp prickling with the electricity in the atmosphere.

She had to admire both the Deverels that evening, for neither of them deviated from the line of calm politeness which Celia had started, but which Fiona found more devastating than if they had thrown the china at each other. Celia had never looked so nearly beautiful. She wore an olive green dress, beautifully cut and moulded to her slender figure, with the narrow gold belt matched to an intricate chain necklace and small drop ear-rings. Perhaps it was the effect of pride and anger inside her which made her grey eyes sparkle so brightly, which emphasised the widely sprung nostrils and challenging curve of lip, and gave her the spirited air of a thoroughbred on its toes. Laurie's face was as though carved in stone, quite impenetrable, but what an uncompromising jaw, thought Fiona, who could see the ship of this marriage running straight on to the rocks but could do nothing about it.

As soon as she had finished coffee, she excused herself on the plea of having letters to write, for she felt that the sooner Celia and Laurie came out with it, the better.

There was silence for a few moments after Fiona left, then Laurie, trying in vain to catch his wife's elusive eyes, said quietly:

'I'm really sorry I had to postpone my arrival, but something important cropped up, my dear.'

'It's quite all right, Laurie. I'm used to that sort of thing by now. I know the Research Station has to come first. Aunt Bea's been taking my place quite satisfactorily, I gather.'

'I wouldn't put it quite like that. It's worked very well, though, and she's excellent with the boys.'

'Yes, she always has been. She knows the Deverel blood and how to tackle it. It'll be lovely to see the imps again. I suppose we're returning on Friday, as originally planned?'

'I haven't decided,' said Laurie deliberately, and was rewarded by seeing his wife pinch her lips together, a habit she had when her control was threatened.

'I see. Perhaps you'll let me know when you have, as I think Aunt Bea should be given as much notice as possible.'

'I told her we should be back on Saturday week.'

Celia's head jerked up at that.

'A whole fortnight's holiday? You haven't taken that much time off from the Station for years.'

'I know. Thought I was due for a break.'

'Then why do you say you haven't decided?'

'I think it's up to you.'

Always, thought Celia furiously, always, he drives me into a corner.

'What do you mean, Laurie?'

'You know damned well what I mean, but you're in such a flaming temper that I doubt whether it will be fruitful to discuss it now. I think good manners, if nothing else, might have induced you to be here when I arrived after three days' travelling to end a separation of two months.'

'You want it all ways, don't you, Laurie? You show in the clearest possible way that you're not interested in me as a person any more, and have done so for the past year or two at least, but you want me playing the loving wife for the benefit of onlookers. It was your pride that was damaged because I wasn't here waving flags for your arrival. What will the Orlais couple think, what will Fiona think?'

'I don't care a damn what they think. You should have been here.'

'For years, Laurie, I have been regarded as your housekeeper and the mother of your children. No more. Your work, the Research Station, are far more important to you than I am, and even during the small amount of leisure you have, you still don't bother to throw off your preoccupation with your work. In the evenings over dinner, you scarcely hear the few remarks I make. In the mornings, you are buried behind *The Times*. You are no more aware of me or interested in me than in an armchair. Very well. I accept that. Marriage can do that to people. Familiarity can kill love, make it into a stale habit. I will accept the roles you have given me—your housekeeper, and the mother of your children. Neither of those roles called for my presence when you arrived here today. Only your arrogance would demand the act of loving wife from somebody who has been treated as an armchair for years.'

'I can't help the claims of my work, Celia. As head of the Research Station, I carry a responsible position, and I wouldn't have it otherwise. Would you?'

'No. But you forget, my father was also head of that same Research Station before you. That didn't de-humanise him. He always had room in his life for me. He talked to me, was interested in me, and he even discussed the affairs of the Station with me. You never talk to me of your work or the running of the Station. Yet I worked there, too, you may remember. I could talk quite intelligently about it, I dare say, but you can't be bothered.'

'I've always treated you with consideration,' said Laurie, shifting his ground, and now his eyes, too, were angry.

'Yes. You treat an armchair with consideration, too. It's useful, it's perhaps decorative, it costs money. You wouldn't kick it around or jump on the springs. I expected and wanted more, that's all. But I've given that up now. I've had time to think during these past weeks, and I'm ready to submit to your idea of a wife's role. I've the boys to think of, and I want a happy home for them. I must just find new interests to fill in the vacuum in my personal life. But don't ask me to act a part in public which you don't give me in private, Laurie. And don't touch me. I'm not in the mood,' she added fiercely as he came across to her and grasped her shoulders.

'Well, since you've thought everything out, including this warm welcome, perhaps you'll tell me where you've decided I shall sleep tonight.'

She looked up at his handsome, flinty face. To love a man and not be loved; to be mastered by his arrogance, as she had so often been in the past; to be insulted by the worst of all insults—indifference: it was humiliation piled on humiliation, and her pride spurred her to hurt him where she could.

'The bed is made up in the little room you used as a dressing-room when you were here. I'm tired tonight after that climb and I'm going to bed now. Perhaps you won't mind using the dressing-room, and then you won't disturb me when you come up.'

'Certainly,' said Laurie, and his face was as grim as his voice.

'Good-night,' said Celia firmly.

'Good-night.'

*   *   *

Fiona spent longer than usual with George the next morning. Breakfast had been as painfully polite as the previous night's dinner, and she was trying to think of a way to break this deadlock between Laurie and Celia. It was evident that whatever had passed between them on the previous evening had not improved the situation. She dared not openly interfere in the private affairs of these two people, so much older and more experienced than she. It would seem an impertinence and Laurie, for one, would not hesitate to tell her so. And yet she longed to help them come to some understanding of each other. They were both such strong-willed people, she thought, sighing as she fondled George's willing head. If only she could make them forget their pride and anger, they could talk things over sensibly together. This way, they stood about as much chance as a matador and a bull of getting together. Then an idea came to her which she thought might prove helpful.

She found Laurie sitting at the table on the little terrace in front of the chalet. He had a map in front of him, but he was holding his head between his hands in a brooding attitude and Fiona doubted whether he saw anything of the map. He gave her a smile as she came up.

'Hullo, Fiona. Afraid you've got to keep me company again this morning. Celia's gone into Chamonix to do some shopping.'

'Oh. Well, are you planning anything ambitious? Because I warn you, I'm no climber. I'm a stroller.'

'As a matter of fact, I feel darned lazy this morning, and quite happy to study the possibilities of being energetic on the map.'

'Then I'll sit with you and be lazy, too. You and Celia used to do a lot of climbing, she told me.'

'M'm. A long time ago.'

'She's looking forward to climbing with you again this holiday. Been talking about it for weeks.'

'Has she?'

'Yes. She was terribly disappointed when you had to postpone your arrival. She'd planned a few days' easy walking to prime you a little before she showed you her paces up the Chasseur. But I guess you'll be able to hold your own with her.'

'I haven't done any climbing for years. Probably find I'm short of wind. Had some grand climbing days when I was younger, though.'

'By the way, did you like the tie-pin Celia bought you?'

Laurie looked blank.

'What tie-pin?'

'Your wedding anniversary present. Hasn't she given it to you?'

'We didn't get round to it. Do you know, Fiona, I completely forgot our wedding anniversary. Oh, Lord! Damn!'

'We quite thought that was why you'd fixed that particular day to arrive,' said Fiona guilelessly. 'I guess Celia's keeping the tie-pin back for another occasion so that you won't be embarrassed at having forgotten it.'

'I've never forgotten it before, but things have been boiling at the Station this past week or two and I was just concentrating on clearing a space to get away.'

'Oh, well, these things happen. I suppose women set more store by anniversaries than men. I know I always have to remind Julian about birthdays—he forgot Aunt Lou's last year, and he never remembers his own. You've a lot more to distract your minds from personal things than we have, I guess.'

'Yes,' said Laurie thoughtfully.

'Well, don't say anything about the tie-pin, then. It'll probably be presented for your birthday or for Christmas. It's a very nice one—coils of rope twined round an ice-axe. Lovely delicate work. Mind you register surprise.'

'I will.' Laurie was looking at her, his chin propped in his hand, and Fiona felt the colour rise to her cheeks.

'This is the route they took up the Chasseur,' she said hastily, tracing it on the map with her finger.

Laurie's hand came down over hers, and when she looked up at him, a little startled, she found an odd little smile on his lips and a twinkle in his eyes.

'You're a nice girl, Fiona, and the delicacy of your touch is appreciated, I assure you. I must try to emulate it. There's no need to blush as though I've made an immodest proposal.'

Fiona laughed, melted, as often before, by the sudden revelation of a warmth in Laurie which his autocratic manner was apt to veil. Other people might be blessed with a consistent and abundant warmth of nature and it would be taken for granted, but at the sight of one streak of it in a harder nature, one found oneself completely disarmed and almost ready to fawn. It was like feeling honoured by the rare manifestations of affection from a cat while the eternal and slavish devotion of a dog was taken for granted, thought Fiona. No wonder Celia found this man a difficult proposition.

'I'm saying no more. You're too clever by half, Dr. Deverel.'

'And what, I wonder, are you up to, staying on here instead of coming home with us? Julian's a little bit foxed by it, I fancy.'

'I'm not ready to come home yet. I've work to do. This is a lovely place, Laurie. I'm very grateful to you and Celia for bringing me here.'

'Well, if I were Julian,' went on Laurie, in no way deflected by her red herring, 'I wouldn't have it. You're too young to be left here on your own, so many miles away from your own country and your friends.'

'Yes, Laurie,' said Fiona meekly, her eyes twinkling. 'I knew you'd forbid it. Celia told me you would.'

'The devil she did. Well, a firm hand is needed with you women sometimes, you know. However, Julian has agreed, so there's nothing I can do except vet this job you're taking on. I promised Julian I'd do that.'

'You can't make Julian into a tyrant, Laurie. He's not made that way. He has other methods.'

'They seem to work well, I must admit. Whatever he says, goes with you. I can't say the same of my female belongings.'

'Force always provokes force.'

'I'm not going to accept your slander of tyrant, my girl. You are a very different proposition from my stormy petrel, and if I didn't take a firm line, I'd be a hen-pecked husband before you could say knife, and a more contemptible object than that, I don't know.'

Fiona smiled but was not taken in by this plausible excuse. He would take the same line with any woman, placid or stormy. The fact that he had married a girl of spirit only added a clearer definition to the line. She liked and respected Laurie, but she could never imagine herself loving or marrying a man of his nature. Perhaps she had been too sickened by the conflict with her father to see any happiness in a clash of wills. The deep sense of harmony which she knew with Julian had seemed like a benediction in her life and she had no liking for battles, and saw no glory in them. Celia and Laurie could perhaps achieve their own kind of happiness in a balance of opposing forces, but it was not and never would be Fiona's kind.

'What are you going to do this afternoon?' she asked.

'I think I shall take my wife climbing. What's your programme?'

'I have a date in Chamonix.'

'Would that be with a young man by the name of Ben? Celia mentioned him in one of her letters.'

'Yes.'

'Rather a nice chap, I gather.'

'M'm. He's joined us on some of our expeditions. A cheerful laddie. Works in a tourist office in Chamonix.'

'Well, bring him along to dinner one evening. I'd like to meet him.'

Fiona turned her attention to the map to hide the little smile that pulled at the corners of her mouth. Laurie evidently wanted to vet the young man as well as the job. Now she thought, he begins to see the light. That is why I'm staying on—a young man. It was typical of his whole outlook that a man would constitute a far more valid reason for her decision to stay on than any other. And, she thought ruefully, in a way he was right, but the man wasn't Ben. However, she would leave Laurie to deduce what he would.

When Celia arrived from the bus, she was surprised to see her husband laughing and chatting to Fiona, evidently in the best of spirits. But then, she thought, why should she be surprised? She had hurt his vanity, no more. And that was quickly forgotten. The lack of her company had not troubled him for months, so why should it trouble him now?

Under her husband's urbane countenance, Celia tried to eat a hearty lunch, but she was not hungry and even the most gallant efforts could not clear her plate. She concealed as much as possible of what she had left by a careful arrangement of her knife and fork. Laurie was evidently enjoying his lunch. I wish it would choke him, she thought, for by now a childish anger covered the deep pool of her unhappiness like a green scum. Busily engaged in cutting off her nose to spite her face, she had deprived herself of his company that morning and had not stopped thinking about him every minute of it. She had real cause for unhappiness, but she knew that the present mood of spite and anger that resulted from her hurts was petty and ridiculous in a woman of her years, and dangerous, but she could not control it. Like a hoop bowling merrily downhill, it took her with it willy nilly.

'I thought, my dear, I'd like you to show me the walk up to the Col du Midi. It looks a pretty easy proposition and there should be a grand view from there of the other side of this range. What about it?'

'How do you feel, Fiona?' asked Celia.

'Count me out. I'm working this afternoon, and at five o'clock I'm meeting Ben in Chamonix. We're going for a swim at the Plage.'

Celia eyed her husband suspiciously. She felt he was up to something.

'We'd better take a flask of tea,' said Laurie. 'I should say from the map that it's a good two hours' trek.'

'Bertrand and I did it in an hour and a half, but it may take you longer.'

'I'll do my best,' said Laurie, with a gleam in his eye.

Fiona watched them go, reassured by Laurie's superb confidence. He obviously felt that he had the whole thing buttoned up now, and although Fiona knew that this was no trivial squabble, his confidence had somehow reassured her, for Laurie was intelligent as well as autocratic, and he understood his wife's temperament. Presenting two erect backs to Fiona, they swung off down the road. Celia had discarded her climbing boots for this unambitious excursion and wore brogues. She was setting a smart pace, and every line of that slender back seemed to spell defiance. She carried her windcheater over her shoulder, and wore a green and grey checked shirt with her grey skirt. Laurie's back was enlivened, too, by a checked tweed sports jacket over his flannels, and he carried the haversack on his shoulder. He stopped to light his pipe, but Celia went on and he had to lengthen his stride to catch her up. They disappeared up the track which wound through the woods, and Fiona turned back into the chalet, feeling lonely. Quarrelling or not, they had each other. Julian was hundreds of miles away....

Celia shot a glance at her husband as they approached the end of the tree-line. He showed no signs of distress, although she had set a fast pace and the path had wound uphill at a pretty steep gradient for most of the way. A hot stony track faced them when they emerged from the woods. They had said little so far, and that little had been confined to remarks about the views, Laurie using the map to sort out the peaks that became visible from time to time as the path twisted round the flanks of their mountain.

'Want a breather?' asked Celia.

'No, I'm all right, if you are.'

The track became the dried-up bed of a tributary which in the spring, when the snows melted, added its own quota of water to the river which rushed down to the right of them, but which was now as uncomfortable a path as one could find. They came out to a small plateau strewn with huge boulders. Here the grass was a deep green and gave a lovely impression of coolness. A giant cascade thundered down a rock face opposite them on the other side of the river gorge and sent spray dancing across, reflecting rainbow colours where the sun played on it. Even Celia could not find it in her angry heart to push on from this delightful oasis without pause.

'What about tea here?' she asked briskly.

'Good idea. There's a rock over there which throws quite a decent patch of shade.'

They sat down with their backs against the rock and Celia busied herself with the haversack. They drank their tea in silence. Celia could feel her skin tauten with nerves.

'That was good,' said Laurie eventually. 'I usually loathe Thermos flask tea, but that was pure nectar.'

'How cool the waterfall looks.'

'And is. I can feel cool air drifting over with the spray. I bet the water's icy. Remember when you thought you'd like to paddle in one of these mountain streams?'

'I do. You didn't warn me, and I nearly got frostbitten.'

'Not the only unpleasant shock I've given you, I'm afraid.'

She was silent, plucking at a piece of grass until his hand covered hers.

'Are you still angry, or can we talk?'

'I'm not angry. I'm unhappy.'

'I know. And it's largely my fault. But we can't hope to put things right while you're still wanting to murder me. I wondered whether it was safe to go climbing with you, because I felt I ran a grave risk of being pushed over a precipice if the opportunity presented itself. That's why I chose this safe route.'

Celia looked at him gravely.

'Love and hate run closer together than you might think, Laurie.'

'True enough. But what you said about me yesterday isn't true, you know.'

'How should I know? There's not a shred of evidence to the contrary.'

'I admit I've been taking an awful lot for granted. You're not the only one who's been doing some thinking these past two months. But however immersed I seem in work, basically you're the centre of my life. Perhaps it's because I've become so sure of that centre that I'm able to give myself up so wholeheartedly to my work. If I felt something was wrong, that our feeling of belonging was weakening, I'd be too worried to be immersed in work.'

'Haven't you realised how unhappy I've been during these past two years of neglect? Yes, neglect, Laurie,' she added, stilling his protest. 'Neglect of me as a person. You've made every provision for my material well-being, but as far as my mind and heart are concerned, you've shown complete indifference, and that wasn't what I wanted from marriage. I didn't want a husband who did things for me, but with me. I know lots of wives would be content with the material comforts. Perhaps I must learn to be. But I wanted so much more than that. Not just a bread ticket. I wouldn't care how poor we were, what material struggles we faced, as long as we were working together. I wanted a close and real companionship with my husband. You said yesterday that you had always treated me with consideration. So you have. As you would treat a good housekeeper. But the real me, the person, you haven't allowed inside the door of your life for a long time.'

He was silent for a few moments, then said quietly:

'Why didn't you say all this before? Why have you let it go on?'

'Why? Love isn't a thing you can ask for. It's either there, alive, or it's dead.'

'You could have asked me if it was there.'

'Perhaps it was pride, perhaps it was a dread of having to face the truth. Then, when your letters seemed more interested and we had this holiday coming, I thought that climbing here together as we used to do, being alone and away from our responsibilities, might bring us together again. I was counting on it so much. And then you . . .'

She stopped, fighting the tears that threatened to overwhelm her.

'I had to spoil everything. I forgot our anniversary and put off coming.'

'And it's happened so often. The claims of the Station override everything. Time and again I'm fobbed off because of them. It wouldn't have been quite so bad if you'd written, but there was only the curt telegram.'

'I'm truly sorry about forgetting our wedding day, my dear. And I should have written to you. But I was up to my eyes trying to clear a space for this holiday at all. And I've been looking forward to it as much as you have. I've missed you terribly these past weeks, even if you find that hard to believe. But I have. And I've realised how incomplete and barren my life would be without you. I've let work obsess me too much. I admit it. And what will it all add up to in the end?'

'If only when you leave the Station, you would come to me, I wouldn't mind. But you don't. You bring it with you. I don't seem to count any more. And the boys can't make up for you, Laurie. But I seem to have lost you.'

'Well, you'll have to find me again, my dear, because I don't intend to be lost. Not having you around for the past two months has taught me a lot. I'm sorry I've been taking so much for granted. Will you give me another chance? Because I love you now as I did when I married you, even if I've let the dust accumulate a bit. What about it?'

Celia nodded blindly, and Laurie put his arm round her.

'All the same, you should have been there to meet me.'

'You didn't deserve it.'

'Perhaps not, but it was Hamlet, wasn't it, who said that if we all got our deserts, who would escape hanging?'

'Yes. I've not been in a nice mood at all. I'm sorry about that. But when I'm hurt, I turn nasty. I can't help it.'

'Well, it's natural enough. Are you interested in getting up that pass this afternoon?'

'Not particularly.'

'Nor am I,' said Laurie, drawing her down beside him. 'I tell you what. We'll make a bargain. We'll come away alone together at least once every year for a few weeks just in case we've managed to mislay each other because of family or scientific preoccupations. We can always park the kids with Aunt Bea, and they'll be going off to boarding school soon, anyway. Good idea?'

'First class. Will you make that a promise?'

'A solemn promise. How young and well you look. That should be a salutary lesson to me. Away from me, and you drop ten years.'

'I don't want to add to your vanity, but it was the prospect of what our dear Fiona calls a second honeymoon that wiped out a few years. You know, it's ages since we had a holiday alone together. Not since Peter was born.'

'A bad mistake.'

'Yes. Have they really been good, Laurie?'

'The boys? Yes. Abnormally so. A slight lapse last week when I had to wallop them both.'

'Oh, no, Laurie! Why?'

'They got in the milkman's cart and drove it half round Marchwood, abandoned it by the War Memorial and vamoosed before the milkman could catch them.'

'Good heavens! They might have been killed.'

'Not with that old nag, dear. I might have let them off lightly if Peter hadn't had the bright idea of foxing me. Aunt Bea had been answering interminable questions about our system of trying criminals, and one of the principles which she had underlined was that of allowing ten guilty persons to escape punishment rather than to convict an innocent person. So when this particular crime was brought to court, Peter blithely informed me that the milkman often allowed them to sit in the cart and only one of them was to blame for driving it off, but they weren't going to tell me which one, and then I couldn't pass any sentence. I wonder if that boy will go in for the legal profession.'

'Well, I suppose it was rational enough,' said Celia, laughing.

'Imagine what a racket they could develop on those lines. I gave them five minutes in which to make justice possible. They stuck it out, though, so I'm afraid injustice ruled the day. I bet they were both in it up to the neck, anyway, although the milkman only saw the back of the cart and didn't know which of them had the reins.'

Laurie pulled out the map and opened it up.

'Let's plan our climbing days. You are the expert, madam.'

'This humility won't last long, so I'll make the most of it. I'd like to try this Aiguille before we go back, but I think we'd better do something a bit easier first.'

They pored over the map until the sun left their retreat and reminded them of the time.

'Heavens, we'll have to move fast, or we'll be late for dinner,' said Celia.

Laurie stood up and gave her a hand, pulling her to her feet. When she was beside him, he cupped her face between his hands and said gently:

'Am I truly forgiven?'

'Yes.'

As he kissed her and her arms went round his shoulders, she knew that she would always forgive him as long as he wanted to be forgiven. When he released her, he did an odd thing. He picked up her hand and held it, palm upwards, in his own, as though reading it. Then he kissed it and closed her hand on the kiss.

'Always remember, Celia, even if sometimes it seems overlooked, that it's there for all time.'

'I'll remember.'

CHAPTER FIVE

Dear Julian,

Here I am at Chez Vincent. Moved in on Sunday and already, after only three days, I feel that I'm an old inhabitant. Madame Vincent is an extremely kind and competent person, and Laurie will give a 'Pass' certificate to you when he sees you. He and Celia spent most of the week-end here, and have already promised Madame to come and stay with her for two or three weeks next summer. So you have no cause to worry about me or my job.

My duties are pleasant enough. I clear breakfast, skip round the bedrooms and downstairs rooms as soon as the holiday-makers are out of the way, and see to the flowers and set the tables in the dining-room for lunch. The rest of the day is my own, and all day Saturday. I have my keep, a very nice bed-sitting-room at the top of the chalet—all eaves and dormer-windows and with heavenly views—and a big enough wage to pay all my personal expenses and have a bit over. I shall be here until early in September. Don't know exactly what my plans will be after that.

Which brings me to the difficult part of this letter, Julian. You have been so wonderfully kind to me—you and Uncle John when he was alive—in giving me a home at Alanbridge all this time, and you know how deeply grateful I am. But I realise now that it is time for me to stand on my own feet and free you from responsibility for me. You will be getting married one day and my presence could only be an embarrassment to you then. Perhaps I am assuming too much, but I have wondered whether if it hadn't been for me, you might by now have been married to Gillian Courtney. Perhaps your kind heart put off telling me in the hope that I would realise for myself that I couldn't go on living at Alanbridge for ever. If I've been dense, I know you will forgive me.

So I shan't be coming back to Alanbridge, Julian dear. But I shall always think of it with love and gratitude. Even if it is not Miss Courtney it will be somebody one day. And I'm not a child any longer, you know. I may stay abroad or I may come back to Elton in the autumn. I don't know yet. But I shall keep writing and know you will, too. I have made good friends here, including one, George, but I will write about him another time as I am due to dine with Laurie and Celia in twenty minutes' time and need some doing over! Our farewell dinner together. They are off in the morning. I shall miss them. They are both in the best of spirits, and Laurie has come down from Mount Olympus and is positively frivolous! The holiday has done them a world of good, in more senses than one. But you will hear all their news yourself.

I shall be looking eagerly for your next letter. Not anxiously, because I know you will understand.

Ever your
FIONA.

P.S. I think Miss Courtney would suit Alanbridge perfectly. Both so lovely.

Fiona read the letter through twice before she sealed it. It had been difficult to keep the balance between appearing heart-broken at leaving Alanbridge, which would make Julian feel guilty, and appearing unfeeling, which would make him think her ungrateful. She hoped she had succeeded, but her heart was heavy as she took the letter to the post. The ache for him grew no less.

She said good-bye to Celia and Laurie that night, but slipped away from her duties the next morning to wave to them from the gate of Chez Vincent as the car went by with loud hootings. Watching the G.B. plate on the back recede until the car turned off on the first of its hair-pin bends down the valley and the road was empty, Fiona felt that her heart went with it.

Although she had denied that she felt anxious, she watched the post for Julian's reply in a state of mind not far removed from anxiety. It came the next week.

My dear Fiona,

To say that I'm amazed by your letter is an understatement. And, frankly, there are one or two aspects of it that I don't understand.

The thing that hits me about it, though, is that you should have come to this decision without talking it over with me. Maybe I've been the obtuse one, but I thought we were so closely in each other's confidence that you would have talked over with me any major step you contemplated. In fact, I would have staked my life on it. You surely don't think I would stand in the way of anything you wanted to do? I've never wanted to rule your life, or anybody else's for that matter. But after all these years together, I don't think it's unreasonable of me to expect to be consulted before you leave my home, which has been your home for so long—ever since you were a child, for Lime Avenue was never a home. However, let's say no more of that.

I can't help thinking that Gillian is something of a red herring, my dear. If there had been any talk of an engagement, you might have thought the time had come to make a change. As it is, I can't believe that such a vague friendship could precipitate your headlong flight. I should have told you if my future and Gillie's were bound together.

I feel that there is something you are keeping from me, and I have had the humiliating experience of having to approach Aunt Lou and Celia to see if they could enlighten me. Celia wouldn't commit herself but Laurie thinks it is Ben who is the reason. Aunt Lou, however, says you had decided not to come back when you left Alanbridge.

Now, my dear, come clean. I never thought I'd have to ask you to be frank with me. If it is a sudden urge to be independent, to try a new way of life, then good luck to you, but I wish you'd told me. I would have helped in any way I could. If Ben is a factor that counts, then I have Laurie's word for it that he's a nice chap and there's no reason to keep it hidden from me.

Your happiness has always meant a great deal to me and I would never do anything to obstruct it. Do I really have to tell you that? I'd like to be in on it, though.

I've had to write this hastily as I am leaving Norah to cope with the last week of the school term and am off to the west country tomorrow for a fortnight, lecturing at a Summer School. A job I like because everybody is always so tremendously keen, but it won't leave me much time for anything else. Am taking your letter with me to see if it becomes more digestible with time!

JULIAN.

P.S. You don't have to marry me off to be rid of me.

Fiona put the letter down with a little gesture of despair. Everything she had done had been for Julian's sake, and all she had achieved by tearing her heart away from where it belonged was to hurt him. And hurt him badly, or he would never have written so severely. It was her first experience of any kind of admonishment from him and she found it devastating. The tears began to trickle down her cheeks as she sat on the bed, the letter still in her hand. Come clean, Julian had said. But what could she add to enlighten him? She could say that Norah's cruel words had helped to drive her away, but it would only be half the truth and that half was something she was pledged not to reveal. If she were to give him the core of the matter, she would have to say, I love you, Julian, as a woman loves a man, not as a child loves her guardian, and I can't go on living under the same roof with you, as a child. That would embarrass him, but perhaps it would hurt him less than what he saw as her secretiveness. She didn't know. But she could not reveal so much to him; it was every woman's right to nurse that unhappy secret. She felt helpless and bereft of any idea of how to put things right. She had fought against the tide of her feeling for so long, ever since that talk with Norah, that now she was exhausted and awash, and must let the sea cast her up where it would. She could make no more effort. And so it was that her reply to Julian only covered one side of a sheet of notepaper.

DEAR JULIAN,

I am so terribly sorry that I have disappointed you. Please forgive me, but I can't add anything more to what I have already told you, and can only ask you to accept it. You are the last person in the world I would want to hurt. I owe you so much. But I can't do anything about it.

I may stay on here and help Madame Vincent in the Winter Sports Season. We get on well together.

I hope the Summer School was a success. I am sure you were, anyway. You are so good at communicating your own love of music. I should like to have heard you.

Please let me have your news from time to time, even if you are angry with me for what I've done.

Ever your
FIONA.

July dragged painfully to a close and August came in with a week of stormy weather, and there was no reply from Julian. She spent a Saturday in Chamonix trying to find a suitable birthday present for him, although she guessed that after the Summer School he had set off for the Continental holiday which embraced Salzburg, and would not be at Alanbridge for his thirty-third birthday. She found it difficult to hit on anything, for her supply of francs was not large and the goods displayed to catch the tourist's eye did not appeal to her. Finally she tracked down a delicate little piece of wood carving in an antique shop: a gazelle standing on a small stone plinth, its head thrown back, the whole no more than five inches in height. But it was beautiful work and would not be cheap.

It took her half an hour of bargaining to get the gazelle,

but she emerged triumphantly although she had to seek out Ben to borrow her bus fare back to the village. When it came to writing a note to accompany it, she confined herself to a few lines of good wishes, conscious that Julian's silence had opened up a gap which she did not know how to bridge.

The days passed and brought no acknowledgment from him, thus confirming her guess that he was on holiday, but the knowledge that she was now a stranger to his movements, that he had not replied to her last letter before leaving Alanbridge, chilled her heart although she knew that her own attitude was the cause. Her only comfort was the knowledge that there was not a shred of ill-nature in Julian and she could be sure that he would not wash his hands of her because she had quitted his home. She knew that she would hear. But she knew, too, that things would never be the same again.

This thought was with her as she returned from a walk up the valley. She had intended to do some sketching but had added nothing to her sketch-book. For weeks now, she had not been able to do any worth-while work. A strange inertia of the spirit seemed to have seized her, and she had spent most of that afternoon lying on the grass watching the river flow by, thinking of the happy days she had spent at Alanbridge. Nothing stood still, she thought, as she made her way back in a melancholy mood. No matter how she had bungled this business, that happy harmony with Julian had been doomed as soon as she left her childhood behind. The old childish hero-worship was by its very nature a limited phase which must cool into friendship, or grow into love. She remembered how Julian had teased her a little about putting him on a pedestal. It was when he asked her to come and live at Alanbridge. She remembered it so clearly. In a way, perhaps he had been trying to warn her. But already it was too late, my dear, she thought. Even then I was on the road which you didn't want me to take, and the milestone of childhood was receding. But because you didn't want it, you wouldn't see it. You seem to want the old footing of adored guardian and child perpetuated for ever. But children grow up, even if you don't want them to.

Already the pastures around her were showing the first pale chalices of the autumn crocuses. Soon she must decide whether to stay on in this Alpine village for the winter. Her original contract with Madame Vincent came to an end in two weeks' time. But she was still unable to throw off this sense of helplessness which had blanketed her ever since she had received that letter from Julian. She could not seem to grapple with anything; and any decision seemed beyond her. As she walked slowly along, the sight of autumn crocuses filled her for the first time in her young life with a sense of the relentlessness of time. If she could have halted it, she would have chosen to stay in her enchanted garden with Julian for ever, like the figures on the Grecian urn. But she was a helpless human being whom time carried on irresistibly, like the river beside her. It would carry her far from Julian, and she could do nothing about it and nor could he, since he wanted the impossible, an eternal unchanging child.

When she arrived back, she found a card awaiting her from Salzburg. It gave no address.

MY DEAR,
Don't worry. Of course you have the right to make your own decisions and I'm sorry I read the riot act. Forget it.

Finished up here after a pleasant tour round, but find that this surfeit of riches is giving me musical indigestion. Rationing, I fancy, is indicated.

All the best,
J.

She put the card with all the other letters she had received from him. Time was carrying her from him even faster than she had foreseen. The new pattern of their relationship was already emerging—a casual friendship thrown like a bridge between two separate shores. Stones for bread. She wondered how long it would take to stop being hungry for the bread. . . .

The holiday season was drawing to a close and Chamonix was emerging from the crowds of tourists and assuming the more peaceful aspect which it had first presented to Fiona in the spring. She had come in to buy some cartridge paper from the art shop and she hesitated now between lingering to have an *apéritif* outside her favourite café and running the risk of being seen by Ben, or returning by the mid-morning bus to the village. She did not want to see Ben. His persistence was tiring and she frequently fell in with his suggestions these days because she had not enough energy to go against them. He often came to this café about eleven o'clock on Saturday morning. She approached it cautiously, and sure enough, there he was at the little table half hidden by the bay tree in a tub. Fiona slid away down a side turning and came out at the bus stop just in time to run and be hauled aboard by the grinning conductor.

Jogging up the valley, she wondered how to spend the day. Would it be any use taking her sketch-book out, or would a strenuous climb help to rid her of this fog of indecision? She would have to make up her mind this week-end. Although the Winter Sports Season did not begin until December, Madame Vincent had offered to keep on the present arrangement without break, for she would find Fiona useful in the coming weeks while the chalet was being refurbished, bed linen overhauled and plans made for the coming season. And still Fiona hesitated, unwilling to commit herself to a further period of exile, but unable, also to see a niche for herself in Elton now that Alanbridge was no longer hers.

The bus swung merrily round hair-pin bends, its gears whining as it climbed up the valley, depositing voluble passengers at various villages *en route* until it drew up with a jerk and a bounce at the stop outside Chez Vincent. It was too lovely a morning to stay indoors, and Fiona left her parcel in the hall and slipped out again. She had time for a stroll along the river before lunch, and this afternoon, perhaps, she would climb up to the little plateau which Celia had revealed to her.

The sun was hot on her head and struck up from the rough road through the thin soles of her sandals as she walked along. Someone was leaning on the little stone bridge watching her. She stopped dead, then was flying down the road, her face radiant. He held out both hands as she came up and she flung herself into his arms.

'Julian!' she gasped. 'Oh, Julian.' And could say no more as she held him tight, her head pressed against his jacket.

'Well, well. Let me have a look at you after all this time.'

He stood her away from him, his eyes searching her face, then a slow smile creased his face and he said gently:

'It's good to see you.'

'But how, when? . . .' began Fiona breathlessly.

'How? By car. When? I arrived ten minutes ago and was informed by Madame that you had gone into Chamonix and would not be back until lunch-time. I said I'd stroll around and return then, and I'd just stopped here to take my bearings when you appeared out of the blue. You came up on that bus, I suppose?'

'M'm. Oh, this *is* a wonderful surprise! I didn't think there was any chance of your coming after I had your card. I know your Continental tours are always pretty crowded,' she added hurriedly. Then, as she caught his eye, 'And I thought you were angry with me.'

'So I was, furious. But it all evaporated at the sight of those large eyes of yours. Anyway, we'll not dwell on that now. I have two more weeks' holiday and I thought I'd like to spend them with you. What about it?'

'No better thought has ever come out of heaven,' she said fervently, aware that her joy at seeing him was so overwhelming that she was only a hair's breadth from tears.

'How are you placed now?'

'I've very little to do. My agreement ends with Madame Vincent at the end of this week and I haven't definitely decided whether to stay on or not. Now you're here, we can talk it over. We haven't many guests left, and we can put you up. It's really a very nice little hotel.'

'I'm sure it is and I've no intention of staying anywhere else. Do you think we'd better see Madame now and fix it up? Then I can unload the car before lunch, and we can be free for the rest of the day.'

Madame was delighted to have another guest; Fiona flew off to prepare his room and by lunch-time Julian was installed. As he sat opposite her at her small corner table in the dining-room, expressing his appreciation of Madame's soup, Fiona felt like pinching herself to make sure that it was true. He told her about his tour, talked of the music festival, filled her greedy ears with news of Alanbridge and the Deverels, and all as easily as if they had never been separated and there was no issue between them. But there was, and Fiona knew it, and wondered when he would bring it up.

For the moment, however, the sheer delight of his presence blotted out everything else and she drank her fill of it.

CHAPTER SIX

MADAME VINCENT generously freed Fiona of all duties, and the first halcyon days of Julian's arrival were spent in showing him the country. They took a picnic lunch with them every day and since Julian, too, shared Fiona's preference for the living world below the snow-line, there was no difficulty about their programme, although if Julian had expressed a wish to attempt the most difficult peak in the area, Fiona would have followed him without question.

It was not until the Wednesday of that first week, when Julian drove into Chamonix, that any reference was made to the clouds between them which had so far been ignored, and this was precipitated by a chance encounter with Ben. They ran into him as they were walking to the *téléphérique* which was to carry them to the heights they were unwilling to climb. Fiona introduced the two men, a little confused but hoping her confusion was not apparent to Julian's very observant eyes. Ben, it appeared, was *en route* to the bank and they walked the short way together.

'Haven't seen you lately, Fiona. Where have you been hiding yourself?' asked Ben, as they stopped at the bank.

'Been busy.'

'What about my offices as easel-bearer? Any prospects?'

'I shan't be doing any work for a bit, Ben. Julian is staying at Madame Vincent's and I'm giving myself a holiday at the same time.'

'I see,' said Ben slowly. Then he turned to Julian with a faint smile. 'You know, I'd heard a lot about you from Fiona, but somehow I thought of you as a cross between Sir Henry Wood and Mark Hambourg. I didn't visualise anybody so young.'

'How disappointing for you,' said Julian, with a grin. 'I'm afraid Fiona's opinion of my prowess in the world of music has always been far too high.'

Fiona's eyes met Ben's and she realised that he knew.

Being in love gave one an additional sensitivity, she thought. She saw his mouth tighten in the rather obstinate way which she had become familiar with recently. She wished he would go into the bank and leave them. It was not her fault that she could not give him what he wanted, and she had never deceived him on that point.

'I guess Fiona's a romantic kid,' said Ben. 'Apt to get spell-bound.'

And at that, she was suddenly angry. She gave no sign of it, however, as she said quietly:

'That's my kind of fun, Ben. But I know it's not yours.'

'Should hope not. I outgrew that when I was ten.'

'What a pity. You miss a lot.'

'Well, I like that! I enjoy this world as it is, my dear. I get a lot of fun out of it. I don't waste my time in a never-never land dreaming of what might have been.'

Julian's eyebrows were raised comically as he surveyed them, and Fiona, realising the absurdity of the situation, laughed and said soothingly:

'Never mind, Ben. I know I exasperate you, but I'm afraid I can't change. Forgive me.'

Ben grinned reluctantly.

'You're a bit of a spell-binder yourself. I must get back to the sordid realities of money. Good-bye, my dear. And good-bye, Mr. Falconer. I'm still a bit sorry about that lack of venerable beard.'

He left them and Julian eyed Fiona wickedly.

'Well, well. I can see it's not Ben. That's one point cleared up. But who the devil is George?'

'George?' Fiona thought a moment, and then smiled. Now it was her turn. 'Ah, George is quite a different proposition. I'll introduce him to you this evening. He's my darling.'

Julian looked at her thoughtfully but her gay face told him nothing more.

'How many scalps have you collected since you've been away? I can see you're a dark horse. You've even got the august Dr. Deverel eating out of your hand now.'

'I was always a bit in awe of Laurie before, but I got to know him better when he was here, and I like him a lot. He's much more human than I thought.'

'He's a good chap. I'm glad he and Celia have come

through that sticky patch all right. I thought they would. I don't know exactly what the trouble was, but I was pretty sure that their marriage had a strong enough base to stand the racket of their lively temperaments.'

'Yes. I suppose if your blood runs like that, you can even bring a certain amount of zest into fighting the person you love, and come out unscathed.'

'Perhaps come out wiser. Who knows? Laurie and Celia have always challenged each other, as well as loved. I think what you are must govern the tone of your life. If Laurie and Celia ever fall into a placid pattern of life together, it will be because they have both grown indifferent to each other. I see no signs of that,' said Julian, smiling, then added, 'That little exchange with your Ben has made us miss our *téléphérique*. Shall we wait for the next, or change our programme?'

'I don't like hanging about. I know. Let's drive a few miles beyond here and I'll show you the coolest, greenest place you've ever seen. We can go up the *téléphérique* another day. I think it would be a bit hot up there today, anyway.'

'Yours to command. If you like to wait here, I'll collect the car.'

'No, I'll come with you. I'm not wasting one moment of your time here.'

'Well, now I come to think of it, that's the prettiest compliment I've ever had paid to me.'

'Silly,' said Fiona, taking his arm as they walked back to the centre of the town where Julian had parked the car.

'Want to look through the telescope?' asked Julian, as the man in charge looked hopefully towards them. '*Il y a des personnes sur Mont Blanc.*'

'No, thanks. I've seen people climbing Mont Blanc at closer quarters than that. He does a very good trade with it, though. Back in July and August the town was swarming with tourists. But it's lovely now,' added Fiona, looking across the half-empty square to the bridge across the tumbling river, and the bronze group nearby depicting de Saussure and his guide looking up at the summit of Mont Blanc. The mountain itself, with its darkly wooded lower slopes, its rock faces and its vast snow-fields, dominated the town with benign grandeur on that still, sunny autumn day.

Julian drove a few miles beyond the town, and under Fiona's direction left the car at a little village, no more than a hotel and two or three chalets, not far from the Swiss border. Then she led him along the river a short way until they came to her green dell, a pocket in a bend of the river where the grass was an intense emerald green, and ferns and larch trees and mossy boulders created a picture of coolness which matched the crystal clear water running fast over its stony bed.

'Isn't this a lovely retreat, Julian?'

'Beautiful. "Annihilating all that's made to a green thought in a green shade." Don't often see these rivers as clear as that; they're usually a bit milky-looking from the glaciers. Where do you want to sit? Sun, shade or dapple?'

'Dapple,' said Fiona.

They found a patch of grass half shaded by a small larch tree close to the water, and Julian stretched himself on his back and closed his eyes.

'Heaven,' he said. 'Pure heaven.'

Fiona sat with her hands clasped round her knees and watched him. The tree cast a dappled pattern across her green linen dress and bare brown legs and threw tongues of shadow across Julian's white shirt.

'Would you like my cardigan under your head?'

'Thanks.'

Fiona folded it into a pad and lifted his head, since he showed no signs of lifting it himself. Her fingers moved through his crisp black hair as she held his head while she adjusted the make-shift pillow and then lowered it.

'Aren't heads heavy?' she observed, suddenly conscious that every nerve in her hand was tingling.

'Mine's extra dense, I think.'

She wondered whether that remark had any special significance but his eyes were closed and he did not enlighten her. He had a good head, she thought, with spare taut lines, ears set close in. A narrow bar of sunlight crossing his face seemed to dust his dark eyelashes with gold. Now that he was with her again, the thought of losing him was so agonising that it was impossible to contemplate. She knew then that if he asked her to go back with him on the old footing she would not have the strength to refuse even though she knew that it would only postpone the inevitable parting. Her only chance of escaping from the heartbreak of frustrated love was to keep at a distance from him. All these weeks she had been trying to make the decision that would cut her off from him, and had shrunk from it. Now she could never do it unless he helped her. He was so dear to her that the thought of a life when she never saw him seemed now impossible to endure, although only starvation would cure her of this love. But what else would it do to her? If only he would help her. She needed his help to do what had to be done. It would have been better, she thought, if she had told him the whole truth. She was suddenly aware of her youth, her immaturity, before a problem which had become too big for her.

Julian opened his eyes, and with the uncanny intuition which he had always possessed where she was concerned, discerned her distress, for he sat up and put an arm round her shoulder.

'My poor Niobe, don't look so forlorn. There are no troubles which can't be sorted out with care and thought. It's when we let our emotions rush in and stampede us that we crash about like bulls in china shops, and that's just what I did when I got that letter of yours. Instead of thinking about it, I went charging round to Aunt Lou and Celia like any stupid outraged parent trying to find out what his offspring had been up to, and then I sat down and dashed off my reply before I'd really thought rationally about it at all. It must have shaken you.'

'Yes, it did. But it was my fault as well. I'm afraid that with the best of intentions, I bungled it all.'

'Well, that's no excuse for the way I reacted. There was I, who had always loathed possessiveness and staked my all on the principle that every individual's birthright is freedom, feeling outraged because you were asserting that right. And to cap it all, I had the humiliating experience of being reminded by Celia, Aunt Lou and Norah that you were no longer a child and that I seemed to have overlooked that fact. Norah's acid postscript that it was only my vanity that was hurt because I enjoyed playing King Cophetua did nothing to soothe me.'

'How dare she say that after . . .'

'After what?'

'Never mind. But your feelings were quite natural, Julian.

You'd always looked after me and advised me, and saw me as the child you'd first known. But twelve years difference in age narrows with time. I was a child when you were a man, and that's the pattern you've always seen. But I'm not a child now. It's natural enough that you shouldn't have realised that, though.'

'Well, I'm sorry about that letter, my dear. Mind you, I still think I had some justification for feeling jarred, to put it mildly, but I'd no right to adopt that attitude. Anyway, your reply made it clear that it didn't cut any ice and that we weren't getting anywhere on those lines, so I took myself off to chew it over and try to work out why I couldn't approach the whole thing rationally and get at what was behind this sudden uprising of my fledgling. Because I felt all the time that there was something you hadn't said. The trouble, poppet, about you and me is that we've always been so close that odd little warning bells ring when the contact is faulty.'

'Yes, I know.'

'And that's why you told Celia that you'd better write it, and then I couldn't see your face.'

'Did she tell you that?'

'M'm. It was the only help she would vouchsafe. That's when I decided that at all costs I was going to see you.'

'I thought your card meant that you'd given me up.'

'I don't give up that easily. I wanted to surprise you, though. Wanted to see your face. It was distinctly reassuring.'

'Julian, you could never have thought for one moment that my affection for you had changed. You couldn't.'

'No, not after I'd had time to think about it. But something has puzzled me about this, my dear. I could have sworn you didn't want to come away with Celia and Laurie. In fact, I did my best to persuade you, I remember, but you were reluctant. Then you suddenly changed your mind, and at the same time, it seems, decided that you would go and not come back. Now what decided you? Until then, you were happy at Alanbridge and never wanted to leave it. You don't have to tell me, but I think it was something Norah said.'

'What makes you think that?'

Julian pulled out his pipe and said, with a faint smile:

'When I'd cooled down and got my mind working on it, I went back to the day when you changed your mind about going away. It was your birthday. Then I remembered seeing you come down the stairs with Norah, looking as white as a ghost. I thought you were over-tired. Norah was wearing that hideous hat with the menacing bird of prey. She was wearing it just before I came away, and that rang a little bell. I suddenly remembered seeing you two come down the stairs. Do I rival Sherlock Homes?'

'Yes.'

'Going to tell me?'

'I can't, Julian. I promised I wouldn't.'

'I see. Well, at a guess I'd say she spun you a yarn about Gillie and suggested that your presence might be an embarrassment. I don't think you would have thought that word up for yourself in that connection. Am I near it?'

'Well, not quite. I was the one who thought Gillian was to be your wife. But Norah did make me realise that I would be a stumbling block in your marriage, that my position at Alanbridge really had become untenable. No, Julian, don't be angry. I should have come to that conclusion myself some time, even if it hadn't come quite so harshly. Please don't let this rebound on Norah.'

'I could wring her neck. Spent all those years trying to give you a sense of security, of belonging, because I knew what your home life was, and she undoes it with her malicious tongue in five minutes.'

'Oh, no. You'd given me the confidence that my home never gave me. You and Uncle John. Norah couldn't undo that. I knew I had your affection and friendship for the rest of my life. Nothing that Norah said could change my confidence in that, Julian. So please forget her part.'

'All right, my dear. But you say that it was you who thought Gillie was in the picture. Why? I've hardly seen her this past year. That visit to Alanbridge was a bolt from the blue. I haven't seen her since. In fact, she's in America. I can't think of anything that could have given you the idea.'

'Those same little bells, Julian. I knew ages ago, before I came to live at Alanbridge, that you and Gillian were close friends. Celia knew, and Norah knew. I'm sorry,' she added with a little smile, 'but we do happen to be interested in you, you know.'

'Go on.'

'I know you've never talked about her, or brought her to Alanbridge, but I guessed what took you to London so often. And then that time last summer when you were so unhappy, I thought things were going wrong for you with Gillian. But when I saw you together at Alanbridge this spring, I knew for certain that you were very close. I could tell. That's all. I know you never wanted me to know about it and I sometimes wished you would tell me. It would have been a sign that you thought I was growing up, and I did so want to help you when you were unhappy. But you didn't say anything.'

'And you respected my rights far more than I've respected yours, and asked no questions. I didn't realise, dear, that you were growing up. I admit it. And my affair with Gillie was at one time too painful to talk about, and later on there seemed no point. However, I think I'd better tell you about it now.'

'Don't, if it's painful.'

'It isn't any longer. I met Gillie five years ago, and fell in love with her almost at first sight. I had her affection, and her love, I think. As much as she would allow herself to love, anyway. But she was honest from the start about devoting her life to her career. She's a great actress, as you know. And like all great artists, she made her art her life. I tried for two years to persuade her to marry me. She wouldn't. I can't tell you about those two years, my dear. They belong to Gillie and me. They were part heaven, part hell, but in the end I began to get burned out with the frustration of it and Gillie found it more and more difficult to keep the conflict in her private life from affecting her work. I think I knew in my heart that I shouldn't win her over to marriage, but I wouldn't admit it until Gillie realised that I'd never be satisfied with half a loaf and broke it off.'

'That was when you were so unhappy, last summer?'

'Yes.'

'How could she do it?'

'She was right. I realise that now. I think I did at the time, but some truths are so unpalatable that we put off admitting them. She is first and foremost an actress. She'll travel a lot, give her best energies to her work. She could never have settled down at Alanbridge. She wouldn't want family life and children. And I couldn't give up Alanbridge and become her stage door Johnny. She appreciated that. It wouldn't have worked. She saw it before I did, and had the courage to act on it. When she came down to Alanbridge, she was saying good-bye before she went off to America. I'd tried to persuade her to come down and see the place many times, but she wouldn't. She was afraid of making things more difficult for herself. But she wanted to see it once before she went away, and when she realised that I'd got over it, she came. I'm glad she did. We were able to say good-bye without regrets and without bitterness. I had a letter from her just before I came away. We shall always be glad we knew each other, and I owe it to Gillie that we split up before frustration and tension had brought the affair to an uglier end. That's all, Fiona.'

'I'm so sorry, Julian. She is a lovely woman. You would have been such a good match for each other, I thought.'

'Perhaps, if Gillie had been less of an actress and I less bound by my inheritance. Anyway, it's over and done with. In fact, I got over it a good deal more easily than I ever imagined I would, and I think you were the reason for that. I didn't realise until you went away quite what a hold you had on my life, Fiona. Alanbridge seemed dead, somehow, without you. I kept expecting you to pop up in the garden or appear from nowhere whenever I arrived home, and I never got used to the emptiness without you. When I heard that you had no intention of coming back, I couldn't believe it. It seemed almost blasphemous: as though one of my best pupils had suddenly taken a pick-axe to my piano. But when my mind came clear, I knew where I stood. And when I saw your face last Saturday, I was pretty sure where you stood. Our little encounter with Ben this morning made me even more sure. But did you really have to run away without saying a word and cause all this heart-burning, dear? I could have told you all about Gillie if you'd told me what you were thinking.'

'But if it wasn't Gillie, it had to be somebody some time, Julian. I didn't feel I could bear to stand by and go through it all again. And would you ever have realised that I was no longer a child if I hadn't gone away?'

'Sooner or later. But perhaps I needed that jolt.'

He took her face between his hands and kissed her gently.

'I've always loved you. You've been part of my life, part of Alanbridge, for so long that you must forgive me for taking it for granted, and not recognising a new stage in its course.'

'I've nothing to forgive, and everything to be thankful for. I love you so much that I don't know how I could have faced losing you again.'

'Well, you're saddled with me now for good. Since we know all about living under the same roof, there is no gilt to be rubbed off and we know exactly what we're taking on, and I for one contemplate the future with abominable complacence. The only danger is that unless you open that haversack, I may die of starvation before I have a chance of enjoying our nuptial bliss. It's nearly two o'clock and Continental breakfasts don't support me that long.'

Julian took champagne back with them that night and invited Madame, her daughter, and the only two remaining holiday-makers, to join them for dinner to celebrate their engagement. It was a very jolly and informal little gathering, with Madame Vincent in a surprisingly rollicking, if not ribald, mood, which caused Julian some amusement, and her daughter, Yvonne, some embarrassment. Yvonne was a tall, dark girl with fine black eyes and an intelligent bony face. The holiday-makers were two university students from Edinburgh, stocky young men who were keen climbers.

When the party had dispersed and they were left alone, Fiona and Julian strolled down to the bridge. It was cold at that altitude once the sun had gone, and Fiona drew her coat closer.

'Well, if you don't feel engaged now, ring or no, you should,' observed Julian, taking her arm. 'Sorry currency shortage means you'll have to wait until we get home before I can buy the ring, but I'm running low and shall only just make out.'

They leaned on the bridge and watched the wavering reflection of the moon in the water.

'I must write to Celia tomorrow. Can I tell her?'

'Of course. Warn her to be ready with a wedding bonnet by the middle of October. That is, if you're willing. Or do you want longer to get used to the idea?'

'The sooner the better. It will be lovely to see Alanbridge again. You know, don't you, that I'm only marrying you because you have such a lovely home and play the piano so beautifully.'

'Of course. Why else?'

She rubbed her head against his shoulder, smiling, but said nothing.

'You've been a remarkably constant nymph, you know. Hasn't Ben or that young art friend, Eric, or anybody else your own age ever tempted you to look elsewhere?'

'No. Nobody has ever counted beside you.'

'And what about George? I still don't know about him.'

'George is a cart-horse, with the most beautiful melting eyes you ever saw.'

He pinched her ear.

'So you were stringing me along, were you?'

'M'm. Talking of Eric reminds me of that dance you took me to. Remember? I was so angry with you because you didn't want to dance with me and absolutely ignored the efforts I'd made to look glamorous.'

He thought a moment, then laughed.

'Good Lord, yes. We got stuck in the ditch coming home.'

'And I finished up in your raincoat, and I don't believe you noticed any difference.'

'Very clottish of me, but it was only the trappings I missed, after all. I always appreciated that wistful little face of yours. You're cold, dear. Let's call it a day.'

But Fiona was not cold, and she wondered for a brief moment whether he would have taken Gillian back so soon on a night like that. But with so much happiness in her heart, the tiny question mark still hovering could be ignored.

Celia and Laurie wired their congratulations, and Celia followed up with a letter asking Fiona to stay with them until the wedding. Fiona discussed it with Julian over breakfast.

'What do you think, Julian? Celia says Laurie is hoping he'll have the privilege of giving me away, and she would love to have me there before you gobble me up.'

'M'm. Very helpful of her. It seems silly not to carry you back to Alanbridge with me, but I suppose convention still means a lot to Mrs. Blakeney, and we'd better consider that. Afraid I shan't be able to get away for more than a few days' honeymoon, ducky. Term starts next week.'

'Where better to spend a honeymoon than Alanbridge, anyway?'

And so it was that Fiona spent the last weeks of her single state at Marchwood with Celia and Laurie, although most days saw her at Alanbridge. Julian was kind and affectionate, as always, but still that little question mark remained in her mind.

On the eve of their wedding, Fiona went to dinner at Alanbridge. She arrived early and was informed by Mrs. Blakeney that Julian was in the garden. It had been a perfect autumn day, calm and sunny, and now as she walked through the garden in search of her groom, the sun was setting above the larch trees, streaking the sky with red and purple and reflecting a rosy sheen on a castle of fleecy clouds in the east. The borders on each side of the long walk were still rich in colour, for the dahlias and chrysanthemums and Michaelmas daisies took on a deeper glow from the setting sun, and one group of red dahlias seemed afire. The leaves of the trees were turning colour, the beech to copper, the birches gold, and a few leaves had escaped Joe's broom and sparsely patterned the grass which was now, with heavy dews morning and night, a more luscious green than at any time of the year. Fiona passed her hand through the spray of the fountain as she passed, the drops of water sparkling to rival the ring on her finger. A few roses still lingered on the bushes in the rose garden, a wistful reminder of their summer glory.

It was in the changing light at dusk that the enchantment of this garden was strongest; at all times and seasons it was a joy, even when frost and snow came to it, even when winter's bareness served only to reveal the beauty of twig and branch and enhance the evergreens, but its spell was never more potent than at twilight, and on that particular evening it seemed to embrace her with a brooding tenderness as though welcoming her home.

She found Julian picking apples from a cordon tree in the walled garden.

'Hullo, my dear. Fruits of the earth. Not bad, are they?' He proffered the basket with some pride.

'Beautiful. Can I help?'

'No, that's the lot.' He kissed her, then picked up the basket as he said, 'You're looking a little pale. Everything organised?'

'Yes. Celia's been fiddling with my veil. I didn't realise that getting married, even with a quiet wedding, was quite so exhausting.'

'You know, I fancy we've allowed our friends, the Deverels, to jockey us into a much more formal affair than we intended.'

'Yes, perhaps. But then, as Celia says, you are somebody in this neighbourhood, and must do your duty.'

'Shucks to that. I always feel that all this flap about weddings is a bit vulgar, and that a marriage is a private and personal affair. But then, I've never liked publicity of any kind.'

'Nor I.'

'Trouble is, we're too easy. However, this time tomorrow it'll all be over, and in a few days we'll be back here and everybody will have forgotten all about us. Nervous?'

'Not really. But I'll be glad when the public part is over. Socially, as my father used to say, I'm a wash-out.'

'If that means you're not conventional or gushing, then thank heavens for that. Nor am I. We don't need the world, my dear, you and I.'

She squeezed his arm, and they walked slowly back through the garden, lingering now and again over some plant or shrub that caught Julian's critical eye and was marked down for attention.

'I love this tangy smell of autumn, don't you?' she said, as the lights of the house reached out to them.

'M'm. Wonder if there'll be a frost tonight. There's a nip in the air.'

After dinner, Fiona asked him to play for her, and she curled up on the window seat and listened, as she had done so many times before. She had not drawn the curtains, for the moon had risen over the beech tree, and the garden was serene and beautiful in its cool light. Now and again a moth fluttered against the glass, pale and insubstantial as a dream.

'I've never known anybody who could look so still and out of this world as you,' observed Julian as he closed the piano and came across to her. 'What were you thinking of just then?'

'Of the past and the present and the future—seeing it all out there in the garden.'

He was watching her profile against the window, turned from him, and his eyes dropped to the line of her throat and followed the slender, graceful curve of her body. He was reminded of the fleeting delicacy of the gazelle she had sent him. For the first time in his life, this quality of escape in her which had always rather intrigued him, now irked and challenged him, and he turned her round to him with a suddenness which startled her.

'Don't escape into that enchanted country of yours and leave me behind, Fiona. You're in my world now, and for always.'

'But I never go alone, Julian. You're always with me.'

'Too nebulous,' he said, and pulled her to her feet, drawing the curtains behind her and shutting out the night.

He was looking at her with an expression which she had never seen on his face before, and as she gave herself up to his searching hands and yielded her mouth to his, she knew that at last he had drawn the curtains on the child.

THE END

IRIS BROMIGE

A HOUSE WITHOUT LOVE

Andrew Courtland was determined to make his granddaughter Jill marry the young man he had chosen for her. A crusty old patriarch, he ruled the household at Holly Hill with a rod of iron. And in his opinion Martin Teviot, the son of an old friend, was just the right man for his granddaughter.

But Jill herself had other ideas. She preferred Paddy Dynard and positively disliked Martin Teviot. Since their first meeting had been precipitated by Jill nearly driving her car into Martin's, he had no reason to like her either. In his opinion she was a silly, thoughtless girl, far inferior to his shy sister Beth. And there the matter stood, with two obstinate people refusing to change their minds ...

CORONET BOOKS

IRIS BROMIGE

THE BROKEN BOUGH

Harriet's fiancé Kevin had spent a whole year away from her in the West Indies. His letters assured her that he still loved her as much as ever. But Harriet had changed inside herself. She knew that she just couldn't marry him.

From the start, Harriet had been so sure about Kevin. She had agreed to their engagement although her beloved father had never liked him, and had blamed Kevin for the accident in which Harriet's mother had died. There was no other man in her life but she wanted independence rather than marriage. "Take a clean break," her father said. But Harriet knew it wouldn't be that easy.

CORONET BOOKS

ROMANTIC FICTION FROM CORONET

IRIS BROMIGE

☐	15107 2	The Tangled Wood	20p
☐	15953 7	Alex and the Raynhams	25p
☐	16078 0	A Sheltering Tree	25p
☐	16077 2	Encounter at Alpenrose	25p
☐	17194 4	The Gay Intruder	30p
☐	18281 4	Rosevean	30p
☐	18612 7	Rough Weather	30p
☐	12947 6	An April Girl	30p
☐	02865 3	Challenge of Spring	30p
☐	18762 X	The Young Romantic	30p
☐	19675 0	The New Owner	40p
☐	19892 3	The Broken Bough	35p
☐	02917 X	A House Without Love	50p

JANE BLACKMORE

☐	17877 9	It Couldn't Happen to Me	30p
☐	17878 7	Bitter Honey	30p
☐	18613 5	A Love Forbidden	30p
☐	18606 2	Two in Shadow	30p
☐	18607 0	Girl Alone	30p
☐	18824 3	Joanna	30p

All these books are available at your local bookshop or newsagent, or can be ordered direct from the publisher. Just tick the titles you want and fill in the form below.

Prices and availability subject to change without notice.

CORONET BOOKS, P.O. Box 11, Falmouth, Cornwall.

Please send cheque or postal order, and allow the following for postage and packing:

U.K. — One book 18p plus 8p per copy for each additional book ordered, up to a maximum of 66p.

B.F.P.O. and EIRE — 18p for the first book plus 8p per copy for the next 6 books, thereafter 3p per book.

OTHER OVERSEAS CUSTOMERS — 20p for the first book and 10p per copy for each additional book.

Name..

Address...

....

Direct Hit!

"Flag, this is *Defiant*," he says. "Enemy ships pursuing. They'll reach your position soon. Too many for us to stop. . . ." He rubs ineffectually at the blood on his face. "There's more of them than anyone thought. We took a grazing hit, with one geodyne damaged and fifty men killed or wounded. Admiral, we can't fight them." It's clear that *Defiant*'s captain knows his ship is doomed.

"Energy pulse from target 027," a voice calls from somewhere behind the battlecruiser's captain. "They're getting ready to—!" With a blinding flash of light and the sound of melting electronics, the transmission ends abruptly. *Defiant* has been hit again, this time fatally.

"Pax Eternal," the communications technician mutters again. Ulnar drops his eyes to the planning tank, where the computer is already updating the symbols. The one representing *Defiant* is fading from powerful battlecruiser to lifeless hulk.

What next? What decisions must be made to save . . .

THE LEGION AT WAR

The Combat Command Books from Ace:

COMBAT COMMAND: **In the world of Piers Anthony's**
BIO OF A SPACE TYRANT, CUT BY EMERALD
by Dana Kramer

COMBAT COMMAND: **In the world of Robert A. Heinlein's**
STARSHIP TROOPERS, SHINES THE NAME
by Mark Acres

COMBAT COMMAND: **In the world of Keith Laumer's**
STAR COLONY, THE OMEGA REBELLION
by Troy Denning

COMBAT COMMAND: **In the world of David Drake's**
HAMMER'S SLAMMERS, SLAMMERS DOWN!
by Todd Johnson

COMBAT COMMAND: **In the world of Jack Williamson's**
THE LEGION OF SPACE, THE LEGION AT WAR
by Andrew Keith

COMBAT COMMAND
IN THE WORLD OF
JACK WILLIAMSON'S THE LEGION OF SPACE

THE LEGION AT WAR
BY
ANDREW KEITH

WITH AN INTRODUCTION BY
JACK WILLIAMSON

ACE BOOKS, NEW YORK

The names, places, descriptions, depictions, and other plot elements used in this game are derived from works copyrighted by and trademarks owned by Jack Williamson. These are used under license and may not be used or reused without Jack Williamson's permission.

This book is an Ace original edition, and has never been previously published.

THE LEGION AT WAR

An Ace Book / published by arrangement with
Bill Fawcett & Associates

PRINTING HISTORY
Ace edition / April 1988

All rights reserved.
Copyright © 1988 by Bill Fawcett & Associates.
Introduction copyright © 1988 by Jack Williamson.
Cover art by Don Dixon.
Maps by James Clouse.
Illustrations by Todd Cameron Hamilton and James Clouse.
This book may not be reproduced in whole or in part,
by mimeograph or any other means, without permission.
For information address: The Berkley Publishing Group,
200 Madison Avenue, New York, New York 10016.

ISBN: 0-441-11431-8

"Combat Command" is a trademark
belonging to Bill Fawcett & Associates.

Ace Books are published by The Berkley Publishing Group,
200 Madison Avenue, New York, New York 10016.
The name "Ace" and the "A" logo
are trademarks belonging to Charter Communications, Inc.

PRINTED IN THE UNITED STATES OF AMERICA

10 9 8 7 6 5 4 3 2 1

To Commander Jay Kalam, Admiral-General Hal Samdu, Giles Habibula . . . and the men of The Legion of Space.

INTRODUCTION
by Jack Williamson

It's a long time since 1933, when I wrote a serial novel I called *The Legion of Space*. That was in the middle of the Great Depression. Times were hard for nearly everybody. Certainly for me. I had been writing science fiction for several years, selling enough of it to let me go on writing science fiction, but the magazines that bought my stories were running into trouble. I had spent the summer before riding freight trains to tour a little of the West.

By fall a couple of delayed checks had come in, money enough to enroll at the University of New Mexico. I recall it as a fine year. The school was small then, and I made good friends. Most of them were anthropologists. Visiting the Indian pueblos with them, watching ceremonials, I got my first glimpse of other cultures, their different beliefs and ways of life.

In 1933 I had gone home from the university with only six dollars left, but an idea for *Legion*. One of my best courses had been a lecture series on "The Great Books," by a great teacher, Dr. George St. Claire. He told us how the Polish novelist, Sienkiewicz, looking for characters for his historical novels, had borrowed the three musketeers from Dumas and Sir John Falstaff from Shakespeare.

If that had worked for past history, I thought it might do as well for the future. Reading Dumas, I had thrilled at the daring exploits of his musketeers. I didn't know Shakespeare so well, but Falstaff's speeches soon gave me Giles Habibula. (Shakespeare, I might add, was the same sort of borrower; Falstaff himself, the old soldier with more courage for talk than action, came from the *Miles Gloriosus*, a stock figure in the theater for two thousand years before Shakespeare transformed him into a real human being.)

Luckily, I could live for nothing on the family ranch, doing a few chores to help pay for my keep. I spent that six bucks for paper and typewriter ribbons and wrote *The Legion of Space*, sleeping and working in an old building with a tarpaper roof. That was before air-conditioning, and I used to work stripped to the waist.

Those summer days were long. I did one chapter each morning, another in the afternoon. Three weeks for the first draft, three more for another—I had been sending stories out in first draft and selling most of them, but the Legion had become something special.

In those days, when the term "science fiction" still bewildered most of my friends, there was no book market for it unless you had already made a name from writing something else. I had hoped to sell the story to the old weekly *Argosy*, which was publishing such heroes of mine as Max Brand, Edgar Rice Burroughs, A. Merritt, but *Argosy* said no. Part of the reason, I think, was that they didn't like stories to contradict one another. My superweapon, AKKA, had destroyed the moon, which they wanted to preserve for other authors.

My best market had been *Astounding*. Its publisher had gone bankrupt, but a stronger firm, the old Street and Smith, soon brought it back to life. Luckily again, when they decided to publish serials, I had *Legion* ready. They ran it, and readers seemed to like it. One fan tabulated comments from the letter columns that ran in the back of the book and found that Giles Habibula had been the most popular character in the magazine during the 1930s.

I'm delighted that he's still alive. When you look back at titles of the best-selling books of fifty years ago, most of them are long forgotten. Somehow—thanks, I guess, to Shakespeare—old Giles had been remembered. All told, I have written four more stories in the series, the latest is about a girl who grows up to be "The Queen of the Legion." The books have stayed in print in several languages. My Italian publisher is just bringing out a four-volume boxed edition.

I'm delighted with the way Andy Keith has continued the history of the Legion through another century in *The Legion at War*. This game form, like the orbital satellite and the station in space and the robot explorer, is another exciting new invention since 1932. The game lets the player become an officer aboard his own space fleet, making his own battle commands.

The Legion stories—including all those that will be invented by players of the game—are "space opera." The term derives from "soap opera" and "horse opera"—that, of course, was a name for the old films of cowboys and Indians in the American West. Some writers I know don't like their work called space opera; they want it to be Literature. Capital L. Myself, I've never denied the name. I've enjoyed writing space opera. A lot of people like to read it. A lot more, I think, will enjoy commanding their battlecraft of space in *The Legion at War*.

I like to defend space opera. The best of it—if not necessarily the Legion books—can even be called literature. When I came across the theory of the epic in college literature classes, it struck me that some of the great pulp writers had a good deal in common with Homer. Without claiming that Max Brand's Westerns are destined to live forever, I can see strong similarities to such hallowed classics as *The Iliad* and *The Odyssey*.

Those great Greek epics, like the Norse sagas, the Anglo-Saxon *Beowulf*, Vergil's *Aeneid* and the myths of many other people, all tell the adventures of some folk hero. Often he's the legendary founder of his race or his nation. He's always drawn larger than life, armed with wits, courage, and sometimes extraordinary powers which he uses to defend great causes. His world is large; his noble missions carry him to unknown frontiers, often beyond. His victories are not for himself, but for a great family or a proud race or all humanity. If he dies, his death is a noble sacrifice.

Odysseus, for a fine example, was a man of craft and courage, equally skilled with words and his bow. Returning from victory in the Trojan War, he met and defeated such monsters as the Cyclops and the enchantress Circe. He wandered the half-known fringes of his world and even visited the underworld. Home at last, after twenty years away, he proved his strength and skill by stringing his old bow and slaughtering the horde of suitors who had been trying to seize his wife and his kingdom.

At least in theory, epic is an oral art, older than the art of writing. It originated as a way of preserving unwritten records, the history and beliefs that had to be saved because they carried the spirit of the nation or the people. The metric form made it easy to memorize. Mastering his art, the epic bard learned patterns of words that he could choose and vary to fill out the meter and fit whatever story he had to tell.

In print by such pulp masters as Max Brand, "horse opera" shows striking similarities. It tells and retells the story of the American West, the drama of a great continent conquered and a proud nation founded. The settings are vast. The values are good and evil, sharply etched and simple. The hero fires a deadly gun. Even his horse is heroic.

If the folk epic was an oral art, pulp was akin to it. Brand was famous for pounding out 4000 words a day, so many that he sold them under twenty-odd pen names—his real name was Frederick Faust. Those millions of words were printed with no revision, in pulp magazines usually no more permanent than the chanting of a bard.

Brand had wanted to be a poet. Looking at his stories, I noticed that long passages of his prose scanned like iambic verse. He repeated patterns of words not very different from the epic similes. His landscapes were vast, his characters heroic enough, his villains sufficiently evil to deserve what they got.

On film most horse operas were cheap Grade B productions, shot in a few days for very little money, but John Ford did better with *The Iron Horse*, the story of the first railroad to cross the continent, and his great classic, *Stagecoach*—his original is better by far than any remake.

I like to think of science fiction, or at least the most popular sort of it, as the epic of a technological age. The hero is heroic; sometimes he saves the world. His mental powers may seem supernormal. More commonly he depends upon his mastery of future science and engineering. Though his alien enemies are seldom magicians, they are armed with their own superscience—I think it was Arthur Clarke who pointed out that really far-out science can't be told from magic.

In the history of American science fiction, Edgar Rice Burroughs prefigures the themes of space opera. Tarzan, brought up by apes in a mythical Africa, has every trait of the epic hero. John Carter crosses space, if only by wishing to, and wins his own kingdom on Mars. Burroughs was no scientist, but he wrote with the speed of a reciting bard, and his tales still grip the reader.

E. E. "Doc" Smith followed with his own brand of space opera. It was my own admiration for his *Skylark of Space* that led me to try doing my own, but I think it was John W.

Campbell who did more than anybody else to mold American science fiction into the epic shape I think it has.

Campbell began writing as a rival of Smith, both of them hammering out space operas that look pretty crude to most of us now. He soon learned to do better, with more care for character and style, and truth to his own optimistic vision of a magnificent human future in space. Editor of *Astounding/Analog* from 1937 until he died in 1971, he shaped science fiction through its Golden Age, sharing that vision with a whole generation of such able writers as Heinlein, Sturgeon, de Camp, and del Rey.

Epic has always been optimistic; even when the hero dies, he dies victorious. Campbell liked forecasts of progress toward a great human destiny—he never cared much for aliens in space. Much of the best science fiction shares that same theme. Clarke's *The City and the Stars* shows mankind surviving for another billion years. Gordon Dickson is still at work on his ambitious "Childe Cycle," a series of novels about human evolution. The list of hopeful dreams could go on and on.

There are, of course, pessimists too. C. P. Snow saw us divided, a culture of science in conflict with a culture of tradition. I think science fiction reflects that division. The scientists are making the future; they understand and welcome it. The traditionalists, on the other hand, have their emotional stakes in the past; they tend to distrust the scientists and fear future change.

Great science fiction has come from both cultures, but space opera clearly belongs to the culture of science. In spite of all the pessimists, its epic appeals are still alive, in countless new novels, in the reruns of *Star Trek*, in the *Star Wars* films.

The world is vastly changed since I wrote that first Legion story in 1933. Men have actually walked on the moon, and such robot explorers as the Mariners, the Vikings, and the Voyagers have gone a lot farther. But the mythic human values that informed those old epics still matter to us. You'll discover them again in this game, as you command your Legion fleet in a desperate defense of the League of Worlds against a brand-new set of utterly evil alien invaders, the ruthless Ka'slaq.

Good hunting!

—Jack Williamson

INTRODUCTION
by Bill Fawcett

You are in command. With a blare of trumpets reverberating off the towering ships that surround you, it's off to battle with civilization's most valiant defenders, the Legion of Space. Marching into their ships are your men, trained spacemen, whose lives depend upon the decisions you are about to make.

Combat-Command books provide more than just another chance to read an exciting military adventure featuring the Legion of Space. You could simply "read" this book, tracing a route through the sections, but these books are also a "game" that lets you make the command decisions. This book is divided into sections rather than chapters. In each section of this game/book a military situation is described. Your choices actually write the book, both the story and the ending being determined by the combat decisions you make.

A careful effort has been made to make these adventures as "real" as possible. You are given the same information as you would receive in a real combat situation. At the end of each section you'll find a number of orders you may give your men. The consequence of the choice you make is described in the following section. When you make the right decisions, you are closer to successfully completing your mission. When you make a bad decision, men die in their shattered spaceships . . . men who are not going to be available for the next battle.

FIGHTING BATTLES

This book includes a simple game system that simulates combat and other military challenges. Playing the game adds an extra dimension of enjoyment by making you a participant in the adventure. You will need two six-sided dice, a pencil, and a sheet of paper to "play" along with this adventure.

COMBAT VALUES

In this book the force you command will consist of a legion of spaceships. Each ship is assigned five values. These values provide the means of comparing the capabilities of the many different military units you'll encounter. These five values are:

Manpower
This value is the number of separate fighting parts of your force. Each unit of Manpower represents one man, one ship, or whatever is firing. Casualties are subtracted from Manpower.

Ordnance
The quality and power of the weapons used is reflected by their Ordnance value. All members of a unit commanded will have the same Ordnance value. In some cases you may command two or more units, each with a different Ordnance value.

Attack Strength
This value indicates the ability of the unit to attack an opponent. It is determined by multiplying Manpower by Ordnance (Manpower × Ordnance = Attack Strength). This value can be different for every battle. It will decrease as Manpower is lost and increase if reinforcements are received.

Melee Strength
This is the hand-to-hand combat value of each member of the unit. In the case of a squad of mercenaries, it represents the martial-arts skill and training of each man. In crewed units such as tanks or spaceships, it represents the fighting ability of the members of the crew and could be used in an assault on a spaceport or to defend against boarders. Melee value replaces Ordnance value when determining the Attack Strength of a unit in hand-to-hand combat.

Stealth

This value measures how well the members of your unit can avoid detection. It represents the individual skill of each soldier or the ECM of each spaceship. The Stealth value for your unit will be the same for each member of the unit. You would employ stealth to avoid detection by the enemy.

Morale

This reflects the fighting spirit of the troops you command. Success in battle may raise this value. Unpopular decisions or severe losses can lower it. If you order your unit to attempt something unusually dangerous, the outcome may be affected by their morale level.

THE COMBAT PROCEDURE

When your unit finds itself in a combat situation, use the following procedure to determine victory or defeat.

1. Compute the Attack Strength of your unit and the opposition, (Manpower × Ordnance or Melee Strength)
2. Turn to the charts at the end of this book that are given in the description of the battle.
3. Roll two six-sided dice and total the result.
4. Find the Attack Strength of the unit at the top of the chart and the total of the dice rolled on the left-hand column of the chart. The number found where the column and row intersect is the number of casualties inflicted by the unit for which you were rolling.
5. Repeat for each side, alternating attacks.
   The unit you command always fires first unless otherwise stated.

When you are told there is a combat situation, you will be given all the information needed for both your command and their opponent.

Here is an example of a complete combat:

Hammer's Slammers have come under fire from a force defending a ridge that crosses their line of advance. Alois Hammer has ordered your company of ships to attack. Your ships have an Ordnance value of 8 and you have a Manpower value of 8 ships.

Slammers fire using Chart B.

Locals fire using Chart D with an Ordnance value of 3 and Manpower of 12 (this gives them an Attack Strength of 36).

To begin, you attack first and roll two 4's for a total of 8. The current Attack Strength of your Slammers is 64.

CHART B

Attack Strength

Dice Roll	1–10	–20	–30	–40	–50	–60	–70	–80	–90	–100	101+
2	0	0	0	1	1	1	2	2	2	3	4
3	0	0	1	1	1	2	2	2	3	3	4
4	0	1	1	1	2	2	2	3	3	3	4
5	1	1	1	2	2	2	3	3	3	4	5
6	1	1	2	2	2	3	3	3	4	4	5
7	1	2	2	2	3	3	3	4	4	4	5
8	2	2	2	3	3	3	4	4	4	5	6
9	2	2	3	3	3	4	4	4	5	5	6
10	2	3	3	3	4	4	4	5	5	5	6
11	3	3	3	4	4	4	5	5	5	6	7
12	3	3	4	4	4	5	5	6	6	7	8

Read down the 60–70 Attack Strength column until you get to the line for a dice roll of 8. The result is four casualties inflicted on your opponents by your company.

Subtract these casualties from the opposing force before determining their Attack Strength. (Combat is not simultaneous.) After subtracting the four casualties you just inflicted on them, the enemy has a remaining Manpower value of 8, (12 – 4 = 8). This gives them a remaining Attack Strength of 24 (8 × 3 = 24).

Roll two six-sided dice for the opposing force's attack and determine the casualties they cause your Slammer's company. Subtract these casualties from your Manpower total on the record sheet. In this case they caused one casualty, giving the Slammers a Manpower of 7 for the next round of combat. This ends one "round" of combat. Repeat the process for each round. Each time a unit receives a casualty, it will have a lower value for Attack Strength. There will be that many less men, spaceships, or whatever firing.

Continue alternating fire rolls, recalculating the Attack Strength each time to account for casualties, until one side or the other has lost all of its Manpower, or special conditions (given in the text) apply. When this occurs, the battle is over. Losses are permanent, and losses from your unit should be subtracted from their total manpower on the record sheet.

SNEAKING, HIDING, AND OTHER RECKLESS ACTS

To determine if a unit is successful in any attempt relating to Stealth or Morale, roll two six-sided dice. If the total rolled is greater than the value listed for the unit, the attempt fails. If the total of the two dice is the same as or less than the current value, the attempt succeeds or the action goes undetected. For example:

Rico decides his squad of Mobile Infantry (M.I.) will try to penetrate the Bug hole unseen. M.I. have a Stealth value of 8. A roll of 8 or less on two six-sided dice is needed to succeed. The dice are rolled and the result is a 4 and a 2 for a total of 6. They are able to avoid detection by the bug guards.

If all of this is clear, then you are ready to turn to section 1 and take command.

TIME

Time is a key factor in this war. You will be told in days how much time each action takes. Be sure to keep a record of the total time that has elapsed, on a sheet of scrap paper.

THE COMBAT CHARTS

After you have made a decision involving a battle, you will be told which chart should be used for your unit and which for the enemy. The chart used is determined by the tactical and strategic situation. Chart A is used when the unit is most effective, and Chart G when least effective. Chart A represents the effectiveness of the Sioux at Little Bighorn, and Chart F, Custer. Chart G represents the equivalent of classic Zulus with aseiges (spears) versus modern Leopard tanks. Even a very small force on Chart A can be effective, while even a large number of combatants attacking on Chart G are unlikely to have much effect.

CHART A

Attack Strength

Dice Roll	1–10	–20	–30	–40	–50	–60	–70	–80	–90	–100	101+
2	0	1	1	2	2	3	3	4	5	6	6
3	0	1	2	2	2	3	4	5	6	7	7
4	1	2	2	2	3	3	4	5	6	7	8
5	2	2	2	3	3	4	5	5	6	7	8
6	2	2	2	3	4	4	5	6	7	7	8
7	2	2	3	4	4	5	5	6	7	8	8
8	2	3	3	4	4	5	6	6	7	8	9
9	3	3	4	4	5	5	6	7	8	8	9
10	3	4	4	5	5	6	7	7.	8	9	10
11	3	4	4	5	6	6	7	8	9	10	11
12	4	4	5	6	7	7	8	9	10	11	12

CHART B

Dice Roll	1–10	–20	–30	–40	–50	–60	–70	–80	–90	–100	101+
2	0	0	0	1	1	1	2	2	2	3	4
3	0	0	1	1	1	2	2	2	3	3	4
4	0	1	1	1	2	2	2	3	3	3	4
5	1	1	1	2	2	2	3	3	3	4	5
6	1	1	2	2	2	3	3	3	4	4	5
7	1	2	2	2	3	3	3	4	4	4	5
8	2	2	2	3	3	3	4	4	4	5	6
9	2	2	3	3	3	4	4	4	5	5	6
10	2	3	3	3	4	4	4	5	5	5	6
11	3	3	3	4	4	4	5	5	5	6	7
12	3	3	4	4	4	5	5	6	6	7	8

CHART C

Dice Roll	1–10	–20	–30	–40	–50	–60	–70	–80	–90	–100	101+
2	0	0	0	0	0	1	1	1	2	2	2
3	0	0	0	0	1	1	1	2	2	2	3
4	0	0	0	1	1	1	2	2	2	3	3
5	0	0	1	1	1	2	2	2	3	3	4
6	0	1	1	1	2	2	2	3	3	3	4
7	1	1	1	2	2	2	3	3	3	4	5
8	1	1	2	2	2	3	3	3	4	4	5
9	1	2	2	2	3	3	3	4	4	5	5
10	2	2	2	3	3	3	4	4	4	5	6
11	2	2	3	3	3	4	4	4	5	5	6
12	2	3	3	3	4	4	4	5	5	6	7

CHART D

Dice Roll	1–10	–20	–30	–40	–50	–60	–70	–80	–90	–100	101+
2	0	0	0	0	0	0	0	1	1	1	2
3	0	0	0	0	0	0	1	1	1	2	2
4	0	0	0	0	0	1	1	1	2	2	2
5	0	0	0	0	1	1	1	2	2	2	3
6	0	0	0	1	1	1	2	2	2	3	3
7	0	0	1	1	1	2	2	2	3	3	4
8	0	1	1	1	2	2	2	3	3	4	4
9	1	1	1	2	2	2	3	3	3	4	5
10	1	1	2	2	2	3	3	3	4	4	5
11	1	2	2	2	3	3	3	4	4	5	5
12	2	2	2	3	3	3	4	4	5	5	6

CHART E

Dice Roll	1-10	-20	-30	-40	-50	-60	-70	-80	-90	-100	101+
2	0	0	0	0	0	0	0	0	0	1	1
3	0	0	0	0	0	0	0	0	1	1	1
4	0	0	0	0	0	0	0	1	1	1	2
5	0	0	0	0	0	0	1	1	1	2	2
6	0	0	0	0	0	1	1	1	1	2	2
7	0	0	0	0	1	1	1	1	2	2	2
8	0	0	0	1	1	1	1	2	2	2	2
9	0	0	1	1	1	1	2	2	2	2	2
10	0	1	1	1	1	2	2	2	2	2	3
11	1	1	1	1	2	2	2	2	2	2	3
12	1	1	1	2	2	2	2	2	2	3	3

CHART F

Dice Roll	1-10	-20	-30	-40	-50	-60	-70	-80	-90	-100	101+
2	0	0	0	0	0	0	0	0	0	0	0
3	0	0	0	0	0	0	0	0	0	0	0
4	0	0	0	0	0	0	0	0	0	0	0
5	0	0	0	0	0	0	0	0	0	0	0
6	0	0	0	0	0	0	0	0	0	0	1
7	0	0	0	0	0	0	0	0	0	0	1
8	0	0	0	0	0	0	0	0	0	1	1
9	0	0	0	0	0	0	0	0	1	1	1
10	0	0	0	0	0	0	0	1	1	1	1
11	1	1	1	1	1	1	1	1	1	1	2
12	1	1	1	1	1	1	1	1	1	2	3

CHART G

Dice Roll	1–10	–20	–30	–40	–50	–60	–70	–80	–90	–100	101+
2	0	0	0	0	0	0	0	0	0	0	0
3	0	0	0	0	0	0	0	0	0	0	0
4	0	0	0	0	0	0	0	0	0	0	0
5	0	0	0	0	0	0	0	0	0	0	0
6	0	0	0	0	0	0	0	0	0	0	0
7	0	0	0	0	0	0	0	0	0	0	0
8	0	0	0	0	0	0	0	0	0	0	0
9	0	0	0	0	0	0	0	0	0	0	0
10	0	0	0	0	0	0	0	0	0	0	1
11	0	0	0	0	0	0	0	0	0	1	1
12	1	1	1	1	1	1	1	1	1	1	1

SHIPS OF THE LEGION

Fleet Morale: 9

You may choose to allocate hits to any ship which is involved in the battle. For damage purposes treat a battle cruiser as two destroyers (i.e., it takes two hits to destroy one) and orbital fortresses as four. A single hit does no damage to either of the larger ships and will be repaired if the ship survives the battle. Any battle cruiser which has received one hit must receive the next hit allocated to battle cruisers.

Battle Cruiser
Ordnance: 4
Stealth: 9

Destroyer
Ordnance: 2
Stealth: 9

Orbital Fortress
(treat for hits and calculations as 4 destroyers)
Ordnance: 8
Stealth: none

The orbital fortress should only be included in battles where the Legion fleet is directly defending a planet. It can only be used if a defensive formation is chosen.

Ka'Slaq Ships

Attack Ships
Ordnance: 3
Stealth: none

Planetoid
Ordnance: 6
Stealth: none

Treat as 4 attack ships for damage.

Section 1

—1—
Top Secret

From: Jon Damor
   Commander, The Legion of Space
To: Vice Admiral David Ulnar
   Commanding Ninth Defense Squadron

Upon receipt of these orders your squadron will proceed to the Orion frontier to seek out hostile alien forces of unknown origin believed heading toward the territory of the League of Worlds. The Ninth Defense Squadron is hereby required to conduct a reconnaissance in force against these aliens to determine their nature, origins, and intentions. You are authorized to engage them in combat at your discretion, but the delivery of recon information to Legion Sector Headquarters is of utmost importance.

Alien forces, identified from intercepted ultrawave messages as "the Ka'slaq," fired upon a lightly armed exploratory mission near the System S.C. 170 two weeks ago, destroying four of five vessels, among them the *Discovery*. Last reported positions and courses will place the aliens at Thule in eight to ten days. The Ka'slaq are presumed to be hostile to all League forces.

Effective this date you are appointed Acting Sector Commander to coordinate frontier defenses and operations in your sector. Admiral J. T. Merros has been assigned as C.O., First Defense Fleet. Upon his arrival you will transfer authority as Sector Commander to him and integrate your forces.
                           Jon Damor
                           Commander of The Legion of Space

Personal Message

From: James Star
To: David Ulnar

Dave:
Commander Damor brought Dad the news about the mobilization orders, and he said he'd enclose this message with the official word to you. They won't pass the whole truth on through channels, so I'd better give you the full story.

* * *

Section 2

Those aliens out there are trouble, maybe the biggest trouble the Legion's tackled since the Cometeers. They shot up a flight of survey cruisers; only *Pioneer* got out, and she was crippled so badly it took a week to reach a port and a working ultrawave relay to warn us. The League Senate met the same day and agreed to bring in the Keeper of the Peace—that gives you an idea of how serious it is.

But when Sis tried to use AKKA, *nothing happened*! She says there's some kind of mental power, like a shield, that protects the aliens from her weapon.

You know, as I do, that AKKA depends on the Keeper's mind to operate. Stephen Orco could do the same thing because he knew the secrets of AKKA and could cancel out the Keeper's power. So these Ka'slaq either know about AKKA or have some other mental or physical powers we cannot comprehend. They say an attempt to use the other "ultimate weapon," the geofractors at contra-Pluto, was blocked by a force screen!

Maybe now you can see how critical things really are, Dave. If we can't beat these guys in a fleet action—and you've got to wonder if we have a prayer of that, with everything else that's gone wrong—we're in *trouble*. "A mortal lot of it," as old Giles Habibula would have said.

So *be careful*. And try not to let Merros get to you—I know he's not been your best friend in the service. But they can't spare Commander Damor, Dad, or Admiral-General Derron yet, and Merros has the seniority. He's a good man, even if he does get rabid when he hears the name "Ulnar."

I can't say it often enough—be careful. And good hunting.

Your friend and kinsman,
James Star

Upon completing this section, go to section 2.

— 2 —

Vice-Admiral David Ulnar, commanding the Ninth Defense Squadron on the Orion Frontier of the Star League, reads his new orders for the third time with a growing unease. Star's enclosure has made it clear that the Legion of Space is about to face the most awesome opponent since the attack of the Cometeers

Section 2

nearly a century and a half ago, and Ulnar is the man who must meet them first. Though his grandfather married a granddaughter of the legendary John Star, the Ulnar name is still associated all too strongly with the Purple Throne and with Eric the Pretender, who sold out his own people to the alien Medusae in his mad quest to claim an empire. Loyal men with the Ulnar name have been paying the price ever since, and anything short of total success will call forth all the old suspicions and accusations of David Ulnar's head.

Even the Legion plays the game of politics. Ulnar has been ordered to fight the aliens, and his decisions can win or lose the campaign. But Merros, long-time enemy and rival, stands ready to step in as Ulnar's superior. If he fails, David Ulnar is a scapegoat, another failure in a long line of traitors and incompetents; such is the reputation of a once-proud family. But if he succeeds, Merros can claim the credit. For a time Ulnar considers resigning his command, but that, too, would tarnish the family name still further.

He calls up a computer record of the ships at his command and a star chart of the frontier worlds threatened by the aliens. Here at the main Legion base of St. Germaine, Ulnar's Ninth Defense Squadron stands ready. But there are at least five frontier worlds in easy range of S.C. (Star catalogue) 170, where the Ka'slaq have already struck. What is his best response to their threat? How should he deploy to meet them?

Examine the map. Each named world is a League colony or a planet explored by humanity. Worlds where ships are initially stationed are noted; only by visiting a planet in person can Ulnar add the ships there to his own force or order them to move in any way. When the story opens, Ulnar commands the squadron at St. Germaine and can order it to move to any of the named systems. He can also order ships under his command to split off and garrison other systems, where they must remain until he personally reattaches them to his main squadron.

Information on the various planets can be obtained by going to the section numbers located in parentheses on Map 1. If Ulnar wishes to move the entire force under his command to a specific world, the entry for that planet gives further instructions for subsequent sections or events which follow.

If Ulnar wishes to strengthen other garrisons by detaching ships from his fleet, record the number and types of ships detached

Section 2

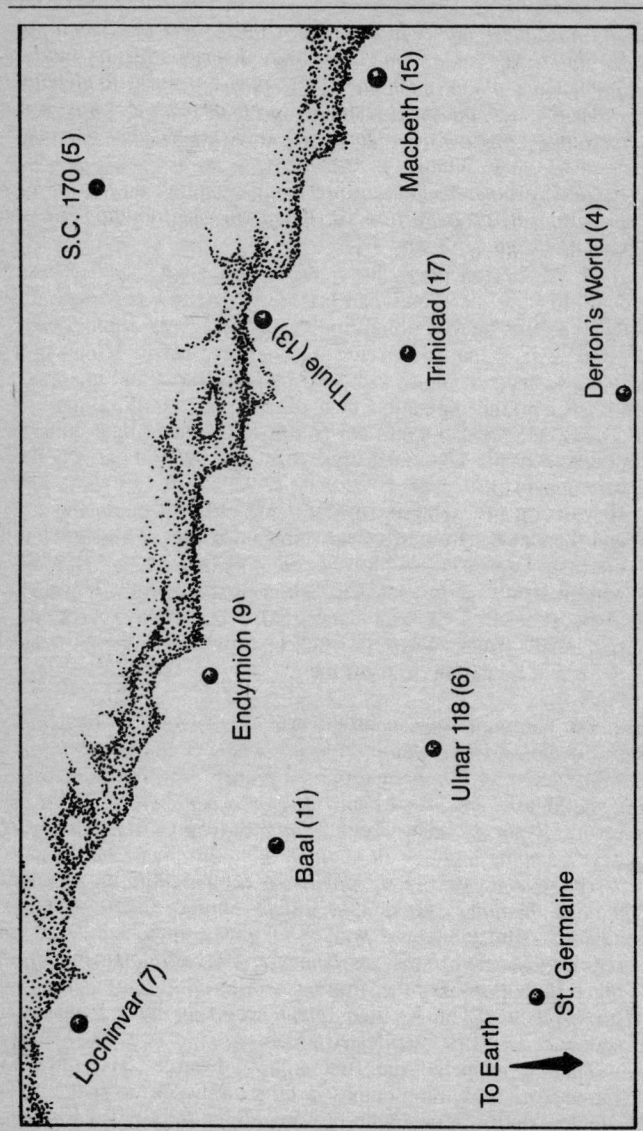

NINTH SECTOR

- S.C. 170 (5)
- Macbeth (15)
- Thule (13)
- Trinidad (17)
- Derron's World (4)
- Endymion (9)
- Baal (11)
- Ulnar 118 (6)
- Lochinvar (7)
- St. Germaine

To Earth →

and note these additional garrisons on a sheet of scratch paper for later reference. Garrisons may help worlds to hold out against the aliens if Ulnar's fleet is not present to defend it. Ulnar must still choose a destination from among the named worlds for himself and whatever forces he keeps under his command.

If Ulnar decides to look up further information on the forces at his disposal, go to section 10. When you are familiar with your command, go to section 3.

— 3 —

Studying the situation and reviewing both forces and options at his disposal, Ulnar realizes that St. Germaine is the key to the entire sector. If the planet were to fall, the loss of the geofractor complex in the star system would cut his fleet off from Merros and the incoming reinforcements and effectively isolate the Ninth Defense Squadron. Moreover, the military and governmental administration centers and the large planetary population all need to be protected. St. Germaine's position makes it possible to respond to whatever reports come in regarding alien movements if the Ka'slaq fleet does not choose to concentrate on this vital target.

The admiral issues his orders accordingly, posting the ships of the Ninth Defense Squadron retained under his command, and the vessels of St. Germaine's permanent garrison as well, in strategic positions to spot alien incursions and report to his own central reserves. The Legion settles down to await further developments.

The worst part of any defensive campaign is the agony of waiting, and the weeks that follow remind Ulnar of the old saying, "Hurry up and wait." Incoming merchant ships and regular ultrawave messages from the garrison commanders and other authorities on the frontier worlds all bring nothing but routine news. The Ka'slaq threat seems to have vanished as suddenly as it first manifested itself.

Then it happens—the first sign of trouble. The ultrawave signal from Endymion comes in faint and weak, as if the power supplies there are uncertain or a huge high-gravity field is creating interference in the transmission. But despite the fading and

Section 3

surging waves of interference that break up his words, Captain Don Larno of the *Audacious* gets enough of his message across to tell Ulnar everything he needs to know.

" . . . to HQ, Endymion garri—HQ . . . alien ships . . . hundred or more . . . from . . . frontier. Garrison out . . . to hold them until . . . forcements. . . . Like a giant planet . . . mobile . . . death ship . . . Cometeers. Repeating: Endymion garrison to . . . spotted alien . . . a hundred . . . coming in from beyond . . . tier. Outnumbered, but we'll try to hold . . . send reinforcements. Most targets cruiser size, but one is like . . . planetoid, except it's mobile . . . a death . . . worse than the comet. . . . Repeating . . ."

But it repeats no further; after the second version of the message, the power from the Endymion communications station fades out for good.

In the face of this message, Ulnar once again ponders the proper dispositions to meet the Ka'slag threat. Captain Larno said he'd try to hold until reinforcements arrive, but the admiral cannot be sure that Endymion can hold out. The squadron can rush to Larno's aid, but risks allowing the aliens to penetrate deeper. But if Ulnar continues to wait at St. Germaine and the Ka'slaq choose a different destination, another world may fall while the Legion waits idle. Can Ulnar outguess the invaders and block their attack?

If Ulnar chooses to remain at St. Germaine, go to section 12.

If Ulnar chooses to go to Endymion, go to section 20.

If Ulnar chooses to go to Baal, go to section 18.

If Ulnar orders his ships to travel to S.C. 170, go to section 68.

If Ulnar chooses to go to any other destination, go to section 14.

Ulnar is free to detach ships to strengthen other garrisons, as before. He is also free to take the mobile elements of the St. Germaine garrison with him when he departs, adding those ships to his squadron. Go to section 10 for a review of the garrisons at various worlds, remembering to add any forces already detached from Ulnar's squadron.

On a piece of scratch paper, note the fact that twenty days have elapsed waiting at St. Germaine.

— 4 —

Derron's World is a small, recently opened colony in the first stages of settlement. Discovered by Mors Derron during his exploration of the frontier region sixty years ago, the planet is notable as a mineralogical treasure house. Exploitation of the planet's natural resources, which include substantial deposits of precious metals, industrial-grade gems, and radioactives, is expected to make the colony self-sufficient (and highly profitable) in a very short time.

Currently only about five hundred colonists are on the planet, most of them miners sent to open the world prior to the arrival of other settlers. Despite its vast potential value to the League, Derron's World is not yet considered an important colony since even the equipment necessary to exploit it has not been entirely deployed. There is no Legion garrison to defend the system, and no major facilities of strategic, economic, or political significance are located in the system.

If Ulnar orders the ships under his command to travel to Derron's World, go to section 25.

If the admiral remains undecided and wishes to review his available options further, go to section 8.

— 5 —

S.C. 170 lies outside the bounds arbitrarily established for the League of Worlds. Ken Star first surveyed this Class G star system during his third exploration of the Orion frontier and noted it as a likely prospect for future expansion. However, development along the Orion Frontier has been slow, and the planet has not yet been scheduled for settlement or development.

The computer record does not contain the latest information on S.C. 170, but briefing material included in Ulnar's orders does. Five lightly armed exploratory vessels—*Pioneer, Discovery, Humbolt, New Horizons,* and *Cook*—were dispatched to conduct

Section 6

a detailed survey of S.C. 170 as the first step toward opening the planet to new colonists. Three months into their mission the ships were attacked with provocation by the alien Ka'slaq. Only *Pioneer* escaped, having suffered severe damage in the process. *Discovery* was crippled and taken in tow by two of the alien ships, so presumably the Ka'slaq have access to all of her computer files as well as any information known to the survivors captured on board. Whether or not they possess the means to translate and act on this data is unknown, but a worst-case assumption must be accepted until evidence to the contrary turns up.

Presumably S.C. 170's planets have been occupied by the invaders, and elements of their fleet may well be present there. It is also possible that the hulks of the Legion expedition' ships remain and might contain more information regarding the aliens, but this is uncertain.

If Ulnar decides to take his fleet to S.C. 170 to investigate the alien attack firsthand, go to section 30.

If Ulnar remains undecided and wishes to spend more time reviewing his options, go to section 8.

— 6 —

Ulnar 118 was first surveyed by Lars Ulnar, Admiral Ulnar's famous grandfather, in company with the equally renowned Ken Star during an early sweep of the region. A harsh wilderness world with a hellish environment, this planet circles a Class F star at a distance too close for human comfort.

Although it lies deep inside the League frontier, Ulnar 118 has never been settled. The planetary surveys yielded no signs of worthwhile resources, and the extreme heat, fierce winds, and dust-swept rocks make it a poor candidate for settlement. Thus, even though the world is technically classed as a marginally Earthlike planet—with native plant and animal life of sorts, and an oxygen atmosphere—it has always been regarded as a "poor relation" among the worlds of the Ninth Sector.

Section 7

If Ulnar decides to visit this deserted, hostile world, go to section 63.

If Ulnar remains undecided and wishes to review his options further, go to section 8.

— 7 —

Lochinvar is a flourishing colony world on the edge of League space, and one of the first planets in the sector to be explored and settled. The original expedition, out of Farhaven in neighboring Sector 8, was commanded by John Samdu, younger son of the great admiral-general of the early days of the Expansion.

Samdu's colony was established as a haven for rugged individualists who resented the commercial exploitation of Farhaven (settled a few years earlier by Samdu to escape overcivilized Earth). For many years the colony remained small, self-isolated, and fiercely independent. Even the discovery of luxenite crystals, the beautiful gemstones that subsequently became a major trade item, was at first suppressed in hopes of preserving the planet's isolation from other worlds. It wasn't until the Great Plague thirty-one years ago, when the population declined by seventy percent in one year, that the old traditions of self-reliance broke down. Calls for medical aid, imported food, and other assistance attracted League attention to Lochinvar, and shortly thereafter word of the gems leaked out. Waves of fortune-hunting colonists quickly filled the void left by the Plague, although many of these succumbed to the lingering remnants of the disease themselves.

The colony has since diversified, although the luxenite crystals remain the major source of off-world wealth. A stable if still somewhat underpopulated planet, Lochinvar is important as the lateral communications link to Sector 8. Legion ships are stationed there, as well as a small ground force to protect the League communications station and the Medical Research center, one of the largest such facilities along the frontier.

If Admiral Ulnar orders the ships under his command to Lochinvar, go to section 25.

If he wishes to review his options further, turn to section 8.

Section 8

— 8 —

Ulnar shuts off the computer summary of the sector and rubs his eyes, tired and more worried than ever. With the entire sector threatened by the alien armada and only a handful of ships to meet them with, he cannot be sure what to do. Should he rush to Thule, where the enemy is reported to be heading, or Baal, the most heavily populated world in the sector? Do the Ka'slaq know about the mineral wealth of Derron's World? Perhaps they are lingering around S.C. 170, where their first attack took place.

Though the commander's orders are supposed to be classified, news like the Ka'slaq invasion can't be kept secret for long. If Admiral David Ulnar is seen as indecisive in the face of this crisis, it can't help but injure the morale of his men. The Ulnar reputation, still so poor despite the redeeming heroism of men like John Star (born on Ulnar) and David's grandfather Lars, is to blame for the delicate state of the men's morale. Uncertainty, hesitation, defeat—any one of them can be a problem. Hotheads like Commodore Benbo, the recon wing commander, would be quick to exploit the slightest weakness on his part.

With a sigh Ulnar leans forward again to flick on the computer screen and resume his work. He knows that he must start issuing decisive orders soon. Once more he plunges into reports and summaries, knowing well that his decision could be crucial to the safety of League and Legion alike.

Continue to examine material, and plan to take action. Map 1 is consulted as before. (See section 2) Each time that this section is chosen, however, there is a chance of trouble. Roll two six-sided dice.

If the total rolled is the same or less than the fleet's Morale value, there is no ill effect and the decision process continues uninterrupted.

If the roll is greater than the fleet's Morale value, go to section 24.

To review the dispositions of Legion forces in the Ninth Sector, consult section 10.

— 9 —

Endymion is a small colony world near the edge of the League frontier, most notable for its extensive port facilities. The planet is a major scout base, the jump-off point for expeditions into the unknown. The settlement of Endymion is less than fifty years old and primarily centers on the port and base complexes.

The Endymion colony is protected by a small Legion garrison, mostly made up of recon ships not currently employed for exploratory voyages. The garrison commander there, Captain Don Larno, is the son of the colony's governor-general, and a former protégé of Ulnar's, who can be counted on to back up his admiral in any situation.

Ulnar can also note that the five ships ambushed at S.C. 170 originally came from Endymion. The capture of one of them, *Discovery*, in the Ka'slaq assault suggests that they might look upon Endymion as a major target.

If Ulnar decides to shift his fleet to Endymion, go to section 16.

If Ulnar remains undecided and wishes to spend more time reviewing his options, go to section 8.

— 10 —

Legion Space Forces

Ninth Sector
Vice-Admiral David Ulnar, commanding

Ninth Defense Squadron, battle wing (St. Germaine)
 7 battlecruisers
  Valiant (flag of Vice-Admiral D. Ulnar)
  Dauntless
  Intrepid
  Legionaire
  Vigilant
  Protector
  Avenger

Section 10

Ninth Defense Squadron, recon wing (St. Germaine)
  10 destroyers
    Corsair (broad pendant of Commodore N. Benbo)
    Freedom
    Kalam
    Star
    Fox
    Voyager
    Hawk
    Juno
    Gorgon
    Rama
St. Germaine Garrison (St. Germaine)
  2 battlecruisers, 2 destroyers, orbital fortress
    Endeavor (BC)
    Triumph (BC)
    Lightning (DD)
    Wotan (DD)
Baal Garrison (Baal)
  3 battlecruisers, 2 destroyers, orbital fortress
    Dreadnought (BC)
    Glorious (BC)
    Defiant (BC)
    Lancer (DD)
    Anthar (DD)
Lochinvar Garrison (Lochinvar)
  2 battlecruisers, 1 destroyer
    Invincible (BC)
    Steadfast (BC)
    Mongoose (DD)
Endymion Garrison (Endymion)
  1 battlecruiser, 5 destroyers
    Audacious (BC)
    Avernus (DD)
    Reiver (DD)
    Arrow (DD)
    Falcon (DD)
    Dragon (DD)
Thule Garrison (Thule)
  3 destroyers
    Viking (DD)
    Hind (DD)
    Iris (DD)

Section 10

MacBeth Garrison (MacBeth)
   2 battlecruisers, 1 destroyer, orbital fortress
      Pride (BC)
      Heroic (BC)
      Ranger (DD)

Trinidad Garrison (Trinidad)
   4 battlecruisers, 5 destroyers
      Remise (BC)
      Shield (BC)
      Sentinel (BC)
      Courageous (BC)
      Buccaneer (DD)
      Javelin (DD)
      Hopeful (DD)
      Dart (DD)
      Memnon (DD)

Orbital fortresses are immobile defense complexes defending specific worlds. Although well-armed, their lack of maneuverability means that they cannot effectively engage enemy forces in concert with mobile ships. They are a line of defense to be used separately from mobile ships and cannot be moved between star systems without the use of massive geofractors.

Destroyers are lightly armed, fast ships designed for reconnaisance duties and the exploration of new planets. Their combat role is customarily a screening one, protecting the heavier elements of a squadron until they are ready to strike a decisive blow, or covering a fleet's withdrawal from battle.

The battlecruiser is the standard fighting ship of Legion fleet. Well-armed but comparatively slow, battlecruisers deliver the decisive blows in combat. They also carry contingents of ground troops to restore order on troubled planets and launch surface assaults against the Legion's enemies.

After reviewing these forces, return to the section you came from. Remember to keep track of forces that have been detached from or attached to the groups listed here. A separate sheet of scratch paper should be used for this purpose. Ulnar is always free to detach ships to his present location or absorb garrison ships (not orbital fortresses) into his mobile squadron while in the garrisoned star system. Be sure to also mark off garrison ships when they are destroyed.

— 11 —

Baal is a major colony world of the Ninth Sector. It has the largest population of any of the planets of the region and is the oldest settlement as well. Circling a Class G star at a distance of 89 million miles, Baal has a warm climate which, coupled with a dense, humid atmosphere, supports extensive agriculture. For the most part it is a quiet, pastoral world, but it does feature extensive commercial interests because of its importance as "breadbasket of the Ninth Sector."

As a major hub of the agro trade, Baal's commercial shipping facilities are excellent and its volume of space traffic impressive. Although St. Germaine was chosen as the sector capital over Baal, the planet's value cannot be underestimated. A substantial Legion garrison is maintained there, although three months ago several Baal guardships were transferred to Trinidad to deal with local civil disturbances there.

Currently, League civil space engineers are busy installing a geofractor system in the outer reaches of the Baal system to facilitate transport of the planet's produce to other worlds, including the overpopulated planets of the Inner League.

If Ulnar chooses to move his main fleet to Baal, go to section 43.

If Ulnar remains undecided and wants to spend more time reviewing his options, go to section 8.

— 12 —

Reports on the fall of Endymion begin to filter in within hours of Larno's original report. A few merchant ships and other private vessels on the fringes of the system were able to escape, but none of Larno's outnumbered garrison had a chance. Ultrawave messages, traveling faster than light but still slow over interstellar distances, only gradually unfold the story of the Ka'slaq onslaught.

They came in fast, and in force. Some reports speak of hundreds of ships, each of them identical in size, speed, and

Section 12

devastating weapons. Sweeping into the system at a speed impossible for any human-built ship to match—not because of engineering problems, since geodyne drives could tear up the light-years that separate the stars, but because no human pilot could have handled the precise maneuvers and sudden vector changes these invaders took as routine—the Ka'slaq descended upon Endymion without even pausing to get their bearings. Their every action made it plain they knew every detail of the colony and its defenders.

Larno's tiny squadron did its best, but it was a handful of ships against a horde that easily outnumbered and outgunned the Legion's defenders. No accounts of his actual attack on the main body of the Ka'slaq fleet reach Ulnar's flagship. An ultrapulse scan picked up a single large object the size of an asteroid or small planet in the heart of the enemy fleet, and Larno plunged into the midst of this overwhelming force. Before all contact was lost, Ka'slaq systems all over the star system broke off their attacks for a time, but it wasn't long before they returned with even more ruthless energy than ever.

Endymion was not just attacked, it was devastated, systematically and without the least mercy. Each city, each town, each homestead was blasted by weapons more powerful than the strongest Legion vortex gun. The ruthless campaign of destruction targeted the human colonists with a precision that could only have stemmed from total familiarity with the computer files captured on board the *Discovery*. One report records that the Ka'slaq annihilated one town as its terror-stricken inhabitants were in the middle of a message of surrender. Except for a few lucky ones in fleeing ships, no one in the Endymion system was spared.

And again the aliens, having overwhelmed their opponents, have disappeared from view. Are they still around Endymion? Or have they decided to strike at some other colony? A destroyer operating out of Baal picked up ultrapulse blips on his long-range scanners between Endymion and Baal, but was this the enemy fleet or some natural phenomena? The fate of Endymion makes clear the total inhumanity of the Ka'slaq, and Ulnar is well aware that their campaign of terror has to be stopped before they destroy another hapless planet. But where will they go next? Where should he try to bring them to battle? And is there any hope for his squadron even if he does meet up with this implacable foe?

Section 13

If Ulnar chooses to remain at St. Germaine even after these new reports, go to section 45.

If Ulnar chooses to go to Endymion, go to section 20.

If Ulnar chooses to go to Baal, go to section 50.

If Ulnar orders his squadron to S.C. 170, go to section 30.

If Ulnar chooses to go to any other destination, go to section 44.

Roll one die and add the number of days shown to the time already spent at St. Germaine.

— 13 —

Thule is a small, recently settled colony near the edge of the League's Ninth Sector frontier. Barely a year old, the settlement is primarily a research outpost coupled with a pioneering team's first-phase landing port and survey center. Legion ships have been assigned to Thule to provide assistance for the settlers in opening up the planet to mass colonization.

The planet is the second of a dim, cool class K star, and it has a chilly climate. However, early surveys discovered that an indigenous animal species, dubbed the tundra bison, was potentially valuable as a food source and export item for human colonists. Plans now project the large-scale establishment of ranches and a ranching industry that should rapidly convert the fledgling colony into a going concern, profitable to commercial and governmental interests alike.

Ulnar's records and reports show that the Ka'slaq ships were on course for Thule from S.C. 170 when a Legion ship last tracked them. Though not an important planet by League standards, it would seem that the world may be the most likely target of further enemy operations in the near future.

Cross-references in the base computer files show that Dr. Maja Benbo, director of the research station on Thule, is the sister of Ulnar's second-in-command, Commodore Nils Benbo.

Section 14

If Ulnar chooses to take his forces to meet the expected Ka'slaq occupation of Thule, go to section 25.

If Ulnar remains undecided and wants to spend more time reviewing his options, go to section 8.

— 14 —

Ulnar issues his new orders, marshaling the ships of the Ninth Defense Squadron for a shift to the star system he believes will next come under Ka'slaq domination. Glad to be doing something—*anything*—after the long wait at St. Germaine, the men of the Legion set out in high spirits to foil the alien attack.

By leaving St. Germaine, the squadron puts itself out of direct communication with the other worlds of the sector. Ultrawave messages to and from fast-moving ships are difficult to send over interstellar distances, where an error of a fraction of a degree can hurl the signal trillions of miles off course away from the intended recipient. As a result, the admiral receives little in the way of new information about events at Endymion during his voyage. One brief message from the base at St. Germaine makes it clear, though, that the Endymion colony has been lost. Full reports will await the admiral when he reaches his destination.

Consult the Travel Time Chart. Cross-index Ulnar's point of origin (St. Germaine) with his intended destination; the number given on the chart is the number of days it will take his squadron to reach that world. Add this number to the time spent waiting at St. Germaine before the Endymion report came in.

If the total time spent is thirty-five days or less, go to section 22.

If the total time amounts to thirty-six days or more, go to section 27.

— 15 —

MacBeth, like Baal and St. Germaine, is a sizable and diversified colony. It is a hospitable planet, third from a Class G star, with a climate much like Earth's. Settlement on MacBeth goes back five decades, and the colony is only slightly behind St. Germaine in population.

The MacBeth colonists were initially drawn from the ranks of the PSP (Pan-Stellar Peace) movement, which was at the peak of its support in that period. Members of the PSP group sought to completely lay aside violence and war as an instrument of League policy. Although their political power was strong, it wasn't sufficient to achieve true disarmament (which, among other things, would have required the complete suppression of the secret of AKKA on which the League was founded). They did, however, obtain exclusive rights to settle MacBeth as a model colony run along completely utopian lines.

Following the crop failures ten years ago, food riots and the short-lived coup of Jol Nolar caused the MacBeth colonists to request Legion intervention. After Nolar's dictatorship was eliminated, a Legion garrison was permanently established in the MacBeth system to help the colonists make a smooth transition to a less utopian but more successful social structure.

The planet has no major military bases or other League facilities. It has little real strategic value, but the population of the planet and its trade ties to the Fifteenth Sector make it a world of some importance in Legion planning.

If Ulnar chooses to move his forces to the MacBeth system, go to section 25.

If Ulnar remains undecided and wishes to review his options further, go to section 8.

— 16 —

Although reports suggest Thule as a likely target for the Ka'slaq fleet, Ulnar has to take other factors into account. The capture of one of five ships at S.C. 170 suggests the possibility, at least, that the aliens have access to the computer records that ship carried. If so, Endymion's prominence as an exploratory base—and the point of origin of the human expedition—makes it a much more likely military target than Thule. At any rate, Endymion offers a better position for covering other vital worlds in the region than most of the other possible destinations.

With this in mind Vice-Admiral Ulnar issues his orders, assembling the ships he needs for the eighteen-day voyage from St. Germaine to Endymion. Ponderous battlecruisers and darting, agile destroyers move slowly out of orbit, cut in their faster-than-light geodyne engines, and speed toward their destination at a pace hard to understand or even imagine.

Eighteen long days in interstellar space pass with maddening slowness. The nature of ultrawave communications makes it difficult to receive more than fragmentary information from any of the worlds of the Ninth Sector; an error of a degree or two in the alignment of transmitters can throw a message at a point light-years from the intended recipient, and the excessive speeds of the geodyne-powered ships makes it even harder to get an accurate fix. In effect, the fleet is cut off from outside contact, from information, orders, or warnings from the star systems that are Ulnar's responsibility. If the choice he has made is wrong, Ulnar won't learn about it until his ships actually reach Endymion and sort through the messages already relayed there, because ultrawave communications are much faster than ships, and they operate efficiently between the predictable orbital coordinates of individual worlds.

As they approach Endymion the ships train their ultrawave receivers ahead; the closer they get, the more chance they have of picking up messages. But the receivers don't pick up any intelligible transmissions—only a steadily increasing and disturbing kind of ultrawave static. One day out from Endymion this static begins to show distinctly artificial patterns and pulses. When the squadron is nearly two hours from planetfall, the static lifts long enough for a weak, fuzzy signal to come through from the garrison.

Section 16

"Endymion garrison to HQ, Endymion garrison to HQ. We have spotted alien ships numbering a hundred or more, coming in from beyond the frontier. Garrison outnumbered, but we'll try to hold them until you can send reinforcements. Most targets are cruiser size, but one is like a giant, mobile planetoid. It's some kind of a death ship, even worse than the Cometeers. Repeating . . ." The message plays again before being swallowed up in static.

"Detector status!" Ulnar rasps from his flag display at the rear of *Valiant*'s bridge.

"Ultrapulse radar systems jammed by interference, Admiral," a young officer replies quickly. "Teleperiscopes operable, but at this range—"

"Get those ultrapulse units working, Captain," Ulnar orders. "We have to see what's going on!"

Captain Sammis, his sharp features set in a dour frown, nods. His stiff bearing and gruff orders to his bridge crew convey his dislike of having the admiral spell out his duty. Ulnar ignores him. Don Larno, captain of the battlecruiser *Audacious* and commander of Endymion's tiny garrison squadron, is facing a vastly superior enemy on his own, and Ulnar is impatient to come to the aid of one of his most loyal friends. Nothing else matters.

"Ultrapulse display coming on line now, sir," the same young officer reports.

The tactical tank beside Ulnar's position comes alive with a confusion of faint lights and traces, some flickering madly. Distorted by ultrawave interference, the signals are poorly defined and could be false readings. Still, the picture they paint is grim.

A handful of yellow readouts represent the positions of the six ships of Larno's squadron, still over an hour away at the fleet's best speed. They are almost completely surrounded in the planning tank by red-colored blips, most of them somewhat smaller than a Legion battlecruiser. One fuzzy blob of light can only be Larno's "mobile planetoid."

And Larno's ships, a battlecruiser and a handful of destroyers, are formed up like an arrow streaking right toward the huge vessel.

"Can we raise the *Audacious*?" Ulnar asks.

Sammis gestures to the crewman manning the communications station. Like a well-oiled machine, *Valiant*'s bridge crew works

Section 16

together with effortless efficiency, with very little chatter and few spoken orders.

Minutes pass, and the symbols in the display tank continue to creep inexorably together. Ulnar opens his mouth to give vent to his impatience.

But Sammis beats him to it. "Wish there was a way to get around the ultrawave time lag," he mutters.

Embarrassed at forgetting something so basic to space travel, Ulnar checks his impatience and concentrates on the planning tank and the smooth, perfectly coordinated movements of each of the enemy ships. No Legion fleet could ever hope to duplicate such absolutely precise maneuvering. Larno's ships don't stand a chance against such teamwork.

"We have contact," the communications technician announces suddenly.

"Patch me in," Ulnar orders. At the crewman's nod, Ulnar turns toward the plotting tank and speaks into the microphone on the console near him. "*Audacious*, this is Flag. Break off the action, Larno . . . break off. You can't fight a whole fleet for an hour or more!"

There is another interminable wait as Ulnar's words, converted into the faster-than-light medium of ultrawave signals, race through space toward Larno's ships. Over these comparatively short distances there is less trouble in aiming messages, but they still take several minutes to cross the distance between the two battlecruisers. Ordinary radio messages, at this range, would take weeks.

Finally Larno's relaxed voice, almost unrecognizable against the background of static, breaks the silence. Ulnar knows he is hearing the voice of a man resigned to death.

"*Audacious* to Flag. Negative on your request—"

"It's not a request, damn it, it's an order!" Ulnar cuts in loudly before he realizes his words won't be heard aboard the other battlecruiser for several more minutes. Seething, he picks up the thread of Larno's message again.

"Can't fight them all, but we can't run either—those beauties are *fast*. My best estimate says that planetoid thing is some kind of flagship. If we can get in a couple of good shots with the vortex guns . . . well, it's all we've got. I can't fight dogfights with a hundred ships and expect to do much of anything.

There is a long pause, and for a moment Ulnar thinks Larno's transmission is done. Suddenly Larno's voice cuts in again, flat and emotionless. "Dave . . . tell Kay—"

Section 16

All at once a shriek of melting electronics cuts off his words. Ulnar doesn't need to see the fading light in the planning tank to know that Larno and the *Audacious* are gone. Don Larno's last message to his wife would never be finished.

Two other Legion ships vanish from the display at the same time. The tiny garrison squadron is falling apart under the enemy onslaught. For a moment Ulnar thinks the enemy ships on the display are becoming uncoordinated in their movements, but suddenly draw back into flawless formations and proceed to destroy the other ships of Larno's squadron. The cloud of Ka'slaq craft seem to coalesce around the larger vessel like a swarm of insects around a lantern. But as the last of the Legion destroyers vanishes from the display, the alien fleet begins to spread out once more, some closing on Endymion's undefended globe, others remaining clustered around the slow-moving planetoid. Another wave, perhaps a third of the total enemy force, turns on a new course—directly toward Ulnar's squadron.

Ulnar hunches forward in his seat, his mind racing furiously. Caution battles a thirst for vengeance as he contemplates the possibility of engaging the Ka'slaq here and now. Larno's force was overwhelmed; if the same fate overtakes Ulnar's squadron now, the whole of the Ninth Sector is opened up to the aliens. But the need to strike a blow in Larno's name is almost too strong to ignore. As the enemy ships close with incredible speed, Ulnar is well aware of the responsibility that hangs over his head like a sharpened blade, threatening not only himself and the men who serve in his handful of ships, but the entire League and Legion who lie behind them.

If Ulnar orders the squadron to engage the enemy fleet, go to section 21.

If Ulnar orders the squadron to avoid the enemy fleet but attack the planetoid, go to section 23.

If Ulnar orders his ships to avoid the enemy fleet but attack the alien force approaching Endymion proper, go to section 26.

If Ulnar orders the Ninth Squadron to stand its ground and defend itself, go to section 28.

If Ulnar orders his command to withdraw, go to section 32.

Section 16

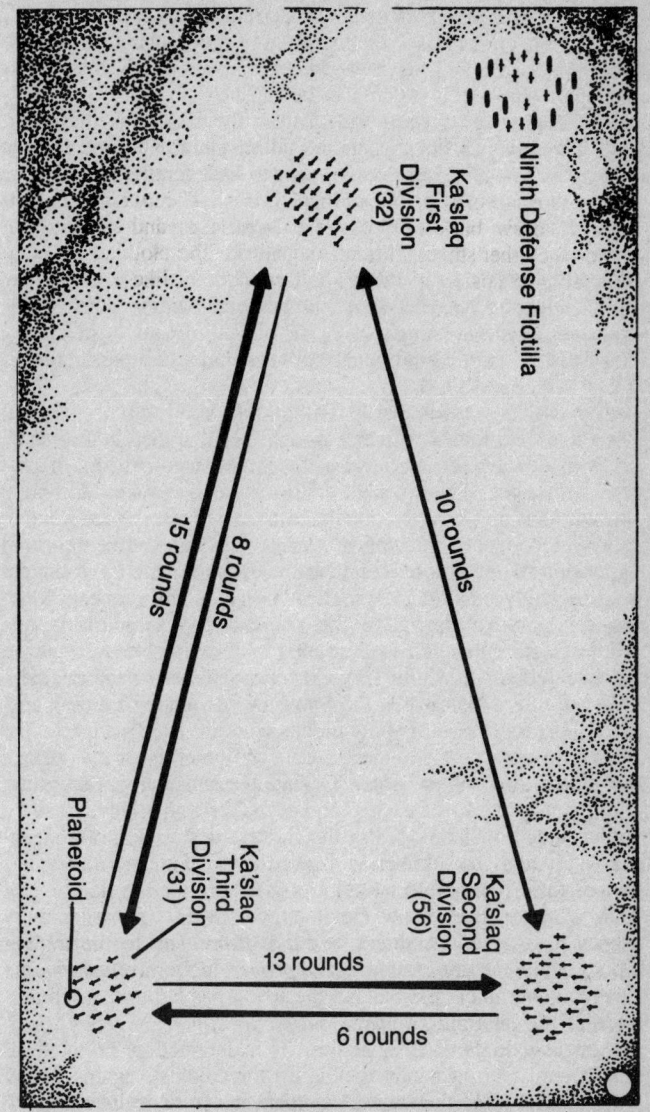

BATTLE OF ENDYMION

Section 17

— 17 —

Trinidad is the biggest troublespot of Ulnar's Ninth Sector. Fifth planet of a Class F star, the planet's highly eccentric orbit makes for extreme changes in climate and geography over the course of one of the planet's long "years." The human colonists planted on the world a decade ago were forced to settle under immense domes that protected them from the worst dangers of radically variable temperatures and dramatic changes in the level of the planet's seas between summer and winter. Some dome cities are undersea complexes in the hottest months of periastron and isolated, land-bound outposts in the midst of a barren tundra when winter sets in.

The settlers were drawn to Trinidad by the discovery of great deposits of exploitable mineral wealth, easily mined during some portions of the year, because of the accelerated process of erosion which goes hand in hand with the harsh climate. Although the world is not heavily populated, it has drawn a fairly large influx of colonists pursuing golden opportunities. But the rapid expansion of the colony combined with the hostile environment to completely outstrip the progress of scouts and pioneers looking for possible threats to the community. As a result, the colonists are entangled in a strange and inexpiable war with a native intelligence whose very existence had been unsuspected.

These aliens, known as the Snow Devils among the humans, are a monstrous race of spiny bipeds who estivate throughout the periastron period of Trinidad's orbit and emerge on the surface during the long, bitter winter. Despite the handicaps of spending significant portions of each year asleep, the Snow Devils have a sophisticated civilization. But the careless destruction of a sleeping vault and its slumbering occupants by human miners has earned their implacable hatred. As a result, for the duration of each winter period Snow Devil attacks against human colony domes pose a serious threat to the settlers—and to the mining work. Diplomacy has failed totally, but a stubborn refusal by the League government to abandon the world has led to the continuation of the intermittent war.

A sizable force of League ships is maintained at Trinidad all year round. During winter they assist the colonists against Snow Devil attacks, and the summer is spent in efforts to locate Snow Devil lairs and so spot their probable bases for the next cam-

Section 18

paign. A proposal to neutralize these lairs has been blocked in the League Council as being nothing short of genocide.

Currently, it is the hot periastron summer period on Trinidad, which means that the ships can be spared from their duties there to serve with Ulnar's fleet if the need arises.

Trinidad's resources could make it an important strategic target. The Legion cannot discount the possibility that the Ka'slaq might seek some kind of alliance with the Snow Devils. Their fleet could well need the support of a technological civilization, and they could choose to support the Ka'slaq as the best weapon against the human interlopers who have so aroused their fury.

If Ulnar decides to order his ships to travel to Trinidad, go to section 25.

If Ulnar remains undecided and wishes to review his options further, go to section 8.

— 18 —

There are several other planets in immediate danger, but no one world is as important as Baal. The key planet of the sector, with its large population and major trade links with other key planets, Baal is the obvious next choice for a Ka'slaq assault if they know anything about the League. The assault on Endymion suggests that the Ka'slaq knew, presumably from records or captives aboard the lost *Discovery* at S.C. 170, that Endymion was the nearest Legion port and base.

Convinced that Baal is the best choice for the Ka'slaq, Ulnar knows it will take both luck and speed to win the race and bring the Ninth Squadron to the defense of Baal. The Ka'slaq are closer, but if they linger around Endymion, the Legion ships might just reach the planet in time to block the enemy advance. No time can be spared; Ulnar issues the orders that will set the squadron in motion at last with scarcely a pause to consider the dangers of the situation.

Accelerating out of orbit, the Ninth Squadron gathers speed as the great geodyne engines run up to their maximum output. Using their power to distort the very fabric of space itself, the ships slide past the speed of light to velocities no human mind

Section 18

could grasp, and shape their course for Baal. But even at these awesome speeds it is an eleven-day journey from St. Germaine to Baal, and that leaves plenty of time for plans, doubts, and second thoughts.

The fleet is cut off from any but the briefest of contacts with the worlds of the sector. Ultrawave transmissions between planets are easy enough because the coordinates of each are well-known and relative motions comparatively low, but the uncertainties of speed and distance between moving ships make communications difficult. Even an error of a degree or two in antenna alignment can cause a transmission to miss the intended recipient by trillions of miles. Except at fairly short ranges or under unusual circumstances, it is almost impossible to broadcast substantial messages to or from a moving ship in interstellar space.

Thus, Ulnar has very little to go on as he lays his plans during the voyage. Except for Larno's first message, he has no information on events at Endymion and no way of knowing what to expect at Baal. But as the squadron finally draws near its destination, it makes contact and begins updating information relayed over the past eleven days from the base at St. Germaine to Baal, as well as news gathered locally.

The word from Endymion is grim. None of Larno's ships escaped, but a few merchant vessels on the fringes of the system were able to watch what happened before they fled. The Ka'slaq onslaught was fast, utterly ruthless, and totally devastating. There were at least one hundred ships (Larno's original estimate, and probably the most accurate), although some reports speak of several hundred, all identical in size, speed, and bearing incredibly powerful weapons. The ships swept into the system at a speed no human ship would have dared maintain (not because human ships couldn't move that fast, but because human pilots couldn't handle the precise maneuvers and sudden vector changes the invaders evidently regarded as routine), and closed in on Endymion almost before anyone was aware of their presence. Their actions made it clear that the Ka'slaq knew every detail of the Endymion colony and its defenses.

According to the reports, the large body of enemy cruisers was followed by one other object, which ultrapulse scans reported as a huge, slow-moving structure the size of a planetoid or small moon. Larno's scanners must have picked up the same data, because the last reported act of the tiny garrison force was a headlong rush into the heart of the enemy fleet, aimed straight at

Section 18

the huge object. The threat was enough to draw off some of the Ka'slaq ships, which closed in on Larno's force with inhuman accuracy and wiped out all the ships before they could either reach the large target or break off and flee. But the slackening attack didn't die away for long; soon the aliens were back in force. There was nothing left to stand in their way.

The Ka'slaq didn't just overawe the helpless colony—they systematically devastated it. Endymion's cities and towns were reduced from orbit without the slightest trace of mercy or a single offer of acceptance of quarter. One town was apparently destroyed even as the inhabitants sent a panic-stricken message of total surrender. Ka'slaq weapons, more powerful than the best vortex guns in the Legion's arsenal, picked off inhabited areas one after another, from the largest town to the newest homestead. It was clear that the aliens had a detailed summary of human habitation on the planet, which made it even more likely that the Ka'slaq had cracked the computer files aboard the captured *Discovery*. A few lucky colonists escaped in merchant ships, but no human escaped from the holocaust at Endymion.

No one knows what happened there; the Ka'slaq might have remained, or they may have moved on to new conquests.

They have not yet taken Baal, although patrol ships operating away from the colony in the direction of Endymion have sent in some disturbing reports. Ultrapulse scans have picked up fuzzy images at the very limit of detection range on a course toward Baal. Some kind of previously unknown ultrawave band static has also been detected in that direction, prompting the captain of the battlecruiser *Defiant* to follow up the reports with a personal reconnaissance. Evidently Ulnar has arrived in time, but just barely . . . if, indeed, these reports are of enemy ships and not more refugees or some other anomaly unconnected with the Ka'slaq.

By the time the squadron makes orbit around Baal, the static reported by the patrols is noticeable to everyone and has begun interfering with communications and ultrapulse scans. The scanners still work, but they aren't very reliable. Several blips have appeared swooping toward the planet, but the distortion makes it hard to gather more than the most basic ideas of speed, headings, and size. Two ships—the destroyer *Anthar* and the battlecruiser *Defiant*—are overdue and still out of contact, and everyone in the squadron is growing increasingly concerned about the situation.

Section 18

"Ultrapulse reports two friendly ships at the limit of detection range," an officer announces.

Ulnar, feigning calm by sipping from a mug of coffee, hands it to a steward and swivels his seat to command a view of *Valiant*'s tactical planning tank, where ultrapulse data is translated by computer to readouts. Moving at maximum speed, the two yellow blips are identified as a battlecruiser and a destroyer. Ulnar watches as the computers update the information and transponder signals identify the two vessels: *Defiant* and *Anthar*, as everyone hoped.

A ragged cheer starts from the crewmen on the bridge, but it dies away quickly. Ultrapulse scans show a whole phalanx of blue-covered lights, representing unknown and presumably hostile ships, closing fast on the two Legion vessels. Ulnar needn't see more to know that tha Ka'slaq have arrived.

"*Defiant* on line, Admiral," the communications technician reports.

"Put it through." Ulnar turns to face the microphone and comm screen on the Flag command console. The screen flickers to life, broken up by static but revealing the strained features of a young captain with a scorched uniform collar and a bleeding gash across one cheek.

"Flag, this is *Defiant*. Enemy ships pursuing. They'll reach your position soon. Too many for us to stop." The captain rubs at the blood on his face. "There's more of them than anyone thought. We took a grazing hit, with one geodyne damaged and fifty men killed or wounded. Flag, Admiral, we can't fight them. . . ."

The captain begins to ramble, his confused words and dazed expression making plain his anguish and fear. *Defiant*'s captain knows his ship is doomed.

"Energy pulse from target 027," a voice calls out from somewhere behind the battlecruiser's captain. "That means they're—" With a flash of light and the sound of melting electronics, the battlecruiser is hit again.

"Pax External," someone on *Valiant*'s bridge mutters. Ulnar drops his eyes to the planning tank, where the symbols that represent *Defiant* as a battlecruiser under power are fading out. Something there still returns a faint ultrapulse echo amidst the lifeless hulk drifting silently through space.

Almost as if an afterthought, an anticlimax following the death of the *Defiant*, the smaller dot that represents the destroyer winks out a few moments later. The Ka'slaq destroyed the smaller ship so thoroughly that no trace remains to bounce back ultrapulse signals.

Ulnar stares at the tank for a long minute, watching thirty blue symbols creep toward the squadron, and, behind the Legion's protective shield, Baal. Two more ships are gone, and the implacable aliens continue their remorseless advance. Ulnar wonders for a moment if it would be better to fight and die or flee and face the shame of running without a fight.

Then, as he stares down at the planning tank, Ulnar feels a dawning resolve. He knows what he should do and how to make it work. All that remains is to give the necessary orders.

If Ulnar decides to attack the Ka'slaq fleet, go to Section 33.

If Ulnar decides to remain near Baal to defend it from attack, go to section 37.

If Ulnar decides to abandon Baal, go to section 41.

— 19 —

St. Germaine has the second largest population of all the League worlds in the Ninth Sector. Fourth planet of a Class F star, it has a cool, pleasant climate which has attracted extensive settlement from Inner League worlds. First surveyed by the exploration team headed by Ken Star and Lars Ulnar, it continues to support a Legion defense complex and scout base. The Ninth Defense Squadron is headquartered at St. Germaine.

As capital of the Ninth sector and center for both League and Legion activities in this segment of the frontier, St. Germaine has an important place in the strategic planning for Legion military operations in the Ninth Sector. It is the major military bastion of the area, with significant ground- and space-based defenses. A geofractor complex ties St. Germaine to Earth and other inner worlds, making the planet the main link for military, exploratory, and commercial traffic connecting the frontier with major League planets.

Section 20

If Ulnar orders the ships under his command to remain on station at St. Germaine and await further developments, go to section 3.

If Admiral Ulnar remains undecided and wishes to review his options further, go to section 8.

— 20 —

Ulnar is well aware of how slim Don Larno's chances of survival are at Endymion. Even at the maximum possible speed, the Ninth Defense Squadron cannot reach Endymion in less than eighteen days. Against a fleet numbering a hundred ships or more, the beleaguered garrison had little hope of survival, barring some kind of miracle. Now Ulnar regrets his caution in keeping his reserves at St. Germaine; if he had been closer to the frontier, there might have been a chance of helping Larno in time.

Ulnar thinks his best move now is to descend on Endymion in force. If the Ka'slaq are still in the system, the Legion can catch them and exact a measure of revenge. And if the main fleet has gone on, the squadron can interrupt their supply lines and draw back the main Ka'slaq strength from wherever it attacks next. Lingering in the back of Ulnar's mind is the faint, irrational hope that the Endymion garrison might somehow survive, an impossible hope, perhaps, but the Legion was dedicated to making miracles happen.

Ulnar wastes no more time. Issuing the necessary orders, he waits in his private office as *Valiant* breaks orbit around St. Germaine, followed in turn by the other ships of the squadron. Under the space-twisting energies of their geodyne engines, the Legion's vessels hurtle from their base and gather speed rapidly, freed from the restrictions of inertia and Einsteinian physics by the local distortion in the fabric of the universe created in the bowels of each ship.

The days pass slowly. Cut off from contact with the worlds of the Ninth Sector, the squadron exists like a separate universe. Ultrawave communications are not hampered much by interstellar distances, but a target the size of a spaceship moving at velocities far in excess of light is hard to pinpoint, and harder

Section 20

still to hold in an ultrawave beam. The seemingly endless time that passes en route to Endymion gives everyone aboard too much time to reflect on everything they've heard about their enemies.

In the final few hours of the approach to Endymion, Admiral Ulnar assumes his bridge position overlooking *Valiant*'s tactical plotting tank, where the ship's computers interpret ultrapulse scans and other sensor information and translate these into a simulation of space around the flagship. The tank has remained clear of anything except natural objects—stars, dust clouds, interstellar debris—throughout the voyage, but now, with Endymion only three hours away, an unknown blip registers on ultrapulse. Unpowered and apparently lifeless, the unknown object still bounces back echoes characteristic of a spaceship or other artificial structure.

Cautiously, Ulnar orders one of his ships to move closer for a direct inspection. On teleperiscope the object proves to be a battered, drifting spaceship, a human-designed vessel identified from shipboard files as a private yacht. A boarding party is sent to the yacht. Their report suggests that the vessel was near a massive explosion, a near miss that tore most of the major structural members apart through the force of expanding gases buffeting the yacht, an effect one expert from the party likens to being "on the fringes of a newborn supernova." A weapon that could induce such an effect is far beyond the vortex guns of the Legion ships.

The boarding party learns that the yacht was a private courier in the service of Endymion's colonial government. On board are detailed accounts of everything the ship's crew could collect regarding the fall of Endymion before they were themselves destroyed.

If Ulnar has had no previous information regarding what happened at Endymion (aside from Don Larno's initial message), and he wants to review the information on board the courier/yacht, go to section 42.

If Ulnar waited to receive information about Endymion before leaving St. Germaine and he wants to review it on board the courier/yacht, go to section 46.

If Ulnar chooses to ignore the information contained on the courier/yacht, go to section 51.

On a piece of scratch paper note that eighteen days are used up in the voyage.

— 21 —

"Open Fleetcomm to all ships," Ulnar orders. "Patch it through to my board." Eyes on the planning tank, the admiral runs through everything he has seen and heard so far. If the Ka'slaq have a weakness, it is up to him to find and exploit it.

"On Fleetcomm, Admiral," the communications technician tells him.

Ulnar switches on his microphone. "Flag to Ninth Defense Squadron. Prepare for battle." He pauses, examining the moving lights in the tank that represent enemy ships closing on the squadron at high speed. Ultrapulse interference still makes things uncertain, but there are at least thirty enemy ships on the way, maybe more.

But the Ka'slaq have divided their forces, their first major mistake. Ulnar knows that a divided foe can be defeated in detail where a united one can be too strong to fight.

"We will attack the nearest enemy ships on my signal," the admiral continues. "Formation and battle orders to follow. Stand by."

Clicking off the microphone, Ulnar leans forward to study the tank. The attack formation his ships adopt could be decisive in the battle to come. He has only minutes to decide and marshal his ships for battle.

If Ulnar orders the squadron to adopt a wedge formation, go to section 55.

If Ulnar orders the squadron to adopt a cone formation, go to section 60.

If Ulnar orders the light destroyers to form a screen ahead of the battlecruisers, go to section 65.

If Ulnar orders the squadron to disperse and fight independently, go to section 70.

— 22 —

The fleet is in a stable orbit around the planet as Ulnar goes through the accumulated reports relayed from St. Germaine. They tell the story of Endymion, and as the tale takes form, the admiral begins to realize just how much danger the League and the Legion face from their evil foes.

None of the ships of Larno's garrison force escaped from the battle at Endymion, but a few merchant ships and other private vessels were able to get away and bring back their impressions of the planet's end. The Ka'slaq assault was fast and merciless, and the only ships that had much of a chance were the ones already near the edge of the system.

Larno's report of a hundred enemy ships is the lowest estimate Ulnar hears; the refugees report varying numbers, but all agree that the Ka'slaq armada was immense. Most also agree that ultrapulse scans showed a very large object moving slowly and purposefully in the wake of the alien cruisers. But it was the cruisers that made the biggest impression, all identical in size and speed and each one armed with weapons far more powerful than a Legion vortex gun.

The cruisers were able to carry out maneuvers no human pilot could hope to duplicate. All accounts emphasize their tight formations and high-speed turns, attributable to the Ka'slaq race's superior mental and physical abilities.

Larno's last battle was fought without witnesses. One transmission, punched through massive ultrawave interference, said that the garrison ships were forming to attack the large planetoid object, which Larno thought might be the alien flagship. The Ka'slaq broke off most of their other operations shortly afterward and closed in around Larno's last reported position; the Legion ships never came back.

But the Ka'slaq did. When their cruisers had finished with Larno, the aliens orbited Endymion. Then, without a trace of compassion or a single demand for surrender, they began to bombard the helpless colony. Their attacks showed familiarity with the planet; every town, every homestead on Endymion's surface was systematically wiped out. One town was destroyed even as its leaders pleaded for their lives and asked to be allowed to capitulate. These reports make it clear that the Ka'slaq, having

Section 23

captured the *Discovery* at S.C. 170, were able to crack the ship's computer files and translate the information they contained.

With the flight of the handful of refugees who escaped the destruction of Endymion, there is no more news of the Ka'slaq. Who can tell where they will strike next?

If Ulnar orders his squadron to remain in its current position, go to section 71. Mark seven more days off your time record.

If Ulnar orders the squadron to travel to Endymion, go to section 53.

If Ulnar orders his ships to Baal, go to section 58.

If Ulnar orders his ships to Ulnar 118, go to section 63.

If the admiral orders the squadron to S.C. 170, go to section 68.

If Ulnar's orders send the squadron back to St. Germaine, go to section 74.

If the squadron is given orders to any other destination, go to section 73.

— 23 —

As he absentmindedly rubs his chin, Ulnar considers the events of the last hour. Don Larno's doomed attack had stood no chance of success, but it pointed the way for the Ninth Squadron. Larno had a reputation for solving problems with an almost instinctive grasp of priorities and probabilities. Admiral Ulnar was sure he had done so again.

Two things stand out about Larno's failed thrust toward the enemy: The Ka'slaq had called in all of their outlying ships to stop the Legion force, and there was a short time when the Ka'slaq fleet's superb coordination seemed to fail. These two points suggested that the giant ship or asteroid might be a sensitive point to be exploited by the Ninth Squadron.

"Open Fleetcomm to all ships, and patch it through to me," Ulnar orders, his determination and tactical insight becoming firm.

"On Fleetcomm, Admiral," the communication technician responds quickly.

The admiral casts a last glance into the tank as he switches on the microphone on his console. "Flag to Ninth Defense Squadron. Prepare for battle."

The readouts in the tank are still uncertain from ultrapulse interference, but he can be sure of at least thirty ships in the force closing on his squadron. Between twenty and thirty more are spread around the planetoid, approximately a half hour away. Ulnar nods in sudden decision, drawing a quizzical look from Captain Sammis. They have to follow up on Larno's last insight. He flicks on the microphone again.

"All vessels, Stealth mode. Repeat, Stealth mode. We will evade the nearest alien ships and close on the large object at grid 320. Formation and battle orders to follow. Stand by."

Stealth mode is a chancy tactic at best, given everything Ulnar has seen of Ka'slaq technology. But if the squadron can jam the alien ultrapulse scans, Ulnar's command can swing out of the path of the attackers and slip past them.

"It has to work," Ulnar says softly, drawing another look from Sammis. "It *will* work."

Roll two dice and compare the result to the squadron's Stealth rating.

If the roll is less than or equal to the rating, go to section 52.

If the roll is greater than the rating, go to section 62.

— 24 —

If Commodore Benbo and the Corsair *are with Ulnar's squadron, go to section 31.*

If Benbo's Corsair *has been detached to any other station, go to section 40.*

Section 25

— 25 —

Making up his mind, Ulnar reaches to his desk communications button. "Bridge, this is Ulnar. Inform the squadron that we will be breaking orbit by 1630 hours. Duty officer, begin preparations. Get me Captain Sammis."

Valiant's sharp-featured captain comes on the intercom screen moments later to receive Ulnar's orders from the squadron. He seems surprised at the destination the admiral has chosen, but characteristically accepts the orders without argument.

At the appointed time the ship seems to come to life as the great geodyne engines power up and thrust *Valiant* out of orbit around St. Germaine. The rest of the squadron follows suit. Gathering speed, it points toward its destination and hurtles outward at speeds made possible by space-twisting geodynes.

The admiral has chosen his destination, and he and his ships are committed. Perhaps, he tells himself more than once during the journey, it is a blessing that the squadron can't receive information from St. Germaine or the other worlds of the sector. The vast distances of interstellar space and the unimaginable speeds of ships under geodyne drive make it almost impossible to align antennas and transmit ultrawave messages to a squadron in interstellar space. Thus, although ultrawave communications are much faster than ships, they can be used between planets (with well-known coordinates and relatively slow speeds) much more effectively than to or from vessels.

Effectively, the Ninth Defense Squadron is out of touch until it reaches its destination and can collect messages relayed from HQ during the voyage. Ulnar and his men have no idea what might await them, but already Ulnar has a growing feeling of dread as he goes over the strategic situation again and again throughout the long voyage.

Consult the Travel Time Chart. Cross-index Ulnar's point of origin (St. Germaine) with his intended destination. The number given on the chart is the number of days it will take his ships to reach the chosen planet. Note this number for future reference before proceeding to section 22.

— 26 —

Ulnar rubs his jaw anxiously. His eyes are on the planning tank while his mind runs through calculations of strength and speed. Now that Larno's garrison has been wiped out, Endymion stands helpless before the Ka'slaq assault. About half the alien fleet, as many as fifty ships or more, are closing fast on the planet. At maximum speed the Ninth Squadron might intervene in time to protect the planet, if they can evade the ships already rushing toward them at high speed. The safety of the colony is Ulnar's highest priority right now.

"Open Fleetcomm to all ships," Ulnar orders. "And patch it through to me." As the communications technician complies with the order, Ulnar continues to study the tank. They'll have to use Stealth mode, jamming ultrapulse scans to avoid detection while dodging the aliens detached to deal with the squadron. Given the advanced Ka'slaq technology, the tactic is risky at best, but it's the only chance they have to save Endymion.

The technician finishes his task. "Fleetcomm open, Admiral," he says.

Switching on the microphone on his console, Ulnar issues his orders.

"All ships, this is Flag," he begins. "Prepare for battle. Set course for planetary flyby over Endymion." He pauses, then continues with forced steadiness. "All vessels to adopt Stealth mode. We will evade the nearest enemy ships and engage the aliens over Endymion. Formation and battle orders to follow. Stand by."

The die was cast. Now the Legion's men and ships would test their mettle against the Ka'slaq.

Roll two dice and compare the result to the squadron's Stealth rating.

If the roll is less than or equal to the rating, go to section 52.

If the roll is greater than the rating, go to section 62.

— 27 —

The squadron reaches its destination after a long, tedious flight, entering orbit around the planet in good order. There is no sign of a Ka'slaq incursion, and Ulnar worries that he has made a wrong choice. As Ulnar wades through the stack of reports beamed here by ultrawave, he soon has his worst fears comfirmed. Not only has Endymion fallen to Ka'slaq raiders, but Baal, the most heavily populated planet in the sector, has as well. Overcoming his anger, Ulnar forces himself to scrutinize each report carefully in hopes of uncovering clues to the alien fleet's abilities, intentions, and weaknesses.

These reports tell much more about the power of the Ka'slaq than they do about weaknesses or opportunities the Legion might exploit. In both cases, the survivors who managed to make coherent observations were most impressed by the speed, coordination, and awesome power of the alien ships. The primary Ka'slaq vessel is described as being about the size of a cruiser, smaller than Ulnar's fighting ships, but armed with weaponry far superior to the Legion's vortex guns. These ships are capable of sustained high-speed maneuvers in extremely tight formations beyond the capability of any human pilots, giving the Ka'slaq a vast advantage in rapid battle movement. Only the cruiser-type ship was noted in reports from Baal and Endymion, although ultrapulse scans showed another gigantic moving object which was probably Don Larno's planetoid.

None of the warships in either of the garrisons escaped the Ka'slaq onslaught. Larno's ships were annihilated as they attempted to punch through the enemy battle lines to threaten the larger object. The ships at Baal, on the other hand, were caught scattered. As testament to the power of the alien guns, there are descriptions of the *Defiant*, a battlecruiser that was reduced to a powerless, lifeless hulk by a single well-placed shot.

Battle tactics adopted by the Ka'slaq differed markedly in the two engagements. At Baal the aliens seemed locked into a rigid plan of battle. Their initial dispositions changed very little as the fighting developed, and some Ka'slaq ships remained out of the fighting even as others were forced to engage in major duels against pockets of resistance among the garrison

Section 27

ships. Although the aliens responded quickly to changing situations on an individual basis, they showed little tendency to support one another through radical changes in deployment or formation.

Endymion was a different kind of fight. Here, the alien fleet acted and reacted almost as one. Near the climax of the action, as Larno's ships surged toward their huge target, the Ka'slaq cruisers seemed to abandon all other targets to mass all their strength against the Legion. The disparate nature of alien actions in the two battles disturbs Ulnar as he reads about them.

If the battles were fought differently, they were exploited in almost identical fashion. Once every fighting ship of the planetary garrison was destroyed, the target world was encircled by a large force of Ka'slaq cruisers and bombarded. In both cases this orbital bombardment was systematic, thorough, and utterly merciless. With an obviously precise knowledge of the layout and organization of the two human colonies, the aliens directed the awesome power of their annihilator guns against the planetary surfaces. They knew the location of every inhabited area of each world, from cities and towns down to individual homesteads, and they destroyed them all. There are accounts from Endymion of one town being reduced to slag even as the inhabitants tried to surrender to their conquerors. The only ones to escape from either world were the crews or passengers aboard a handful of merchant ships already near the fringes of the systems when the attacks began. The ships were able to bring back some word of the assaults, but the remoteness that allowed them to avoid the Ka'slaq also obscured the details of these engagements.

Two planets, one of them a thriving colony world with over a hundred million inhabitants, have fallen to the ruthless assault of the alien Ka'slaq, and through it all, Ulnar's actions have proven worse than useless. If his next choice goes no better, more of the people he is pledged to defend may die. Pain and guilt twist Ulnar's features into an anguished frown. He reaches for the communications switch to issue new orders to the squadron. This time his orders must be right.

If Ulnar orders the squadron to go to Endymion, go to section 53.

If Ulnar orders the squadron to Baal, go to section 66.

Section 28

If Ulnar sends the squadron to Ulnar 118, go to section 63.

If Ulnar issues orders to move the squadron S.C. 170, go to section 68.

If Ulnar gives orders to return the squadron to St. Germaine, go to section 74.

If the squadron receives orders to go to any other destination, go to section 73.

If the squadron remains at its present location, go to section 71.

— 28 —

"I want Fleetcomm open to all ships," Admiral Ulnar orders. "Put it through to my board." Ulnar watches the planning tank, balancing the computer readouts against everything he has learned about the Ka'slaq. He must find a weakness to exploit in the battle ahead.

"You're on Fleetcomm, Admiral," the technician informs him.

Ulnar switches on the microphone at his station. "Flag to Ninth Defense Squadron. Prepare for battle." Pausing, he examines the enemy dispositions again. The Ka'slaq have divided their forces, a mistake he could take advantage of. If the squadron can deal with the thirty-odd ships closing first, the Legion might be able to deal with the other two alien divisions in turn. "We'll let them come to us," Ulnar continues. Perhaps Larno's attack had attracted the main strength of the enemy. "Formation and battle orders to follow. Stand by."

Ulnar shuts off the microphone and leans forward to study the tank. He has a matter of minutes to assemble the squadron to fend off the enemy.

If Ulnar orders the ships to form a defensive globe, go to section 57.

If the squadron is ordered to adopt a defensive cylinder, go to section 67.

If Ulnar orders the light destroyers to screen the battlecruisers, go to section 65.

If Ulnar orders the destroyers to take refuge behind a battlecruiser screen, go to section 81.

If Ulnar orders the squadron to scatter and fight dispersed, go to section 70.

— 29 —

With Admiral Merros dead, his fleet shattered, and Ulnar's squadron no longer capable of offering resistance, the Ka'slaq fleet orbits St. Germaine and subjects it to the same devastating bombardment as Endymion and Baal already suffered. Apparently invincible, the aliens continue their drive into human space, spreading destruction and devastation in their wake. Star League scientists advance many theories to explain the single-minded campaign of annihilation the Ka'slaq pursue, but no one can be sure of their purpose. Xenophobic and genocidal, the Ka'slaq exterminate the inhabitants of dozens of planets as they plunge deeper and deeper into the Star League.

Another Legion fleet meets them near the Solar system, but is no better prepared than the last one. Brushing aside all opposition, the Ka'slaq bombard Earth and the other planets around the Sun. The Legion had triumphed over the Medusae, the Cometeers, the treachery of Stephen Orco, and the malice of the evil Basilisk, but against this power, they proved impotent. Over the years to follow, humanity slowly delines to extinction, hunted ruthlessly by the aliens from beyond Orion. The story of mankind eventually ends.

David Ulnar's name is remembered in the twilight years. Refugees from St. Germaine passed on the story of his campaign, portraying him as a coward, a traitor, and an ineffectual incompetent. Before the last human colony falls, his name has surpassed those of his infamous ancestors, the Lords of the Purple Hall, and even that of Eric the Pretender, as mankind's greatest betrayer. For although Vice-Admiral Ulnar never actually collaborated with the foe, all of his efforts in the campaign against the Ka'slaq are seen as a betrayal of the Legion's trust. It

Section 30

is a failure Ulnar himself felt as he died, fighting to the end but incapable of stopping humanity's alien scourge.

Because Ulnar failed to find and exploit the weaknesses of the aliens, the campaign was lost. To try again, go back to section 1 and start over. Good luck!

— 30 —

Contemplating everything he has learned so far, Ulnar finds himself thinking more and more of S.C. 170, the system where all the trouble started. The place where the Ka'slaq first appeared might provide information that would help Ulnar defeat the aliens. Moreover, he reasons, a blow at S.C. 170 might threaten the Ka'slaq supply lines back into whatever region they came from. If so, that could blunt their advance into the Ninth Sector and buy more time for Merros to prepare.

Satisfied that his reasoning is sound, Ulnar issues his orders. Within minutes *Valiant* comes alive as her geodyne engines lift her out of orbit around St. Germaine. The other ships of the squadron follow her lead and gather speed as the space-twisting engines alter the laws of inertia and Einsteinian physics around each of the Legion warships. Setting their course outward, they begin the long journey out of League space toward the world where four vessels have already been lost.

The journey is a long one, twenty-six days in all, even at the unimaginable speeds achieved in interstellar travel, during which the squadron is out of contact with any of the League worlds. Although ultrawave transmissions are even faster than the ships themselves, interstellar distances and velocities make it almost impossible to keep antennas aligned to exchange meaningful amounts of data. Only at short ranges, or between planets where positions and relative speeds are easily calculated and compensated for, can interstellar contact be effectively maintained.

The long voyage gives Ulnar plenty of time to brood and reconsider. What is happening in the sector as his squadron pushes toward its destination? Was his decision the right one?

If Ulnar decides to stop at Thule instead of going all the way to S.C. 170, go to section 79. This trip takes twenty-two days, which should be noted on a piece of scratch paper. Morale drops by 1 point.

If Ulnar chooses to stick to his original decision, proceed to section 54.

— 31 —

Ulnar's desk communicator buzzes. He thumbs the accept call button, and his star chart and planetary readouts are replaced by the image of an angry, saturnine man with a livid scar across his left cheek. Commodore Nils Benbo, one of the youngest wing commanders in the Legion, is an outspoken hothead who loves action and military display. Benbo wastes no time in pleasantries.

"I've heard about *Pioneer*, Admiral. When do we get under way for Thule?"

"Back off, Nils," Ulnar tells him. "When I'm ready to issue some orders, I'll tell you. Until then, stay where you are and keep your ships ready for action."

The commodore's face flushes darkly. "It's plain enough that Thule's the next enemy target! It's closest to where *Pioneer* was attacked, and the report said the aliens were heading there. What more do you need, a signed invitation and a road map?"

"I told you, Commodore, *back off*," Ulnar repeats harshly.

"That's easy for you, *sir*. I've got a sister on Thule, and I don't plan to let you throw her life away. *My* squadron is breaking orbit in one hour for Thule, whatever you decide."

"Who's in command here, Nils?" Ulnar demands.

"The recon wing will obey me. You can *accept* it or not, as you wish, but I'm going to Thule. So will you, if you know what's right." The screen goes blank.

Ulnar realizes Benbo isn't making idle boasts. His popularity with his own wing is on par with his popularity with Admiral Merros, Benbo's mentor and patron in the Legion. Short of ordering an attack on his own light forces, Ulnar hasn't much hope of bringing Benbo to heel.

Damn him, Ulnar thinks bitterly. The man's aggressiveness makes him a brilliant recon wing commander but an untrustworthy subordinate. Ulnar's options are to fight him (almost unthinkable), ignore him, back him, or join him. No matter

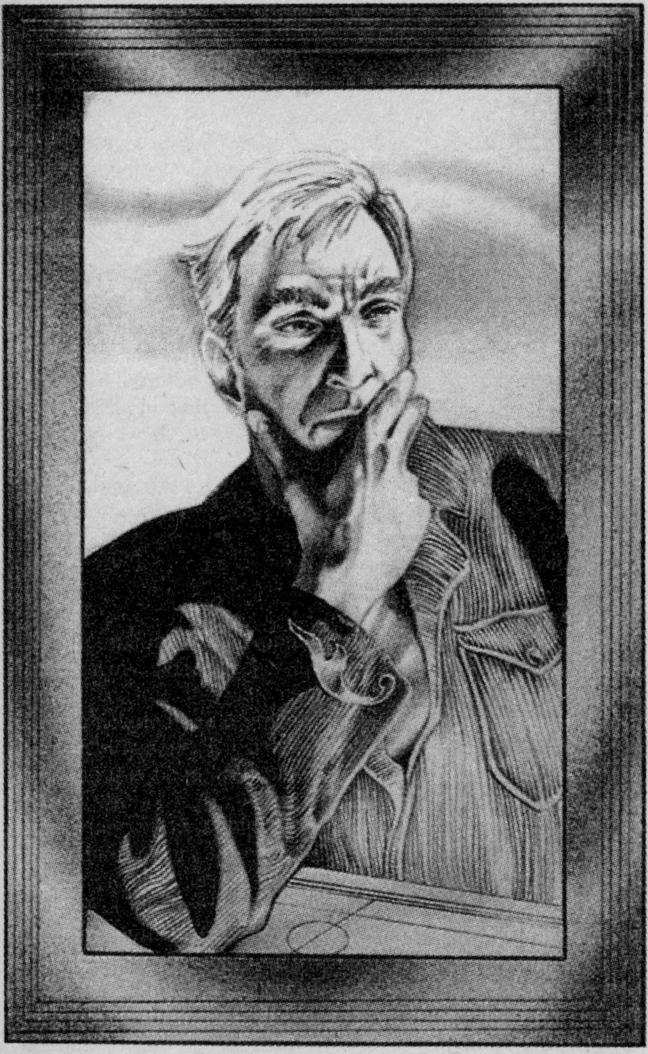

what, Ulnar is bound to lose face. And if Benbo uses his connections against him, Ulnar stands to lose even more.

If Ulnar chooses to try to stop Benbo from going to Thule, go to section 34.

If Ulnar decides to ignore Benbo and allow him to go to Thule but does not wish to join him at this time, go to section 40.

If Ulnar decides to travel to Thule with the Ninth Defense Squadron, go to section 35. However, the morale of all ships in Ulnar's sector drops by 1.

Ulnar can also choose to back Benbo by ordering the entire recon wing to Thule, but he must still choose a destination of his own. Go back to section 8.

— 32 —

Ulnar rubs his chin nervously. He scans the information displayed in the planning tank with worried eyes. Even though the Ka'slaq have split their forces, Ulnar doesn't like the odds. Even if he defeats the first attack, there are enough aliens at hand to destroy is ships before they can escape. Larno's ships were overwhelmed so quickly . . . can the Ninth Squadron expect to do better?

"Open Fleetcomm to all ships and patch it through to me here," Ulnar orders curtly. He doesn't like the decision he feels compelled to make now; Merros will certainly see it as cowardice. But the safety of Earth's first line of defense is more important than Ulnar's personal feelings or reputation.

"Ready on Fleetcomm, Admiral," the communications technician tells him.

Ulnar switches on the microphone at his elbow and tries to make his tone as cold and remote as possible. His words are difficult to force through his dry throat. "All ships, this is Flag," he says reluctantly. "Withdraw at once . . . repeat, withdraw at once. This isn't the time or the place for a showdown." But it will be soon, he promises himself wordlessly. "Adopt Stealth mode and disperse for a general withdrawal. Stand by for further orders."

Section 33

Stealth mode uses ultrawave and ultrapulse generators to jam the enemy's tracking systems. If it doesn't work, the superior speed and maneuverability of the Ka'slaq ships will make withdrawal impossible. Given the way the aliens are jamming the squadron's equipment, Ulnar wonders how well they can deal with the Stealth mode transmissions. Ulnar believes Stealth mode is the squadron's only hope of escape.

Roll two dice and compare the result to the squadron's Stealth rating.

If the roll is less than or equal to the rating, go to section 52.

If the roll exceeds the Stealth rating, go to section 62.

— 33 —

"On Fleetcomm," Ulnar orders the communications technician. As he waits, Ulnar sizes up the situation from the planning tank.

Despite the disruptive static on ultrapulse frequencies, the computers estimate that the aliens have thirty to thirty-five ships in a curving wall, sweeping inexorably toward Baal. They are keeping perfect formation, but their dispositions seem entirely concerned with an attack on the planet. The giant planetoid vessel from Endymion is nowhere in sight. Unless the Ka'slaq are setting some kind of trap, Baal is facing only a part of their strength.

"Fleetcomm ready and patched to you, Admiral," the technician tells him.

Ulnar nods once and keys in his microphone. "Flag to all ships. We're going to attack. Prepare for battle. Stand by for formation orders."

If Ulnar orders the squadron to adopt a wedge formation, go to section 80.

If Ulnar orders the ships to adopt a cone formation, go to section 85.

Section 34

If Ulnar orders the destroyers to provide a screen for the battlecruisers, go to section 90.

If the admiral orders his ships to scatter and fight dispersed, go to section 95.

— 34 —

Angrily, Ulnar attempts to raise Benbo again, but the wing commander refuses to accept his calls. The young upstart seems intent on deliberately provoking more trouble. Ulnar considers threatening Benbo and his men with violence, but he dismisses the idea at once. The squadron's battlecruisers wouldn't fire on the destroyers, and Benbo's men know it. The days when members of the Legion would turn their guns on one another are dead and gone, with Eric the Pretender and the android Orco.

Ulnar realizes he has very little way to enforce his authority. As long as Merros backs his youthful protégé, Benbo won't have to worry about repercussions for disobedience.

"Damn politics!" Ulnar says aloud, smashing his fist against the top of his desk.

Perhaps Merros would place discipline ahead of his feud with Ulnar. A slim chance, but it's Ulnar's only hope of backing Benbo down. He reaches for the intercom, then hesitates at getting involved with Merros. Suddenly resolve wells within him.

If Ulnar asks Admiral Merros to stop Benbo, go to section 77.

If Ulnar reconsiders and decides to order the squadron to accompany Benbo to Thule, go to section 35. However, the Morale of Ulnar's ships drops by 2 due to his display of indecisiveness.

If Ulnar reconsiders the call to Merros and allows Benbo to take his wing to Thule unopposed, go to section 40.

If Ulnar backs Benbo by formally ordering him to Thule, but does not accompany him, detach the whole recon wing in the usual manner, go back to section 8 and choose a destination.

Sections 35, 36

— 35 —

Ulnar stares at the blank monitor, his mind in turmoil. He doesn't see any way to stop Benbo, and once on his own, the hotheaded commander would be unlikely to rejoin Ulnar voluntarily. Removing the recon wing to Thule would rob the battlecruiser wing of a valuable advantage; light ships were essential for scouting, for screening the heavier ships as a battle developed, for delivering the first strokes of a battle as well as the final shots of a hell-for-leather pursuit.

Unable to bring Benbo to heel, Ulnar feels he must give in to his blackmail. Reluctantly, Ulnar reaches for the desktop communications switch once again, resigned to joining Benbo on his voyage to Thule.

Proceed to section 79. Note that the trip to Thule will take twenty-two days.

— 36 —

From his station on *Valiant*'s bridge, Ulnar studies the tactical planning tank. The computers deep in the flagship's core, analyzing ultrapulse scans and other sensor data, record no trace of activity in the system. Neither human ships nor Ka'slaq cruisers are exposed by the squadron's long-range probes. The system appears dead and deserted, but Ulnar knows better than to trust appearances. Perhaps alien ships are lying in ambush somewhere near Endymion, or maybe they have a method of hiding from ultrapulse scans.

Unwilling to expose the entire squadron to a trap, Ulnar passes orders to the squadron's light destroyers, the recon wing. "Investigate Endymion for signs of life, human or alien," he tells the chosen captains. "But at the first sign of trouble, *withdraw*. The battle wing will cover you."

The destroyers dart ahead while Ulnar and the rest of the squadron watch and wait.

Proceed to section 64.

Section 37

— 37 —

"Patch me in on Fleetcomm," Ulnar orders the communications technician. He glances around the bridge once before turning his attention back to the planning tank beside his flag console. Waiting for the crewman to comply, he tries to size up the situation.

The ship's computers, interpreting as much as they can through a haze of disruptive static, have estimated enemy strength via ultrapulse scans; they report between thirty and thirty-five enemy ships. That's a far cry from the hundred cruisers from Endymion. Nor is there any sign of the giant planetoid object here. The Ka'slaq have divided their fleet and sent only a fraction of their total force against Baal—a significant fraction, but a fraction nonetheless. That gives the Legion a chance to fight on more even odds for a change.

"On Fleetcom, sir," the technician says.

Keying in his microphone, Ulnar weighs his decision carefully before speaking to the captains in the squadron. "This is Flag to all ships. Prepare for battle. The squadron will adopt a defensive posture; let's make them come to us. Stand by for formation and battle orders."

By standing on the defensive, they can disrupt the enemy formations more easily. They form a perfect, curved wall sweeping down on Baal in formation, seemingly oblivious to anything but the planet.

He pauses for a long moment, still contemplating the tank. Finally, he reaches for the microphone again.

If Ulnar orders the squadron to form a defensive globe, go to section 78.

If Ulnar orders the ships to adopt a defensive cylinder formation, go to section 83.

If the admiral orders the squadron's destroyers to form a screen ahead of the battlecruisers, go to section 90.

If Ulnar orders the squadron to allow the orbital fortress around Baal to take the first wave of enemy attacks, go to section 93.

Sections 38, 39

If they should deploy into Phalanx and attack, turn to section 88.

If the squadron is ordered to scatter and fight dispersed, go to section 95.

— 38 —

From his station on *Valiant*'s bridge Ulnar studies the tactical planning tank. Deep inside the bowels of the flagship computers analyze and interpret ultrapulse scans and other sensor inputs, but they can detect no sign of activity in the Endymion system. Neither human nor alien ships appear to be moving in space, and the planet seems as devoid of life. Though appearances can be deceiving and a trap is always a possibility, Ulnar would rather keep his ships together. If the Ka'slaq spring a trap, they'll find the Legion ready for action.

"All ships to proceed on a flyby of Endymion," he orders over the Fleetcomm communications hookup. "Stay alert, and notify Flag of any anomaly. Deploy full sensor arrays and transmit reports on flyby completion." He pauses. "We're here to learn what we can . . . not to fight. Avoid battle if possible. Engage only on my orders."

Forming into a tight group, the ships drop toward Endymion. Tense and ready for anything, the men of the Legion wait to see what the planet holds in store for them.

Proceed to section 64.

— 39 —

Ulnar issues orders to hold the squadron at St. Germaine. It is a solid, conservative plan, not flashy by any means, but by far the best way to keep the squadron intact and in a position to guard the base and geofractor link, the linchpins to the sector's hope of survival.

But he reckons without one complicating factor: the hotheaded

Section 39

commander of the squadron's recon wing, Commodore Nils Benbo. Benbo is a protégé of Admiral Merros and a popular leader among his wing's destroyer captains. He and Ulnar have clashed before. Only minutes after Ulnar issues his orders, the commodore places an angry call to the admiral.

"What's this nonsense about staying in port?" he demands without preamble as Ulnar accepts his call. As usual, he ignores every military courtesy, a habit he can afford to indulge in because of his patronage from Merros. "Endymion's been destroyed. We have to take some kind of action!"

Wearily, Ulnar reminds his subordinate of the time lag involved. It's been two days since Larno sent his message. It will take eighteen more days to get the squadron to Endymion. "Or would you rather we just chose a world at random and risked missing the Ka'slaq entirely?" he concludes, growing angry.

Benbo looks disgusted. "So you'll write the campaign off just like that! An excuse to stay here, where it's safe!"

"Another word, Commodore," Ulnar says coldly. "Just one more word and even your patron won't save you from a court-martial. You have my orders. They're final."

"Are they indeed, *sir*?" Benbo responds with an unpleasant smile. "I'm getting ready to file a report with Admiral Merros. Are you sure you want to sit and do nothing? I'm sure the admiral would prefer that the squadron make some kind of attempt to stop the aliens. Baal's our most important colony—I vote we shift the squadron there. It's the only reasonable thing to do."

"When this is a democracy," Ulnar shoots back, "I'll consider your vote."

"Ah, but it *is* a democracy, Admiral. But Admiral Merros carries all the votes." Benbo smiles again, even more unpleasantly than before.

Benbo's threat, Ulnar realizes, is far from an idle one. He pauses for a long moment before replying, knowing that he is staking everything on his answer to the young commodore's blackmail.

If Ulnar backs down and orders the squadron to go to Baal, word of Benbo's manipulation of Ulnar circulates quickly. Ulnar's reputation with his men suffers, reducing the Morale value of the squadron by 1 point. Go to section 82.

If Ulnar stands by his decision, turn to section 49.

Section 40

— 40 —

A discreet knock interrupts Ulnar again. "Enter," he barks irritably, switching off the computer monitor and rubbing his eyes.

The crewman's uniform bears the symbol of the communications section. "Message capsule for you, sir." Ulnar takes the finger-sized spool from the technician with a gruff word of thanks. The crewman leaves the cabin as Ulnar drops the spool into a receptacle on his desk and punches up the message.

As he suspected, the message is from Admiral Merros on Earth. Ultrawave communications link planets, but though they could pass messages at many times the speed of light, the ultrawave signal was far from instantaneous. Over interstellar distances it could take days or even weeks to transmit information or orders.

But the League's geofractors, once so hideously misused by the evil criminal who had called himself the Basilisk, could move objects (although not ultrawaves) over vast distances in an instant. They could be used to move things almost anywhere, but the safest use of geofractors required a unit on each end of the trip. So a world like St. Germaine was connected to other geofractor-equipped planets, and it was practical to send tapes or couriers back and forth between these when ultrawave messages would be entirely too slow. It was a pity the Ka'slaq had some sort of defense against geofractors; every graduate of the Legion Academy knew how awesome a weapon a geofractor could be. The Basilisk had proven that.

Admiral Merros always reminds Ulnar of a basilisk. As his taped image forms on the screen, Merros turns his malevolent stare directly into the camera. There is something snakelike in his thin, drawn features and dry skin; his wispy hair and sunken eyes add to the serpentine image. Old before his time, he is still energetic when he wants to be and decisive when he has to be. Energy and decision always characterize the admiral's dealings with people he doesn't like, as Ulnar has discovered more than once.

"Vice-Admiral Ulnar," Merros begins, licking dry lips with a quick flick of his tongue. "I have had several complaints of inactivity and indecision on your part. Obviously you have an insufficient grasp of the gravity of the current situation.

Section 41

"Having seen the same reports you received, I fail to see how you can have any cause for uncertainty," the tape continues. "The alien armada is reported on course for Thule. Plainly that is the best place for our forces to meet them. May I strongly suggest that you deploy the bulk of your fighting forces to that star system at the earliest possible instance? As an alternative, of course, you may wish to step down from your command and allow an officer with a better grasp of strategic imperatives to take command in the Ninth Sector. I'll leave it to you to judge the most expedient choice." Merros pauses and offers a cold, cheerless smile. "And you can be sure, Admiral, that I will be taking a keen interest in your handling of your duties. Message ends."

Ulnar stares at the screen even after it goes blank. Damn Merros! And damn Nils Benbo, whose hand is all too clearly in this. The last thing Ulnar needs is this kind of ill-considered order from Admiral Merros. But the man is his superior, and Merros's orders leave him little choice.

Or do they?

If Ulnar complies with the admiral's order, go to section 79. The trip takes twenty-two days; note this on a piece of scratch paper for future reference.

If Ulnar decides to defy orders by remaining at St. Germaine or going to any world other than Thule, return to section 8 and select a destination. However, if the destination Ulnar ends up at is a planet still under League control and not threatened by the Ka'slaq at the time of Ulnar's arrival, go from the section that records the squadron's arrival directly to section 125, rather than following the regular choices for the section in question.

— 41 —

"Put me through on Fleetcomm," Ulnar orders.

The curving wall of Ka'slaq ships is moving inexorably across the planning tank, and Ulnar stares at them with the fascination of a helpless bird watching a predatory snake. There are only about thirty alien ships, with no sign of the rest of the fleet that

Section 42

attacked Endymion or of Larno's planetoid ship. Where were they? Ulnar senses a trap, and he doesn't intend to fall into it. Even if he's condemned as a coward, Vice-Admiral David Ulnar isn't going to throw away his command in a hopeless cause. The specter of the shattered *Defiant* looms fresh in his mind, stiffening his resolve to keep the squadron intact and wait for a better time to strike.

"Fleetcomm patched through to your board, Admiral," the communications technician says quietly.

Ulnar nods briskly and switches on his microphone. "Flag to all ships. The squadron will withdraw on my signal. Repeat, all ships are to avoid engaging and withdraw. Switch to Stealth mode. Further orders to follow. Stand by."

Ulnar sees the angry glances from crewmen around *Valiant*'s bridge; even the usually phlegmatic Sammis looks disgusted. But, angry or not, they comply with his orders. Ulnar ignores their reaction. Right now the squadron's duty is to remain intact and look for an opening to exploit later.

"Engaging Stealth mode," the captain reports. "Ultrawave and ultrapulse jamming signals in operation."

The admiral acknowledges the information with a vague gesture. Now comes the real test—would the jamming work? If the squadron can't elude the Ka'slaq, they will fight whether they want to or not. The next few minutes will decide their fate.

Roll two dice and compare the result to the squadron's Stealth rating.

If the roll is less than or equal to the rating, go to section 97.

If the roll is greater than the Stealth rating, go to section 100.

— 42 —

The records on board the yacht give Ulnar information about what happened on Endymion. Dispatched from the planet even as Larno's ships were engaged in their desperate fight to the death, the ship contains information collected at the planet's scout base as well as supplemental observations recorded by the

Section 42

crew as they fled the system. An abrupt and ominous end to these shipboard observations comes shortly after the crew noticed the lone Ka'slaq cruiser pursuing them at a speed even their powerful geodynes couldn't match.

Speed is one of the hallmarks of the Ka'slaq. Their first appearance at Endymion was totally unexpected, and the alien ships swooped down on their prey in tight-formation, high-speed maneuvers no human pilot could have hoped to duplicate. The reports here bear out Larno's transmission that there were a hundred or more enemy ships in the attacking fleet, and they also confirm the presence of some larger object, never actually seen, but showing up plainly on ultrapulse scanners. The cruisers made up the real threat of the Ka'slaq assault, each identical in size, speed, and powerful armaments.

Larno's last fight was not witnessed by any of the people who contributed to the courier's records, but some of the reports suggest that the garrison drove into the heart of the enemy fleet to try to reach the large object. The Ka'slaq ships gathered around the battle site, concentrating all their power on the Legion ships; nothing more was heard of the Legion ships thereafter. But the Ka'slaq came back, and they proceeded to reduce the Endymion colony.

Their subsequent actions made it clear that they knew everything they needed to know about the colony, down to the location of the smallest, newest homestead. This could only mean that the *Discovery*, reported captured at S.C. 170, has yielded up its computer files to the aliens. Using their powerful energy weapons— each of them far more powerful than Legion vortex guns— the Ka'slaq bombarded the planet's surface in a ruthless, systematic campaign on eradicate any sign of human habitation on Endymion. They neither offered quarter nor accepted surrender, destroying one town even as its helpless inhabitants broadcast their agreement to capitulate unconditionally. With the exception of a few ships—and many of those were probably dealt with in the same fashion as the courier itself—no one escaped from the holocaust on Endymion.

There is nothing in the yacht's files to suggest whether the Ka'slaq are still in the system or not, and no clue as to their ultimate purpose or immediate plans.

Transferring the data to his files, Ulnar turns to Captain Sammis and orders the squadron to resume its previous course and speed toward Endymion and gather more information.

Proceed to section 51.

Section 43

— 43 —

The population, commercial value, and central location of Baal are major factors in Ulnar's decision. He perceives the colony to be crucial to the defense of the entire sector, and the need to shift his squadron to Baal is obvious. The admiral issues his order accordingly.

Soon *Valiant*'s powerful geodynes begin to hum with barely suppressed power, lifting the battlecruiser slowly out of orbit ahead of the rest of the Ninth Squadron. Twisting the very fabric of space around each of the vessels, the geodynes accelerate them to unimaginable speeds through realms where accepted physical laws have been suspended. Setting the course Ulnar has ordered, the squadron steers for Baal.

The voyage from St. Germaine to Baal takes eleven days, and throughout that time the squadron is cut off from contact with the rest of the universe. Ultrawave communications link planets with each other and can contact ships across short distances, but a ship is an infinitesimal target across interstellar distances, and moves at such high speeds that it is almost impossible to maintain contact. Ulnar hears nothing of events in the sector as the squadron plunges on toward Baal. It is a tense time, for no one knows what to expect upon their arrival. Doubts assail the admiral, forcing him to realize just how much his decisions can mean to the future of the League. A wrong choice could cost the lives of innocent colonists.

As the squadron draws near to Baal, it is plain that the worrying has been for nothing. There is still no news of the Ka'slaq fleet, and the only thing to do is wait. Now that he has chosen Baal as his temporary base, Ulnar knows he has to stay with it; jumping from world to world without a clear-cut purpose is worse than useless, and bad for morale as well.

Another nine days pass at Baal before news comes in. A wavering, static-broken message from the commander of the garrison at Endymion finally reaches Ulnar. Don Larno is an old friend and protégé of Ulnar's, a reliable man with a flair for solving problems and inspiring subordinates and superiors alike. But the message he sends is far from inspiring.

". . . to HQ, Endymion garri— Alien ships . . . hundred or more . . . from . . . frontier. Garrison out . . . to hold them until . . . forcements. . . . Like a giant planet . . . mobile . . .

Section 44

death ship . . . Cometeers. Repeating: Endymion garrison to . . . spotted alien . . . a hundred . . . coming from beyond . . . tier . . . outnumbered, but we'il try to hold . . . send reinforcements. Most targets cruiser size, but one is like . . . planetoid, except it's mobile . . . a death . . . worse than the . . . Repeating . . .''

But there are no further repetitions; the Endymion communications station fades out shortly thereafter.

Endymion is eight days from Baal at maximum geodyne thrust, which leaves scant hope of actually reinforcing Larno's garrison in time to do any good. Ulnar, going over the message again and again, debates the best course to follow. Should he try to support Larno, or would his ships be better employed somewhere else? Whatever Ulnar does now, he must act for the best good of the League and the Legion, and he must choose correctly if he is to carry out his duty effectively.

If Ulnar chooses to go to the aid of the Endymion colony, go to section 53.

If Ulnar orders his ships to Ulnar 118, go to section 63.

If Ulnar orders the ships in his command to S.C. 170, go to section 68.

If Ulnar chooses to return with the squadron to St. Germaine, go to section 74.

Should the admiral wish to remain at Baal, go to section 61.

If the squadron is given orders to proceed to any other destination, go to section 73.

— 44 —

Ulnar makes his choice and begins to issue orders. The destination he has chosen seems a likely target for Ka'slaq attention, and he is determined to beat them to the punch. Led by the *Valiant*, the squadron boots out of orbit and accelerates away from St. Germaine. Urged forward by space-twisting geodyne

Section 45

engines, the ships defy the laws of inertia and Einsteinian physics as they leap across the light-years at a speed beyond human ken.

The squadron exists in isolation, unable to communicate effectively with St. Germaine or any other League world. Ultrawave messages are ten times faster than ships carrying information between the stars, but a ship in flight is so small and moves so fast that it is almost impossible to maintain contact except over comparatively short ranges. Transmissions between worlds are easier, because the relative speeds and current positions of antennas on each end are simple to calculate. But a ship or a squadron in deep space might as well be in a separate universe for all the contact it can make with worlds or distant vessels.

Without information to go on, Ulnar spends the long days of the voyage struggling with doubt and concern. He has no way of knowing how events are developing at Endymion or elsewhere, and if he has guessed wrong concerning the next Ka'slaq target, there will be more destruction, more deaths on his conscience. But the journey must continue until the squadron reaches its goal and makes contact with the outside once again.

Consult the Travel Time Chart. Cross-index Ulnar's point of origin (St. Germaine) with his chosen destination, and add the number shown to the number of days spent previously at St. Germaine. Note this total time spent on a piece of scratch paper for future reference. Then go to section 71.

— 45 —

If Commodore Benbo and the Corsair *are with Ulnar's squadron, go to section 39.*

If Benbo's Corsair *has been detached to any other station, go to section 49.*

— 46 —

As Ulnar skims through the material relayed from the wrecked ship's records, he finds nothing he hasn't heard from other sources, but the material he examines does confirm the reports collected before the squadron's departure from St. Germaine. He files the material with the other reports and clears his computer screen.

"Order the squadron to resume previous heading, Captain," he tells Sammis curtly. "We will proceed to Endymion now."

Proceed to section 51.

— 47 —

By some miracle the squadron manages to elude the alien fleet and escape from Endymion. They are alive and ready to take steps to ensure no reptition of Larno's disaster.

Later, when he has more time, Ulnar ponders the full implications of what he found at Endymion. There were some anomalies that deserved attention: the ultrawave static that seemed random sometimes but quite deliberate at others. The repeated pulse that the computer transphonated as "Ka'slaq"—was that the name of the race, as the survey team first assumed, or was it something more? What caused the alien ships to lose coherence in their maneuvering after the squadron went into Stealth mode?

For now, Ulnar turns his attention to other matters. He must set a course out of harm's way and yet move to protect the sector from fresh assaults.

"Incoming message, Admiral," the weary communications technician tells him. "From the merchant ship *Errant Night*. It's a high-density pulse transmission, coming in at five hundred to one." HD pulses crammed a lot of information into a short ultrawave burst. Few merchant ships bothered with that sort of transmission; they left it to Legion technicians and spies.

Ulnar has the pulse tape slowed to an understandable playback speed and takes time to skim through it while he thinks about destinations and plans. The merchant ship, unnoticed near the

Section 47

fringes of the system, has been watching the Ka'slaq in the aftermath of the squadron's withdrawal, and the things they were seeing weren't pretty. Not by a long shot.

With Endymion left totally undefended, a large group of Ka'slaq cruisers moved into close orbit. Then they began the next phase of their attack, a concerted bombardment of the helpless colony. Their targeting was precise, suggesting that they were intimately familiar with every aspect of the human settlement—proof that the Ka'slaq capture of the *Discovery* near S.C. 170 had been followed by penetration and translation of that vessel's computer files. The aliens knew the location of every town, every homestead on the surface of Endymion. Their bombardment systematically destroyed each of these. One town was obliterated even as it tried to surrender.

This proof of Ka'slaq savagery is all the admiral needs to strengthen his own determination to resist the enemy. They must not be allowed to spread their campaign of terror and destruction deeper into human space. Switching on the computer terminal at his bridge position, Ulnar begins to consider his options.

If Ulnar orders the squadron to remain at Endymion, go to section 99.

If Ulnar wishes to move the squadron to Baal, go to section 58.

If the squadron is ordered to Ulnar 118, go to section 63.

If the admiral orders the squadron to S.C. 170, go to section 68.

If Ulnar chooses to return to St. Germaine, go to section 74.

If he gives orders to go to any other destination, go to section 73.

Section 48

— 48 —

Hoping either to block the next enemy attack or to get a better clue to their further intentions before committing the squadron to another voyage, Ulnar decides to remain in orbit and see what happens. It is another tedious wait, hard on the squadron's crews and on Ulnar himself. But without information, strategic decisions are reduced to little more than guesswork. Caution and care are Ulnar's watchwords.

At last word comes in, but it's the worst information imaginable. The Ka'slaq have struck again, and in striking they have overwhelmed the most populous colony in the sector. Baal has fallen to the alien fleet.

According to reports broadcast by refugees, the alien attack on Baal was more in the nature of a raid than an all-out onslaught, but it was a raid that reduced the colony as completely and as ruthlessly as Endymion had been. Only about thirty Ka'slaq cruisers were reported, as opposed to the hundred or more said to have been involved in the first encounter of the invasion. Moreover, there was no sign of Larno's huge planetoid ship. Evidently only a portion of the alien strength was turned against Baal, but it was enough.

The garrison was caught dispersed. Trying to get the earliest possible warning of an attack, patrols were flung out to search the volume of space in the direction of Endymion. After some ambiguous readings of moving vessels and some odd ultrawave static, the patrols were stepped up, but the garrison ships had too much territory to cover. Two of them—the battlecruiser *Defiant* and an escorting destroyer—made contact with a phalanx of enemy cruisers and were destroyed as they warned the colony. *Defiant* was reduced to a wreck by a single well-placed shot from the Ka'slaq annihilator guns.

The Ka'slaq assault on Baal followed a whole different tactical pattern as compared to their attack of Endymion. They showed little of their previous flexibility and responsiveness, keeping rigidly to a single formation as they closed on Baal. As ships of the garrison rushed into battle, a very haphazard engagement developed. But the aliens lent one another very little support; some of the Ka'slaq cruisers encountered heavy resistance, while others, in easy supporting range, never fired a shot during the whole approach to Baal. Having taken measure of their human

Section 48

foes, the Ka'slaq perhaps saw no need to use their full capabilities. It didn't make any difference to the garrison. The ships at Baal fought hard and held on with feverish tenacity, but in the end superior numbers and superior weapons defeated them.

Once the garrison, including Baal's powerful orbital fortress, was wiped out, the aliens repeated the Endymion atrocity. Orbiting cruisers began the systematic elimination of inhabited sites on the colony's surface. They spared no one and nothing. After the colony was devastated in this merciless style, the Ka'slaq raiders boosted out of the system again. They did not even pause to search out the merchant ships that had escaped.

If Ulnar is not at St. Germaine, but receives these new reports and decides to stay at his present location longer, go to section 71.

If the squadron is ordered to Endymion, go to section 53.

If Ulnar orders the squadron to Baal, go to section 66.

If Ulnar orders the squadron to Ulnar 118, go to section 63.

If S.C. 170 is Ulnar's destination, go to section 68.

Should Ulnar issue orders to return to St. Germaine, go to section 74, (if the squadron is not already there).

If the squadron is ordered to any other destination, go to section 73.

If the squadron is already at St. Germaine and Ulnar decides to remain in orbit there, go to section 115.

— 49 —

A crewman is admitted to Ulnar's cabin late in the evening. "Message capsule for you, Admiral," he tells Ulnar apologetically. "It's just through the geofractor from Earth, from Admiral Merros, sir." The man is young, diffident . . . more like a schoolboy than a warrior. Had the heroes of the great days of the Legion ever been like this youngster? It seemed almost impossible.

"Thank you, Lomis," Ulnar acknowledges, proud of himself for remembering the man's name. "Dismissed."

Lomis leaves, relieved. As the cabin door closes silently behind the crewman, Ulnar slips the capsule into a receptacle at the computer station across from his bed. Switching on the monitor, he keys in a playback order and leans forward to see what his hostile superior has sent through the instantaneous matter transmitter from the Legion base at the New Moon orbiting the Earth.

The screen lights up with an image of Admiral Merros, neat and impeccably dressed as always. With a slender frame, narrow face, and sparse white hair, he looks like a corpse decked out in a dress uniform for burial.

"Reports have reached me," Merros says without preamble, "of your continued inactivity in the face of the recent reports of alien attacks at Endymion. I find your refusal to take an active part in the defense of the squadron a totally inexplicable dereliction of duty which shows a want of initiative or sufficient resolve to carry out your orders." The older man pauses, his sunken eyes glaring into the camera with a mixture of indignant outrage and smug satisfaction at the way Ulnar has set himself up for a fall.

"Our strategic planners believe that an attack on Endymion must surely herald an invasion of Baal, the nearest major population center. I believe there are those among your own officers who believe the same, even if you are too blind to see it. Therefore, I am officially ordering you to move your squadron to Baal to defend it against any Ka'slaq incursion. Moreover, you are required to take active steps against the enemy wherever they may be encountered. Further inaction on your part shall certainly be grounds for remedial action on the part of the Legion High Command. I trust, Admiral, that I have made myself clear? Message ends."

The screen goes blank, leaving Ulnar to switch it off and sink

Section 50

back into his chair with a sigh. Merros will watch him like a hawk, eager to catch a hated upstart in a breach of duty. As Ulnar feared from the start, the deck is stacked against him. No matter what David Ulnar does or doesn't do in the days and weeks ahead, Merros will be waiting for any excuse to intervene; any mistake will be enough.

It isn't a position Ulnar enjoys, but he must either accept the admiral's orders or be ready to face the man's anger over the slightest disobedience.

If Ulnar decides to comply with the admiral's order, go to section 50.

If Ulnar defies orders and remains at St. Germaine, go to section 125.

If Ulnar defies Merros to go to Endymion, go to section 20.

If Ulnar defies Merros and orders the squadron to S.C. 170, go to section 68.

If Ulnar defies Merros and goes to any other destination, go to section 44.

In the case of any *defiance of orders, the first contact with a Legion garrison following Ulnar's disobedience will lead to section 125 (rather than the usual choices open at that location), unless Ulnar's squadron engages in a battle with Ka'slaq ships prior to the time that it reaches a garrisoned planet.*

— 50 —

The fall of Endymion endangers several other planets, of which Baal is the most important. With its sizable population, its commercial value, and a position of obvious strategic value in the interior of the sector, Baal strikes Ulnar as being the obvious next target of the alien fleet.

It will take speed—and no small amount of luck—to beat the Ka'slaq to the planet. Ulnar can't help but berate himself for waiting for the detailed reports on Endymion; he begrudges

Section 50

every hour wasted. The admiral issues the orders that will send the Ninth Defense Squadron to Baal. As he goes through the steps to get the ships moving, he silently prays that the action won't end up being too little, too late.

Pushed out of orbit by their mighty geodyne engines, the ships of Ulnar's squadron follow the *Valiant* away from the planet and set their course for Baal. Twisting the fabric of space and sweeping aside the normal physical laws that govern velocity and inertia, these engines carry the Legion across interstellar space at a speed the human mind could neither imagine nor comprehend.

The voyage takes eleven days, and during most of that time there is no chance of communication between the squadron and the worlds it protects. Although ultrawave messages can speed through space in a tenth the time it takes a ship to travel an equivalent distance, the technology is far more useful for sending information between planets than it is for maintaining contact with moving vessels. Individual ships are such minuscule, fast-moving targets over interstellar distances that it is virtually impossible to keep up a link for any length of time. Planets have much lower relative speeds and have positions calculated so carefully for any portion of their orbits that communication involving them is relatively easy. Moving ships, like the Ninth Squadron en route to Baal, are easier to contact when they are comparatively close by or moving very slowly.

Ulnar spends the whole time out of touch with the rest of the League. As the ships speed through deep space, the Ka'slaq might strike again and kill more unprepared civilians. Will Baal still be a human colony when the squadron reaches it, or will it share Endymion's fate? Or are other worlds under attack even as Ulnar leads a wild-goose chase to a quiet, unthreatened planet? Only time will tell.

Add eleven days to the total number accumulated waiting at St. Germaine, and note the new total somewhere for future reference.

If the new total is thirty-three days or less, go to section 69.

If the new total is thirty-four days or more, go to section 76 instead.

— 51 —

The shattered hulk of the yacht drops astern, and the squadron approaches Endymion at last. As the Legion ships near their goal, they turn all their facilities to keeping watch for a sign of danger. But there is nothing, no echo on ultrapulse scans and no message on ultrawave from friend or foe. The squadron, closing in on the star system, seems to be alone, and Ulnar imagines the dangers and traps that might lie ahead. Could the Ka'slaq have simply destroyed the colony and moved on? If so, why? Why attack if they did not want mankind's planets or resources?

Perhaps a closer look at Endymion will tell them something more. Something worthwhile.

If Ulnar orders light ships from the recon wing to investigate the planet more closely, go to section 36.

If Ulnar orders the entire squadron to close on Endymion, go to section 38.

— 52 —

"Stealth mode, Admiral," Sammis tells him. "Ultrawave and ultrapulse generators on feedback setting, maximum output." Green lights on Ulnar's console report compliance by the other ships in the squadron.

"Thank you, Captain," Ulnar acknowledges, his formal tone matching his subordinate's grave manner. Sammis was a stickler for proprieties on the bridge.

The other officers and crewmen in the control center are quiet, hunched over their consoles with every nerve focused on their duties. The tension in the air is almost palpable; they all know what is at stake. Larno's fate is a grim reminder of what could happen in battle.

Minutes drag by. Given the speed and maneuverability of the alien forces, running is out of the question. The Stealth mode system is the squadron's only hope of eluding the enemy. The

Section 52

next few minutes will determine the fate of the Ninth Defense Squadron.

An ultrapulse operator breaks the silence. "Drawing away, Sir," he says hoarsely. Ulnar looks back at the tank and nods once.

"Confirmed," someone else says. "The jamming has thrown 'em off!"

A ragged cheer goes around the bridge, cut off abruptly by Sammis. "As you were!" the captain snaps. He turns toward Ulnar. "We seem to be dodging them, Admiral," he reports unnecessarily.

"So it seems," Ulnar replies gruffly, his eye still on the tank. Is it just his imagination, or are the alien formations looser, less coordinated?

"I'd swear those bastards look *confused*," someone else comments audibly. "They look like a bunch of dogs casting around for a scent."

"Quiet there," Sammis says angrily. He looks offended at the breach of discipline.

But Ulnar is happy to hear the talk; it confirms his own observations. Whatever else the squadron has done, it may have uncovered an important fact about the Ka'slaq. Not only had the aliens lost track of his ships, but it seemed as if they were actually having trouble operating in the vicinity of ships under Stealth mode. A slow smile spreads across Ulnar's face. He turns back to his console and prepares for the next step in the campaign against the alien invaders.

If the squadron is to attack the aliens around Endymion, go to section 102.

If the squadron is to attack the alien planetoid and its defenders, go to section 112.

If the squadron changes its course to attack the first alien division (the ships they have just eluded), go to section 122.

If the squadron withdraws from Endymion, go to section 47.

Sections 53, 54

— 53 —

It may be too late to do the colonists at Endymion any good. But the devastated colony world may well be the key to the campaign. For one thing, it might contain a clue to the aliens and their purpose. Perhaps their forces are still concentrated there, which would allow the Legion to strike a blow against them before they have a chance to threaten another world. If the Ka'slaq have already moved on, a threat to their channels of communications could induce the aliens to turn back, thus sparing their next target from sharing Endymion's fate.

With all these possibilities in mind, Ulnar orders *Valiant* to lead the squadron back into deep space once more. Again the mighty geodynes focus their space-warping energies to thrust the Legion's ships across the light-years. Their destination is Endymion, but no one can be sure what else they may find, aside from a ruined world and a dead colony.

Along the way the squadron encounters a wrecked yacht drifting in space, its hull torn apart by the nearby explosion of some powerful weapon. The hulk obviously attempted to escape from Endymion's ruin but failed. Records on board supplement but do not significantly change the information Ulnar has already gathered on the colony's loss.

Consult the Travel Time Chart. Cross-index the squadron's point of origin with its destination (Endymion). The result is the number of days the new voyage takes. Add this number to the number accumulated in the previous journey(s) the squadron has undertaken. Record this number for future reference and then proceed to section 51.

— 54 —

The ships of the Legion's Ninth Defense Squadron approach their goal, the distant world designated by the catalogue number S.C. 170. Straining every sensor and scanner to detect some sign of alien activity, they advance cautiously to the outer fringes of the system. There is no sign of danger, no trace of any artifacts or vessels that might belong to the Ka'slaq. There isn't even a sign of the lost survey ships. S.C. 170 seems completely deserted.

Appearances can be deceiving, Ulnar knows, but he is beginning to think this journey has been a mistake. Not only does the main fleet appear to have moved on, presumably into League space, but they evidently don't have a supply line to threaten. This makes Ulnar's whole strategy invalid.

But perhaps this judgment is too hasty, Ulnar tells himself hopefully. A closer look at this system might turn up something the long-range scans have failed to uncover. From his station on *Valiant*'s bridge, Ulnar issues orders feverishly to follow up on this faint hope.

If Ulnar orders the destroyers in his squadron (if any are available) to scout the system, holding his battlecruisers in reserve, go to section 56.

If Ulnar orders all the ships in his command to mount a reconnaissance into the system, go to section 59.

— 55 —

"Flag to all ships," Ulnar says, the microphone on. "Adopt standard wedge formation and attack the enemy." He touches a combination of pads on the flag computer console and watches as his monitor begins scrolling through the detailed battle orders for the squadron. It is one of dozens of deployments Ulnar has worked out over the past days in space, and it is being transmitted to every ship in the squadron at once.

In the three-dimensional planning tank, the yellow lights representing the Legion ships draw together into a tight formation and begin changing course. Now they are closing fast with the blobs of blue that mark the enemy formation. Lighter ships are in the lead, while the battlecruisers, *Valiant* among them, are shown farther back in the broader section of the wedge. The alien cruisers form a loose globe, the perfect target for a well-used battle wedge. But Ulnar knows how effective the Ka'slaq are in responding to threats; he's seen too much evidence of their ability to maneuver and coordinate attacks effectively.

Minutes pass slowly as the two forces come together for a

Section 56

decisive clash. Ulnar sees the two distant Ka'slaq forces changing course to back up their first wing and knows he must win quickly or not at all.

"Contact in five minutes," someone reports.

"Weapons ready," an officer adds, reporting to the captain. Ulnar tries to shut it all out, to concentrate on his task. Admirals do not handle ships, he reminds himself with a hint of wistfulness. His job is to handle the whole squadron, to make sure that it works together, as he's seen the aliens do.

The resolution of the battle is governed not only by the formation already chosen, but also by which of the enemy groups is engaged first. Find out the division that fights initially by following the guidelines presented below.

If the squadron is attacking the closest group of enemy ships, the Ka'slaq First Division is engaged first.

If the squadron is remaining on the defensive, the Ka'slaq First Division is engaged before the others.

If Ulnar has ordered the squadron to move to shield Endymion from attack, the Ka'slaq Second Division is engaged first.

If the squadron has been sent against the alien planetoid, the Ka'slaq Third Division will be the first group to be engaged.

If the squadron attempts to elude the nearest alien force but failure of Stealth mode movement brings it to battle anyway, the Ka'slaq First Division will be engaged first.

To resolve the battle of Endymion, Ulnar can choose to fight a conventional space battle by going to section 130.

If Ulnar prefers to try using the squadron's Stealth mode during the actual battle, go to section 135.

— 56 —

"Flag to recon wing," Ulnar says, speaking into the Fleetcomm microphone at his station on *Valiant*'s bridge. "Investigate S.C. 170 for signs of enemy activity. Do not, repeat, *do not* engage enemy vessels encountered unless absolutely necessary." Destroyer captains begin acknowledging his orders, and the lighted symbols that depict their ships begin to separate from the main bulk of the squadron's battlecruisers.

Ulnar is reluctant to divide his force, but if there is a trap waiting somewhere in the system, he would rather flush it out with something less than his entire squadron. Destroyers are designed for this sort of work. The Legion's ace in the hole is the battle wing, which Ulnar can bring up quickly to support the destroyers.

He reminds himself that that plan is the textbook solution to an uncertain situation like this one. His concern now is that the Ka'slaq haven't read any of the same textbooks. The apparent lack of a supply line or base here has made him begin to doubt that this alien armada can be overcome by conventional means at all.

The only thing he can do for now is sit back and wait, hoping the recon wing uncovers something worthwhile.

Proceed to section 75.

— 57 —

"All ships, this is Flag," Ulnar begins again, reopening the Fleetcomm channel once more. "Form defensive globe and stand by for action. Recon wing to retire within the globe." The admiral's fingers dance over the keyboard on the console before him, punching in the combination that brings the Flag computer into the Fleetcomm link and calling up a string of detailed battle orders. On his monitor Ulnar watches a scrolling readout of vectors, positions, and speeds that will tell each captain in the squadron how to deploy his ship for the conflict ahead.

This is only one of many preprogrammed deployments Ulnar has put together since the squadron left St. Germaine. The battle orders on his monitor are being repeated on the bridge of each vessel, while the Legion captains translate them into actions to place every ship in battle readiness.

In Ulnar's planning tank the yellow lights that represent his ships are creeping slowly to form a new pattern, reflecting the slow redeployment into the new positions he has assigned them.

Section 57

A defensive globe is considered the ideal formation for the employment of strictly defensive tactics, giving ships the maximum support against almost any kind of attack. The globe's effectiveness against the Ka'slaq, though, remains to be seen.

The clash of fleets is inevitable, but it won't necessarily be quick. Even at tremendous speeds it takes time to span the vast distances involved in a space battle. Minutes pass at a crawl while yellow and blue lights draw nearer with agonizing slowness. It is the hardest part of battle—this period of watching and waiting before the ships actually join in combat. Ulnar has the worst role of all; other officers and men have jobs to concentrate on during the approach, jobs that help take their minds off their fear. Ulnar's job is to concentrate on those worries, to try to anticipate the difficulties and dangers before they happen and plan ways to overcome them all.

The movements of the other two Ka'slaq divisions recorded by the tank, for instance, must be considered. Those two Ka'slaq forces have changed course to reinforce the division already closing on Ulnar's tight-knit globe of battlecruisers. If the Legion can't defeat the initial alien wave quickly, these newcomers will boost the enemy's strength to overwhelming levels. Against those numbers Ulnar's forces won't stand much more of a chance than Don Larno's in their fight to the death.

The resolution of the battle is governed not only by the formation already chosen, but also by which of the three enemy groups is engaged first. Find out the division that fights initially according to the guidelines below.

If the squadron attacks the closest group of enemy ships, the Ka'slaq First Division is engaged first.

If the squadron remains on the defensive, the Ka'slaq First Division is engaged first.

If Ulnar decides to move the squadron to shield Endymion from attack, the Ka'slaq Second Division is engaged first.

If the squadron is sent against the alien planetoid, the Ka'slaq Third Division is the first to be engaged.

If the squadron attempts to elude the nearest alien force but is brought to battle anyway, the Ka'slaq First Division is the first force engaged. This happens if Stealth mode fails while the squadron tries to escape this force (for whatever reason).

Section 58

To resolve the battle at Endymion, Ulnar can choose to fight a conventional battle by going to section 130.

If Ulnar would rather try using the squadron's Stealth mode tactic during the actual battle, go to section 135.

— 58 —

With the fall of Endymion, several other worlds are vulnerable to alien attack. Of them all, Ulnar fears most for Baal. Its population, commercial value, and strategic position in the very heart of the sector all combine to suggest that this vital world could become the next Ka'slaq target. Angry at himself for already being outguessed in his every move, Ulnar vows not to choose wrong again. The admiral issues his new orders, and the Ninth Squadron boosts under geodynes for Baal.

It's a long trip, and Ulnar can't help but be concerned. If the Baal colony is the next Ka'slaq target, Ulnar could easily be too late to help. Will the Legion find a flourishing colony, or a world reduced to a lifeless desert by the power of the Ka'slaq?

Consult the Travel Time Chart, cross-indexing the squadron's planet of origin with Baal, the intended destination. Add this number to the time accumulated previously in traveling and/or waiting.

If the new total is thirty-one days or less, go to section 69.

If the new total is thirty-two days or more, go to section 76 instead.

Sections 59, 60

— 59 —

Seated at his command console on *Valiant*'s bridge, Ulnar masters his initial indecision. He didn't bring the squadron all the way to S.C. 170 to waste the effort in half measures. As long as there is even the slightest chance of finding Ka'slaq ships, a base, even some trace of their passage, it is vital to investigate more closely. He has the duty communications technician open up the Fleetcomm channel so he can pass orders to the whole squadron.

"All ships, this is Flag," he begins. "Proceed at maximum speed on a standard hyperbolic approach past the system's primary. All scanners to maximum sensitivity." He pauses. "Stay alert, and notify me of any unusual readings or signs of alien activity. This is a recon mission, and if there is some sign of trouble, I want all ships to disengage and withdraw as quickly as possible. Avoid battle unless absolutely necessary, or on my orders."

Forming into a tight, wedge-shaped formation, the ships of the Ninth Squadron drop toward the star, scanning the system for anything out of the ordinary. Ulnar wants his force kept close together, determined not to fall into the cardinal error of dividing his squadron in the face of a possible enemy ambush. Ready for whatever they might find, the men of the Legion turn their full attention to S.C. 170.

Proceed to section 75.

— 60 —

"All ships, this is Flag," Ulnar continues after a few more minutes studying the planning tank. "Adopt standard cone formation and attack the enemy."

Sweeping his fingers over a series of keys on the console before him, Ulnar activates the Fleetcomm computer link. His monitor shows a scrolling list of orders governing the position and function of each ship in the squadron. One of dozens of

Section 60

tactical plans worked out by Ulnar during the recent voyage, it is being relayed to each vessel in his command.

The yellow lights that represent the squadron's ships begin to rearrange themselves, slowly but with great precision and determination. The cone begins to form with the battlecruisers at the base and the lighter ships forming the rim. In the battle to follow, the lighter ships will have the most vital job, englobing the alien force while the battle wing holds their attention. The Ka'slaq, in a loose defensive sphere, are well-deployed to block the cone, but with luck and the Legion's well-known fighting spirit, the cone englobement tactic could make short work of the aliens.

The distance between the two forces is still wide enough to leave the combatants several minutes before the battle can be joined. Watching the slow tracks of lights in the tank, Ulnar wonders what his opposite number might be thinking right now. What is the Ka'slaq leader like? Is he worrying about the lives soon to be lost in battle, about service politics and the consequences of defeat? Or were the Ka'slaq so alien that they had nothing in common with Ulnar and his men?

"Closing to contact," someone reports. Ulnar continues to study the tank intently, looking for a weakness, a way to clinch a quick victory. But all he sees are the traces that show the other two alien forces beginning to turn in support of the first wave. Time favors the Ka'slaq, and unless Ulnar can win a quick victory, the squadron will soon be outnumbered and overwhelmed, just like Don Larno's garrison ships.

The resolution of the battle is governed not only by the formation already chosen, but also by which of the three enemy groups is engaged first. Find out the division that fights initially according to the guidelines below.

If the squadron attacks the closest group of enemy ships, the Ka'slaq First Division is engaged first.

If Ulnar decides to remain on the defensive, the Ka'slaq Second Division is engaged first.

If the squadron is sent against the alien planetoid, the Ka'slaq Third Division is the first to be engaged.

If the squadron attempts to elude the closest alien force, but is brought to battle anyway by failure of the Stealth mode tactic, the Ka'slaq First Division engages first.

Section 61

To resolve the battle at Endymion, Ulnar can choose to fight a conventional battle by going to section 130.

If Ulnar instead decides to use the squadron's Stealth mode tactic in the actual battle, go to section 135 instead.

— 61 —

Glumly, Ulnar contemplates his choices. Endymion is too far away for him to save Larno or the colonists from the Ka'slaq armada. Rushing in without further information would be little short of suicide. But it seems equally foolish to shift the squadron anywhere else without good reason. The same factors that brought Ulnar to Baal continue to hold true, and until he learns of some other possibility to the contrary, the admiral realizes he is best off remaining right here.

More information about Endymion trickles in over the next several days, relayed by merchant ships that escaped the disaster that engulfed the system. They tell a horrible story; Endymion has not just been captured by the alien Ka'slaq, but utterly destroyed.

The attack developed with startling speed. From the reports Ulnar reads, it seems clear that the Ka'slaq have a significant advantage over their human opponents in speed—not because of any superiority in technology (the enemy uses geodynes of roughly the same capabilities as those aboard Legion ships), but because Ka'slaq pilots are capable of conducting high-speed, tight-formation maneuvers no human pilot could hope to duplicate. This is but one of several significant advantages displayed by the alien armada in their assault.

Another is numbers. As Larno's original report indicated, the aliens had at least a hundred ships. Some stories are obviously wild exaggerations, but Larno's figure is borne out by the vast majority of the other observations that reach Ulnar. No one else was actually close enough to the action to see the mobile planetoid Larno spoke of, but many accounts noted a moving object that showed up on ultrapulse scans as an immense artifact the size of a small moon. The actual fighting was carried on by cruiser-sized vessels, larger than a Legion destroyer, but smaller than *Valiant* and her sister battlecruisers, and armed with annihi-

Section 61

lator weapons that far outmatched the heaviest vortex guns of the Star League.

Larno's last fight left no human survivors, and no one actually witnessed the battle at firsthand. The last transmissions to punch through some weird, previously unknown kind of static or jamming put out by the alien ships reported that Larno intended to form up his ships into a tight wedge and drive toward the planetoid. The Ka'slaq ships responded to his threat by breaking off their other attacks and closing in on the garrison, surrounding and overwhelming them. Ka'slaq cruisers returned, went into orbit around Endymion, and proceeded to destroy the colony completely.

From the way they prepared and launched their orbital bombardment, it was clear they knew a great deal about the colony. The Ka'slaq knew the location of every town, installation, settlement, even the smallest homesteads, evidence that they had managed to translate the computer files on board the captured *Discovery*. Every center of human habitation on Endymion was bombarded by Ka'slaq annihilator weapons. The colonists were not even allowed to surrender; one town was devastated as it broadcast an offer to capitulate on any terms the conquerors cared to name. The attack was systematic, ruthless, and utterly complete. Except for a handful of people on ships far enough away to avoid alien notice, no one escaped this holocaust.

These reports show all too clearly the character of the Legion's opponents and the fate awaiting any world they succeed in dominating. With this evidence of Ka'slaq intentions and evil at hand, Ulnar takes time to review his options and position. He knows he has to stop the alien armada before it can strike again.

Roll one die and add the indicated number of days to the time accumulated in the campaign.

If Ulnar chooses to remain at Baal, go to section 69.

If Ulnar chooses to travel to Endymion, go to section 53.

If Ulnar orders the ships in his command to Ulnar 118, go to section 63.

If Ulnar chooses to travel to S.C. 170, go to section 68.

Section 62

If Ulnar chooses to have the squadron return to St. Germaine, go to section 74.

Should the admiral order the squadron to proceed to any other destination, go to section 73.

— 62 —

"Stealth mode, Admiral," Sammis reports formally. "Ultrawave and ultrapulse generators are on feedback setting, maximum output."

"Thank you, Captain," Ulnar acknowledges, matching his tone.

Around him *Valiant*'s bridge crew is quiet, hunched over their control consoles as they focus all their attention on their work. The tension in the air is almost palpable. Everyone knows what is at stake; they'd seen Larno's ships snuffed out by the aliens. Would the newcomers fare any better?

The waiting drags on. Given the enemy speed, it would be impossible to outrun the Ka'slaq. Stealth mode is the only alternative, the only hope of dodging the alien attack. The next few minutes will determine the whole nature of the battle . . . and probably the fate of the Ninth Defense Squadron.

"They're matching us," an ultrapulse operator says at last. "Jamming isn't working, damn it! They're swinging around to engage."

Ulnar looks into the tank, seeing the truth in the crewman's words as he takes in the changing dispositions. Stealth failed. Hastily he thumbs the microphone to issue new orders, hoping against hope that there is still time to meet the enemy in some kind of battle order. "All ships, this is Flag. Formation change. Formation change. Prepare for enemy attack!"

As Ulnar frantically issues new orders for a defensive formation, something in the planning tank catches his eye. The Ka'slaq ships are closing inexorably, as before, but their formation seems looser, their maneuvers and response times slower. What is happening—and why? The admiral shakes his head abruptly. There is no time for more analysis; it is essential that the Legion prepare to fight.

Section 63

Roll two dice and compare the result to the squadron's current Morale level.

If the roll is less than or equal to the Morale value, go to section 28.

If the roll is greater than Morale, go to section 72.

— 63 —

Acting on a hunch, Ulnar has been devoting a lot of thought to the planet that bears his family name. Ulnar 118 is uninhabited and rarely visited, easily ignored by strategic planning as a worthless piece of rock that isn't worth fighting for. But the admiral can't help but wonder if this is really true.

Even in the aftermath of victory a fleet has to have time and resources to refit and consolidate. If the Ka'slaq have the files from the captured *Discovery*, they know that Ulnar 118 is one place they can recover from battle without much risk of interference from a human fleet. And the deserted world lies at the very doorstep of the sector base at St. Germaine, an ideal place from which to strike the next logical blow of the war once the Ka'slaq are ready to resume the campaign.

Ulnar thinks that the planet is worth a look. Although the captains in his squadron all seem startled by the decision, he frames his orders accordingly. Soon the ships are in motion again, plunging through interstellar space toward the planet explored by the admiral's famous ancestor.

Consult the Travel Time Chart. Cross-index the planet of origin with Ulnar 118, the squadron's destination, to find the duration of the voyage in days. Add the resulting number to the previous accumulation of time spent waiting or traveling in the course of the campaign. Note this new total for future reference. Then go to section 103.

— 64 —

The scanner reports pour into *Valiant*'s computer banks, but as Ulnar sifts through them, he grows increasingly dismayed and irritated. The reports are negative, consistently and frustratingly negative. There is no sign of life in the Endymion system, either human or alien. The planet itself is uninhabited, the colony's towns and settlements blasted to ruin. But the Ka'slaq fleet has gone on, leaving behind neither garrison nor base. Ulnar's expedition has been in vain.

Then Ulnar comes to one report that might, perhaps, be worth following up. One of the destroyers has discovered and plotted an orbit for a hulk, a wrecked starship of nonhuman design. Presumably it is a Ka'slaq cruiser destroyed by Larno's garrison during its last defiant struggle. Thorough examination of the wrecked ship may help the Legion's scientists discover more about the opposition.

Ulnar leans back in his command chair, brow furrowed in concentration. His ships could investigate the wreck or they could take it in tow; either way will slow them down. Is it a clue worth following up?

If Ulnar decides to have the wrecked Ka'slaq cruiser investigated, go to section 104.

If Ulnar decides to ignore the cruiser and leave Endymion, go to section 136.

— 65 —

"Flag to all ships," Ulnar says, switching on the Fleetcomm microphone again. "Recon wing, form screen and prepare to engage. Battle wing, adopt close formation and await my signal to attack."

The admiral enters a combination of letters and numbers through the keyboard on his console, bringing the Flag computer into the Fleetcomm link and calling up a preprogrammed string of battle orders. The monitor shows the scrolling readout of vectors,

Section 65

speeds, and positions that will guide each ship of the squadron into place, one of many plans Ulnar has prepared since leaving St. Germaine. Captains on each vessel in the squadron are reading the same information and translating the data into orders preparing their individual commands for action.

The yellow lights in the planning tank creep slowly into a new pattern, mirroring the slow movement of the Legion ships to their assigned places. A destroyer screen is a risky formation to adopt against an enemy as powerful as the Ka'slaq, but it offers advantages. If the destroyers can hold the aliens back, Ulnar can bring up his battlecruisers for a decisive blow at just the right time to turn the tide. If necessary, the destroyers can also be sacrificed to cover the withdrawal of the heavier ships if things get bad.

Minutes pass with painful slowness as yellow and blue lights slowly converge, hurtling toward one another at incredible speeds, kept apart by the sheer vastness of space itself. Waiting is the hardest part of a space battle, especially for an admiral. Other officers and crewmen have their own jobs to do, but Ulnar's role is to consider every variable, every fear.

Right now, fear twists his guts as he sees the farthest two alien forces altering course toward the squadron. Time favors the Ka'slaq now; if Ulnar doesn't quickly overcome the first enemy force, the other two will soon close in and bring their superior numbers into play against the Legion. If that happens, his ships will have little more hope of surviving the onslaught than Don Larno and his garrison had.

The resolution of the battle is dictated not only by the formation already chosen, but also by which of the three enemy groups is engaged first. Find out the division that fights initially according to the guidelines given below.

If the squadron attacks the closest group of enemy ships, the Ka'slaq First Division is engaged first.

If Ulnar decides to remain on the defensive, the Ka'slaq First Division is still engaged first.

If Ulnar moves the squadron to shield Endymion from attack, the Ka'slaq Second Division is engaged first.

If the squadron moves to fight the force around the alien planetoid, the Ka'slaq Third Division is first to be engaged.

If the squadron attempts to use Stealth mode to elude the

Section 66

nearest aliens but are brought to battle because Stealth fails, the Ka'slaq First Division engages first.

To resolve the battle at Endymion, Ulnar can choose to fight a conventional space battle by going to section 130.

Ulnar can also choose the more unorthodox approach of using Stealth mode during the actual battle; if so, go to section 135.

— 66 —

The loss of Baal is a serious blow, not only to the Star League, but to David Ulnar personally. He feels the deaths of all those people keenly. His inability to stop the alien armada before it could descend upon the helpless colony condemned those settlers as surely as any death warrant.

Baal is gone, but Ulnar is drawn to the planet. Perhaps the aliens are there, preparing for their next move. If so, a sudden attack by the Ninth Squadron might take them by surprise. And even if the Ka'slaq are no longer in Baal's star system, Ulnar hopes to find clues there regarding Ka'slaq intentions or limitations.

At his command, the squadron sets out. The ships lift from orbit, set their course, and once again leave behind the relative security of a planetary system for the lonely chill of interstellar space.

Consult the Travel Time Chart, cross-indexing the planet of origin with Baal, the destination world. Add the duration of the voyage given from the chart to previously accumulated time spent in the campaign and record this amount for future use. Then proceed to section 76.

— 67 —

"Flag to all ships," Ulnar continues a few minutes later. "Formation order: adopt defensive cylinder. Detailed battle orders follow by computer link. Stand by." As he speaks, his hands move over the keyboard on the console before him. The combination Ulnar punches hooks the tactical computer into his Fleetcomm ship-to-ship network, sending to the rest of the squadron via computer a string of orders detailing speeds, vectors, and positions to be adopted by the squadron in forming the cylindrical deployment he has chosen.

Now Ulnar watches the plan unfold in the tank as the yellow lights representing the Ninth Squadron crawl slowly to arrange themselves in a new pattern. The defensive cylinder is supposed to be a solid, flexible defensive formation that brings the entire firepower of a squadron into action, but it can be disrupted by a well-organized attack. Ulnar has no illusions about the quality of the opposition, but his outnumbered squadron needs to bring as much strength as possible to bear if the enemy is to be thrown back.

Ship movements in the planning tank are slow and deliberate. Even at geodyne-induced speeds, the vessels preparing to clash are maneuvering through a vast battlefield. Waiting can be the worst part of a battle in space, although the officers and men have duties to distract them from their fears—with one notable exception. David Ulnar's duty demands that he concentrate on every possible problem and threat and plan reactions to them before the battle is joined. At times like this Vice-Admiral Ulnar would gladly trade roles with the most junior spaceman on board.

Symbols in the tank attract his attention. According to computer interpolations of sensor information, the farthest two divisions of Ka'slaq ships have altered course. Projections of their new vectors show that they will join the first attack wave soon after the battle is joined. The squadron will have to defeat the First Division before the other two divisions arrive or the Legion stands no chance of winning.

The resolution of the battle is determined by the formation already chosen, as well as which of the three alien forces is

Section 68

engaged first. Determine which division fights first by following the guidelines given below.

If the squadron attacks the closest group of enemy ships, the Ka'slaq First Division is engaged first.
If Ulnar remains on the defensive, the Ka'slaq First Division is still engaged first.
If Ulnar orders the squadron to shield Endymion from attack, the Ka'slaq Second Division is engaged first.
If the squadron is sent to fight the enemy near the alien planetoid, the Ka'slaq Third Division is the first group to be engaged.
If the squadron attempts to use Stealth mode to elude the nearest aliens but are brought to battle because Stealth fails, the Ka'slaq First Division engages first.

To resolve the battle of Endymion, Ulnar can choose to fight a conventional space battle by going to section 130.

Ulnar can also choose the less orthodox alternative of using Stealth mode during the actual battle. Go to section 135.

— 68 —

The Ka'slaq pose a threat to humanity's Star League, a serious menace made even more deadly by the mystery that surrounds the aliens. Their invasion into League space could well prove impossible to turn back.

"If only the Legion knew more about them!" Ulnar mutters angrily.

The aliens first appeared at S.C. 170. Perhaps there are clues on S.C. 170 concerning the Ka'slaq's intentions and weaknesses, Ulnar reasons. There might even be information aboard the wrecks of the human expedition destroyed there.

There may also be some strategic value to a visit to the distant planet. As the scene of the first Ka'slaq assault, the system is the logical location for an alien base or supply link. If so, an attack on a sensitive point in the rear of the alien advance would draw the Ka'slaq back to defend it.

Could S.C. 170 be the answer to all their problems? Ulnar

allows himself the luxury of hope as he issues the necessary orders. Within hours the Ninth Squadron is under way, the pervasive hum of the geodynes filling the *Valiant* and her sister ships with purpose.

It is a long way to their new destination. Cut off from the League by the problems of interstellar communications, the voyage gives everyone too much time to brood. But the die is cast. Ulnar forces himself to ignore his doubts and to maintain an air of confidence befitting an admiral.

Consult the Travel Time Chart. Cross-index the squadron's port of origin with its intended destination (S.C. 170) to find the length of the journey and add this amount to any time already accumulated from previous sections. Record the new total on a piece of scratch paper for future reference, and proceed to section 54.

— 69 —

"All clear, Admiral. No report of alien activity," the duty officer says as Ulnar enters *Valiant*'s bridge. His bored tone speaks volumes. Since their arrival at the colony world, the days have rolled by tediously without a trace of the Ka'slaq. Ulnar is beginning to wonder at the wisdom of his decision. While the squadron waits idle at Baal, the alien armada could be almost anywhere.

But Ulnar is not yet ready to admit error. The Ka'slaq could still come, and if he feels foolish sitting in orbit here, he would feel more foolish still if he left, only to have the aliens arrive after his ships are out of contact and range. He crosses the bridge to the Flag console, the admiral's position for monitoring squadron activities in or out of battle, and sinks into his seat with weary resignation. The wait hasn't done his confidence any good.

"Patrol status?" he asks the duty officer. Ulnar is already calling up the relevant information on his monitors, but he prefers to get his briefings from a man rather than a machine, an idiosyncracy the flagship bridge crew has become accustomed to.

"Four ships deployed on long-range patrols, Admiral," he is

Section 69

told. "Two of them are five minutes overdue for check-in, but—"

"That's nothing unusual," Ulnar finishes for him. He glances at the monitor readout and takes note of the two ship names. "Communications, patch my board through and raise *Defiant* and *Anthar*. Perhaps we can instill a sense of proper timing in them."

"Aye-aye, sir," the technician answers, oblivious to the admiral's sarcasm. Suddenly, one hand to his earphone, the technician stiffens and swivels to face Ulnar. "Pax Eternal," he mutters, a perplexed look on his face.

"What is it?" Ulnar asks quietly.

"Static, sir, on the ultrawave channels," comes the reply. "I've never heard this kind of static. There's a *pattern* to it, Admiral."

Ulnar bends over his own board and turns up the volume on his speaker to the crackle of an unfamiliar form of ultrawave static. Textbooks claim that ultrawave static is not possible.

". . . *Defiant* . . . Mayday . . ." Tiny, distant, almost overpowered by background noise.

Ulnar whirls on the duty officer. "Call Captain Sammis to the bridge," he orders curtly. "And sound the call to general quarters."

While Sammis prepares the ship, Ulnar places the rest of the squadron on guard, but without more information, there isn't much they can do. The static grows worse and begins to affect the ultrapulse tracking system and communications. Scanners and ship-to-ship contact remain usable but are unreliable.

Finally, the tension is broken by another report. "Ultrapulse shows two friendly ships at the limit of detection range," an officer announces.

Ulnar, feigning calm by sipping from a mug of coffee, hands it to a steward and swivels his seat to command a view of *Valiant*'s tactical planning tank. There, ultrapulse data is translated by computers to symbols. Two yellow blips identified as a battlecruiser and a destroyer appear at the edge of the tank, moving inward at maximum speed. The computers identify the transponder signals of these two newcomers, updating the readouts to show that they are, as everyone hoped, *Defiant* and *Anthar*.

A ragged cheer starts from the bridge crew, but it dies away as another computer update supplements the previous one. Not far behind those two ships, and gaining fast, are a whole phalanx of

Section 69

blue-colored lights representing unknown, presumably hostile ships. The Ka'slaq have arrived.

"*Defiant* on line, Admiral," the communications technician reports.

"Put it through." Ulnar turns to the microphone and comm screen on the command console. The monitor flickers to life, broken by static. Between bursts of distortion, the strained features of a young captain with a scorched uniform collar and a bleeding gash across one cheek appears.

"Flag, this is *Defiant*," he says. "Enemy ships pursuing. They'll reach your position soon. Too many for us to stop. . . ." He rubs ineffectually at the blood on his face. "There's more of them than anyone thought. We took a grazing hit, with one geodyne damaged and fifty men killed or wounded. Admiral, we can't fight them. . . ." It's clear that *Defiant*'s captain knows his ship is doomed.

"Energy pulse from target 027," a voice calls from somewhere behind the battlecruiser's captain. "They're getting ready to—" With a blinding flash of light and the sound of melting electronics, the transmission ends abruptly. *Defiant* has been hit again, this time fatally.

"Pax Eternal," the communications technician mutters again. Ulnar drops his eyes to the planning tank, where the computer is already updating the symbols. The one representing *Defiant* is fading from powerful battlecruiser to lifeless hulk.

As an anticlimax to the death of the *Defiant*, the smaller dot representing the destroyer *Anthar* winks out altogether a few moments later. The Ka'slaq destroyed the smaller ship so thoroughly that nothing large enough to bounce back ultrapulse symbols is left.

Ulnar stares into the tank for long minutes, watching thirty-odd blue symbols creep toward the squadron, and, behind them, Baal. Two more ships are gone, and the implacable aliens continue their advance. He wonders for a moment if it would be better to fight and die or flee and face the shame of running without a fight.

He feels his resolve hardening and begins mentally framing the orders to carry out the decision he has made.

If Ulnar decides to attack the Ka'slaq fleet, go to section 33.

If Ulnar decides to remain near Baal to defend the planet from attack, go to section 37.

If Ulnar decides to abandon Baal and withdraw, go to section 41.

— 70 —

"All ships," Ulnar says, activating the Fleetcomm microphone once more. "This is Flag. Disperse and prepare to engage. Repeat, disperse for battle. Orders coming on-line." His fingers tap in a quick code on the Flag computer console in front of him, hooking the computer to the Fleetcomm transmitter and calling up the preprogrammed battle orders stored there. Lines of information scroll across the monitor, giving precise vector and positioning information for each ship in the squadron, and Ulnar's readout is repeated on the bridge of each ship. The captains stand ready to translate that data into action, preparing each individual vessel for the battle to come.

In the planning tank the yellow lights that represent Legion ships creep slowly into a new pattern. The ships are scattering to form an extremely loose and irregular wall to meet the aliens. It's a dangerous formation to adopt against an enemy as well-coordinated as the Ka'slaq, but perhaps it will divide the tight alien groups and even the contest.

Battles in space take time to develop since the size of the battlefield slows actions to a crawl. The minutes go by like hours, and Ulnar's wait is hardest of all. Officers and crewmen throughout the squadron at least have duties that distract them from waiting and worrying.

Suddenly the scanners detect changes in the vectors of the two distant Ka'slaq divisions. The alien divisions are moving toward the squadron to support the nearest alien ships. Ulnar's squadron must win quickly if it is to win at all, or the Ka'slaq strength will grow to overwhelming levels.

The resolution of the battle is determined not only by the formation already chosen, but also by which of the three alien forces is first to be engaged. Determine which alien division fights first by following the guidelines given below.

If the squadron attacks the closest group of enemy ships, the Ka'slaq First Division is engaged first.

If Ulnar decides to remain on the defensive, the Ka'slaq First Division is still the first to engage.

If the squadron is ordered to shield Endymion from attack, the Ka'slaq Second Division is engaged first.

Section 71

If Ulnar has the squadron fight the enemy near the alien planetoid, the Ka'slaq Third Division will be the first group they engage.

If the squadron attempts to use Stealth mode to elude the nearest aliens but are brought to battle because Stealth fails, the Ka'slaq First Division engages first.

To resolve the battle of Endymion, Ulnar can choose to fight a conventional space battle by going to section 130.

Ulnar can choose a less orthodox alternative, using Stealth mode during the actual battle. Go to section 135.

— 71 —

Admiral Ulnar is unwilling to leave the system, feeling that little purpose will be served by moving without a clear idea of enemy intentions. The Ninth Squadron remains in orbit, awaiting orders. Ulnar studies incoming information and news for clues about what to do next.

Add one day to the total number of days in the campaign thus far.

If the new total is thirty-three days or less, and no League planets have fallen yet, go to section 22.

If the new total is thirty-four to forty-five days and only one League planet has fallen, go to section 48.

If the new total is forty-six to fifty-five days and no messages have been received from St. Germaine, go to section 98.

If the new total is fifty-six days or more, go to section 121.

If none of the conditions noted above apply, go to section 107.

— 72 —

"Enemy closing fast," the ultrapulse operator announces dispassionately. Ulnar curses inwardly. His improvised formation orders are nowhere near complete, and the other ships are reacting too slowly. He thinks fleetingly of how useless the tactical planning computers really are in a case like this; they are only as good as the programs stored within them, and they can only provide battle plans for situations that have been worked out in advance. Without a prepared program, Ulnar is reduced to human speeds. *How* do the Ka'slaq react so fast and so smoothly?

Fingers dancing on the computer keyboard, he cancels his previous orders and quickly enters new instructions.

Proceed to section 70.

— 73 —

The latest developments worry Ulnar. He reexamines enemy movements up until now, but can find no real pattern. He projects the dangers to the sector; from that he chooses his destination. He hopes to forestall an enemy thrust, *and* add ships in the local garrison to his force.

The geodynes hum to life, and the squadron sets out once again. As always, the voyage is long, and the lack of news does nothing to ease tensions. Eventually the ships of the Legion approach their goal. Ulnar prepares for the worst while hoping desperately for the best. He needs a break that will turn the campaign in his favor at last.

Consult the Travel Time Chart. Cross-index the planet of origin with the destination world to yield the duration of the voyage in days. Add this to the time spent in previous stages of the campaign and note the new total.

If the new total is thirty-three days or less, go to section 91.

If the new total is thirty-four to forty-five days, go to section 89.

If the new total is forty-six to fifty-five days, go to section 98.

If the new total is fifty-six days or more, go to section 121.

— 74 —

Ulnar is beginning to regret leaving the base at St. Germaine. He tells himself again that the capital is the best place to concentrate his ships in view of the most recent developments. And the geofractor complex there is the sector's one link with the League's inner planets and the larger fleet Admiral Merros is assembling. St. Germaine is the logical target for the next Ka'slaq thrust, and its strategic importance makes Ulnar's decision an easy one.

Issuing orders to the squadron, Admiral Ulnar begins to feel better about the situation. The Legion ships set their new course and let their geodyne engines thrust them out of orbit and into deep space. As before, the passage is a long one, with plenty of chances for uncertainties and doubts. Eventually Ulnar's ships approach their home base again, slipping into orbit with quiet precision. Ulnar is already busy catching up on the news in preparation for the next moves of the campaign.

Consult the Travel Time Chart by cross-indexing the planet of origin with the squadron's destination (St. Germaine). Add the result to the number of days already accumulated from previous voyages and note the new total.

If Endymion is the most recent planet attacked by the aliens, go to section 48.

Otherwise, go to section 115.

— 75 —

Ulnar goes through the reports from the ships engaged in the sweep through the S.C. 170 system, staying up to date on their findings. The scouting run proves to be a major disappointment; there is no trace of the Ka'slaq fleet and no sign of a base or a depot anywhere in the system. Ulnar's hope that S.C. 170 would exercise a strategic pull on the Ka'slaq leadership has been thoroughly dashed by the lack of significant discoveries here. Now Ulnar is worried; this long-range strike at the Ka'slaq rear was his one chance to draw the aliens away from the Star League, and now that it has failed, the sector is sure to suffer the ravages of war on a grand scale.

But depressed though he is by these thoughts, Ulnar is quick to notice one item that could have a far-reaching impact. One of his destroyers did find signs of the Ka'slaq passage: the hulk of a cruiser-sized vessel of totally nonhuman design orbiting at the fringes of the system's asteroid belt. The cruiser is powerless, though the reason is undetermined. The vessel could furnish League scientists with more information on the aliens.

Ulnar's one concern is time. Even if they tow the hulk, the squadron will be slowed considerably. Does the information it might hold make the investment in time worthwhile?

If Ulnar decides to have the wrecked Ka'slaq cruiser investigated further, go to section 104.

If Ulnar decides to ignore the alien ship and leave S.C. 170, go to section 138.

— 76 —

Approaching Baal, the ships of the Legion turn all their sensors toward the star system in an effort to discover what, if anything, is still happening there. Scanners and ultrawave communications bands remain obstinately silent. By the time the fleet reaches the outer fringes of Baal's system, it is clear that the colony is not going to respond. There is no sign of any activity.

Section 77

"Appearances can be deceiving," Ulnar says to Sammis, *Valiant*'s hawk-featured captain. "We may turn up something worthwhile by taking a closer look." But behind his optimistic mask, Ulnar begins to suspect that he was wrong in choosing Baal. If the Ka'slaq have struck and moved on without leaving a garrison behind, the squadron's trip here has been completely wasted.

But Ulnar can't be sure without a closer look. From his station on *Valiant*'s bridge he begins issuing orders to examine the system more closely.

If Ulnar orders the destroyers in his squadron (assuming he has destroyers available) to scout the system while the battlecruisers are held back in reserve, go to section 111.

If Ulnar orders all the ships in the squadron to move into the Baal system in a reconnaissance in force, go to section 116 instead.

— 77 —

Ulnar composes himself and reaches for the intercom again. "Bridge. This is Admiral Ulnar. Prepare a courier boat to carry a message to the geofractor complex."

"Bridge, aye-aye," the duty officer responds, unsurprised.

Switching off, Ulnar turns back to his computer and communications desk. It takes only minutes to create a message capsule for Admiral Merros. A small, spindle-shaped object, the capsule contains a brief video recording of Ulnar stating the Benbo case, including transcripts of the commodore's message. Ulnar is requesting disciplinary assistance.

The capsule is the only practical way of communicating with Merros back on Earth, but even as Ulnar turns it over to a courier, he can't refrain from feeling gloomy. Chances are that Merros will back Benbo, not him. By now the hot-tempered commodore may well have sent his own version of the confrontation. After the courier leaves, Ulnar tries to get back to work, but he expects more trouble to come.

Proceed to section 40.

— 78 —

"Flag to all ships," Ulnar continues, reopening the Fleetcomm microphone. "Form defensive globe. Recon wing to take shelter within the globe." He punches in a combination on his computer keyboard; battle orders for each ship begin to scroll across his monitor, and simultaneously the Fleetcomm hookup relays them to each of the other vessels in the Ninth Squadron.

In the planning tank the yellow symbols that represent the squadron's ships begin to shift slowly into the globe formation Ulnar has ordered, their relative positions reflecting those of the actual ships around *Valiant*. With a defensive globe, Ulnar reasons, he can maintain the closest possible support for all the ships under his command and thus offset the Ka'slaq coordination.

Movements are slow despite the incredible speeds possible; space battlefields are infinite. The fleets draw together slowly, deliberately, but with the inevitability of two juggernauts set in motion against one another.

Although the Ka'slaq have an advantage in numbers, Ulnar's squadron has every chance of defeating them if handled properly. A failure now would be a crippling blow to the defense of the Star League.

To resolve the battle of Baal, Ulnar can choose to fight a conventional battle by going to section 120.

If Ulnar prefers to use the unorthodox tactic of employing Stealth mode during the actual battle, go to section 128.

— 79 —

Twenty-two days pass during the voyage to Thule. By the end of the journey everyone aboard is hungry for news and concerned about what they might find at Thule. The fear that the Ka'slaq might reach Thule first and overwhelm its small garrison is a common topic in *Valiant*'s wardroom.

At last the squadron comes back into communications range, and those fears are quickly laid to rest. Although Thule and its garrison are both intact, the news is not all good. Early transmissions from the colony relay word of the fall of Endymion to the alien armada. This trip has proven to be a wild-goose chase after all, one that could cost the League and the Legion dearly.

But the time the squadron is in orbit around chilly Thule, Ulnar is already collecting detailed reports of the Ka'slaq invasion at Endymion. He needs to formulate a new strategy quickly if he is to stop the aliens from penetrating deeper into the League.

Proceed to section 22. Mark forty-four days off your time record.

— 80 —

"All ships, this is Flag," Ulnar continues, speaking into the Fleetcomm mike once more. "Adopt standard wedge formation for an attack on the enemy." He runs his fingers over the Flag computer keyboard in front of him, calling up detailed battle orders for the squadron and hooking the computer into the Fleetcomm transmission. The preprogrammed description of vectors and positions governing the squadron's movements scrolls across his monitor slowly, and it is repeated aboard each other vessel under Ulnar's command.

The three-dimensional planning tank shows yellow lights marking the positions of each Legion ship. These begin to shift slowly as the ships assume their proper places, forming into the wedge-shaped pattern Ulnar has selected for the coming battle. With the destroyers forming the tip of the wedge and the battlecruisers clustered behind, the squadron is ready to fly like an arrow into the phalanx of loosely-deployed Ka'slaq vessels. The wedge will bring a great deal of Legion firepower to bear in a concerted attack, although the flexible Ka'slaq fleet might find it easy to engulf and surround the compact formation.

Time passes slowly, with the opposing ships drawing gradually but inexorably together. It takes time, even at the high speeds possible under geodynes, to cross the volume of space. The Ka'slaq are maintaining a rigid formation, as if they don't know or don't care about the Legion ships thrusting like a spear toward the center of their phalanx.

Section 81

Ulnar focuses on the planning tank and the Flag console. Victory is essential, for a defeat here could have catastrophic consequences.

To resolve this battle using conventional tactics, go to section 120.

If Ulnar chooses the unorthodox use of Stealth mode during the actual battle, go to section 128.

— 81 —

Ulnar switches on the Fleetcomm microphone once more. "Flag to all ships," he begins. "Battle wing, form phalanx and prepare to engage. Destroyers will retire behind the battlecruiser screen and remain out of combat." His fingers dance quickly over the keyboard on the console before him, entering in a combination that brings his Flag computer into the Fleetcomm hookup and calls up a set of detailed battle orders. His monitor begins to scroll through a readout of positions, vectors, and speeds for each ship in the squadron to adopt. This program is only one of dozens Ulnar has prepared during the outward voyage. Now relayed through the Fleetcomm net, it is being repeated on each of the other vessels, where the squadron's captains are busy translating these guidelines into orders preparing their commands for the action to come.

The idea of a heavy screen, a battlecruiser phalanx, is comparatively new and untried, but Ulnar's memory of the quick destruction of the destroyers in Larno's garrison has left him with little respect for the fighting abilities of light ships against Ka'slaq cruisers.

Despite the awesome speeds achieved by ships under geodyne drives, space battles are slow to develop because of the size of the battlefield. This gives Ulnar every opportunity to watch, wait, and worry: Where the other officers and men have jobs to keep them distracted, Ulnar's job is to study the situation and concentrate on all the problems that might arise.

Suddenly the other two alien divisions change course and move in to reinforce their comrades. If Ulnar doesn't win quickly, the Ka'slaq will have reinforcements. If that happens, the Ninth Squadron would be hard-pressed to survive.

The resolution of the battle is decided by not only the formation already chosen, but also by which of the three enemy groups is engaged first. Determine the division that fights initially according to the guidelines provided below.

If the squadron attacks the closest group of enemy ships, the Ka'slaq First Division is engaged first.
    If Ulnar decides to remain on the defensive, the Ka'slaq First Division is still engaged first.
    If Ulnar moves the squadron to shield Endymion from attack, the Ka'slaq Second Division is engaged first.
    If the squadron is ordered to move against the enemy force around the alien planetoid, the Ka'slaq Third Division is first to be engaged.
    If the squadron attempts to use Stealth mode to elude the nearer alien force but is brought to battle because Stealth fails, the Ka'slaq First Division engages them first.

To resolve the battle of Endymion, Ulnar can choose to fight a conventional space battle by going to section 130.

Ulnar can also choose the more risky and unorthodox approach of utilizing Stealth mode during the actual battle: Go to section 135.

— 82 —

Ulnar knows he can't win in a battle of wills with Benbo, not when Admiral Merros is certain to be waiting for a good excuse to relieve Ulnar of his command. A showdown would end with the Ulnar name dragged through the mud again, and with some useless appointee—maybe even Benbo—installed in Ulnar's place. A good officer knows when to retreat, even if it costs him the respect of some of his men.

"Very well, Commodore," Ulnar says at length. "We'll try it your way. But if your guess is wrong and the aliens don't strike at Baal, you'd better hope for a glorious death in battle,

Section 83

because I'll make your life so miserable you'll wish you were dead."

Ulnar breaks the connection angrily and begins to revise his orders. By the time he's ready, he can see advantages in falling in with Benbo's plan. Perhaps, he tells himself as he reaches for the communications panel, Benbo's temper will be worth something after all.

Proceed to section 50.

— 83 —

"All ships, this is Flag," Ulnar continues, switching the Fleetcomm microphone on again. "Form cylinder and prepare for defensive combat. Battle orders are on the computer link." He switches the computer into the communications network and calls up the appropriate tactical instructions. As he finishes, a scroll of vectors and positions begins to unwind on his monitor, showing the data being received by captains on each ship in Ulnar's squadron.

In the planning tank yellow lights begin to move, showing Legion ships redeploying in obedience to orders. The cylinder is a good defensive formation, utilizing the squadron's whole combat strength in the best possible way. Unfortunately it can be easily disorganized and overwhelmed by a determined assault. Ulnar hopes his ships can keep the formation intact in the battle ahead.

The battle takes time to develop, with ships closing at a crawl. Ulnar tries to tune out all the distractions of *Valiant*'s bridge, focusing all of his attention on his control console and the planning tank where the engagement is beginning to unfold. A victory for the Legion is essential to the defense of the sector. Success could score a major blow against the invaders, but failure could spell the end of everything for the defenders.

To resolve the battle using conventional space combat tactics, go to section 120.

If Ulnar prefers to use the more unorthodox approach of using Stealth mode to partially conceal his ships during the battle, go to section 128.

— 84 —

The battle has an unreal quality to it, as if it were just another simulation in the planning tank. It is hard to realize that each of the lights that flickers and fades out on that screen represents the death of a whole shipload of men, some of them friends or acquaintances, and all of them leave behind families, friends, loved ones.

The detached, analytical side of his mind registers the losses the squadron is suffering. Even though the Legion is fighting back with spirit and resolution, Ulnar can project the situation through to its conclusion. If he doesn't take action, the squadron will eventually be overwhelmed.

"Flag to all ships," he orders at last. "Discontinue the action. I say again, discontinue the action." He keys in the confirmatory computer-signalled battle order before continuing. "Break off and withdraw. Regroup at rendezvous point seven. All ships are to withdraw at once."

The Legion ships begin to peel off and accelerate, using Stealth mode to cover their attempted flight. As *Valiant* pulls away from the battle, Ulnar notices that Stealth mode jamming coincides with a loss of coordination in the alien fleet. He nods with satisfaction, but continues to keep a close watch on the tank. Stealth mode is not infallible, and the aliens can still outrun any of his ships. It will take several minutes to determine whether this retreat will actually carry them to safety.

Roll two dice and compare the result to the Stealth value for the Legion ships. If the result is greater than the value, return to the preceding section and resume combat resolution.

If the result is less than or equal to the Stealth value, go to section 94.

When the squadron attempts to withdraw at the end of a round in which no enemy ships fired on it, go to section 94 automatically. No Stealth roll is needed. This will normally occur after one Ka'Slaq force is destroyed and before another is engaged.

— 85 —

"Flag to all ships," Ulnar continues, speaking on the Fleetcomm circuit again. "Adopt standard cone formation and prepare to attack. Battle orders coming through on Flag computer hookup." He keys in the alphanumeric code that places his computer on the Fleetcomm circuit and calls up one of the dozens of preprogrammed sets of combat instructions stored in its files. The monitor above the keyboard comes alive with scrolling readouts of vectors and positions, information relayed at the same time to the bridges of each ship in the squadron.

The planning tank's yellow lights, depicting Legion vessels, begin to move in response to Ulnar's orders. The battlecruisers are assembling at the vortex of the cone, with the destroyers spreading out into a wider circle ahead of them. Against the Ka'slaq phalanx the cone formation will be hard-pressed to carry out its usual function of englobing the opposition, but Ulnar believes that it can be effective in carving the alien fleet into manageable chunks and defeating them in detail.

Ulnar focuses on the planning tank, blocking out the activity on the bridge around him. Slowly the two groups of ships are closing the gap. A Legion victory at Baal might not drive the Ka'slaq out of the sector altogether, but it would be a moral and strategic victory for the hard-pressed Star League. But if Ulnar and his squadron are defeated here, it could be a blow from which the Legion might never recover.

Ulnar can choose to fight a conventional space battle at Baal by going to section 120.

If Ulnar decides to fight while under the cloak of Stealth mode, go to section 128.

— 86 —

Reports filter to Admiral Ulnar's station on *Valiant*'s bridge from each of the ships of the Ninth Squadron, keeping him current on the progress of their sweep through the Ulnar 118 star system. Unfortunately, the reports aren't much use. There's no trace of enemy activity—virtually no sign that they have ever been here.

Evidently Ulnar's hunch about the system was wrong. Discouraged and irritable, the admiral scans the information over and over again. Finally he begins to consider new options in light of this failure and the rest of the strategic situation as he knows it. He cannot afford to choose wrongly again.

If he decides to remain at Ulnar 118, go to section 152.

If Ulnar orders the squadron to return to the base at St. Germaine, go to section 74.

If the squadron is ordered to Baal, go to section 58.

If Ulnar orders his ships to travel to Endymion, go to section 53.

If Ulnar orders the squadron to move to S.C. 170, go to section 68.

If any other destination is selected, go to section 73.

— 87 —

It is a long, hard-fought battle. Although the Ka'slaq manage to inflict heavy damage to the squadron, Ulnar's ships hang on. Eventually the battered survivors of the Ninth Defense Squadron realize that they have run out of alien opponents. The last of the enemy cruisers vanish in the atomic fire of the squadron's vortex guns.

But ahead, looming like a small planet, is the last gigantic Ka'slaq ship, Larno's planetoid. It is no asteroid, no natural

Section 88

formation somehow made mobile. The Ka'slaq mother ship is an immense artifact, a dizzying assemblage of angles, planes, and soaring towers. Through the entire battle it has not fired once, and even now it seems slow and unable to defend itself. This lumbering target remains an enigma, and, to Ulnar's mind, a threat.

The admiral leans forward in his seat, studying a computer projection of the alien mother ship on his monitor screen. He has scored a victory, but as long as this massive structure remains intact, that victory may only be an incomplete triumph.

If Ulnar orders his squadron to fire on the Ka'slaq planetoid, go to section 143.

If Ulnar orders the squadron to attempt to board the alien station, go to section 114.

If Ulnar does nothing about the planetoid, go to section 147.

If the admiral attempts to communicate with the alien leaders, go to section 172.

— 88 —

"This is Flag," Ulnar continues a few moments later, the Fleetcomm microphone switched on again. "Battle wing, form battlecruiser phalanx and prepare to engage. Recon wing, deploy behind the phalanx. Destroyers are to remain out of combat. Battle orders coming." The admiral enters an alphanumeric code that brings the computer into the Fleetcomm net and calls up one of his prepared lists of deployment instructions from the computer's storage files. He watches the monitor readout information on vectors and positions; the other captains in the squadron are picking out the instructions that apply to them and translating these into the commands that will prepare their vessels for actions.

The orders are carried out efficiently, although Ulnar suspects the destroyer captains, an unruly lot at best, are reluctant to comply. Yellow lights depicting Legion ships in the planning tank move into new patterns that reflect Ulnar's chosen deployment. Ulnar is relieved; he doesn't feel the destroyers have much of a chance in battle against the Ka'slaq, and the battlecruiser screen is specifically intended to protect light ships in such circumstances.

However, that plan will deprive him of the entire Recon wing when the shooting starts, and Ulnar can't help entertaining second thoughts. Ignoring the temptation to tamper with a delicately-balanced situation, Ulnar concentrates on trying to predict enemy moves and project suitable responses to them. The battle for Baal could be a turning point in the war, a chance for the Legion to inflict an important check on their opponents. But if Ulnar loses, the battle could spell the end of the Legion of Space and the Star League.

Ulnar can choose to fight a conventional space battle at Baal by going to section 120.

If Ulnar decides to use less orthodox tactics and adopt Stealth mode during the actual fighting, go to section 128 instead.

— 89 —

Reaching their destination, the officers of the Ninth Squadron anxiously search for news of the Ka'slaq.

If Endymion is the only League world that has been attacked by the invaders, go to section 48.

Otherwise, go to section 107.

— 90 —

"All ships . . . Flag calling all ships," Ulnar says, the Fleetcomm circuit open again. "Recon wing, form screen and stand by to engage the enemy. Battle wing, adopt close formation and await my orders to attack."

Ulnar hooks the tactical computer into the Fleetcomm network

Section 91

and calls up his preprogrammed battle orders with a few quick strokes on the keyboard. A monitor screen shows the instructions scrolling upward, as it does on every ship in the squadron.

The tactical planning tank's yellow lights, representing Legion ships, begin to shift, reflecting the redeployment of the actual ships into the positions Ulnar has allocated. By creating a screen of destroyers, Ulnar hopes to tie down the Ka'slaq cruisers long enough to give his battlecruisers a chance to choose the best moment to counterattack them. This kind of formation can be risky when the enemy is as powerful as these aliens. But the Legion fields good ships, tough crews, and officers with the courage and determination to see the fight through.

The minutes drag by. Officers and men run through the last prebattle checklists and preparations. Ulnar tunes them out, his attention channeled to the Flag command console and the planning tank itself. The Star League cannot afford to lose at Baal. A win here could be the turning point in the war. But failure could spell the end of Legion and League alike.

To resolve a conventional space battle, go to section 120.

If Ulnar chooses the unorthodox use of Stealth mode during the battle, go to section 128.

— 91 —

Reaching their objective at the end of a long voyage, Ulnar and his men immediately search for fresh information on Ka'slaq activities in the sector.

If no League worlds have yet been attacked, go to section 22.

Otherwise, go to section 107.

— 92 —

Ulnar watches the planning tank in horror as Ka'slaq annihilators pick off Legion ships one after another. Although the squadron is able to mete out its fair share of destruction, the odds are against them. The aliens have too many advantages—superior technology, better cooperation and coordination, above all, superior numbers. The Ninth Defense Squadron gives a fine account of itself, performing its duties in the very best traditions of the Legion of Space. But their supreme effort is still too little to turn the tide against the Ka'slaq.

As ship after ship goes down before the might of the Ka'slaq, David Ulnar knows what it is to face total disaster. He tastes fear and almost welcomes it, for it is the last thing Ulnar has left to tell him he is still alive.

With most of the other ships in the squadron destroyed and *Valiant*'s defensive screens glowing from the titanic energies of Ka'slaq beams, the admiral thinks with curious detachment about the future. Will Merros, so stolid and unimaginative, pay heed to any of Ulnar's reports? Can he draw the conclusions Ulnar himself is only now really beginning to understand? And can he learn to apply new tactics in time to prevent disaster? The pieces of the puzzle are growing obvious to Ulnar, too late to help him.

The alien planetoid ship, the stories of alien performance during attacks on Legion ships, the superb battle coordination displayed by the Ka'slaq, even the mysterious static draw together in Ulnar's mind. He can see now how to stop the Ka'slaq, but he knows all too well that he has no hope of passing on his solution to anyone who can use it. He is too late.

Valiant's overstrained defenses glow brighter under the Ka'slaq onslaught. Finally, deep in the bowels of the battlecruiser, circuits whine under an intolerable overload. With a shower of sparks and a cloud of acrid smoke to mark their passing, the defense fields fail. Instants later annihilator beams tear through the flagship.

The ravening energies engulf the bridge, consuming Ulnar and all the others manning the dying ship. David Ulnar's last thoughts before his fiery death are of duty . . . to himself, to his family, and to the Legion he served with body, soul, and life itself.

Go to section 159.

— 93 —

"All ships, this is Flag," Ulnar continues, speaking on the Fleetcomm channel again. "Withdraw to planetary orbit and maintain opposition maneuvering." He pauses before continuing. "Flag to Baal Space Defense Station. Channel alpha six." He switches channels quickly and watches as colors on the monitor screen swirl briefly before coalescing into the head and shoulders of an elderly officer wearing the insignia of a Legion commandant.

"Alpha six," the officer growls. "Commandant Rovin."

Rovin—that explained the man's air of perpetual hostility. Old for his rank, Rovin's career had faltered after his brutal mistreatment of rebel troops at Alborak nearly two decades before. He had the reputation of being utterly fearless, as well as having a short temper and a long-standing grudge with the politicians who rejected his harsh but successful policies and condemned him to a dead-end career in charge of posts usually reserved for up-and-coming youngsters.

After today, Ulnar tells himself, Jak Rovin will be a hero . . . alive or dead.

"Commandant, I intend to use your fortress as an anvil," Ulnar says quietly. "I want you to draw the Ka'slaq into assaulting your defenses, then keep them occupied. When the time is right, we'll join in and break them."

Rovin is no fool; he knows the aliens' reputation by this time. But he just nods, a grim smile on his face. "As you wish, Admiral. I'll pretend they're commanded by the Board of Inquiry from Alborak." His tone isn't bitter; in fact, he sounds relieved, glad to be back in action at last and to distinguish himself before he dies. The screen clears abruptly. The waiting game begins.

It takes time to marshal the squadron, organizing it into a compact body in a tight orbit around Baal. The essence of Ulnar's strategy is to make it seem as if the Legion has withdrawn, using the planet to shield his ships from the enemy until they are committed. Rovin and various posts on the planet's surface keep the admiral updated. After a long and tense wait, the word comes in. The orbital fortress is under attack.

Section 94

Begin resolving the battle at Baal by pitting 10 Ka'slaq cruisers (firepower 3 each, attack value of 30) against the orbital fortress. The fortress fires once per round on Chart C. The aliens fire each round on Chart D. At the end of any round Ulnar can order his ships to attack, withdraw, or hold fast.

If he decides to attack, go to section 33. If the squadron is ordered to withdraw, go to section 41. If it holds fast, continue to resolve the battle as before.

If the orbital fortress is destroyed before Ulnar orders an attack, the squadron must either launch an attack, defend itself, or attempt to withdraw. An attack is still resolved in section 33. A withdrawal is handled in section 41. If the squadron defends itself, go to section 37.

Ka'slaq ships are replaced each round out of the total force of 34 ships in their attacking flotilla. Only 10 ships attack in any given round. When no more ships are available as replacements, reduce this number as further losses occur. If by some miracle the fortress eliminates all of the alien ships without Ulnar's help, go to section 146.

Once events cause the battle to move to another section of the text, the fortress can never be used to screen the squadron or participate in any sort of combat for the remainder of this battle.

— 94 —

Hard-pressed by the alien fleet, the ships of the Legion fight with all the determination and skill that can be expected of the Star League's finest. But it isn't enough. The Ka'slaq are too powerful, too well-coordinated, and Ulnar knows that the battle is already as good as lost. Can the squadron pull out before it disintegrates, or should it keep on fighting and go down in the annals of the Legion as the stalwart warriors who fought and died heroically in a lost cause?

Ulnar doesn't want to be a dead hero. Stabbing the Fleetcomm microphone's switch savagely, he orders the squadron to withdraw. Under the cloak of Stealth mode, which distorts ultrapulse scans and ultrawave communications, the squadron breaks off and begins to retreat.

Ulnar watches the scanners closely, trying to make sense out of the chaos Stealth mode imposes on the squadron's own tracking systems. But the enemy seems even more confused by the jamming. After a long, tense wait, an ultrapulse operator straightens up and says, "I think we've lost them."

His words are quickly confirmed. A wave of cheering sweeps around *Valiant*'s bridge. Ulnar wishes he could join in, but he has other things to do, other decisions to make. It's his job to make sure that this check doesn't cost them the whole war.

Reduce the morale of all surviving Legion ships by 1. Go to section 47.

— 95 —

"This is Flag, calling all ships," Ulnar continues over the Fleetcomm microphone. "Disperse and prepare for battle. Repeat, disperse for engagement. Battle orders coming on-line." Ulnar enters in the alphanumeric combination that summons up the preprogrammed list of battle orders from the tactical computer and feeds them into the Fleetcomm network. He watches the instructions scroll across his monitor, knowing that the captains of each ship under his command are watching the same data and preparing their vessels for battle according to his orders.

Valiant's planning tank show the slow scattering of Legion ships as they obey these instructions, the yellow lights drawing apart. By dispersing his ships, Ulnar is deliberately sacrificing the advantages of mutual support and concentrated firepower that most formations are intended to promote. It offers the one chance he can see, though, of forcing the alien ships to break their own formation up, which might help combat the advantages of speed and coordination they enjoy. But Ulnar doesn't kid himself: It's a dangerous way to tackle an enemy as good as the Ka'slaq have proven to be.

He has plenty of time to contemplate his decision, to raise and discard alternatives, flaws, and doubts. The bridge crew runs through their final checklists, while Ulnar tunes out everything but the planning tank and the Flag command console. This battle is crucial to the war effort; success would give the Legion a significant boost in morale and strategic position.

To resolve the battle at Baal using conventional tactics, go to section 120.

Ulnar can also choose a more unorthodox approach, using Stealth mode during the actual battle. If he chooses to do so, go to section 128.

— 96 —

The destroyers dart into the system, falling toward the star as fast as their geodyne engines can carry them. The admiral watches their progress on the planning tank and listens on ultrawave to the chatter between ships.

Then, abruptly, Ulnar's attention is drawn to static building on the ultrawave channels. Before Ulnar can shout a warning or an order to break off, the destroyers are under attack. Just as Ulnar had feared they might, the aliens detected his ships approaching the system and shut down their ships so completely that they escaped all notice—until the trap was sprung.

The destroyers are outnumbered by the aliens. Their scanners report a fleet of seventy or more cruisers as well as the huge ultrapulse echo that must be the planetoid ship seen at Endymion.

There is no way the destroyers can escape. Ulnar asks himself if he should allow them to fight alone and be destroyed, or should he try to help them by committing the battle wing to support them? Neither alternative looks promising.

If Ulnar chooses to withdraw, go to section 170.

If Ulnar decides to support the destroyers, it will take 8 combat rounds for the battlecruisers to arrive. During that time the destroyers fire once per round on Chart D. The Ka'slaq have a total of 74 ships but launch their attack with only 15. Each round, they fire on Chart A. Any Ka'slaq ships lost are replaced back up to the initial figure of 15 as long as they have more ships in reserve. Their planetoid ship does not participate in the battle. When the Legion's battle wing arrives, they break off the action long enough to let the surviving destroyers join these reinforcements.

Once this happens, go to section 151 if Ulnar orders his ships to attack the aliens.

If the squadron stands on the defensive, go to section 156.

If the reunited squadron tries to withdraw, go to section 170.

— 97 —

"Ultrapulse and ultrawave generators to feedback setting, maximum output," the captain orders curtly. As his instructions are obeyed and confirmed by technicians at posts all around *Valiant*'s dimly lit bridge, Sammis nods slowly. When the last station finally checks in, he turns to Ulnar. "Stealth mode, Admiral." Green lights on Ulnar's command console report compliance by the rest of the squadron.

"Thank you, Captain," Ulnar responds.

Silence falls over the bridge. The next few minutes will determine whether the squadron fights or escapes.

The waiting continues. Ulnar begins to feel optimistic; in the planning tank, alien ships are already dropping out of the tight formation and veering off in unexpected directions. The alien fleet is rapidly degenerating into a confused rabble, an effect far out of proportion with the disappearance of the Legion squadron from the alien scanners. There is more to the Ka'slaq confusion than just the loss of their opponents.

"We've lost them!" an ultrapulse technician cries. A wave of cheers sweeps the bridge, but the captain's gruff orders quickly silence them.

"Stealth mode successful, Admiral," Sammis announces pompously, bringing a smile to Ulnar's lips.

Valiant has eluded them, making clear inroads into the Ka'slaq organization. Ulnar shifts his attention back to his own console, ready to make the next move in this dangerous game of human chess against the alien commander.

If the squadron changes its course to turn and attack the Ka'slaq force it has just eluded, go to section 33.

If Ulnar continues the withdrawal as originally planned, go to section 117.

— 98 —

A message from St. Germaine changes the complexion of the war.

"Merros to Ulnar. There has been no other sign of the aliens. Our strategic planners estimate a ninety-plus percent probability that St. Germaine will be the next Ka'slaq target. I have assembled a fleet at St. Germaine and require the presence of your squadron here. Return to St. Germaine as soon as practicable Merros, commanding defense Fleet, ending message."

Ulnar must weigh duty against his own ideas about where the aliens will strike. The safe course is to return to St. Germaine as ordered; Merros is in charge now and bears the responsibility as well as the authority for future actions. But Ulnar has little confidence in Merros, and his conscience would not be assuaged by duty and obedience if Merros were wrong and Ulnar right about the next Ka'slaq target.

If Ulnar returns to St. Germaine with the squadron, consult the Travel Time Chart and add the time used for the journey home to the accumulated total for the rest of the campaign. If the new total is fifty-four days or less, go to section 140.

If the new total is fifty-five days or more, go to section 121.

If Ulnar disobeys orders and remains at his present location, go to section 121.

If Ulnar disobeys orders and moves to a different location, go to section 73.

Sections 99, 100

— 99 —

Admiral Ulnar studies the situation carefully and comes to the conclusion that his withdrawal from Endymion was premature. With the devastation of the colony, the Ka'slaq have total control of the system. If the aliens follow conventional strategic thinking, they are likely to create a base for themselves in the conquered system before they moved on. Since they have seen the Legion run, the Ka'slaq are likely to be complacent and not about to immediately seek further conflict.

Or are they? Ulnar hesitates. Perhaps they are even now preparing an ambush to discourage new visitors. After a few minutes Ulnar reaches for the Fleetcomm microphone once more. The squadron has had time to regroup and recover; it's ready to pay the enemy a second visit.

Add one day to the accumulated time consumed by the campaign so far.

Ulnar chooses to send his destroyers (if any are available) to scout out enemy positions around Endymion. Go to section 36.

If Ulnar decides to send the entire squadron to the system in a reconnaissance, go to section 38.

— 100 —

"Ultrapulse and ultrawave generators to feedback setting, maximum output," Sammis orders curtly. As his instructions are confirmed from technicians at their posts around *Valiant*'s bridge, the flagship's captain nods slowly to himself. Finally, as the last station checks in, he turns to Ulnar. "Stealth mode, Admiral," he announces formally. Green lights on Ulnar's command console proclaim compliance by the other ships.

"Thank you, Captain," Ulnar responds.

Silence falls over the bridge. The next few minutes will determine whether they will fight or escape.

The waiting continues. But as Ulnar watches the planning

Section 101

tank, he makes his own predictions. He hopes fervently that the tracking crew's estimates will contradict his own observations. But they don't.

"They're matching us," a crewman says, defeat heavy in his voice. "The jamming's not working . . . they're still closing in on us."

Ulnar reaches hastily for the Fleetcomm mike and the computer keyboard. Without a preprogrammed plan to cover the precise situation, some fast improvization and adaptation will be necessary. He must regroup the squadron for a fight.

Ulnar's side has one advantage: The alien ships don't seem to be responding as fast or as effectively as Ulnar expected. Their formations are looser, their maneuvers and response times slower and more hesitant. And they seem to be showing a marked reluctance to deviate from their original headings. It may be enough to make the difference between meeting them in formation and having to scatter and fight without organization or coordination.

Roll two dice three times, noting each of the three totals as separate numbers.

If any of these three rolls yields a result less than or equal to the Morale value of the squadron, go to section 37.

If all three rolls are greater than the squadron's Morale value, go to section 101.

— 101 —

"Enemy ships are closing fast," an ultrapulse operator reports. Whispering a curse, Ulnar swivels his chair to face the planning tank and takes in the situation with a hasty glance. He won't have time to complete his hastily composed formation orders, given the chaos reigning in most of the squadron's ships. Lacking proper coherence, demoralized by failure, the squadron is not able to react quickly enough. The lack of backup battle orders to cover every contingency adds to the confusion. Ulnar finds himself wishing that his vessels could operate with the elegant efficiency displayed by the aliens.

Shaking his head, Ulnar rejects the thought. Clearing the computer of his improvised battle orders, Ulnar sends new general instructions via the computer hookup.

"Flag calling all ships," he says. "Cancel previous orders. Scatter and fight dispersed. Prepare to engage the enemy!"

Proceed to section 95.

— 102 —

The squadron continues under the cloak of Stealth mode, pushing on toward Endymion and the alien detachment already entering orbit there. They seem oblivious to Ulnar's approach, which is just how Ulnar wants it. Perhaps the Legion has a chance to avenge Don Larno after all, he thinks hopefully.

Staring into the planning tank, Ulnar reads the symbols there with practiced ease. He plans to reveal a surprise or two that should have quite an impact on the Ka'slaq. Smiling in anticipation, Ulnar turns to his command console and prepares to issue his orders.

If Ulnar decides to attack the aliens, go to section 21.

If Ulnar wants to stand on the defensive and make the Ka'slaq come to him, go to section 28.

If the admiral loses his nerve and decides to withdraw while he has the opportunity, go to section 32.

— 103 —

Lacking a League colony or even a communications station to record and relay messages, there is no way of telling the situation to Ulnar 118's planetary system. This makes the squadron's job tricky. The admiral suspects that the aliens may use the world as an advanced base, but the only way to find out is to actually check into it.

Section 104

As the squadron arrives on the fringes of the system, Ulnar assumes his battle station at the Flag command console on *Valiant*'s bridge. Long-range scans of the region have revealed nothing of interest, but scans from this distance are usually unreliable, unlike evidence gathered by ships sweeping the system on a detailed reconnaissance probe.

After careful consideration Ulnar prepares to issue the orders to launch that probe.

If Ulnar orders the squadron's destroyers to scout the Ulnar 118 system, go to section 123.

If the admiral orders the entire squadron to probe the Ulnar 118 system together, go to section 131.

— 104 —

Weighing delay against knowledge of Ka'slaq capabilities, Ulnar decides to investigate the wrecked alien cruiser. Shortly, shifts of trained technicians and intelligence officers are involved in an organized examination of the alien vessel.

The final analyses in his hands, Ulnar smiles in satisfaction. These findings explain a great deal about the aliens and suggest ways to use their own strengths against them. Ulnar's concern is that when Merros arrives to take command, the conservative admiral may not be willing to accept the recommendations Ulnar's people have compiled. They call for highly unconventional tactics, and "Bulldog" Merros has never been known to consider the unorthodox.

The squadron's researchers have concluded that the Ka'slaq armada is not crewed by ordinary living beings at all. Instead the ships are controlled by a combination of sophisticated technology and transplanted living brains from an alien organism (believed to be an oxygen-breathing, multilimbed race with tentacular appendages), housed in life-support tanks on board their ships. Many brains are assigned to each vessel, where they are hooked up as cyborg controllers to operate every aspect of the shipboard systems. The brains aboard a single cruiser share a collective consciousness, making each individual vessel a formidable opponent in battle.

Section 104

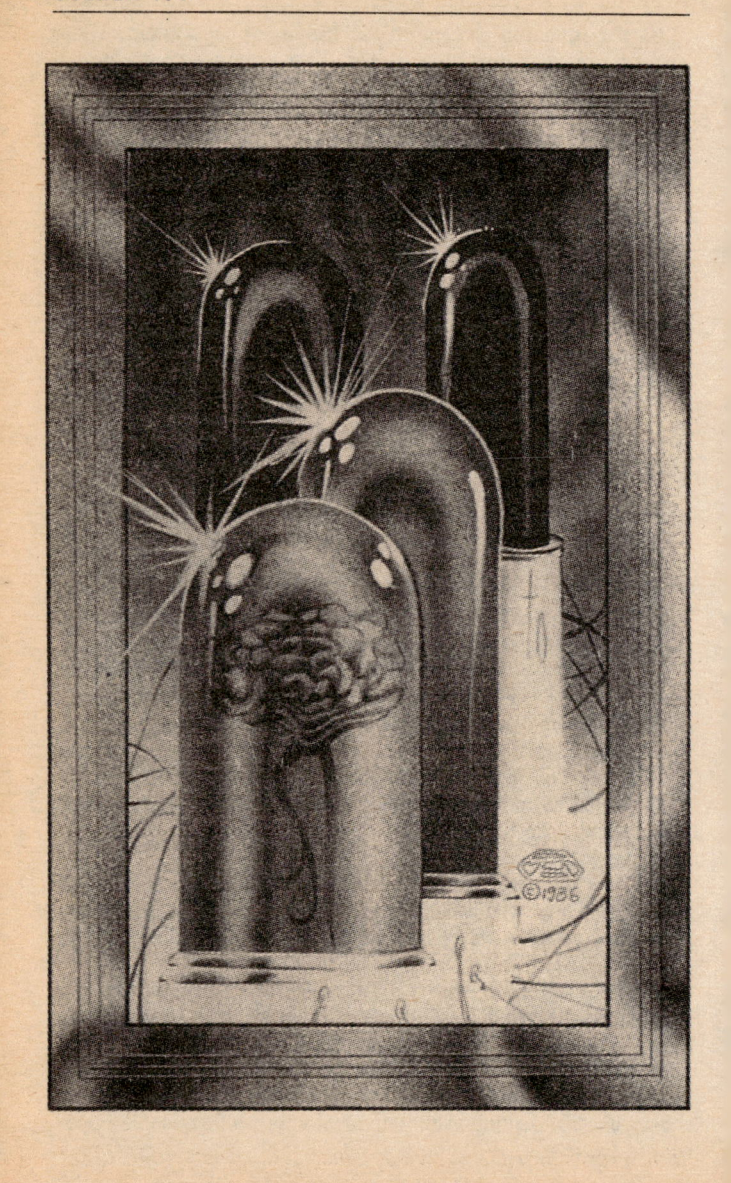

Section 104

These "living machines" communicate via ultrawave just as human ships do, but they can exchange information and orders at the speed of thought. This accounts for their impressive displays of coordination and close-formation maneuvering. However, because their telepathy is conducted on ultrawave channels, it should be possible to jam their communications through the use of the Legion's Stealth mode technique, which uses ultrawave and ultrapulse signals to confuse enemy tracking systems.

Further, the Legion research team has tentatively identified the planetoid structure as a sort of flagship, where a vast collective intelligence directs the fleet as a whole. If so, the planetoid is responsible for every major strategic and tactical decision made. Thus, the elimination of this central core would effectively disrupt the Ka'slaq armada.

The reports are less certain of alien motivations or intentions. The size of the planetoid suggests that it could carry not only military resources, but a body of ordinary, living alien civilians. Such life forms might be necessary as a source of replacement brains for the armada. One intelligence officer, going on admittedly slim data, has theorized that the cyborg brains rule the entire Ka'slaq civilization with ruthless efficiency, probably having lost most emotional traits as a result of their bodiless forms. If they have come as refugees from some natural disaster far off across space (which seems distinctly possible, since a command ship this large and slow is impractical if the aliens are a raiding party or conventional war fleet), their intentions may be genocidal. Seizing planets suitable to their kind, these dispassionate machine beings would probably have no compunctions about exterminating the present inhabitants.

Even if these suppositions don't hold up, Ulnar has learned enough to fight the Ka'slaq on more even terms. Now he must apply this knowledge effectively.

If the cruiser was discovered at Endymion, go to section 136.

If the cruiser was discovered after the fall of Baal, go to section 137.

If the cruiser was discovered at S.C. 170, go to section 138.

If the cruiser was discovered at Ulnar 118, go to section 139.

Section 105

If the cruiser was discovered after a Legion victory at any world, go to section 169.

In any event, add the roll of one die to the number of days consumed so far in the campaign before proceeding further.

— 105 —

The ambushers close fast, giving Ulnar's ships very little time to react. Before the last captain is able to confirm his position in the squadron's formation, the first annihilator beams tear through the vacuum, projecting the fury of a matter/antimatter reaction into the Legion's battle lines. The battle of Ulnar 118 has begun.

Map #4 shows the relative positions of the two forces, although it is not integral to the resolution of the battle. Resolution of combat varies according to the formation adopted by the Legion, as noted below.

Wedge: *The Legion destroyers attack on the first round of Chart D. They may not attack again so long as battlecruisers are available, although combat losses can always be taken from either wing. After the first round, battlecruisers fire on all subsequent rounds on Chart C.*

The Ka'slaq begin with 5 cruisers (total combat strength = 15). They fire on Chart A. After all fire is exchanged, the Ka'slaq receive 10 more cruisers each round (combat strength = 30) to add to their surviving forces, until all 74 cruisers have been committed to battle and/or lost.

Cone: *Roll one die. The Legion battlecruisers fight for this number of rounds, firing on Chart D and suffering any losses inflicted by the enemy. After these rounds have been completed, roll another die and fight with destroyers on Chart D for this number of rounds. Continue alternating in this fashion for the remainder of the battle.*

Ka'slaq cruisers fire on Chart A. They begin with 10 ships (total combat strength = 30). After all fire is exchanged, the Ka'slaq receive 10 more cruisers each round (combat strength

Section 105

= 30) to add to their surviving forces until all 74 cruisers have been committed and/or lost.

Globe: *Legion battlecruisers fire every round on Chart C. Destroyers can only fire or suffer losses if all the battlecruisers are first eliminated: Destroyers use Chart D if they have to engage.*

The Ka'slaq receive 5 more cruisers (total combat strength = 15) to add to their surviving forces until all 74 cruisers have been committed and/or lost.

Cylinder: *Legion battlecruisers fire on the first round of combat, using Chart D. The destroyers fire on the same chart on the next round, and the two wings continue to alternate in the same way until the battle is over. Losses are taken by the wing that fired during the round.*

The Ka'slaq begin with 10 cruisers (total combat strength = 30). They fire on Chart B. After all fire is exchanged, the Ka'slaq receive 5 more cruisers each round (combat strength = 15) to add to their surviving forces until all 74 cruisers have been committed and/or lost.

Heavy Screen: *Legion battlecruisers fire on Chart C and take all losses inflicted by the Ka'slaq. If all the battlecruisers are eliminated, the destroyers can begin fighting using Chart D.*

The Ka'slaq begin with 10 ships (total combat strength = 30). They fire on Chart B. After all fire is exchanged, the aliens receive 5 more cruisers each round (combat strength = 15) to add to their surviving forces until all 74 cruisers have been committed and/or lost.

Destroyer Screen: *Legion destroyers engage first, using Chart D and suffering all losses inflicted by the enemy. They continue to fight until the battle ends, the Ka'slaq eliminate all of the destroyers, or Ulnar launches a special attack using the battlecruisers.*

The battle wing can launch a special attack once during the battle, providing they have not engaged already and there are still destroyers in the screen. The special attack allows two *rolls on Table A during* one *round, using the battlecruisers. Thereafter the battlecruisers continue to fight, firing once per subsequent round on Chart B. The same chart is used if the battlecruisers are drawn into the battle (through the loss of all the destroyers) before their attack can be launched. Surviving destroyers still in*

Section 105

action when a special attack is launched can only engage again if all the battlecruisers are destroyed.

Throughout the entire action, the Ka'slaq fire once per round on Chart A. They begin with 10 cruisers (total combat strength = 30). After all fire is exchanged, the aliens receive 5 more cruisers each round (combat strength = 15) to add to their surviving forces until all 74 cruisers have been committed and/or lost.

Dispersed: *Legion destroyers attack on the first round, firing on Chart D. Battlecruisers fire on Chart C on the next round, and the two wings continue to alternate fire thereafter until all of one wing's ships are lost; then the survivors fire every round. Losses are taken from whichever wing fired in the current round.*

The Ka'slaq begin with 20 ships (total combat strength = 60). They fire on Chart B. After all fire is exchanged, roll two dice and add that number of cruisers each round (each at firepower = 3) to the surviving engaged forces until all 74 cruisers have been committed and/or lost.

In all cases reduce the total number of alien ships available (but not the initial numbers) by the number of cruisers eliminated by destroyers prior to the main battle, if applicable.

Resolve the battle according to the game rules, within the framework provided above.

The squadron can attempt to withdraw at the end of any combat round. To resolve a retreat, go to section 118.

The squadron may be required to attempt a retreat. At the end of any round in which Legion losses exceed Ka'slaq losses, roll two dice and compare the result to the squadron's Morale value. If the roll is greater than the Morale value, go to section 118. Results less than or equal to this value have no effect, so retreat remains voluntary.

If the squadron continues to fight until all Legion ships have been destroyed, go to section 92.

If the Legion ships eliminate all of the Ka'slaq cruisers, go to section 87. This is the only situation in which the alien planetoid ship can actually be attacked; it cannot be involved in battle until all defending cruisers have been eliminated.

— 106 —

During the search sweep, reports pour in constantly to keep the admiral up to date. The star system that bears his name—or rather the name of his famous grandfather—is scrutinized by every kind of detection apparatus known to Legion science. But all the scanners and sensors available are not able to locate targets that simply are not there.

Nothing. Negative. Zero. Ulnar reads each report and grows more and more depressed. His hunch about Ulnar 118 was wrong. There is nothing here, no alien fleet. Once again they have outmaneuvered him.

Then a new item comes in, and all at once doubt and depression vanish. From his station on the bridge Ulnar reviews the report. One of the ships has stumbled across the drifting hulk of a Ka'slaq cruiser near the edge of the system's asteroid belt, the apparent victim of a collision with a sizable chunk of rock. The cruiser is a golden opportunity to gather more information about the aliens. But it is also proof that the Ka'slaq have been here. Was this a lone scout, or was it left behind during a visit by the entire Ka'slaq fleet?

Ulnar is tempted to order a closer examination of the wreck. But whether he waits while it is investigated here or arranges to tow it in flight, the alien vessel will cause serious delays. Yet if the Ka'slaq have been here and departed already, every second counts toward trying to overtake them before they can attack another League colony. Ulnar's decision could be crucial to the outcome of the war. Which is more vital: speed or knowledge?

If Ulnar decides to have the wreck investigated, go to section 104.

If Ulnar chooses to ignore the cruiser, go to section 139.

Sections 107, 108

— 107 —

No fresh information has come in so far. The Ka'slaq have not attempted any new attacks that he knows of, and Ulnar has nothing further to go on. Any decision he makes now will have to be made without the benefit of recent intelligence.

If Ulnar decides to remain in his present location, go to section 71.

If Ulnar decides to return to St. Germaine, go to section 74.

If Ulnar orders the squadron to travel to Ulnar 118, go to section 63.

If the squadron receives instructions to go to S.C. 170, go to section 68.

If Ulnar wants to travel to Baal, go to section 58.

If the squadron is ordered to visit Endymion, go to section 53.

If Ulnar orders his ships to travel to any other destination, go to section 73.

— 108 —

No fresh information has come in so far. The Ka'slaq have neither appeared at Ulnar 118 nor, to Ulnar's knowledge, attacked any other world. Ulnar has nothing further to go on. Whatever decision he makes now he must make blind.

If Ulnar decides to remain at Ulnar 118, go to section 152.

If Ulnar chooses to return to the squadron's base at St. Germaine, go to section 74.

Section 109

If the squadron receives instructions to go to S.C. 170, go to section 68.

If Ulnar wants his ships to travel to Baal, go to section 58.

If the squadron is ordered to visit Endymion, go to section 53.

If Ulnar orders his squadron to travel to any other destination, go to section 73.

— 109 —

Closing in fast, the Ka'slaq ambushers give the squadron very little time to prepare for battle. The captains are still reporting their completion of the evolutions Ulnar has ordered when the first annihilator beams begin to tear through the vacuum toward the Legion ships. Ulnar grabs his microphone one last time and switches it on.

"Engage Stealth mode during combat," he sputters. "Good luck all!" Ulnar is certain that Stealth mode will cause more confusion to the aliens than to the Legion fleet. He prays it will be enough to offset their advantages in battle.

The map shows the relative positions of the two forces, although it is not integral to the resolution of the battle. Resolution of combat varies according to the formation adopted by the Legion, as noted below.

Wedge: *The Legion destroyers attack on the first round on Chart D. They may not attack again as long as battlecruisers are available, although combat losses can always be taken from either wing. After the first round battlecruisers fire on Chart C.*

The Ka'slaq begin with 5 cruisers (total combat strength = 15). They fire on Chart D. After all fire is exchanged, the Ka'slaq receive 10 more cruisers each round (combat strength = 30) to add to their surviving forces until all 74 cruisers have been committed to battle and/or lost.

Cone: *Roll one die. The Legion battlecruisers fight for this number of rounds, firing on Chart D and suffering any losses*

Section 109

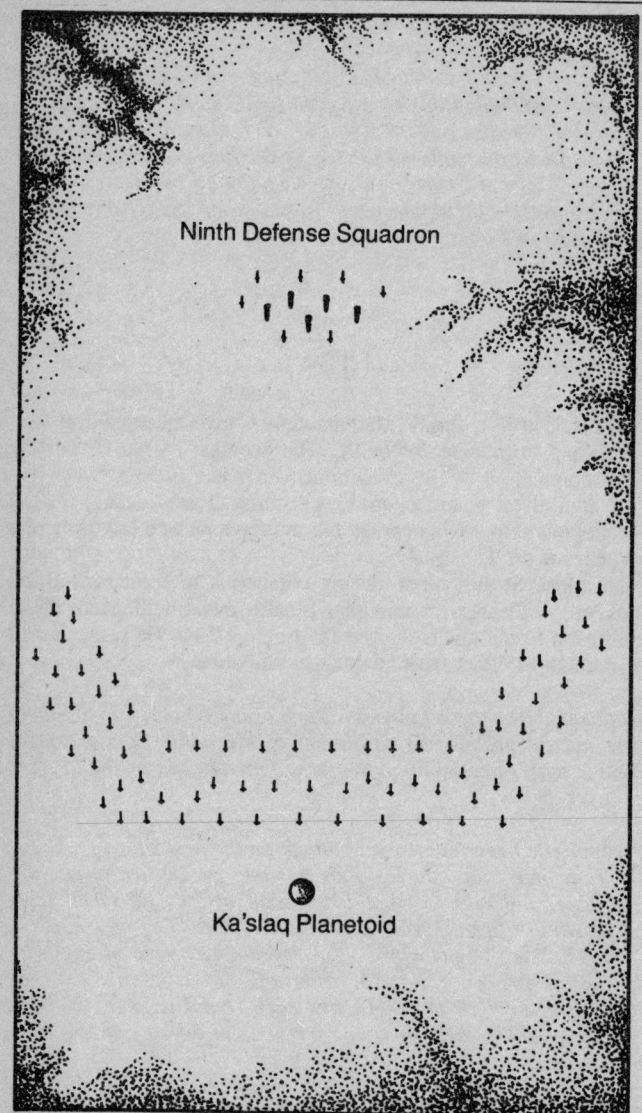

Ninth Defense Squadron

Ka'slaq Planetoid

BATTLE OF ULNAR 118

Section 109

inflicted by the enemy. After these rounds have been completed, roll another die and fight with destroyers on Chart D for this number of rounds. Continue alternating in this fashion for the remainder of the battle.

Ka'slaq cruisers fire on Chart D. They begin with 10 ships (total combat strength = 30). After all fire is exchanged, the Ka'slaq receive 10 more cruisers each round (combat strength = 30) to add to their surviving forces until all 74 cruisers have been committed and/or lost.

Globe: *Legion battlecruisers fire every round on Chart C. Destroyers can only fire or suffer losses if all the battlecruisers are eliminated first, and they use Chart D if they must engage.*

The Ka'slaq begin with 10 cruisers (total combat strength = 30). They fire on Chart E. After all fire is exchanged, the Ka'slaq receive 5 more cruisers each round (combat strength = 15) to add to their surviving forces until all 74 cruisers (combat strength = 15) have been committed and/or lost.

Cylinder: *Legion battlecruisers fire on the first round of combat, using Chart D. The destroyers fire on the same chart on the next round, and the two wings continue to alternate in the same way until the battle is over. Losses are taken by the wing that fired during the round.*

The Ka'slaq begin with 10 cruisers (total combat strength = 30). They fire on Chart E. After all fire is exchanged, the Ka'slaq receive 5 more cruisers each round (combat strength = 15) to add to their surviving forces until all 74 cruisers have been committed and/or lost.

Heavy Screen: *Legion battlecruisers fire on Chart C and take all losses inflicted by the Ka'slaq. If all the battlecruisers are eliminated, the destroyers can begin fighting. They use Chart D.*

The Ka'slaq begin with 10 ships (total combat strength = 30). They fire on Chart E. After all fire is exchanged, the aliens receive 5 more cruisers each round (combat strength = 15) to add to their surviving forces until all 74 cruisers have been committed and/or lost.

Destroyer Screen: *Legion destroyers engage first. Using Chart D, they suffer all losses inflicted by the enemy. They continue to fight until the battle ends, the Ka'slaq eliminate all of the*

Section 109

destroyers, or Ulnar launches a special attack using the battlecruisers.

The battle wing can launch a special attack once during the battle, providing they have not engaged already and there are still destroyers in the screen. The special attack allows two rolls on Table A during any one round, using the battlecruisers. Thereafter, the battlecruisers continue to fight, firing once per subsequent round on Chart B. The same chart is used if the battlecruisers are drawn into the battle (through the loss of all the destroyers) before their attack can be launched. Surviving destroyers still in action when a special attack is launched can only fight again if all the battlecruisers are destroyed.

Throughout the entire action the Ka'slaq fire once per round on Chart D. They begin with 10 cruisers (total combat strength = 30). After all fire is exchanged, the aliens receive 5 more cruisers each round (combat strength = 15) to add to their surviving forces until all 74 cruisers have been committed and/or lost.

Dispersed: *Legion destroyers attack on the first round, firing on Chart C. Battlecruisers fire on Chart B on the next round, and the two wings continue to alternate fire thereafter until all of one wing's ships are lost; then the survivors fire every round. Losses are taken from whichever wing fired in the current round.*

The Ka'slaq begin with 20 ships (total combat strength = 60). They fire on Chart E. Each round, after all fire is exchanged, roll one die and add that number of cruisers (each one with a firepower of 3) to the surviving engaged forces until all 74 cruisers have been committed and/or lost.

In all cases reduce the total number of alien ships available (but not the initial numbers) by the number of cruisers eliminated by destroyers prior to the main battle, where applicable.

Resolve the battle according to the game rules, within the guidelines provided above.

The squadron can attempt to withdraw at the end of any combat round. To resolve a retreat, go to section 118.

The squadron may be required to attempt a retreat. At the end of any round in which the Legion loses more ships than do the Ka'slaq, roll two dice and compare the result to the squadron's Morale value. If the roll is greater than the Morale value, go to section 118. Results less than or equal to this value have no effect, so retreat remains voluntary.

If the squadron continues to fight until all Legion ships have been destroyed, go to section 92.

If the Legion ships eliminate all of the Ka'slaq cruisers, go to section 87. This is the only situation in which the alien planetoid ship can actually be attacked. The ship remains uninvolved in the battle until all defending cruisers have been eliminated.

— 110 —

The united squadron plunges into the star system, every scanner and sensor array reaching out to examine Ulnar 118, its planets, and the vast empty tracts of space that surround and separate them. Looking around *Valiant*'s bridge, Ulnar is aware of the air of tense expectation that fills the whole control center. On the flagship, and on all the other vessels of the squadron, the men of the Legion are eager to fight the enemy. If the Ka'slaq are here, the admiral will have his hands full controlling them. And if the aliens aren't here, the blow to morale will be a severe one. Ulnar has already made mistakes; if he is wrong about Ulnar 118 now, his authority over these men will be weaker still.

"Mass detectors report objects bearing 163 by 092," a crewman reports.

"Verified," an ultrapulse operator adds. A series of lights in red appear in the holographic tank. A few crewmen look up expectantly.

"Asteroid belt," Captain Sammis remarks.

Ulnar nods. "The bearing's correct," he replies.

"Probably just random junk," the captain continues. He pauses. "Of course . . ."

"If you were going to hide a fleet," Ulnar says, picking up the thought, "an asteroid belt is the best place to do it."

"Concentrate scanning on those objects," Sammis barks to the bridge crew. "I want them analyzed down to the last atom!"

Thinking back over Endymion and Baal, Ulnar swivels toward the communications console. "Anything odd on ultrawave?" he asks.

Section 111

The operator shakes his head, uncomfortable at the admiral's direct attention.

"First approximations coming in," another scanner technician announces. "Nearest object. Composition: metallic. Ultrapulse echo indicates a regular shape. Temperature and radiation levels anomalous . . . it's definitely an artifact."

"I'm getting energy surges at bearing 163 by 092," another technician chimes in.

The ultrawave operator puts a hand to his ear. "Static, sir. Regular patterns—it's not natural either."

With a great show of nonchalance, Sammis turns to Ulnar. "Admiral, we have found the aliens."

In the planning tank red lights rapidly switch to blue on all sides. The Ulnar 118 system is an elaborate trap, and the Ka'slaq have sprung it perfectly. Now Ulnar must attempt to keep his squadron from being overwhelmed by seventy or more ships.

If Ulnar orders his squadron to attack the enemy, go to section 151.

If Ulnar instructs the squadron to stand on the defensive, go to section 156.

A withdrawal is not possible at this time. The Ka'slaq will be able to get in at least one round of combat first. Retreat during combat may still be possible.

— 111 —

"Recon wing, this is Flag," Ulnar says, speaking on the Fleetcomm circuit. "Destroyers to deploy sensor arrays and probe the Baal system. Scan for any sign of activity, human or alien, and report the presence and location of any vessel. All ships of the battle wing will remain in reserve." He pauses, rubbing his forehead briefly. "Don't try to be heroes; this is a scouting mission, not the charge that wins the war. Avoid battle if possible, unless you hear different from me."

Admiral Ulnar breaks the communications link and settles back into his seat. He had struggled long and hard with his conscience before deciding to send in the destroyers by themselves. Splitting his forces in this manner worries him, but the possibility of an ambush wiping out the entire squadron in a single blow worries him even more. This way he can preserve a few options if the enemy attack his ships. He can support the destroyers or withdraw his battlecruisers intact as the situation dictates. But he doesn't relish the thought of leaving the recon wing.

In the planning tank the symbols representing the squadron's destroyers slowly pull away from the main body of the squadron. Watching them begin their plunge starward, Ulnar finds himself wishing he could be with them. It would give him something to do besides watch them fly on perhaps their last mission.

Proceed to section 126.

— 112 —

The squadron continues under the cloak of Stealth mode, pushing on toward the mysterious alien planetoid and the Ka'slaq ships clustered around it like drones. They seem totally oblivious to Ulnar's approach, which is just how Ulnar wants it. Perhaps the Legion has a chance to avenge Don Larno, he thinks hopefully.

Staring into the planning tank, Ulnar reads the symbols there with practiced ease. For the battle ahead he plans to reveal a surprise or two that should have quite an impact on the Ka'slaq. Smiling in anticipation, Ulnar turns to his command console and prepares to issue his orders.

If Ulnar decides to attack the aliens, go to section 21.

If Ulnar wants to stand on the defensive and make the aliens attack the squadron, go to section 28.

If Ulnar loses his nerve and decides to withdraw while he has the opportunity, go to section 32.

— 113 —

In the planning tank a handful of Legion ships show the characteristic fuzzy patterns of vessels in Stealth mode and begin to split off from the main body. But the majority of the squadron doesn't change course at all, and the Stealth generators remain off. They continue to steer straight for the core of the ambushing alien fleet.

Ulnar curses silently. "Flag to all ships," he spits. "Repeating orders. Withdraw immediately. I *repeat*, withdraw!"

Sammis is beside him, the sharp angles of his face holding a mixture of diffidence and grim determination. "They won't respond, Admiral," he says quietly.

"Why not?" Ulnar demands. "What's wrong?"

"There was talk of this during the last passage. They plan to fight. Whether you want to or not."

"Do you know what the penalty for mutiny is, Captain?" Ulnar asks.

"There are higher duties, Admiral."

"And *Valiant*? Do you plan to fight against orders, as well?"

"I would rather fight under orders, sir," he says reluctantly.

"That's no answer."

"It's all the answer I can give you, Admiral." Sammis is clearly determined to carry out this strange mutiny. He leans past Ulnar and switches on the microphone. "All ships, Flag calling. Cancel previous orders. Stand by for new instructions."

He switches if off again. "Who should issue those orders, Admiral?" he asks evenly.

If Ulnar chooses to change his instructions and order an attack, go to section 151.

If Ulnar relents and orders the squadron to adopt a defensive formation, go to section 156.

If the admiral refuses to acknowledge this mutiny and does not change his withdrawal order, go to section 181.

— 114 —

Ulnar studies the computer's graphic simulation of the gigantic alien ship. Scans have pinpointed a powerful source of ultrawave signals located in a complex of towers and domes extending over an area almost a mile across. The computer has assigned an eighty percent chance that the main control center for the vessel is somewhere within this large area. The admiral cannot find any other obvious targets within easy reach; the ship's geodynes are buried somewhere deep in the core of the structure, and the purpose and layout of the rest of the planetoid is unclear.

He could order a bombardment, but that could reduce the control center to slag, condemning the beings aboard the alien vessel to death. Just retribution, perhaps, for the destruction the Ka'slaq had caused, but Ulnar was reluctant to go that far. The aliens might not revere life, but the Legion had higher standards.

Ulnar must ensure that the huge structure has no more power to harm the Legion or the Star League. He intends to secure the vessel by sending men on board. In his tired mind he likens his plan to sending a swarm of mosquitoes to land on an elephant, but he can see no other way to secure the alien vessel without destroying it. He begins to issue orders.

The battlecruisers close in first, ready to unleash a bombardment at the first sign of trouble. But the alien ship does nothing, and soon troops in space armor issue onto the surface of the structure. Seeking a way into the area identified as a command center, they use proton drills to open a hole in the hull, then disappear into their improvised doorway.

Listening to the ultrawave circuit the boarders are using, Ulnar can follow their progress into the heart of a wondrous chamber, a room so large that it might be an open prairie on a planet's surface. Inside they find row upon row of tanklike containers filled with liquid and living tissues. The medical officer refers to them as brains. These brain tanks are connected to a complex array of circuitry: miles of wires, computer boards, and instruments of unknown purpose, all of them evidently controlled by the bodiless creatures in the nutrient tanks.

The boarding party also finds a race of multilimbed beings similar in appearance to starfish. Ten tentacular appendages are

Section 114

Section 115

used for motion and manipulation. Wielding crude clubs, these aliens have burst into the command center and begun smashing the brain tanks. One of their number, speaking through a translation device, tells the Legion party that his people have endured the tyranny of these "masters," an oligarchy of brain-machine hybrids whose emotionless rule has relegated the race from which they sprang to slavery. In the crisis that accompanied the loss of their cyborg-controlled cruiser fleet, the rulers relaxed their control over the slave race, allowing a long-smoldering rebellion to burst into flames at last.

With Legion aid, the aliens can be liberated from this tyranny; the threat of the Ka'slaq invasion can be put to rest for all time.

Proceed to section 171.

— 115 —

Ulnar feels that little purpose would be served by moving again; in his mind, St. Germaine is still the best place to anticipate further Ka'slaq advances. He is fairly sure that the aliens will attack here sooner or later. The Ninth Squadron remains in orbit, awaiting the word that will send them into action once more. Meanwhile, the admiral studies incoming news and information in hopes of discovering a clue that will help him decide how to defeat the aliens.

Add one day to the total accumulated number of days in the campaign so far.

If the new total is less than thirty-six days, go to section 124.

If the new total is thirty-six through forty-five days and Baal is the last place where the Ka'slaq were seen, go to section 127.

If the Ka'slaq were last seen somewhere else, go to section 124.

If the new total is forty-six through fifty-five days, go to section 119.

— 116 —

"Flag calling all ships," Ulnar says, speaking on the Fleetcomm circuit. "The squadron will conduct a reconnaissance of the star system. Deploy all sensors and scan for any activity. Report any contacts to me at once." Ulnar licks his dry lips before continuing.

"This is a scouting mission. Battle is to be avoided unless there is no way out or you receive orders to the contrary from me. I want no heroes, so stick to the mission and stay out of trouble." There were the usual number of hotheads in the squadron, and Ulnar wants them to know just where they stand *before* they start for Baal.

The admiral gives the necessary orders to send the whole squadron plunging into the star system, then leans back in his chair and closes his eyes momentarily. If his worst fears are right, the Ka'slaq may have set an ambush somewhere in the system. It has taken all his resolve to hazard the squadron this way. Though he has never been a believer in dividing his forces unnecessarily, Ulnar can't help but wonder if it would have been better to follow the standard doctrine and employ the recon wing destroyers to scout separately from the main body.

Valiant and the rest of the squadron all gather speed together as they plunge toward Ulnar 118. Everyone knows they are committed now. If the Ka'slaq are here, the squadron will discover them soon.

Proceed to section 126.

— 117 —

Clear of Baal, the squadron escapes disaster. But the cost is high, in morale as well as in lives. The retreat from Baal is a defeat, pure and simple, and even though the squadron is preserved to fight again, Vice-Admiral David Ulnar feels like a traitor to his commission, his planet, indeed to the entire human race. Merros will undoubtably feel the same when the news reaches him.

Staring at the ceiling of his cabin a few hours after the

Section 117

reassembly of the squadron in the fringes of the Baal system, Ulnar thinks back over the Ka'slaq assault and its aftermath. After the retreat of Ulnar's ships, the planet's defenses had proven unequal to the alien onslaught. The orbital fortress, commanded by the bitter but stubborn Commandant Rovin, held out for a long time after its offensive weapons were silenced, but eventually determination and Legion traditions were overcome by sheer firepower; without the orbital fortress, the linchpin of the colony's defenses, Baal was unable to mount any kind of resistance.

The final ultrawave messages from Baal would haunt Ulnar until he died, filled with the final recriminations of doomed people. As at Endymion, the Ka'slaq had settled into orbit to launch a savage bombardment against carefully selected targets. From the tenor of the last transmissions it was likely that Baal had been reduced as completely and as ruthlessly as the earlier colony.

Ulnar has retired to consider his next move. With Baal destroyed, the aliens threaten a number of other planets. Which will be their next target? And where was the bulk of the Ka'slaq fleet while their detached flotilla was attacking here? If Ulnar allows another planet to fall to the invaders, the sector will collapse completely. And so, too, will the Star League's hopes of holding the aliens along the frontier. To protect the Earth from the fate that has overtaken Baal, Ulnar has to outguess his enemies and stand against them. There is no other choice.

If Ulnar chooses to remain at Baal, go to section 167.

If he decides to have the squadron return to St. Germaine, go to section 74.

If the admiral orders his ships to Ulnar 118, go to section 63.

If the squadron is instructed to travel to S.C. 170, go to section 68.

If Endymion is selected as the squadron's next destination, go to section 53.

Should the admiral issue orders sending the squadron to any other destination, go to section 73.

In any event, reduce the squadron's Morale value by 1 point.

— 118 —

The ships of the Legion put up a desperate resistance to the superior numbers of their enemies, but for all their determination and spirit, they are outmatched. Ships are consumed by the fireballs of induced antimatter reactions from the touch of Ka'slaq annihilators, and their darting cruisers drive deep into the Legion battle line. Finally Ulnar can take no more of it.

"Flag to all ships," he orders at last. "Discontinue the action. Repeat, discontinue the action." The computer is signaling the same order as he speaks, confirming his directive. "Break off and regroup at rendezvous point six eight. All ships are to withdraw immediately. Message ends."

He knows the fireaters among them will resist his order, but even the most hotheaded captain in the squadron will recognize their situation is hopeless. Sure enough, the Legion's ships begin to sheer off and pick up speed while Stealth mode jams enemy tracking systems to help them escape. The Ka'slaq ships seem confused by the jamming, breaking formation and casting about like bloodhounds searching for a scent. There is no guarantee that Stealth mode will mask the squadron's retreat, but Ulnar can see that there is a good chance. A few more minutes will tell them for sure.

Roll two dice and compare the result to the Stealth value for the Legion ships. If the result is greater than the value, return to the battle resolution process as before.

If the result is less than or equal to the Stealth value, go to section 174.

— 119 —

The massive geofractor complex in the St. Germaine system provides a link to the rest of the League, a matter-transport network that allows items large and small to be transferred instantaneously across countless parsecs. The geodesic technology of this ultimate achievement is understood little better today than it was in the time of Dr. Eleroud, the genius who discovered the principle, but geofractor complexes have played an important part in opening the stars to humanity.

Now those same geofractors are being harnessed to defend the Star League. Although their potential as weapons has been defeated by the science of the Ka'slaq, these long-range transporters work to funnel in ships, supplies, and men to defend St. Germaine from attack.

Now, as Ulnar's squadron finishes final refitting and resupply chores at the Legion orbital base, the geofractors bring a magnificent new ship into existence nearby. She is the *Pax*, the newest and largest battleship in the Legion, twice the size and firepower of *Valiant*, and the pride of the Star League. On board, arriving to take personal command in the battles to come, is Admiral J. T. Merros.

Although Merros and Ulnar have been on bad terms for years, they have no need to cooperate closely at St. Germaine. Ulnar retains control over his old squadron and the mobile elements of the St. Germaine garrison, which Merros has formed into a reserve. There are three other squadrons of equal size assigned to front-line defenses, ready to go into battle when the aliens arrive. Ulnar isn't happy with the arrangement. His squadron has been closer to the aliens than any of these newcomers, and ought to be more qualified to deal with them, but he knows enough to avoid protesting openly. For the moment, Ulnar and his squadron concentrate on efficiency and preparedness, and keep out of their new leader's way.

Ulnar dutifully files reports and recommendations based on the data his ships have collected, calling attention to those elements of each encounter on record that might provide a clue to Ka'slaq weaknesses. Merros, however, seems more concerned with having the proper reports of inventories, personnel changes, and requisitioned equipment.

Then the Ka'slaq arrive.

The first warning is from lightly armed picket ships posted on the fringes of the system. Their detection apparatus notices the ultrawave disturbances first, and four separate ships promptly relay a warning to the fleet. Admiral Merros reacts promptly, ordering his three front-line squadrons to break orbit immediately and set course toward the area of the disturbance. Ulnar and his squadron receive curt orders to remain in the vicinity of St. Germaine and await further orders.

Called to *Valiant*'s bridge out of a sound sleep and a pleasant

Section 119

dream of home, Ulnar has trouble believing the orders. He sits heavily in the chair at his command console. The full impact of what Merros is doing hits him and he feels years of anger and frustration boiling up all at once.

"Pax Eternal!" he says, the words loud in the sudden silence that descends on the bridge. His clenched hand slams down on the console. "Get me Admiral Merros," Ulnar continues to the communications technician. "And hurry!"

Merros had been exuding confidence in his messages and news broadcast appearances these last few days. He commanded one of the largest forces ever assembled by the Legion of Space, a force that included several new and powerful vessels. Confidence, and contempt for David Ulnar, was making Merros sally forth against the enemy with nearly a quarter of his ships held back so far from the battle that they would be totally useless. Ulnar knew what the aliens could do; Merros would need every ship at St. Germaine to have a hope of success.

"Admiral Merros," the technician says. Ulnar's monitor lights up to show the narrow features and wispy white hair of the admiral.

"What is it, Ulnar?" the older man asks irritably.

"Admiral," Ulnar begins, trying not to let his anger show. "About your orders for the reserve squadron . . ."

"Well?" Merros snaps as Ulnar hesitates.

"Sir, based on everything I've seen of the Ka'slaq, I feel we cannot afford to underestimate their abilities. I believe my squadron should be employed in the battle line—"

"You've had your chance to stop the aliens, Ulnar," Merros responds maliciously. "Now you'll obey orders and stay out of my way! You will remain at St. Germaine as instructed, and that is final! Ending message." The screen goes blank before Ulnar can reply.

There is silence on the bridge. All eyes are on David Ulnar. Most of them have seen the battle orders Merros has already issued; he's sending his ships against the Ka'slaq in a battlecruiser phalanx, with orders to engage the enemy cruisers in a straightforward, conventional battle. He seems to have taken no notice of past clashes between Ka'slaq and human ships, ignoring every anomaly, every clue to their strengths and weaknesses, and every recommendation Ulnar and his officers have submitted to him. Ulnar knows, as surely as if he had already watched it played through, that Merros has no hope of winning.

Ulnar knows by now what Don Larno knew when the aliens

first appeared at Endymion. The Ka'slaq planetoid or mother ship is the real key to the invading fleet. As long as it remains out of combat, the enemy is secure. And conventional tactics have no chance against the coordination and power of the Ka'slaq. Merros doesn't seem to realize this, and he is about to throw away the last chance the Legion has for a victory in this war.

That leaves David Ulnar with a painful decision to make. Every impulse of a long and dedicated career urges him to obey orders, to let Merros call for assistance as or when he needs it. But another part of him wants to ignore Admiral Merros and take the squadron into battle against the alien planetoid ship, to save Merros and the ships he commands from certain disaster. The wrong choice could ruin Ulnar's career, lose the battle and St. Germaine, and even shatter the whole Star League. But it is a choice Ulnar must now make.

If Ulnar decides to take the safe course and follow the admiral's orders, go to section 154.

If Ulnar disobeys Merros and leads his squadron into battle against the alien planetoid, go to section 176.

If Ulnar chooses to withdraw from St. Germaine rather than standing and awaiting the battle's outcome, go to section 164.

— 120 —

The ship symbols in the planning tank draw slowly together and begin shifting color as they come within combat range. Ulnar adjusts the scale of the tank to show a close-up of the battle. Suddenly the tank comes alive with new symbols that record the energy discharges of Legion vortex guns and Ka'slaq annihilators. It's far too late now for second thoughts; the battle for Baal has begun.

The map shows the deployment of the alien ships. They are formed into a rigid phalanx, and throughout the engagement they deviate from this formation and their assigned missions only if actually in battle with Legion ships. They are divided into six groups, as shown.

Section 120

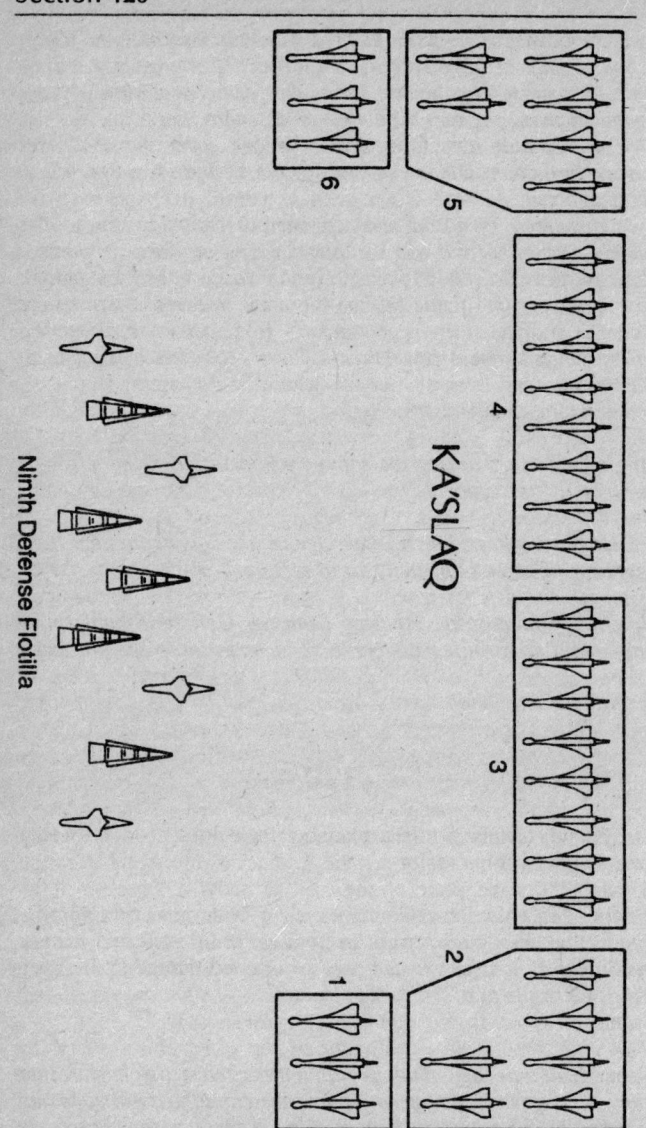

KA'SLAQ

Ninth Defense Flotilla

Section 120

If the Legion ships have adopted a defensive formation (globe, cylinder, battlecruiser screen), the force they engage first will be chosen randomly by the roll of one die. The enemy attackers are found by using the sector number on the map.

If the squadron is formed in a wedge, cone, or destroyer screen formation, Ulnar chooses any one of the enemy groups to fight against.

A dispersed squadron must spread out to engage the entire enemy flotilla. Ulnar may allocate his ships in any manner desired, provided each of the six sectors is engaged by at least one Legion ship. If this option is in use, the resolution of the battle is conducted under a special set of guidelines, described later, which differ somewhat from the standard methods of combat resolution.

Normally, though, only one enemy force is engaged at a time. Once the Legion is matched with an opponent, resolve the battle conventionally. The Legion fires first with whichever wing is eligible to fire; then the Ka'slaq cruisers fighting them return fire. One exchange of this kind is a combat round.

The Legion forces include all of Ulnar's ships, plus the Baal garrison. However, one battlecruiser (Defiant) and one destroyer (Anthar) are deleted from the garrison before the battle, and Baal's orbital fortress cannot engage in a conventional space battle. Ka'slaq forces attack in the numbers shown for each group. If the aliens suffer casualties due to combat with the orbital fortress, their losses are subtracted from group 3 first, then group 4, then group 2, then group 5, and so on. A group must be completely wiped out before losses can be taken from another group. If there are groups reduced to zero ships, they are not eligible as targets for battle. Roll again when random assignment matches the squadron with such a group. Each Ka'slaq cruiser has a firepower of 8.

Wedge: *Legion destroyers attack on the first round on Chart C. They may not attack again so long as battlecruisers remain available, although combat losses can be subtracted from either wing. After the first round, battlecruisers fire for the remaining rounds on Chart B. Ka'slaq cruisers use Chart C.*

Cone: *Roll one die. The Legion battlecruisers fight for this number of rounds, firing on Chart C and suffering any losses inflicted by the enemy in response. After these rounds are completed, roll another die and fight with destroyers on the same*

Section 120

chart for this number of rounds. If necessary, continue alternating in this way until the end of the battle. The Ka'slaq cruisers fire back on Chart B.

Globe: *Legion battlecruisers fire every round on Chart B. Destroyers can only fire or suffer losses if all the battlecruisers are first eliminated; they use Chart D if they must engage. The Ka'slaq cruisers fire each round on Chart B.*

Cylinder: *Legion battlecruisers fire on the first round of combat, using Chart C. The destroyers fire on the same chart on the next round, and the two wings continue to alternate in the same way until the battle is over. Casualties are absorbed by whichever wing has fired in the current round. The Ka'slaq use Chart B for their attacks.*

Heavy Screen: *Legion battlecruisers fire on Chart B and take all losses inflicted by the Ka'slaq. If all the battlecruisers are eliminated, the destroyers can enter the fray, firing on Chart D. The Ka'slaq cruisers fire on Chart B.*

Destroyer Screen: *Legion destroyers engage first, using Chart C and suffering all losses inflicted by the aliens. They continue to fight until the battle is over, the Ka'slaq eliminate all of these light ships, or Ulnar launches a special attack using the battlecruisers.*

The battle wing can launch a special attack once during the battle, provided they have not suffered any losses and there are still destroyers left to cover them. The special attack allows two rolls on Table A during one round, using the battlecruisers. Thereafter the battlecruisers continue to fight, firing once per subsequent round on Chart B. The same chart is used if the battlecruisers are drawn into the battle (through the loss of all the destroyers) before their attack can be launched. Surviving destroyers still in action when a special attack is launched can only engage again if all the battlecruisers are destroyed.

Throughout the entire action, the Ka'slaq cruisers fire once per round on Chart B.

Standard Battle Notes: *When any of the formations detailed above is used (but see Dispersed below), the engagement is limited to the Ka'slaq group in contact with the squadron. The*

Section 120

Ka'slaq do not receive reinforcements. If all the ships of a given Ka'slaq group are eliminated, the squadron can engage another group if (and only if) it is in wedge, cone, destroyer screen, or heavy screen formation. Cylinders and globes cannot engage additional Ka'slaq groups after the first force is eliminated.

Each group in engaged separately, but in the same formation. A destroyer screen can have only one special attack in the whole battle no matter how many groups are fought. Ka'slaq groups cannot be attacked until the previously encountered force is completely eliminated, and only one unit at a time can be involved in battle. Dispersed squadron formations are handled differently, as discussed below.

Dispersed: *One or more ships are deployed against each enemy group. During each combat round one exchange of fire is conducted with each of the six Ka'slaq sectors, beginning with #1 and proceeding in numeric order to #6. In each of these exchanges the Legion fires first, choosing which type of ship (destroyers or battlecruisers) will fire and take losses there. Not all engagements need to use the same ship types. Legion battlecruisers fire on Chart C, destroyers on Chart D. Ka'slaq in all engagements use Chart B.*

If all Ka'slaq ships in a given group are eliminated, all Legion ships engaged against them may shift to any other part of the battle where vessels of both sides are still fighting one another. If the Ka'slaq eliminate all opposing Legion ships in a sector, they may not be attacked again.

Resolve the battle as discussed above, using standard game rules with the described modifications.

The squadron can attempt to withdraw at the end of any combat round. To resolve a retreat, go to section 141.

The squadron may be required to attempt a retreat. At the end of any round in which total Legion ship losses exceed the total of Ka'slaq losses, roll two dice and compare the result to the Morale value of the squadron. If the roll is greater than the Morale value, go to section 141. Results less than or equal to the Morale value have no effect, leaving retreat a voluntary, not mandatory, action.

Section 121

If all Legion ships are destroyed in battle, go to section 92.

If there are any Ka'slaq sectors containing ships not engaged by the Legion, at any time on or after 20 combat rounds have passed, go to section 166. Note that this happens automatically once the fighting is concluded when the Legion ships are in globe or cylinder formation, since they cannot attack any group after the first combat is resolved.

If the Legion succeeds in wiping out all of the Ka'slaq ships before the aliens can accomplish the provisions of the paragraph above, go to section 146.

— 121 —

Ulnar has made a fatal mistake. While he keeps his ships waiting on the wrong side of the sector, the Ka'slaq assembled near St. Germaine launch a ruthless attack on the sector capital. Although Admiral Merros has assembled his battle fleet, it is outmatched. Perhaps with Ulnar's squadron or the specialized knowledge of combat against the aliens it has acquired during the campaign, the Legion might fare better. As it is, Ulnar's squadron survives intact . . . but it can do no good. The decisive battle is already under way, and nothing Ulnar can do now will alter the battle or retrieve the situation after the inevitable defeat of Admiral Merros.

Under ordinary circumstances David Ulnar would be court-martialed on charges ranging from gross negligence to deliberate disobedience of orders to cowardice in the face of the enemy. As it is, no court is likely to try him, because a Ka'slaq victory will probably mean the reduction of the human race through the same type of merciless devastation already directed at Endymion and Baal. In all likelihood Ulnar won't face a court, but when the Ka'slaq finally catch and kill him, he will die knowing that any surviving pockets of human refugees are likely to revile him as a bigger traitor than Eric the Pretender.

Go to section 159.

— 122 —

Under the cloak of Stealth mode the squadron eludes the alien ships sent to attack them. As Ulnar watches their tracks in the planning tank, he pays close attention to the way Stealth mode seems to hamper their coordination. The tight formations and flawless cooperation between ships, the whole essence of Ka'slaq superiority, seems to have vanished.

Ulnar grins wolfishly. With this unexpected advantage he has a weapon worth using. Perhaps now the Legion will have a chance to avenge Don Larno and his men. At any rate, it offers a chance to strike a telling blow against a confused, disorganized foe. Ulnar switches on the Fleetcomm microphone.

"All ships, this is Flag," he says. "Cancel previous orders. We will turn on the nearest enemy division, after all. They're in for the surprise of their lives."

He stares into the planning tank, reading the symbols there with practiced ease. For the battle ahead he plans to teach the Ka'slaq a lesson in Legion fighting skills they won't soon forget. Still smiling, he turns back to the command console and prepares to issue his orders.

If Ulnar decides to attack the aliens, go to section 21.

If Ulnar wants to stand on the defensive and make the enemy attack the squadron, go to section 28.

If the admiral reconsiders again and orders his ships to move to the defense of Endymion, reduce the squadron's Morale value by 1 and go to section 26.

If Ulnar reconsiders yet again and orders the squadron to move against the alien planetoid, reduce the squadron's Morale value by 1 and go to section 23.

If the admiral loses his nerve and decides to withdraw while he has the opportunity, go to section 32.

— 123 —

"This is Flag," Ulnar begins, speaking on the Fleetcomm command circuit. "Recon wing, investigate the star system. Deploy sensor arrays and scan for enemy ships or activity. Squadron battlecruisers are to remain in reserve. Avoid battle if possible, unless I order otherwise. This is a scouting run, not a chance to play hero." Too many of Ulnar's destroyer captains were more interested in glory than common sense.

Sending in the recon wing alone had been a difficult choice to make. It is never wise to split a squadron when there is a chance of enemy attacks, but Ulnar is painfully aware that this one squadron is all that can defend the sector until Merros mobilizes. If there is an ambush in the star system, he can't afford to let all of his ships be overwhelmed. Such cold, calculated sacrifice of men's lives doesn't do Ulnar's self-image any good, but it's the kind of choice a good leader must steel himself to make.

The tactical planning tank shows the squadron's destroyers pulling away from their heavier consorts, bound inward on their mission. Ulnar gives a brief, silent prayer that they will all return safely.

If the total time elapsed in the campaign so far amounts to less than thirty-six days, go to section 86.

If the total time elapsed in the campaign is from thirty-six to fifty days, go to section 96.

If the total time consumed thus far by the campaign amounts to fifty-one or more days, go to section 106.

Sections 124, 125

— 124 —

No fresh information has come in thus far. The Ka'slaq have attempted no new attacks, to Ulnar's knowledge. With no further data to go on, Ulnar's options seem more like shots in the dark than reasonable possibilities, but he must make a decision. What should the squadron do now?

If Ulnar decides to remain at St. Germaine, go to section 115.

If Ulnar wants to have the squadron visit S.C. 170, go to section 68.

If the squadron is ordered to travel to Ulnar 118, go to section 63.

If Ulnar's orders are to travel to the Baal system, go to section 58.

If the admiral chooses to send the squadron to Endymion, go to Section 53.

If the Ninth Defense Squadron is ordered to any other destination, go to section 73.

— 125 —

By violating orders, Ulnar places himself in a dangerous position. He is gambling everything—his career, his honor, the much-maligned family name, and, above all, the safety of the Ninth Sector and of the Star League itself—on knowing better than Admiral Merros. It is essential that the gamble pay off; success is the one sure justification for any act, even disobedience.

But the days stretch on with no sign of the Ka'slaq fleet. However, word of disasters elsewhere arrive, along with Admiral Merros's displeasure at his subordinate's disobedience. Vice-Admiral David Ulnar is ordered in no uncertain terms to lay down his command in favor of the next-highest ranking officer in

Section 126

the Ninth Squadron. Ulnar is to take a fast courier ship to the geofractor complex at St. Germaine, and from thence to the Solar system. While he faces a Court of Inquiry into his conduct, the new squadron commander will continue efforts to slow down the Ka'slaq so Merros can assemble his fleet for decisive action.

The Legion encourages dedication to ideals rather than to individuals, and Ulnar's officers are too well-trained to consider ignoring Merros. For Vice-Admiral Ulnar the war against the Ka'slaq is over. It is no consolation to the ex-squadron commander that his replacement lacks the imagination and the talent to exploit the weaknesses he has perceived in the aliens' tactical capabilities. While Ulnar watches disaster unfold, the ultimate triumph of the Ka'slaq is virtually guaranteed because Ulnar discounted the possibility that his enemies in the Legion might be more dangerous than the alien Ka'slaq.

Go to section 159.

— 126 —

Reports from the squadron keep Ulnar updated on the progress of the sweep through the Baal system. They confirm the complete destruction of what was once the largest, most thriving colony in the Ninth Sector, but they also dash the admiral's hopes of finding Ka'slaq here. There is no sign of their fleet, their planetoid ship, not even a suggestion that they have a base or depot here. Baal is dead, abandoned, and the whole basis of Ulnar's strategy has died with it.

As he reaches a low point in self-confidence and composure, he notices something he overlooked before. One of his destroyers has located a vessel of decidedly nonhuman design drifting in orbit, unpowered and apparently lifeless. His men believe it to be a Ka'slaq cruiser wrecked during the battle with the Baal garrison. Undoubtedly, Legion scientists could use it to discover more about the opposition.

Leaning back in his seat, Ulnar contemplates the report. Whether his ships investigate the wreck in the Baal system or tow it and examine it on the way to their next destination, a thorough probe of the alien cruiser will slow the squadron down by several days.

Section 127

Can his researchers learn enough about the Ka'slaq to justify a delay? Ulnar needs to consider the facts carefully before he gives the word.

If Ulnar decides to order the wrecked Ka'slaq cruiser investigated further, go to section 104.

If Ulnar chooses to ignore the cruiser and leave Baal, go to section 137.

— 127 —

The survey ship *Serendipity*, registered to the prestigious Derron Foundation, is commanded by a stubborn skeptic who has always struck Ulnar as the stereotypical, slightly shady merchant skipper; he never seems quite at home in command of a mobile laboratory. Most private survey ships would stay quietly in port during a crisis like the Ka'slaq invasion, but Rik Joval's ship simply ignores the crisis and carries on.

Ulnar is too involved in strategy to be overly worried about a single vessel, so *Serendipity* is the last thing on his mind—until the message comes in. Ulnar is on *Valiant*'s bridge at the time.

"Derron Foundation vessel *Serendipity* to Ninth Defense Squadron," the ultrawave message begins, a wavering, badly-regulated signal. "Ship in danger. Holed in four places, geodynes out. Losing air. Encountered hostile ships . . . dozens of them. Attacked . . . heavy damage. Using last power reserves for transmission. Location of alien fleet is Ulnar . . . Ulnar 118. Power fading . . . Good luck, Legion . . . hope yours is better than ours . . ."

The message was transmitted days ago. A ship as badly damaged as *Serendipity*, in an uninhabited star system occupied by a hostile fleet, could not have survived. Ulnar hopes Joval used his remaining power to self-destruct, a cleaner death than the slow agony of losing air, heat, and light in a drifting coffin.

Joval's dying gesture gives Ulnar a lead on the Ka'slaq. How should Ulnar use it?

If Ulnar is currently at St. Germaine and wants to remain there, go to section 115.

Section 128

If he is at Baal and the colony there is intact, go to section 144 and remain in orbit.

If he wishes to remain in orbit anywhere else (including Baal if the colony there has fallen) go to section 71.

If Ulnar wishes to travel to St. Germaine, go to section 74.

If the admiral orders the squadron to Ulnar 118, go to section 63.

If Ulnar decides to travel to Endymion, go to section 53.

If Ulnar instructs the squadron to travel to S.C. 170, go to section 68.

If the squadron is ordered to visit Baal, go to section 58.

Should the admiral choose to take his ships to any other destination, go to section 73.

— 128 —

Ulnar switches on the Fleetcomm microphone one last time before the squadron comes within combat range of the aliens. "All ships, Flag calling," he says. "Engage Stealth mode during combat. I say again, use Stealth mode when fighting. Good luck to all!" Even though this unorthodox tactic will hamper the coordination of his own ships, Ulnar is sure that it will cause even more havoc to the alien flotilla.

The battle for Baal is under way!

The map shows the deployment of the alien ships. They are formed into a rigid phalanx, and throughout the engagement they deviate from this initial formation, and from their assigned missions, only if actually in battle with Legion ships. They are divided into six groups, as shown by the map.

If the Legion ships have adopted a purely defensive formation (globe, cylinder, battlecruiser screen), the force they engage first will be chosen randomly by rolling one die. The enemy

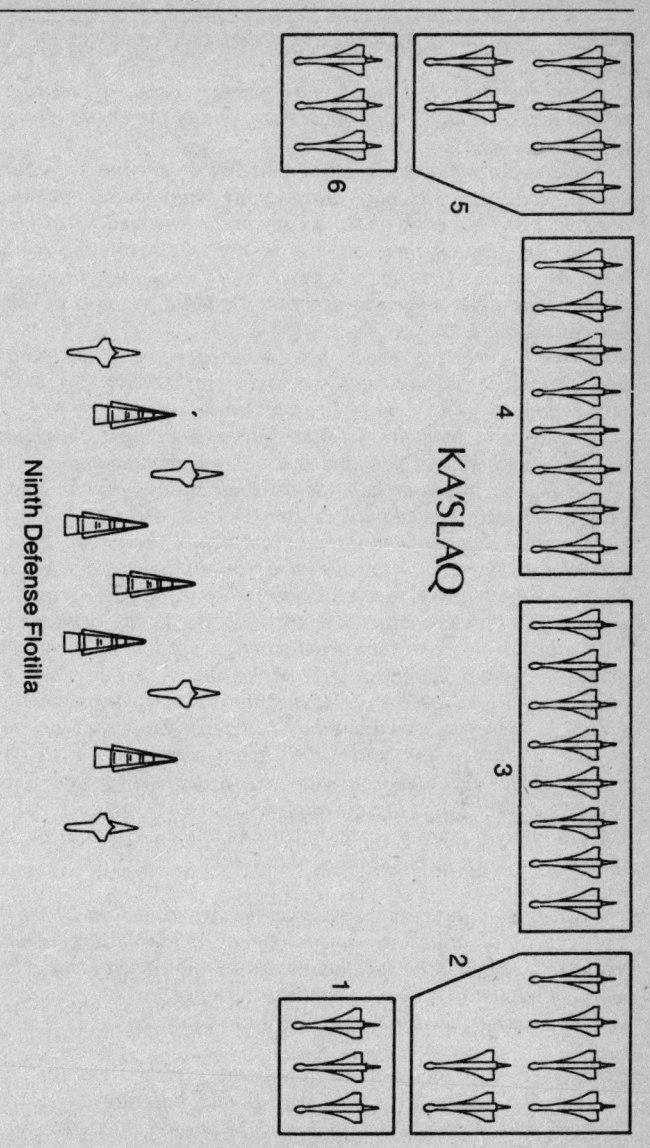

Section 128

KA'SLAQ

Ninth Defense Flotilla

1
2
3
4
5
6

Section 128

attackers are found by using the sector/group number on the map.

If the squadron is formed into a wedge, cone, or destroyer screen deployment, Ulnar chooses any one of the enemy groups to fight against.

A dispersed squadron must spread out to engage the entire enemy flotilla. Ulnar may allocate his ships in any manner desired, provided each of the six sectors is engaged by at least one Legion ship. If this option is in use, the resolution of the battle is conducted under a special set of guidelines described later, which differ somewhat from the standard methods of combat resolution.

Normally, only one enemy force is engaged at a time. Once the Legion is matched with an opponent, resolve the battle conventionally. The Legion fires first with whichever wing is eligible to fire; then the Ka'slaq cruisers fighting them return fire. One exchange of this kind is a single combat round.

The Legion forces include all of Ulnar's ships plus the Baal garrison. However, one battlecruiser (Defiant) and one destroyer (Anthar) are deleted from the garrison before the battle. Baal's orbital fortress cannot engage in a conventional space battle. Ka'slaq forces attack in the numbers shown for each group. If the aliens suffer casualties due to combat with the orbital fortress, their losses are subtracted from group 3 first, then from group 4, group 2, group 5, and so on. A group must be completely wiped out before losses can be taken from another group. If there are groups reduced to zero ships, they are not eligible as targets for battle. Roll again when random assignment matches the squadron with such a depleted group. Each Ka'slaq cruiser has a firepower of 8.

Resolution of combat varies according to the Legion formation in use, as shown in the sections that follow.

Wedge: *Legion destroyers attack on the first round on Chart D. They may not attack again so long as battlecruisers remain available, although combat losses can be subtracted from either wing. After the first round, battlecruisers fire for the remaining rounds on Chart C. Ka'slaq cruisers use Chart E.*

Cone: *Roll one die. The Legion battlecruisers fight for this number of rounds, firing on Chart D and suffering any losses inflicted by the enemy in response. After these rounds are completed, roll another die and fight with the destroyers on the same*

Section 128

chart for this number of rounds. If necessary, continue alternating in this way until the end of the battle. The Ka'slaq cruisers fire back on Chart D.

Globe: *Legion battlecruisers fire every round on Chart C. Destroyers can only fire or suffer losses if all of the battlecruisers are first eliminated. They use Chart E if they have to engage. The Ka'slaq cruisers fire each round on Chart D.*

Cylinder: *Legion battlecruisers fire on the first round of combat, using Chart D. The destroyers fire on the same chart on the next round, and the two wings continue to alternate in this way until the battle is over. Casualties are absorbed by whichever wing has fired in the current round. The Ka'slaq use Chart D for their attacks.*

Heavy Screen: *Legion battlecruisers fire on Chart C and take all losses inflicted by the Ka'slaq. If all the battlecruisers are eliminated, the destroyers can enter the fray, firing on Chart D. The Ka'slaq cruisers fire on Chart D.*

Destroyer Screen: *Legion destroyers engage first, using Chart D and suffering all losses inflicted by the aliens. They continue to fight until the battle is over, the Ka'slaq eliminate all of these light ships, or Ulnar launches a special attack using the battlecruisers.*

The battle wing can launch a special attack once during the battle, provided they have not suffered any losses (as long as there are still destroyers left to cover them). The special attack allows two rolls on Table B during one *round by the battlecruisers. Thereafter, the battlecruisers continue to fight, firing once per subsequent round on Chart C. This chart is also used if the battlecruisers are drawn into the battle (through the loss of all the destroyers) before their special attack can be launched. Surviving destroyers still in action at the time of a special attack can only fight again if all the battlecruisers are destroyed first.*

Throughout the entire action the Ka'slaq cruisers fire once each round on Chart D.

Standard Battle Notes: *When any of the formations detailed above is used (but see Dispersed, below), the engagement is limited to the Ka'slaq group in contact with the squadron. The*

Section 128

Ka'slaq do not receive reinforcements. If all the ships of a given Ka'slaq group are eliminated, the squadron can engage another group if (and only if) it is in wedge, cone, destroyer screen, or heavy screen formation. Cylinders and globes cannot engage additional Ka'slaq groups after the first force is eliminated.

Each group is engaged separately, but always in the same formation. A destroyer screen can have only one special attack in the whole battle, no matter how many groups are fought. Ka'slaq groups cannot be attacked until the previously encountered force is completely eliminated, and only one unit at a time can be involved in battle. Dispersed squadron formations are handled differently, as discussed below.

Dispersed: *One or more ships are deployed against each enemy group. During each combat round one exchange of fire is conducted within each of the six Ka'slaq sectors, beginning with #1 and proceeding in order to #6. In each of these exchanges the Legion fires first, choosing which type of ship (destroyers or battlecruisers) present will fire and take losses there. Not all engagements in a given combat round need to use the same ship types. Legion battlecruisers fire on Chart B, destroyers on Chart C. Ka'slaq vessels in all sectors use Chart D.*

If all Ka'slaq vessels in a given group are eliminated, all Legion ships engaged against them may shift to any other part of the battle where vessels of both sides are still fighting one another. If the Ka'slaq eliminate all opposing Legion ships in a sector, they may not be attacked again.

Resolve the battle as discussed above, using standard game rules with the described modifications.

The squadron can attempt to withdraw at the end of any combat round. To resolve a retreat, go to section 141.

The squadron may be required to attempt a retreat. At the end of any round in which total Legion ship losses exceed the total of Ka'slaq losses, roll two dice and compare the result to the Morale value of the squadron. If the roll is greater than the Morale value, go to section 141. Results less than or equal to the Morale value have no effect, leaving retreat a voluntary action.

If all Legion ships are destroyed in battle, go to section 92.

If there are any Ka'slaq sectors containing ships not engaged by the Legion (after 20 combat rounds have passed) go to section 166. This happens automatically once the fighting is concluded when the Legion ships are in globe or cylinder formation, since they cannot attack any group after the first combat is resolved.

If the Legion succeeds in wiping out all of the Ka'slaq ships before the aliens can accomplish the provisions of the preceding paragraph, go to section 146.

— 129 —

The jaws of the trap are closing rapidly, and Ulnar has very little time to organize the squadron for battle. He examines the planning tank for a few seconds before he finally makes his decision. He swings back to the command console and switches on the Fleetcomm microphone again.

"Flag to Ninth Squadron," he says. "Adopt standard wedge formation and attack the enemy."

With hardly a pause, the computer comes on-line, feeding a list of preprogrammed vectors and positions to the rest of the squadron. Ulnar watches the data scroll across his monitor screen. On the console green lights begin to flash, signifying that the ships are receiving and complying with his orders. The holographic display in the planning tank begins to shift as the ships start to move into position.

In theory the wedge formation is a perfect solution to the Ka'slaq trap; it will keep the squadron in a tight, mutually supporting group that could push through the enemy's wall of cruisers and either escape or turn back to continue the battle. But the Ka'slaq have proven that textbook theories aren't always valid, and Ulnar knows that he is taking a risk. If the aliens englobe his compact formation, the Legion ships will face a serious problem.

The battle is developing too fast to allow much time for second thoughts. The wedge is still forming up as the blue lights in the tank close in. The Squadron is committed now; its fate rests entirely on its skill in battle.

Section 130

To resolve this battle using conventional tactics, go to section 105.

If Ulnar chooses the unorthodox use of Stealth mode during the actual battle, go to section 109 instead.

— 130 —

The two forces close in on one another, and Legion vortex guns flare with blinding light in a challenge quickly answered by the massive antimatter-induction explosions set off by the Ka'slaq annihilators. Battle has been joined!

The nature of the battle depends on the formation adopted by the squadron and on the forces they are fighting first. Study Map 2 for the initial deployment of alien forces.

When the battle first begins, the Legion ships face the Ka'slaq division noted in the previous section. The arrows on the map show how long it takes for the other two divisions to come up as reinforcements. A combat round is one attack by each side; after fire has been resolved, determine how many rounds have passed, and, if appropriate, add any Ka'slaq reinforcements shown as due. The Ka'slaq divisions always move to reinforce a division involved in battle as quickly as they can.

To resolve the battle, Legion ships fire first, followed by return fire by any surviving Ka'slaq ships. Either the Legion destroyers or the battlecruisers (not both) will fire in a given round; all Ka'slaq cruisers fire in every round. The Ka'slaq planetoid never fires and cannot be fired upon. The formation adopted by the Legion ships governs which ships fire when and the firing charts used by each side. Each Ka'slaq cruiser has a firepower of 8.

Wedge: *Destroyers attack on the first round on Chart C. They may not attack again as long as any battlecruisers remain, but they can suffer losses if the Legion commander so desires, sparing the battlecruisers. After the first round, Legion battlecruisers fire during each round of combat on Chart B. The Ka'slaq cruisers generally use Chart C, but any time the Third Division is engaged, they use Chart A.*

Section 130

Ninth Defense Flotilla

Ka'slaq First Division (32)

Ka'slaq Second Division (56)

Ka'slaq Third Division (31)

Planetoid

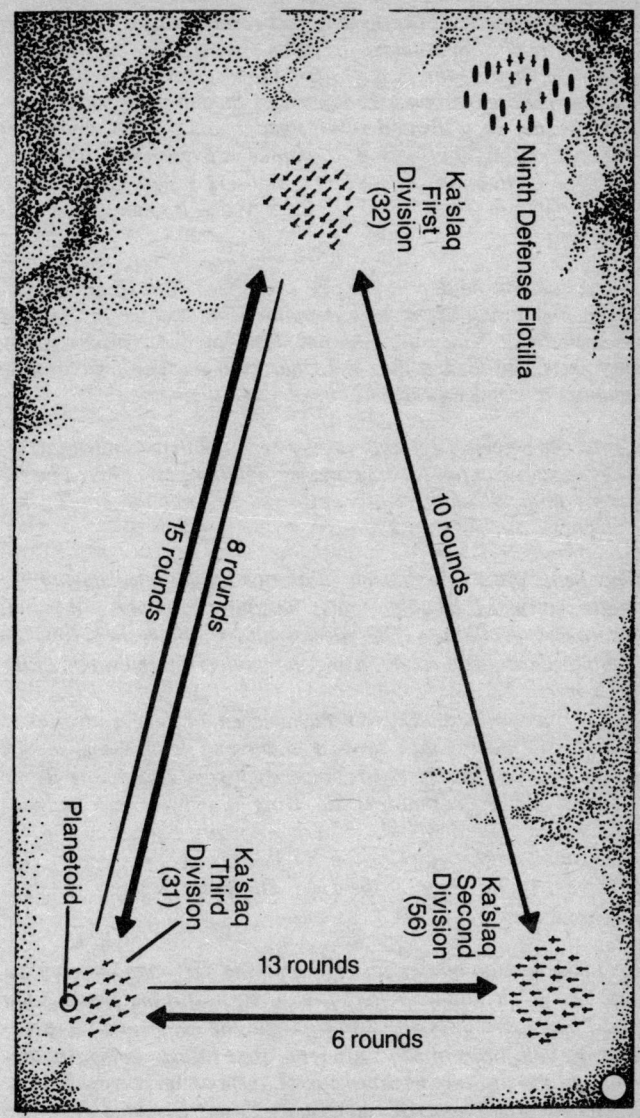

15 rounds
8 rounds
10 rounds
13 rounds
6 rounds

BATTLE OF ENDYMION

Section 130

Cone: *Roll one die. The Legion battlecruisers bear the fighting for this number of rounds, firing on Chart C and suffering all losses inflicted by the enemy. After the last of these rounds, roll another die and resolve this number of rounds using the destroyers instead. They also fire on Chart C and absorb any losses inflicted during this period. Continue alternating in this way until the battle ends. The Ka'slaq cruisers generally use Chart B, but they use Chart A if the Third Division is among the forces engaged.*

Globe: *Legion battlecruisers fire every round on Chart B. Destroyers can only fire or take casualties if all battlecruisers have been destroyed; they use Chart C. The Ka'slaq cruisers generally use Chart C, but they use Chart A if the Third Division is among the elements currently involved in the battle.*

Destroyer Screen: *Legion destroyers engage first using Chart C. They continue to fight, firing and taking all losses inflicted by the enemy until all of them are destroyed or until the battle wing launches a special attack.*

The battle wing can launch a special attack once during the battle, provided they have lost no ships (and there are still destroyers available.) The special attack allows two rolls on Table A during one round, using the battlecruisers instead of the destroyers.

After the special attack has been launched, or if the battlecruisers take losses before they have a chance to launch the special attack, the battlecruisers fire once each round on Chart B and take all further casualties. Surviving destroyers can only be engaged again if the battlecruisers are wiped out.

Throughout the entire action Ka'slaq cruisers fire each round on Chart B. However, if the Third Division is among the ships engaged, they use Chart A instead.

Cylinder: *Legion battlecruisers fire on the first round of combat, using Chart B. The destroyers fire on the next round on the same chart. On subsequent rounds continue the same alternation as long as both types of ships are left. Ships lost to enemy fire in a given round are taken from the ranks of whichever wing fired.*

The Ka'slaq fire each round using Chart B, but if the Third Division is involved in the battle, use Chart A instead.

Section 130

Heavy Screen: *Legion battlecruisers fire on Chart B and take all ship losses inflicted by the Ka'slaq. If all battlecruisers are eliminated, the destroyers can begin firing and taking losses; they fire on Chart D.*

The Ka'slaq cruisers fire each round on Chart C, but if their Third Division is among the forces engaged, use Chart A instead.

Dispersed: *Legion destroyers attack on the first round, firing on Chart D. Battlecruisers fire on Chart C on the next round, and the two wings continue to alternate fire until all of one wing's ships are eliminated; thereafter, the survivors can fire every round. Losses are taken from whichever wing fired in the same round.*

The Ka'slaq fire once each round on Chart C, but if their third Division is involved in the fighting, they use Chart A instead.

Resolve the battle according to the game rules, using the guidelines given above.

The squadron can attempt to withdraw at the end of any combat round. To resolve a retreat, go to section 84.

The squadron may be required to attempt a retreat. At the end of any round in which Legion losses exceed Ka'slaq losses, roll two dice and compare the result of the Morale value of the squadron. If the roll is greater than the Morale value, go to section 84. Results less than or equal to the Morale value have no effect, making retreat voluntary.

If the squadron remains engaged until all Legion ships have been eliminated, go to section 92.

If the Legion ships eliminate all of the Ka'slaq cruisers in the division they first engage before any enemy reinforcements come, they may choose to continue the battle, or they can withdraw. To continue the battle, simply go on with combat resolution against the next wave of aliens. To withdraw, go to section 84.

Should the squadron manage to eliminate every Ka'slaq cruiser in all three alien divisions, go to section 87. This is the only

Section 131

situation in which the alien planetoid can actually be attacked. There is no time to organize an assault on this structure before reinforcements can come up if there are other Ka'slaq ships still present in the star system.

— 131 —

"Flag to all ships," Ulnar begins, speaking on the Fleetcomm command circuit. "The Ninth Squadron will investigate the star system. Deploy sensor arrays and scan for enemy ships or activity. Battle is to be avoided except on my order, or as absolutely necessary."

Ulnar is sure the Ka'slaq are near, and he does not intend to make any mistakes. Conventional doctrine calls for him to send the squadron's recon wing into the system while his battlecruisers stay out of danger, but he has too much respect for the aliens to consider dividing his squadron and allowing them the chance to defeat it in detail. He would rather expose all of his ships to the risk of an attack, and thus have the strength and flexibility to turn back the enemy, than send his ships into danger piecemeal and perhaps have them all destroyed before his people could react.

Valiant and the rest of the Ninth Defense Squadron gather speed as they plunge toward Ulnar 118, every officer and crewman tense with expectation. Ulnar can only hope this reconnaissance in force won't end in disaster.

If the total time elapsed in the campaign so far amounts to thirty-five days or less, go to section 86.

If the total time elapsed in the campaign so far comes to thirty-six through fifty days, go to section 110.

If the total time consumed thus far by the campaign amounts to fifty-one or more days, go to section 106.

— 132 —

The Ka'slaq trap is closing around Ulnar's squadron, leaving the admiral little time to organize his ships. Studying the planning tank, he quickly weighs the possibility before making a final decision. Then he swivels his chair to face the command console. He switches on the Fleetcomm microphone before moving both hands to the flag computer keyboard, where swift, practiced movements call up the plan he has chosen.

"Flag calling Ninth Squadron," he says as he punches in the coded combinations needed to bring the computer into the Fleetcomm network. "Cone formation. Repeat, adopt cone formation, and attempt to englobe the enemy. Target coordinates to follow."

The computer takes over. On Ulnar's monitor screen the prepared list of vectors and positions appears, scrolling upward as it is transmitted to the other ships of the squadron. Almost immediately they begin to acknowledge the instructions, and Ulnar turns back to the planning tank to watch the squadron shift into the cone formation he has ordered.

A cone is a tricky formation to use when outnumbered and an unlikely choice to adopt against an ambush. But Ulnar isn't striving to escape; he wants to turn the tables and annihilate at least part of the enemy fleet while it is within his grasp. Then the squadron can run or continue to fight, but in either case the aliens will feel the strength of the Legion before it is all over.

The battle develops quickly, without the usual waiting that makes time for doubts and uncertainties to shake a commander's self-confidence. The cone is barely stabilized when the Ka'slaq cruisers begin their final approach. Ulnar has no time for second thoughts, no opportunity to consider the alternatives. The squadron is committed now.

To resolve the battle of Ulnar 118 using conventional tactics, go to section 105.

If Ulnar chooses the unorthodox use of Stealth mode during the actual battle, go to section 109 instead.

— 133 —

The destruction of the Ka'slaq mother ship marks the end of the invasion crisis. Thanks to Ulnar and the Ninth Defense Squadron, the alien threat is over. Merros, of course, grabs the lion's share of the credit, but Vice-Admiral Ulnar is not totally ignored. His part in the victory draws attention and praise from people high in the Legion, officers whose opinions matter. Even though Merros gets the adulation and public acclamation, Ulnar gets the rewards that really matter—promotion, recognition, reassignment to a post where his skills and experience count. Any attempt his erstwhile superior makes to block his progress is killed quietly, so that even Ulnar hears no hint of doubt or scandal.

League scientists are frustrated by the loss of the alien vessel. From the remains of wrecked cruisers a sketchy picture of the enemy emerges, but there are many gaps to fill in. The aliens were led by an artificial life form, an organic/machine clique that controlled all facets of the Ka'slaq war effort by a direct interface with their ships and weapons. They were totally self-sufficient, with a race of ordinary life forms kept aboard the mother ship but excluded from any important function in society. Their sole purpose was to perpetuate the cyborg oligarchy by providing new brains at need. The cyborgs, linked by ultra-wave communications, and transmitting orders and ideas at the speed of thought itself, were capable of amazing military feats, but the brain/machine combination was heartless, soulless, incapable of emotion or compassion. In the end it was this lack of feeling that really destroyed them, along with inherent weaknesses in the machine interfaces. But it was a close battle.

The Legion of Space triumphed over their most dangerous foe since the days of the Cometeers. For a time, at least, the Star League can continue to flourish in peace and prosperity . . . until the next threat arises to endanger humanity once more.

Although the Legion has won a victory, its triumph is marred by the fact that so little real information on the aliens survived the loss of their mother ship. This may cost them some day, should they be forced to fight similar enemies without a full understand-

ing of what motivates them. Still, the Legion's success is better than the fate they might have met if fortune had gone against them.

To try to achieve a more complete victory, go back to section 1 and play again. Good Luck!

— 134 —

Ulnar has little time to organize an effective defense; the Ka'slaq trap is fast closing around his ships. He weighs the possibilities quickly, eyes focused on the moving lights in the planning tank, before he comes to a decision. Swiveling his chair to face the command console, the admiral switches on the Fleetcomm microphone. Both hands begin moving over the keyboard to summon up the battle orders he has decided upon.

"Flag calling all ships," he says with studied calm. "Form globe and prepare for enemy attack. Battle orders on-line now."

He stabs a final button on the keyboard, and the computer takes over. His monitor screen lights up with a readout of ship vectors and positions which are being transmitted simultaneously to the entire squadron. The other ships acknowledge his instructions at once. Ulnar turns back to the planning tank to watch as the squadron shifts into a defensive globe formation.

The globe is the best formation to use against a superior enemy, according to the textbooks. It is particularly useful against an opponent's attempt to surround the defenders, providing equal, all-around firepower. The Ka'slaq trap is a perfect example of the situation globes are supposed to counter best. Ulnar finds himself hoping sardonically that the Ka'slaq have read the same textbooks.

He doesn't have much time to worry since the battle develops more quickly than most. The globe is still settling into final form as the enemies begin to close in. Ulnar's ships and men are committed to battle.

Section 135

To resolve the battle of Ulnar 118 using conventional tactics, go to section 105.

If Ulnar chooses the unorthodox use of Stealth mode during the actual battle, go to section 109.

— 135 —

As the two forces close, Ulnar switches on the Fleetcomm microphone to give one last order. "All ships, this is Flag," he says quietly. "Engage Stealth mode during battle. Repeating, engage Stealth mode during battle. Maintain Stealth mode until further notice. Good luck!" It was a tactic that would hamper the squadron's coordination somewhat, but Ulnar was sure it would hurt the superb Ka'slaq synchronization even more.

Vortex guns flare with blinding light, signaling the opening of the Legion bombardment. Moments later the hellish fires of antimatter-induction explosions unleashed by the Ka'slaq annihilator guns answer the challenge. Battle has been joined!

The nature of the battle depends on the formation adopted by the squadron, and on which enemy force they have chosen to fight first. Study Map 2 for the initial deployment of the alien divisions.

When the battle first begins, the Legion ships face the Ka'slaq division noted from the previous section. The arrows on the map denote how long it takes for the other two divisions to come up as reinforcements. A combat round is one attack by each side. After firing has been resolved, determine how many rounds have passed and, if appropriate, add any Ka'slaq reinforcements shown as due. Ka'slaq divisions always move as quickly as possible to reinforce a division that is involved in battle.

To resolve the battle, Legion ships fire first, followed by return fire by any surviving Ka'slaq ships. Either the Legion destroyers or the battlecruisers (not both) will fire in a given round; all Ka'slaq cruisers fire every round. The Ka'slaq planetoid never fires and cannot be fired upon. The formation adopted by the squadron governs which ships fire when and the firing charts used by each side. Each Ka'slaq cruiser has a firepower of 8.

Section 135

Wedge: *Destroyers attack on the first round on Chart D. They may not attack again as long as any battlecruisers remain, but they can take losses during any round even though they cannot fire, thus sparing the battlecruisers at the Legion commander's option. After the first round, Legion battlecruisers fire on each subsequent combat round, using Chart C. If all battlecruisers are lost, surviving destroyers can engage again using Chart D.*

The Ka'slaq cruisers use Chart E, but if their Third Division is among the forces engaged, they use Chart D instead.

Cone: *Roll one die. Legion battlecruisers bear the brunt of the combat for this number of rounds, firing on Chart D and suffering all losses caused by the enemy. After the last of these rounds, roll another die and resolve this number of rounds using the destroyers (also firing on Chart D) instead. Continue alternating in this way until the battle ends, losing ships from whichever wing is currently permitted to fire.*

The Ka'slaq use Chart E to fire unless the Third Division is part of the enemy force currently engaged, in which case they use Chart D.

Globe: *Legion battlecruisers fire every round on Chart C. Destroyers can fire or take casualties only if all battlecruisers have been destroyed; they use Chart D. Ka'slaq cruisers fire on Chart E, but if their Third Division is among the alien forces currently involved in the conflict, Chart D is used instead.*

Destroyer Screen: *Legion destroyers engage first, using Chart D. They continue to fight, firing and taking all losses inflicted by the enemy until all of them are destroyed or until the battle wing launches a special attack.*

The battle wing can launch a special attack once during the battle, provided no battlecruisers have yet been lost (that is, the destroyers have not been totally eliminated). The special attack allows two rolls on Table B during one round, using the battlecruisers instead of the destroyers.

After the special attack has been launched, or if the battlecruisers take losses before they have a chance to launch the special attack, the battlecruisers fire once each round on Chart C and take all further casualties. Surviving destroyers can only be engaged again (on Chart D as before) if the battlecruisers are eliminated.

Section 135

Throughout the entire action, Ka'slaq cruisers fire each round on Chart E, but if the Third Division of Ka'slaq ships is involved in the battle, Chart D should be used instead.

Cylinder: *Legion battlecruisers fire on the first round of combat, using Chart C. The destroyers fire on the next round on the same chart. On subsequent rounds continue the same alternation as long as ships of both types remain. Ships lost to enemy fire in a given round are taken from the ranks of whichever wing fired.*

The Ka'slaq fire each round using Chart E. If the Third Division is involved in the fighting, use Chart D instead.

Heavy Screen: *Legion battlecruisers fire on Chart C and take all ship losses inflicted by the Ka'slaq. If all battlecruisers are eliminated, the destroyers can begin firing on Chart E and take all further losses.*

Ka'slaq cruisers fire each round on Chart E, but if the Third Division is taking an active part in the battle, Chart D should be used instead.

Dispersed: *Legion destroyers attack on the first round, firing on Chart C. Battlecruisers fire on Chart B on the next round. Thereafter, these two groups continue to alternate fire in the same way. Obviously if one group is completely eliminated, no alternation is possible and the surviving force fires on every round. Losses are taken from whichever wing fired in the round.*

The Ka'slaq fire once each round on Chart E. If their Third Division is actively participating in the engagement, Chart A should be used instead.

Resolve the battle according to the game rules, using the guidelines given above.

The Squadron can attempt to retreat at the end of any combat round. To resolve a retreat, go to section 84.

The squadron may be required to attempt a retreat. At the end of any round in which Legion losses are greater than those of the Ka'slaq, roll two dice and compare the result to the Morale value of the squadron. If the roll is greater than the Morale value, go to section 84. Results less than or equal to the Morale value have no effect, leaving retreat voluntary.

Section 136

If the squadron remains engaged until all Legion ships have been eliminated by the aliens, go to section 92.

If Legion ships eliminate all of the Ka'slaq cruisers in the division, they engage first, prior to the arrival of reinforcing divisions. The squadron can either continue the battle or withdraw from the action. To continue the battle, simply go on with combat resolution against the next enemy wave as before. To withdraw, go to section 84, as above.

Finally, should Ulnar's squadron somehow manage to eliminate every Ka'slaq cruiser from all three divisions, go to section 87. This is the only situation in which the alien planetoid can actually be attacked. There is no time to organize an assault on this structure before reinforcements can come up if there are other Ka'slaq ships still present in the star system.

— 136 —

The squadron accelerates away from Endymion, leaving behind the shattered hulk of the Ka'slaq cruiser. Where should it go next? Endymion holds no advantage now, and it seems unlikely that the aliens will return here. Where will they strike? The answer David Ulnar comes up with could spell the difference between victory or defeat in this war with the faceless enemy from Orion.

If Ulnar decides to remain at Endymion, go to section 71.

If Ulnar decides to have the squadron return to St. Germaine, go to section 74.

If the squadron receives instructions to go to S.C. 170, go to section 68.

If Ulnar orders his ships to travel to Ulnar 118, go to section 63.

If the admiral orders the Ninth Defense Squadron to any other destination, go to section 73.

If Ulnar orders ships to Baal, turn to section 58.

— 137 —

The squadron accelerates away from Baal's central star. The wrecked Ka'slaq cruiser drops farther and farther astern. Where should Ulnar take the squadron now? It seems unlikely that the aliens will return to Baal. Ulnar must decide where they are likely to strike next or devise a strategy for stopping their thrust into Star League territory. His choice may make the difference between triumph and total destruction for the entire human race.

If Ulnar decides to remain at Baal, go to section 71.

If Ulnar decides to have the squadron return to St. Germaine, go to section 74.

If the squadron receives instructions to go to S.C. 170, go to section 68.

If the admiral orders his ships to travel to Ulnar 118, go to section 63.

If Ulnar wants the squadron to go to Endymion, go to section 53.

If the admiral orders the squadron to any other destination, go to section 73.

— 138 —

Boosting away from S.C. 170, the squadron leaves the shattered hulk of the alien cruiser drifting in solar orbit behind them. Ulnar must now decide where his ships will best be employed. S.C. 170 yielded few clues and even less strategic value. It seems improbable that the aliens will return. If the Ka'slaq drive into League territory has developed during the squadron's sojourn at this distant planet, the Legion must deploy properly or the war will surely be lost.

If Ulnar decides to remain at S.C. 170, go to section 71.

If Ulnar decides that the squadron should return to St. Germaine, go to section 74.

If the squadron receives instructions to travel to Ulnar 118, go to section 63.

If Ulnar takes the squadron to Baal, go to section 58.

If the admiral orders his ships to Endymion, go to section 53.

If the squadron is given orders to travel to any other destination, go to section 73.

— 139 —

The squadron leaves the hulk of the Ka'slaq cruiser drifting in orbit around Ulnar 118 and accelerates away from the star. Finding no sign of the alien fleet at Ulnar 118 after all, Ulnar must determine where the Squadron can best be employed. Was the alien cruiser an advanced scout for a fleet that hasn't arrived, or was it left behind when the main armada set out for a new destination? Where should Ulnar post his ships now to stop the Ka'slaq invasion?

If Ulnar chooses to remain near Ulnar 118, go to section 152.

If Ulnar orders his ships to return to St. Germaine, go to section 74.

If the admiral instructs the squadron to travel to S.C. 170, go to section 68.

If Ulnar orders the squadron to Baal, go to section 58.

If the admiral's orders send the squadron to Endymion, go to section 53.

If Ulnar orders the squadron to any other destination, go to section 73.

— 140 —

Despite his doubts, Ulnar cannot disobey Admiral Merros over vague suspicions or hunches. His duty is to follow the admiral's orders and return to St. Germaine. Without evidence to the contrary, he must base his decision on that duty.

At Ulnar's command, *Valiant* boosts out of orbit on a new voyage, the rest of the squadron trailing the flagship. The Ninth Defense Squadron plunges through interstellar space once more, headed for St. Germaine.

Aboard each vessel there is mounting excitement. Everyone knows the voyage is leading to the climax of this war, the final confrontation between human and Ka'slaq. When the opposing fleets meet next, their clash will decide the fate of the Star League. No one seems willing to admit that this could also be the squadron's last trip, but by the time it reaches St. Germaine, the tense, expectant mood is evidence that each man aboard has made his peace with himself and his deity.

They arrive at the Sector capital to find the system preparing for invasion, bristling with new defenses and new ships. At long last the final phase of this struggle for survival is about to begin.

Proceed to section 119.

— 141 —

The squadron puts up a fierce fight against the Ka'slaq flotilla. It is an odd battle; the aliens seem utterly indifferent to the humans except when actually attacked, and there is none of the precise coordination and tight mutual support that Ulnar was expecting. The attackers might have been a different race from the victors of Endymion. Still, their weaponry is taking its toll against the ranks of Ulnar's command. He admits to himself that the enemy will wear the Ninth Squadron down. And if the squadron is wiped out here, nothing else stands between the sector and the Ka'slaq fleet.

At last he gives the orders. "Flag to Ninth Squadron," he

says reluctantly. "Discontinue the action. Repeat, discontinue the action." The computer signals the fail-safe withdrawal code simultaneously to confirm his words. "Break off and retreat. Regroup at point one nine. Pull out immediately. Message ends."

One ship after another acknowledges his instructions. In the tank Legion blips grow less distinct, simulating the output of ultrawave and ultrapulse jamming by ships attempting to escape under the cloak of Stealth mode. The Ka'slaq ships seem to lose interest in the humans as contact is lost, resuming their arrow-straight course toward Baal like machines programmed to ignore everything but their goal. There seems little doubt that the squadron will escape them.

Roll two dice three times and compare the results to the Stealth value of the squadron. If any one result is less than or equal to this value, go to section 117.

If all three rolls exceed the Stealth value, they will be attacked by the Ka'slaq. Return to the section you read immediately before this one.

— 142 —

Ulnar focuses his attention on the planning tank, swiftly weighing the possibilities. He has little time to prepare the squadron to meet the Ka'slaq trap closing around his ships. Every vessel will be needed, making his decision a simple one. The admiral swings his chair around to face his command console, flicking on the Fleetcomm microphone. While his hands move over the computer keyboard to call up his chosen battle orders, Ulnar frames his instructions and begins to speak.

"Ninth Squadron, this is Flag. Adopt cylinder formation and prepare for enemy assault. Battle orders coming . . . now."

He keys in the last digit of the code to bring the computer into the Fleetcomm network, and the machine takes over. He watches the orders scroll across his monitor for a moment, repeating the vector and position data being sent to the other ships. As the squadron begins to acknowledge, Ulnar turns back to the planning tank to watch as the formation takes shape.

The decision to use a cylinder was a hard one to make.

Section 143

Weaker than a globe in terms of overall structure, the cylinder is a compromise formation that allows the squadron's destroyers to contribute their firepower to the battle. Like all compromises, its virtues are also its weaknesses; Ulnar hopes those weaknesses won't prove disastrous. At least the destroyers will give him sufficient strength to meet the aliens on less disadvantageous terms.

He doesn't have much time to dwell on his uncertainties, since this battle is developing more quickly than most engagements. The squadron is committed now, and only the battle itself can determine its fate.

To resolve the battle of Ulnar 118 using conventional tactics, go to section 105.

If Ulnar decides to use Stealth mode during the actual battle, go to section 109.

— 143 —

Ulnar studies the computer's graphic simulation of the alien mother ship. Scans have pinpointed a powerful source of ultrawave signals located in a complex of towers and domes extending over an area almost a mile across. The computer has assigned an eighty-six percent chance that the main control center for the vessel is somewhere in this area. The admiral can find no other obvious targets; the planet ships' geodynes are buried deep in the giant vessel's structure, and the rest of the huge artifact defies analysis.

"Cut off the head," Ulnar mutters, "and the body can't survive."

"Admiral?" Sammis, standing nearby, raises a quizzical eyebrow.

Ulnar doesn't answer him directly. Instead he leans toward the Fleetcomm microphone. "This is Flag," he says slowly. "The Ninth Squadron will attack the alien complex. Bombardment coordinates coming on-line." He shifts the flag computer read-out on the target into the network and enters positioning orders for the ships in the squadron. Soon the Legion is ready to deliver the final blow.

Section 143

"Commence bombardment . . . now," Ulnar orders at last.

Flaming balls of pure energy, like miniature suns, streak from the vortex guns of the squadron's remaining ships, raining down on the surface of the huge mother ship. They create an eerie false dawn over the target area, followed by a chain of explosions across the area identified as the control complex. The heat and unchained atomic energies of these opalescent spheres is devastating; huge towers and soaring spires crumble and melt, while vast, glassy craters and jagged fractures spread over the surface of the structure. As the intense bombardment continues, surges of ultrawave static alternate with heartrending cries for mercy and assistance.

"The masters are gone," one transmission announces, using League Anglic. "Please, you've destroyed them. . . . We had no choice but to obey them. Don't—"

But the message ends in an electronic shriek of overloaded, melting circuitry.

Horrified, Ulnar orders the bombardment stopped, but his instructions come too late. The explosions continue rippling along the surface of the alien ship, spreading outward from the original target area in chain reaction. The squadron witnesses the death throes of a ship, and perhaps an entire civilization.

"Pull back," Ulnar orders, reading a warning from the computer's correlation of sensor readings. "It's going to blow." The tiny squadron accelerates away from the doomed mother ship. As the squadron's geodynes strain, a final liberation of energy somewhere in the heart of the alien structure shakes it with a last, agonizing earthquake.

The end is an implosion—a collapse of the ship's structure into a central pit of antimatter fire. The energy released is awesome, and for a few minutes, the alien craft radiates heat and light like a new star.

The Legion barely wins free of the catastrophic end of its enemies. Behind them the radiance begins to fade, lacking the energy or mass to burn longer.

The war with the Ka'slaq is over.

Go to section 133.

— 144 —

No further information has arrived to help Ulnar make a decision. Having held the aliens at Baal, he is reluctant to leave the colony exposed. But as long as he stays, the rest of the sector is open to attack. Word of such attacks may be on its way even now.

Where will the squadron be best employed? Ulnar needs that answer if the Legion is to follow up the success at Baal. But the continued silence, the total disappearance of the alien invaders, has the ominous air of the calm before a Ka'slaq storm.

If Ulnar chooses to remain at Baal, go to section 149.

If the admiral orders the squadron to leave Baal, choose a destination and go to section 180.

— 145 —

With little time to organize the squadron in the face of the fast-closing Ka'slaq trap, Ulnar knows he has to act quickly. He studies the planning tank, weighing the possibilities as he strives to find the best way to buy time. He nods in satisfaction before swinging around to face the command console. One hand flicks on the Fleetcomm microphone even as the other taps in the first codes on the computer keyboard to call up the prepared plan he has selected.

"Flag to all ships," he says, continuing to peck at the keyboard. "Recon wing, establish destroyer screen and engage the enemy. All battlecruisers to assemble behind the destroyer screen and counterattack on my order."

The computer takes over. The monitor reads out the battle orders as they are transmitted to the other ships across the Fleetcomm channel. Green lights on his board flash as individual captains acknowledge his instructions. Ulnar turns back to the planning tank and watches the squadron reorganize according to his plan.

The destroyer screen may buy him time. Though they are

poorly matched against the alien cruisers, Ulnar hopes the destroyers will hold on while he studies the enemy attack and picks the right moment to mount a counterthrust of his own. The battlecruiser attack should temporarily turn the tide—*if* the destroyers can hold long enough . . . *if* the battle wing attack is perfectly timed. Too many ifs, perhaps, but the plan is still the squadron's best hope.

The battle is starting faster than most engagements. Ulnar doesn't have time to order a different formation or worry about his choice. The Ninth Squadron is committed.

To resolve the battle of Ulnar 118 using conventional combat, go to section 105.

If Ulnar decides to use Stealth mode during the actual battle, go to section 109.

— 146 —

It is an odd battle. The Ka'slaq flotilla drives straight forward, ignoring the Legion ships. Unless actually fired upon, the aliens pay no attention to Baal's defenders, and the cooperation they displayed in their attack on Endymion is conspicuously absence here. As Sammis, *Valiant*'s captain, comments at one point: the enemy ships are rushing toward the colony with the single-mindedness of a poorly trained animal.

Their strange behavior makes Ulnar's work easy. Concentrating on each portion of the enemy fleet in turn, the squadron makes short work of them. The men of the Legion find that the battle is easily won, at no real losses by the defenders.

When it is all over, though, Ulnar realizes that this victory may not be the turning point he was counting on. True, the Legion proved they could handle the Ka'slaq, and the men were elated with their success. But this was only one part of the Ka'slaq fleet; their force at Endymion was more than triple the flotilla the Legion just disposed of. And there was no sign of the planetoid; Ulnar is certain it's the key to the war.

Moreover, the alien behavior at Baal was disconcerting. They were ruthless, fearless, and utterly contemptuous of death. The Ka'slaq work together with awesome efficiency, or totally ignore

Section 147

one another in a berserk rush to their objective. Ulnar does not like the unexplained differences between the alien actions at Endymion and those at Baal. Why did they enter the latter battle so poorly coordinated? How can Ulnar duplicate these conditions again? Until Ulnar can answer these and other questions, he won't be able to share in the general euphoria over the outcome of the battle.

He has one lead, though. In the aftermath of the fighting, one of the battlecruisers came across the shattered hulk of a Ka'slaq cruiser drifting in interplanetary space. It had been blasted open by a grazing hit from a vortex gun, but was intact enough to yield useful information. It would take time to have the technical and scientific experts go over the wreck, but it might be worthwhile.

If Ulnar remains at Baal or takes the captured cruiser in tow, it will delay him six days to investigate it right away. If he adopts this course, go to section 104.

If Ulnar leaves the cruiser at Baal, go to section 169. He can have local experts look at it there and send their reports to his next destination. This saves time, but if anything goes wrong, Ulnar may lose any knowledge the ship contains.

In any event, raise the squadron's Morale value by 1 point.

— 147 —

With the alien fleet gone, the Ka'slaq ship is a viper with its fangs pulled. Ulnar feels safe in ordering the squadron to watch it, blocking any aggressive moves the survivors may try. It's up to the League Council to decide what to do with the monstrous vessel now that it seems unable or unwilling to continue hostilities.

But if Ulnar prefers to ignore the alien vessel, it shows no willingness to ignore him. Within an hour of the battle's end, haphazard ultrawave signals emanate from several parts of the ship. The messages are fuzzy and confused, with stilted language that almost certainly comes from a translation device. They purport to come from a faction of rebels on board, self-proclaimed slaves fighting against the tyranny of their masters.

They ask for aid from the Legion. If they don't get technical help, they say, their rebellion will destroy the huge ship, though they don't explain how. As they begin to give coordinates for a Legion landing, the signals suddenly go dead.

If Ulnar decides to bombard the alien vessel, go to section 143.

If Ulnar chooses to send troops on board the ship, go to section 114.

Should the admiral attempt to open negotiations, go to section 172.

If Ulnar does nothing in response to the message, go to section 163.

— 148 —

The Ka'slaq trap is beginning to close, leaving Ulnar little time to prepare the squadron against them. He scans the planning tank, weighing the possibilities and discarding impractical plans. Finally, he reaches a decision and turns from the tank to the the computer keyboard and the Fleetcomm microphone. He switches it on and moves his hands to the keyboard.

"Ninth Squadron, this is Flag," he tells them. "Battle wing, from phalanx and prepare to engage. Destroyers retire behind the battlecruiser screen. All destroyers will remain out of combat."

As he finishes, he stabs one last button to bring the computer into the Fleetcomm circuit. Then the machine takes over. Ulnar nods in satisfaction as the readout of vectors and positions scroll past on his monitor screen, as they appear on the bridges of all the other ships. Green lights on the console signal acknowledgments. The admiral's attention is back on the planning tank and the shifting lights that show the squadron taking up the positions he has ordered.

By holding back the destroyers, a sizable fraction of his strength, Ulnar is taking a calculated risk. But the light-armed destroyers are ill-matched against Ka'slaq cruisers; screened by

Section 149

the battlecruisers, they have a chance to escape and warn St. Germaine of the alien fleet if everything goes wrong.

Once the orders start going out, there is no way to change them. The squadron is committed, and the battle already getting under way before the battlecruiser screen is fully assembled.

To resolve the battle using conventional tactics, go to section 105.

If Ulnar chooses the unorthodox use of Stealth mode during the actual battle, go to section 109 instead.

— 149 —

With no new information to go on, Ulnar feels he must continue guarding the Baal colony from the threat of a renewed Ka'slaq thrust. Baal still seems a likely place for the aliens to seize before they continue deeper into the sector. If so, Ulnar plans to be ready to stop them again.

Add one day to the total time consumed in the adventure so far. Mark this on your scrap paper.

If the new total of time passed is less than or equal to forty-five days, and the last sign of the Ka'slaq was at Baal, go to section 127.

If the new total is forty-six days or more, go to Section 98.

If the Ka'slaq were not last at Baal, and the total time since the start of the adventure is forty-five days or less, turn to section 144.

— 150 —

With the alien trap closing fast, Ulnar has to act fast if he is to prepare the squadron to block the Ka'slaq thrust. Examining the planning tank, he quickly weighs the alternatives before making his final decision. Then he swings back to face the command console, stabbing savagely at the Fleetcomm microphone to switch it on.

"Flag to all ships," he says urgently. "Scatter and engage. All ships will disperse for combat. Do not await battle orders."

Ulnar swings back to watch the planning tank as the Legion ships begin to spread out in a cloud. By dispersing, more ships will have a chance to win free and the Ka'slaq will have to break up their own formation to deal with his maneuver. But it also means his ships are moving out of supporting distance to fight on their own.

Ulnar is tempted to change his mind, to call back the squadron and try to improvise some standard formation. But there isn't time for second thoughts now; this battle is developing much faster than most, and the Ka'slaq will soon be on top of the diffused squadron. The squadron is committed, and the next hour will settle things, one way or another.

To resolve the battle at Ulnar 118 using conventional space battle tactics, go to section 105.

If Ulnar chooses the more unorthodox use of Stealth mode during the fighting, go to section 109.

— 151 —

The alien ambush is well laid, and they have a large fleet available. But Ulnar doesn't allow their numbers to shake his determination. The Ka'slaq want a battle at Ulnar 118, and the admiral intends to give them one. On *his* terms, not theirs.

"Put me on Fleetcomm," he orders, his eyes on the holographic tactical display in the planning tank. Moments later, at

Section 152

the communications technician's signal, he switches on his microphone.

"All ships, this is Flag," he begins, speaking precisely and evenly. "We will attack the enemy. Prepare for battle, and stand by for formation and combat orders." Ulnar can imagine a few of his captains grinning as they hear his instructions; some of them have been impatient for a chance to fight the aliens.

There are at least 70 alien ships in the Ka'slaq fleet, most of them clustered to guard their huge planet-sized vessels. An attack at such odds is a risk, but Ulnar is ready to cast caution to the winds. The invaders will pay dearly for the damage they have caused.

If Ulnar orders the squadron to adopt a wedge formation, go to section 129.

If Ulnar orders his ships into a cone formation, go to section 132.

If Ulnar orders his destroyers to screen his heavy ships, go to section 145.

If Ulnar orders the squadron to disperse and fight without a coherent formation, go to section 150.

If Ulnar orders the Legion ships into cylinder formation, turn to section 142.

— 152 —

Although nothing has turned up to support Ulnar's original suspicions, he is reluctant to leave the star system. This is a good place to mount an attack on St. Germaine, and the admiral is convinced that the Ka'slaq will appear eventually. He plans to be here when they do.

Add one day to the total time consumed in the adventure thus far. Note the new total.

If the new total is less than thirty days and no worlds have fallen to the invaders, go to section 22. If a world has fallen already, roll two dice; a result of 2 or 3 requires a turn to section 167. Otherwise go to section 108.

If the new total is between thirty-one and fifty days and only one world has been reported as attacked, go to section 48. If two worlds have fallen, roll two dice and add the number of days that have passed since day thirty-one. If the result is 12 or more, go to section 168. Otherwise go to section 108.

If the new total is fifty-one days or more, go to section 98.

— 153 —

Ulnar's hand reaches out to the Fleetcomm microphone switch.

"Flag calling all ships," he says. "Form standard wedge. Proceed at full speed against the enemy. Make the large enemy vessel in their rear your final target."

He sweeps his fingers over the flag computer keyboard and nods approvingly as the monitor screen lights up with the scrolling readout of his chosen vector and position orders. As the other ships begin acknowledging their compliance, Ulnar swivels to watch the planning tank. The squadron, closing on the almost stationary Ka'slaq reserve at maximum speed, is also beginning to shift formation to assemble the wedge. Like a knife blade, the ships of the Legion prepare to thrust into the heart of the alien position.

Larno's tiny force used a wedge at Endymion, trying like Ulnar to reach that planet-sized vessel shielded by the Ka'slaq reserve. The wedge is a good formation for penetrating an enemy battle line; it concentrates firepower and focuses a squadron's whole strength at a single vital point. But, as Larno had discovered, a wedge is easy to surround and annihilate when the enemy has superior numbers. Ulnar hopes his force will be strong enough to avoid Larno's fate.

As usual, it seems to take forever to approach the enemy fleet. Ulnar's success or failure here can spell the difference between triumph or disaster in the war against the Ka'slaq. For Merros, fighting against overwhelming odds; for St. Germaine and its

Section 154

helpless population; for the very survival of the Star League and humanity itself, the burden rests squarely on David Ulnar's shoulders as the clash of fleets begins.

To resolve a conventional battle, go to section 161.

If Ulnar uses Stealth mode in the actual battle, go to section 173.

— 154 —

In the end, duty is something Ulnar is unable to reject, not after a lifetime in the service of the Legion. The squadron has been ordered to wait in reserve at St. Germaine, and that is precisely what Ulnar plans to do.

Combat is joined along the fringe of the St. Germaine system. The Ka'slaq have more ships than expected—nearly two hundred in all. Either an alien reserve was hidden inside their huge mother ship, or they were capable of manufacturing and crewing new vessels as needed. Even the losses they suffered against Legion ships in previous encounters doesn't seem to have affected them.

Reports take several minutes to travel back from the battle lines. Ulnar can't help now; Merros has seen to that. All the Ninth can do is listen to the messages that cross the system and try, from the meager information these can give them, to piece together a full picture of what is happening.

The news isn't good. The situation deteriorates faster than anyone predicted. Ka'slaq cruisers swarm around the outnumbered ships of the Legion, using their annihilator beams to carve up the battle line faster than Merros can order his beleaguered fleet to regroup against their brilliantly executed strikes. Suddenly Merros isn't coordinating anything any more; the battleship *Pax* and all hands aboard are lost after receiving the devastating fire of ten Ka'slaq cruisers in a perfectly timed combination.

With the loss of *Pax*, command in the St. Germaine system falls to Ulnar once again, but he cannot control a battle seventeen minutes (or three hours, by ship) away. Local commanders attempt to salvage what they can, but the loss of their proud flagship hastens the inevitable collapse of the Legion defense. In

Section 155

the rout that follows, a few ships shift to Stealth mode and escape, but most go down fighting. A few sacrific themselves by ramming enemy cruisers.

Ulnar is left in charge of the Ninth Defense Squadron, facing overwhelming numbers, with the sector capital at his back and the fate of the Star League in his hands. He knows the battle is lost. There is no hope now, nothing to cling to. All that is left to him is the choice of how he meets the final disaster.

Subtract 3 points from the squadron's Morale value.

If Ulnar wishes to fight the alien fleet, go to section 177.

If Ulnar wants to withdraw from St. Germaine, roll two dice and compare the result to the Stealth value of the squadron. If the result is less than or equal to this value, go to section 178. If the result is greater than the Stealth value, go to section 177 instead.

— 155 —

Ulnar takes his time pondering the decision. Making his choice, the admiral reaches out to tap the switch that turns on the Fleetcomm microphone.

"All ships, this is Flag calling," he says. "Form cone and increase speed to maximum. Englobe the enemy ships and maintain attack until further notice."

His fingers dart across the Flag computer keyboard. In seconds the monitor screen lights up to show the scrolling readout of his chosen vector and position orders. Nodding approvingly as the other ships begin acknowledging the instructions, he swivels back to watch the planning tank. The Ka'slaq reserves are almost stationery, while the Ninth Defense Squadron presses toward them at maximum speed. The Legion ships begin to shift their formation into the open-mouthed cone called for by Ulnar's commands.

Cones are intended to allow a fleet to surround an enemy force. Against superior numbers in a well-managed phalanx, it is a risky proposition at best, but a carefully selected plan that Ulnar hopes will disorganize the Ka'slaq. In striving to avoid being encompassed, a defending fleet often scatters too far and

Section 156

leaves an opening for the attacker. If this happens here, it will help offset the Ka'slaq superiority.

If it fails, Ulnar may end up shattering his own fleet instead.

As always, the minutes drag out into hours, but the squadron closes the gap steadily. This battle is the crucial one, the fight that will end it all one way or another. If Ulnar loses, so will Merros; St. Germaine will fall and the route to the inner worlds will be open. The Star League might never recover. But if Ulnar wins and helps Merros hold on, they might just end the Ka'slaq threat for all time.

To resolve the battle using conventional tactics, go to section 161.

If Ulnar uses Stealth mode in the actual battle, go to section 173.

— 156 —

The alien ambush is well laid, and they have a large fleet available. But the bulk of their cruisers seem to be grouped to defend their planet-sized consort, well away from the scene of their attack. If the Ka'slaq are concerned enough about security to hold back some of their strength, it may be possible to face them in manageable groups—perhaps to defeat them.

"Put me on Fleetcomm," Ulner orders, studying the holographic tactical display in the planning tank. In moments the communications technician signals him, and the admiral leans forward to switch on his microphone.

"All ships, this is Flag," he begins. "Prepare for battle. We will adopt a defensive stance and let them come to us. Stand by for formation and combat orders." There would be a few captains who would rather attack than stand back and defend themselves, but Ulnar was sure the prospect of a good fight would be enough for most of them.

There are at least seventy Ka'slaq ships out there, but with luck, most of them will hold back for awhile. If they don't, they will make short work of the Ninth Squadron. But it is a calculated risk Ulnar is willing to take as long as there is a chance at winning today.

If Ulnar orders the squadron to adopt a globe formation, go to section 134.

If Ulnar instructs his ships to adopt a cylinder formation, go to section 146.

If Ulnar orders his destroyers to screen the battlecruisers, go to section 145.

If the admiral orders the squadron's destroyers to retire behind a screen of Legion battlecruisers, go to section 148.

If Ulnar orders the squadron to disperse and fight without a coherent formation, go to section 150.

— 157 —

Ulnar considers all the options carefully before he finally reaches for the switch that turns on the Fleetcomm microphone.

"Ninth Squadron, this is Flag," he begins. "Recon wing, form destroyer screen and move forward to engage the enemy. Battle wing, form on *Valiant* and attack on my signal."

As he speaks, his fingers move deftly across the Flag computer keyboard. The monitor screen comes to life to show the scrolling readout of vector and position orders that match his plan. Ulnar gives an approving nod as ships begin to send acknowledgments. He swings his seat back to watch the planning tank. The Ka'slaq reserves wait, almost stationary, while the Ninth Squadron drives toward them at maximum speed. Without pause the Legion ships begin to shift their formation, the battlecruisers dropping behind a loose wall of destroyers.

The destroyers will be outmatched, of course, but their job is not to win the battle. The Recon wing's job is to force the enemy to engage, to throw in reserves, to become thoroughly committed before the battlecruisers launch an attack that, properly timed, may settle the battle. The risks that go with the formation center around how long the destroyers can hold. If the screen collapses too early or if Ulnar doesn't time the battle wing's attack perfectly, the squadron will be in very bad shape indeed.

Section 158

As always, the minutes pass very slowly. The squadron closes the gap steadily. Ulnar is staking everything on this gambler's throw; if he wins here, it will give Merros the opening to beat the main Ka'slaq fleet. But if the squadron is defeated, Merros, St. Germaine, the Star League itself will be in a hopeless position.

To resolve the battle using conventional tactics, go to section 161.

If Ulnar uses Stealth mode in the actual battle, go to section 173.

— 158 —

With most of the Ka'slaq fleet concentrated against Merros, the Ninth Defense Squadron is faced by alien ships held back as a reserve to protect the immense mother ship. Although this reserve still outnumbers his force by a fair margin, Ulnar is happy enough with the odds. As long as the main Legion fleet holds out, his ships have a fighting chance. And his knowledge of enemy weaknesses gives the humans an edge in this final confrontation.

So the crucial battle is joined, the darting Ka'slaq cruisers working their way into the Legion battle line only to be met by determined, heroic human opposition. Ulnar is fighting not only the aliens, but the clock; Merros cannot hold out forever. As the hard-fought battle proceeds, it becomes clear that the Legion is gaining the upper hand. One after another the alien ships vanish, consumed by the atomic suns of vortex guns.

Finally, the weary survivors of the Ninth Squadron realize no more cruisers are left to challenge them. The Ka'slaq reserve has been defeated, although ultrawave traffic makes it clear that fighting continues between the two main fleets. Exultant messages from the Legion battle line also make it clear that the aliens are trying to break off and retreat, but Merros and his captains are hounding their opponents and maintaining the pressure. Victory is within mankind's grasp.

Ahead of Ulnar's battered squadron looms the Ka'slaq mother ship. It is thousands of miles across and all gleaming metal, soaring towers, angles, planes, domes, and projections totally alien to the human eye. It has not fired once during the whole battle. It seems unwilling or unable to defend itself, and moves too slowly to run. It is enigmatic but still vaguely threatening, with room inside for a hundred more battle fleets bigger and better-armed than the one now falling before the admiral's attacks.

Ulnar leans forward over his command console, calling up a computer projection and analysis of the alien structure on his monitor. The Ka'slaq fleet is no longer an immediate concern, but now he must follow through on the victory he has won and deal with this last bastion of alien power.

If Ulnar orders his squadron to bombard the Ka'slaq mother ship, go to section 143.

If he orders boarding parties to secure the alien structure, go to section 114.

If Ulnar endeavors to open communications with the Ka'slaq leadership, go to section 172.

If Ulnar does nothing, waiting for Admiral Merros to assume responsibility for the mother ship, go to section 147.

— 159 —

Confident of victory, Admiral Merros assembles a fleet around St. Germaine to stop the relentless Ka'slaq advance. His is the largest collection of warships ever gathered under the command of a single officer wearing the green uniform of the Legion of Space. Although Merros believes his force more than capable of dealing with the invaders, they, too, have increased the size of their fleet. When they meet near the edge of the St. Germaine system, the Ka'slaq have vastly superior numbers. Merros draws little useful intelligence from Ulnar's reports and suggestions, so the Legion's defenders can do nothing in response to the alien advantages of coordination and tactical precision.

If Merros thinks of Ulnar at all, it is with scorn. His greatest regret is the waste of a fine fighting squadron under the incompetent command of a man unworthy of the Legion. By ignoring Ulnar's last reports and suggestions, Merros seals the doom of his fleet. When the battle is finally joined, the superb Ka'slaq fleet cuts through the Legion defenses with barely a pause. Merros himself dies on board his flagship, the great battleship *Pax*. In the wake of his death, his squadrons break and scatter and the Ka'slaq emerge triumphant.

Proceed to section 29.

— 160 —

Ulnar makes his choice. He reaches again for the switch that controls the Fleetcomm microphone.

"Flag to Ninth Defense Squadron," he says. "All ships, scatter and fight dispersed. Repeat, all ships will disperse for combat. Do not await battle orders."

In effect, Ulnar is handing the battle to the squadron's captains to fight. Some might call it a renunciation of authority or accuse him of moral cowardice. But Ulnar knows his is a good squadron, unruly sometimes, but capable, experienced, and dedicated. The men understand what this battle means to the Legion and the Star League, and will fight all the harder for being given some independence.

The Ka'slaq, whose success seems to depend so heavily upon coordination and central control, might have more trouble handling a scattered enemy fighting according to the dictates of individual initiative instead of stilted formations and centralized command. So Ulnar is hoping as he turns his gaze down into the planning tank, where the ships of the squadron are moving apart like an expanding cloud as they continue to plunge at maximum speed toward the enemy reserves.

By dispersing, Ulnar guarantees that none of the ships will be in a position to support each other, which may cost lives later. But an unorthodox approach seems most likely to yield results. This battle is crucial; the survival of Merros's Legion fleet, of St. Germaine, of the whole League could depend on a victory in the next hour or two.

The minutes tick by, and the squadron closes steadily on

Section 161

the almost stationary Ka'slaq reserves. Whether heading toward victory or defeat, the men of the Legion of Space are ready to fight.

To resolve the battle using conventional tactics, go to section 161.

If Ulnar uses Stealth mode during fighting, go to section 173.

— 161 —

The Ninth Defense Squadron drives forward at full speed, aiming straight at the alien mother ship. But between the Legion ships and their target lie the Ka'slaq cruisers, sleek and deadly. Ulnar hears Sammis give the order to open fire; the ship shudders perceptibly as the vortex gun unleashes the first ball of atomic fire into the heart of the alien fleet. The eerie light of Ka'slaq annihilator beams lance out in return, and the climactic battle is under way.

The map shows the basic situation at St. Germaine, although it plays no direct role in the formulation of battle tactics.

Resolution of combat varies according to the formation adopted by the Legion, as described in the sections that follow.

Wedge: *The Legion destroyers attack on the first combat round, using Chart C. Thereafter, they may not attack again as long as there are battlecruisers available, although combat losses can always be taken from either wing. After the first round, battlecruisers fire on all subsequent rounds on Chart B.*

The Ka'slaq begin with 25 cruisers. They attack each round on Chart A. Keep a record of total Ka'slaq casualties suffered over the course of the battle; at the end of each round, if a roll of two dice is less than or equal to the accumulated number of Ka'slaq casualties, an additional 17 cruisers are added to the Ka'slaq force. After this second group appears, no more Ka'slaq reinforcements are available, so losses need not be tracked further or appearance die rolls made.

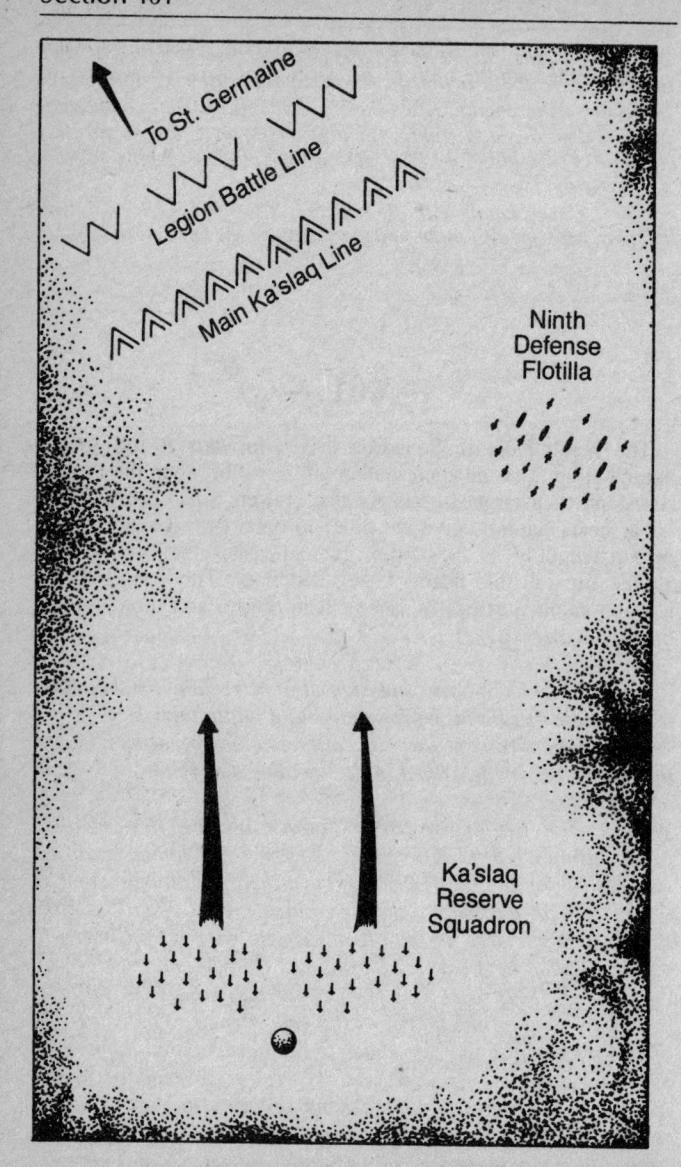

Section 161

To St. Germaine

Legion Battle Line

Main Ka'slaq Line

Ninth Defense Flotilla

Ka'slaq Reserve Squadron

Section 161

Cone: *Roll one die. The Legion battlecruisers fight for this number of rounds, firing on Chart C and suffering any losses inflicted by the enemy. After these rounds have been completed, roll another die and fight with destroyers on Chart C for this number of rounds. Continue alternating in this fashion for the entire battle.*

The Ka'slaq begin with 30 cruisers. They fire each round on Chart A. Keep a record of total Ka'slaq casualties accumulated over the course of the battle; at the end of each round, if a roll of two dice is less than or equal to the total number of alien ships lost, an additional 12 cruisers are added to the Ka'slaq force. After this group appears, no more Ka'slaq reinforcements are available, so losses need not be tracked further or appearance die rolls made.

Destroyer Screen: *Legion destroyers enter the fighting first, using Chart C and suffering all losses inflicted by the enemy. They continue to fight until the battle ends, the Ka'slaq eliminate all of the destroyers, or Ulnar launches a special attack with his battle wing.*

The battlecruisers can launch a special attack once during the battle, providing they have not fired already and there are still destroyers in the screen. The special attack allows two rolls on Chart A during the first round (only) of battlecruiser attacks. Thereafter, the battle wing continues to fight, firing once per subsequent round on Chart B. The same chart is used if the battlecruisers are drawn into the battle (through the loss of all the destroyers) before their attack can be launched. Surviving destroyers still in action when a special attack is launched can only fight again if all the battlecruisers are destroyed.

Throughout the entire action, the Ka'slaq fire once per round on Chart A. They begin with 20 cruisers. Keep a record of total Ka'slaq casualties suffered over the course of the battle; at the end of each round, if a roll of two dice is less than or equal to the accumulated number of alien ships lost, an additional 22 cruisers are added to the Ka'slaq force. After this second group appears, no more Ka'slaq reinforcements are available, so losses need not be tracked further or appearance die rolls made.

Dispersed: *Legion destroyers attack on the first round, firing on Chart C. Battlecruisers fire on Chart B on the next round, and the two wings continue to alternate fire thereafter (until all ships*

Section 161

in one wing are lost; then the survivors fire every round). Losses are taken from whichever wing fired in the current round.

The Ka'slaq begin with 30 ships. They fire on Chart B. Keep a record of total Ka'slaq losses accumulated over the course of the battle; at the end of each round, if a roll of two dice is less than or equal to the total number of cruisers lost, an additional 12 cruisers are added to the Ka'slaq force. After this group appears, no more alien reinforcements are available, so losses need not be tracked further or appearance die rolls made.

Resolve the battle according to the usual game rules, within the framework provided above. Track the total number of rounds of combat as they pass, as this can be of crucial importance.

Voluntary withdrawal from the battle is possible only if the squadron's morale permits it; the do-or-die traditions of the Legion and the crucial nature of the battle make the other captains unruly and difficult to control. At the end of a round Ulnar can retreat only if a two-die throw is less than or equal to the squadron's current Morale value. If the roll exceeds this value, no retreat is possible and the battle continues as before. To retreat, go to section 162.

However, after 30 combat rounds, the defeat of Admiral Merros releases over a hundred Ka'slaq ships from the main battle line. If this happens, go to Section 182.

If Ulnar's squadron fights until all Legion ships are destroyed, go to section 159.

If the Legion ships manage to eliminate all of the alien cruisers before the 30 rounds are fired, go to section 158. Note that this is the only way in which Ulnar can attack the Ka'slaq mother ship; it cannot be brought to battle until all the defending vessels have been wiped out.

Note that Ulnar is never required to retreat from the battle at St. Germaine.

— 162 —

The main strength of the Ka'slaq armada is committed against the Legion fleet; they outnumber Merros by a wide margin. But they have retained enough ships around the immense, planet-sized mother ship to guard it from a strike like Ulnar's. The fighting is furious; Ulnar's men fight like demons, but their opponents are no less determined and no less skilled in the arts of war. For a time it seems an even fight, but an even fight works in the long run against the Ninth Defense Squadron. In the distance the Ka'slaq are overwhelming Merros, and when they finish with his ships, Ulnar will be trapped and crushed. Meanwhile he watches ship after familiar ship vanish in the fury of matter-antimatter reactions.

The battle is a lost cause; Ulnar can see that. His squadron can fight and die, or it can pull out and perhaps, by remaining intact, pose some future threat to the Ka'slaq. At length, unable to keep watching his command being torn apart by the enemy, Ulnar gives the word to retreat.

The officers on *Valiant*'s bridge are horrified by his decision. It is only with the greatest reluctance that Sammis gives the orders to pull out of the battle, cloaked by Stealth mode and followed by equally reluctant crews in the other surviving ships.

Roll two dice and compare the result to the squadron's Stealth value.

If the result is less than or equal to this value, go to section 178.

If the result is greater than the Stealth value, return to the battle and continue resolving it as before.

— 163 —

They hear no more messages from the alien vessel; outwardly, it shows no sign of life or activity. But sensing instruments trained on the structure do detect trouble on board. Wildly varying fluctuations in environmental conditions, surges and sudden failures in power supplies, inexplicable bursts of ultrawave static . . . something has gone badly wrong aboard the vessel, and Ulnar grows increasingly disturbed as he remembers the message requesting technical assistance. Has he allowed caution to become paranoia, and thus condemned innocent lives as well as guilty ones to certain death?

His worst fears are confirmed from two sources almost simultaneously. First, the sensor readings prompt *Valiant*'s computer to begin issuing a warning. Instability in the alien ship's geodynes is reaching critically dangerous levels. If it progresses too far, the engines could twist space so violently around the vessel that it would surely be destroyed.

As he begins ordering the squadron to back away before catastrophe overtakes them all, a second confirmation comes in. This takes the form of an ultrawave message. No longer wavering or tentative, this message is a full-scale audio-visual transmission from the huge ship. Ulnar finds himself looking into the weirdly stalked eyes of a being that resembles a ten-limbed starfish. The translator it speaks through conveys nothing in the way of emotion, so that the being's words of upcoming Armageddon seem curiously detached and remote.

"Aliens," the being says, "my brethren have overthrown the masters, and we are slaves no longer. Their tyranny over us is at an end, and even though it means our own destruction, we have enjoyed the chance to die free. Had we done so sooner, much evil might have been averted by both our peoples."

It blinks, the eyes startlingly humanlike in a nightmare face. "The masters controlled everything here: our food and air and climate. So they controlled us for many generations. By destroying their brains, and the machines they controlled, we have unleashed powers our people cannot. With your help, perhaps . . . but we can understand your reluctance to trust us. My people have no regrets. We are free, now and forever. . . ." The

Section 163

Section 163

translated voice trails off. After a long pause, the alien continues. "We suggest you withdraw a great distance. Our antimatter power source is likely to liberate a sizable quantity of energy when the end comes.

"Aliens, our masters have wronged you, as they have wronged others. Our fate is just, for once they were like us."

The screen goes blank.

Every eye on the bridge is riveted on the teleperiscope displays. Seconds pass like hours, with no outward change in the alien ship. The squadron continues drawing away, accelerating outward to avoid the explosion that has become inevitable, unstoppable.

Then it happens. A series of flashes across the surface of the structure herald the final disaster; the unstable fields projected by the runaway geodynes are literally tearing the vessel apart. All at once the ship shudders and seems to collapse inward like a deflating balloon. With equal suddenness a blinding light consumes the collapsing structure and flares outward, a new star in the heavens burning with the power and fury of an antimatter chain reaction. It continues to expand, but by now the squadron is safe. Lack of sufficient mass and energy causes the reaction to falter, and it begins to fade almost immediately. But the Ka'slaq vessel will probably continue to burn for days more, until every particle of matter and antimatter has been consumed.

Ulnar repeats a childhood prayer in a faint whisper, saddened by the passing of the aliens who had bought their freedom by paying the highest price. Their spokesman had absolved him of guilt. It will take longer for David Ulnar to accept that absolution—or to forget the horrors he has witnessed on this ill-omened day.

Proceed to section 133.

— 164 —

By launching an attack as poorly planned and as ill-supported as the one he has ordered, Merros has made defeat inevitable. Ulnar can see no way of making a difference in the battle, and he fully expects the destruction of Merros and all his ships. Reports from the pickets indicate that the Ka'slaq are fielding their largest fleet ever, close to two hundred ships. Even the losses they have suffered in their previous encounters with the sector's defenders haven't had any permanent effect; the mother ship, as large as a small planet, either carries sizable reserve fleets or manufactures facilities on hand for just such an eventuality.

Against such an armada, even after they have closed with Merros, Ulnar's squadron has no hope of survival. And if they wait for the aliens to break through the battle line and crush Merros, it may well be too late to escape. To remain is to virtually guarantee the destruction of every man and ship in the Ninth Squadron.

Ulnar cannot face such an outcome. With no options but death on one hand and flight on the other, he decides that his duty now is to save what lives he can. As Merros moves into battle against the Ka'slaq, Ulnar begins issuing orders for the formation of a refugee fleet to take off as many of St. Germaine's inhabitants as possible. At the same time, he has the Ninth Defense Squadron ready to withdraw. There is no question of retreat against the orders of Admiral Merros—that kind of cowardly withdrawal wouldn't work with his ships and crews. But if and when Merros dies, command will again devolve on David Ulnar, and he doesn't intend to waste time trying to redeem a battle his superior lost before the fleet even left orbit.

When word of the battle reaches St. Germaine, it is much as Ulnar expected. Legion and Ka'slaq ships clashed in a conventional battle, and the aliens were able to outmaneuver Merros at every turn. *Pax* was destroyed early in the battle, and the rest of the battle line was quickly overwhelmed. A few lucky human vessels won free, shifting to Stealth mode to escape. But most were simply annihilated, knocked down like insects before the unstoppable Ka'slaq advance.

Ulnar's advance preparations pay off; within an hour of the destruction of the *Pax*, his squadron and its refugee charges are ready to move out. They lift out of orbit well ahead of the

Section 165

Ka'slaq armada's descent on St. Germaine. Without his initiative, they might well have been caught in orbit, still preparing to flee, and annihilated there. This way they have a chance of escape, a chance to regroup and try again to mount a campaign. It's a slender enough hope, but hope is all Ulnar and his men have left.

Reduce the Squadron's Morale by 3 points. Then go to section 178.

— 165 —

Captain Sammis is out of his chair, pacing back and forth behind the ultrawave and ultrapulse operators. "Set up generator feedback, maximum setting," he tells them, his voice deceptively soft. Their replies are almost inaudible to Ulnar, but Sammis nods approvingly as the technicians lean forward to comply with his orders. He pauses in his restless movement to bend over the communication board, studying a reading. When he straightens, he turns toward Ulnar. "Stealth mode established, Admiral," is his report.

Green lights on Ulnar's console are signaling the obedience of the rest of the squadron. One by one the other ships check in, until none remain. The Ninth Defense Squadron, cloaked by ultrafrequency jamming, begins to alter course in its attempt to elude the alien ambushers. The dimly lit bridge falls silent as everyone waits, wondering if the maneuver will be successful. Failure means battle, perhaps at even worse odds than before, if the attempt to escape scatters the squadron too much to allow it to regroup to defend itself. But the die is cast, and all anyone can do is wait and hope.

The aliens are spreading out in an unconventional search pattern. Their fleet has lost its cohesion; their maneuvers are disjointed, tentative, even chaotic. Ulnar watches with satisfaction; they aren't perfect after all. He knows how to use their weakness against them now. Time ticks by slowly, the Ka'slaq dropping farther astern.

"Losing contact," an ultrapulse operator announces. A cheer sweeps across the bridge but dies away as quickly as it started under the withering eye of the captain. He waits in silence until a second operator confirms the report; then he turns to the admiral.

"Stealth mode successful, sir," he says. "Out of contact."

"Thank you, Captain," Ulnar replies gravely, but his mind is already far away from *Valiant*'s bridge, grappling with the question of what to do next.

If the squadron is ordered to turn about and attack the force it has just eluded, go to section 151.

If Ulnar orders the withdrawal to continue as originally planned, go to section 174.

— 166 —

By every human rule of war, the battle in the Baal system is totally wrong from start to finish. The Ka'slaq flotilla drives straight forward, ignoring the Legion ships as if in contempt. In this odd conflict only those alien vessels actually brought into contact with the squadron pay attention to their opponents. It seems impossible that these are the same invaders who so impressed eyewitnesses at Endymion with their superb cooperation and coordination. Sammis, captain aboard *Valiant*, compares their strike toward Baal with a stampede of single-minded animals—or the tactical plans of a particularly stupid computer.

Ulnar's work should be easy because of their strange behavior, but the formation he has adopted proves just a little too inflexible to allow him to deal with all of the alien ships in time. Where the Legion fights, they win—but they don't have time to regroup after each victory and move on. Some of the Ka'slaq make it through to Baal despite everything the squadron can do. And before they can react, the aliens reduce Commandant Rovin's orbital complex to dust and begin to turn their weapons on Baal. Their annihilator beams play freely across the planet's surface, leveling cities and towns, and then it is over. The Ka'slaq leave as quickly as they had come, leaving Baal in ruins and the Legion squadron demoralized. What should have been an easy victory turned out to be a costly defeat. The largest colony in the sector is nearly extinguished, and there is no way of knowing where the enemy will strike next.

Section 167

And this flotilla had only been a fraction of the total Ka'slaq force; there was no sign of the full fleet or the giant ship seen at Endymion. Ulnar is certain that huge craft is an important element of the alien armada, and its absence is disquieting. So is the fact that the Ka'slaq are evidently as contemptuous of their own lives as they are of their opponents'; given their other advantages, that is yet another nail that might be driven into the Star League coffin any time.

Finally, there are the unanswered questions. Why the startling difference in performance and tactics between Endymion and Baal? Is there a way the Legion can force the aliens to fight that way again, but with suitable preparations to take advantage of enemy disorganization? And where is the next target to be?

Ulnar has one possible clue to the alien activities and behavior. In the aftermath of the fighting, one of the battlecruisers came across the shattered hulk of a Ka'slaq cruiser drifting in interplanetary space. Blasted open by a grazing hit from a vortex gun, it is still in good enough shape to yield useful information. It will take time to have the technical and scientific experts go over the wreck, but it might be worthwhile.

If Ulnar remains at Baal or takes the captured cruiser in tow, he can investigate it right away at a cost of up to six days' delay in reaching a new objective. Should he adopt this course, go to section 104.

If Ulnar decides to ignore the cruiser, go to section 137 instead.

In either case, reduce the squadron's Morale value by 1 point.

— 167 —

The ships remain in a solar orbit, unwilling to leave the system, but knowing full well that nothing awaits them on the lifeless planet. Abruptly, sensors pick up a minor disturbance: a single ship darting toward them. All scans directed toward it confirm one crucial fact: the ship is a Ka'slaq cruiser, alone and unsupported, but driving toward the Ninth Squadron. Looking for them? Scouting ahead of the alien fleet? Ulnar doesn't know, but he does know a good opportunity when he sees one.

His orders are brief and concise: attack. The alien vessel seems taken by surprise by the sudden onslaught, and though it puts up a furious fight, it does not destroy any of the Legion ships. Neither does it surrender, though Ulnar's communication technicians give it several opportunities to do so. Finally half a dozen hits shatter the cruiser's defenses and pierce the hull, and power readings on sensors fade abruptly. A Legion ship closes in slowly, ready for a trick, but there is no further sign of resistance, or of life. The Ka'slaq cruiser has been reduced to a shattered hulk, drifting in deep space.

Now Ulnar is left with a decision. He is eager to investigate the wreck; it might give the Legion more information on the aliens and their weaknesses. But such a close study of the hulk will take time, perhaps several days; even if he takes it in tow, it will slow the squadron down as they travel and make them easy prey to Ka'slaq pursuers. Knowledge versus speed . . . an old problem, and one the admiral must settle now, and quickly.

If Ulnar chooses to order an investigation of the wreck, go to section 104.

If the admiral decides to ignore the wreck and the squadron is currently at Baal, go to section 137.

If Ulnar ignores the wreck while the squadron is at Ulnar 118, go to section 139 instead.

— 168 —

Ulnar is in his cabin, eating a solitary meal and studying the latest messages from St. Germaine on his computer monitor, when the warning sirens sound. "General quarters, general quarters," the loudspeakers boom. "Hands to quarters, condition three. Captain Sammis to the bridge, please."

Flicking off the message readout, Ulnar thumbs the intercom switch. The monitor screen swirls briefly, the patterns coalescing into the face and shoulders of an officer who looks too young to be standing watch on a battlecruiser. "Bridge, Duty Officer Harro speaking," he says calmly enough.

"This is Admiral Ulnar. What's the situation?"

Section 169

The young man swallows. "Multiple targets reported at the extreme limit of our scanners, Admiral. Estimating fifty-plus units, including one the size of a moon or a small planet. We're also getting heavy static on all ultrafrequency channels. Reports confirmed by all ships, sir." He seems about to say more when an indistinct voice says something from out of camera range. Harro turns, then disappears from the screen.

Moments later the hawk features of Captain Sammis appear, a frown creasing his forehead. "Admiral," he says slowly, "I think you should get up to the bridge. We now have seventy-plus targets, some closing in from each flank. Looks like trouble."

"On my way," Ulnar replies, already out of his chair and halfway to the door before the monitor clears.

As he makes his way to the bridge, his mind is already turning over his options. His hunch was right; part of the enemy fleet, at least, had come to Ulnar 118. Now that they are here, it is up to him to deal with them. And from the captain's description, the Ka'slaq are closing the jaws of a trap around the squadron already. By the time he reaches *Valiant*'s control center and sits down at his command console, he knows what he must do.

If Ulnar orders his ships to attack the aliens, go to section 151.

If Ulnar orders the squadron to stand on the defensive, go to section 156.

If Ulnar decides to withdraw from Ulnar 118, go to section 170.

— 169 —

The wreck of the alien cruiser drops astern of the squadron as it accelerates away from the star. Ulnar must now begin to think of his next move. Should he continue to cover the colony against a possible second attack? Or have the Ka'slaq finished with Baal? If so, where will they strike next? It is the sort of dilemma that gives an admiral ulcers, and Ulnar has to give careful consideration to the question. His choices could help exploit a

Section 170

victory, or they could wipe out the success he has won and leave the squadron worse off than before.

If Ulnar decides to remain at Baal, go to section 144.

If Ulnar chooses to leave the Baal system, go to section 180.

— 170 —

There are too many of them, too many Ka'slaq cruisers concentrated on this ambush. Ulnar leans forward, his eyes fixed on the planning tank while his mind, a whirl of conflicting emotions, grapples with the decision he must make. The system is so close to St. Germaine that it is a perfect base to be used against the capital. If the squadron is destroyed here, nothing will stand against the aliens when they attack there. An intact fighting force might at least hold them until the base geofractors can bring in reinforcements from the inner worlds. Even if people like Merros call him a coward, Ulnar knows his duty is to get away with as many ships as he can, not cast everything away on a gesture of worthless heroism.

"Open Fleetcomm to my board," Ulnar orders sharply. He knows how his shipmates will take his orders, how the rest of the squadron will react, but he cannot afford to give in to personal feelings. At the technician's signal, he switches on his microphone and speaks again. "This is Flag," he says slowly. "The Ninth Squadron will withdraw. I say again, all ships will withdraw. Adopt Stealth mode, scatter, and pull out. Regroup at point 968 and await further orders."

Under the cloak of Stealth mode, his ships might elude this trap. Or so he hopes.

If the destroyers have been ambushed while the battlecruisers remained in reserve, roll two dice and compare the result to the squadron's Morale value. A result less than or equal to this value means that Ulnar is obeyed. The destroyers are wiped out, but the battlecruisers escape automatically. Go to section 174. When the result exceeds the Morale value, go to section 113.

Section 171

If the whole squadron was ambushed together, roll two dice and compare the result to their Stealth value. If the result is less than or equal to this value, go to section 165. A result greater than the Stealth value leads to section 175 instead.

— 171 —

With the liberation of the Ka'slaq mother ship, the invasion crisis is at an end. Ulnar and his Ninth Defense Squadron have played a pivotal role in the defense of the sector—and the entire Star League—from a threat that rivaled the evil of the Cometeers. Merros manages to grab most of the credit, at least publicly, but within the Legion Ulnar's role does not go unnoticed. His part draws the attention of officers whose opinions matter, and it doesn't take long for recognition, promotion, and other rewards to be granted to the man who stopped the Ka'slaq.

Most fulfilling of all is Ulnar's new assignment. The squadron receives a new commander—Sammis, freshly promoted to commodore, and given an admiral's responsibilities in recognition of his skill and valor—while Admiral David Ulnar becomes, for a time, a combination scientist and diplomat in his new post as Director of Liaison with the League embassy to the Ka'slaq planetoid. In this role he heads up the efforts to study Ka'slaq technology and help the former slaves now liberated from the tyranny of their masters.

It had been a near-run thing to save the alien vessel. The ruling class of Ka'slaq society, known as the masters or the Overmind, were disembodied brains connected directly to the controlling systems of their world-ship. When their slaves rebelled and began to destroy the cyborg beings, shipboard systems began running wild. Luckily the Legion boarding party had enough technical experts to bring the vessel back under control before catastrophe broke loose. Now the erstwhile slaves need training and advice to build a new society and a new control system to replace what is gone. The League, meanwhile, is interested in their technology.

Already there have been some amazing discoveries. The alien cyborg rulers, linked by ultrawave transmitters and able to share their thoughts mechanically, had achieved the beginnings of practical telepathy and were unlocking other powers of the mind;

it was their mental strength that had detected and neutralized the powers of AKKA. Their ability to harness antimatter as a power source gave them their superior weaponry, the engineering prowess to control a spacecraft the size of a small moon, and a method of stabilizing their craft against the power of the Legion's geofractors. Because they had direct control of every aspect of their ship, they could manipulate environment, gravity, and other essentials on board, so they maintained perfect dominance over their slaves. And their cruisers, operated by other cyborg entities, were capable of cooperation and coordination that seemed impossible, because they were able to pass information and orders back and forth with the speed of thought—and they were backed up by the strategic and tactical planning of a thousand massed minds. But with their ultrawave signals distorted, and in the absence of central direction from the mother ship, the Ka'slaq were much less effective.

The alien cyborgs ruled their society with ruthless efficiency. They needed a caste of living slaves to perform menial tasks that machines were unable to do, and to serve as a source for new brains to add to their cyborg hierarchy. But though their brains were organic, they had lost all emotion and compassion and were more like thinking machines than living computers.

League investigators were only slowly uncovering their history. Apparently the huge mother ship and its cyborg controllers were the products of an advanced civilization somewhere in the direction of Orion. Peaceful and unambitious, these creatures had never been concerned with the exploration of space until an instability developed in their sun. The ship was the end result of a crash program to build a refuge for the aliens, with cyborg controls to handle the vast complexities involved in running the huge vessel. They had set out generations ago with instructions to seek out a new world and perpetuate the race.

The cyborg controllers, though, failed to perform their duties as expected. The machine, not the living brain, dominated, and with typical machine efficiency the masters sought to carry out their instructions without regard to life or liberty. From running the ship, they soon moved to running the society; instructions to protect the refugees became a determination to extinguish any alien intelligence they encountered. Although they were dispassionate, they were also arrogant, until at last they were unable to contemplate any course but mass direction. Even in defeat they could not acknowledge another course.

Reading these findings as he waits for a courier ship to take him from St. Germaine to the refugee ship's new home in orbit around Ulnar 118, the admiral shakes his head sadly. So much death, so much devastation . . . but at least it is over now. And the Legion of Space is still there, to guard the Star League from any new threat that might someday appear from the depths of space.

Ulnar has achieved the highest possible success. But there were many options open in the war against the Ka'slaq. Could he do as well again by following a different strategy? To find out, go back to section 1 and try again. Good luck!

— 172 —

"Try to contact them," Ulnar says quietly, his eyes resting on the computer's graphic model of the huge Ka'slaq vessel. "Surely their leaders will listen to reason."

The ultrawave operator goes to work, running up and down the frequencies, repeating his call for the aliens to talk. Listening, Ulnar thinks of the ruthlessness the Ka'slaq have displayed. They do not negotiate . . . but the Legion won't stoop to their level. Let the invaders have a chance to speak for themselves, he tells himself silently. Negotiate.

The chance of getting a response seems slim, but suddenly there is a roar of static and feedback. It subsides into a deep, reverberating voice, the flat tones reminiscent of a computer [voder]. "We hear your words," the voice proclaims emotionlessly. "Cease your transmissions and withdraw from the presence of the Overmind."

Ulnar motions the technician to patch the transmitter to his board, then leans forward to speak into his microphone. "This is Vice-Admiral David Ulnar, commanding the Ninth Defense Squadron of the Legion of Space," he says confidently. "We have defeated your warships; your vessel is at our mercy. You are required to surrender to the authority of the Star League Council—"

The feedback whine rises again, until it drowns out all other sounds on the bridge. "The Overmind does not treat with lesser beings," the voice cuts in, arrogant and brassy. "We are the masters, and we shall allow no further communication. The

Overmind is done with you." Their transmission cuts off as suddenly as it began, and no amount of calling will make the aliens speak again.

Ulnar rubs his chin thoughtfully. The alien "Overmind" is either supremely arrogant or they have power in reserve to defend themselves. Their refusal to negotiate places the burden of action back in his lap. And if the Overmind does have hidden powers at their command, a false step now could undo everything the Legion has gained.

If Ulnar chooses to bombard the Ka'slaq vessel, go to section 143.

If the admiral decides to put a boarding party on the alien structure, go to section 114.

Should Ulnar choose to take no further action against the aliens, go to section 147.

— 173 —

As the Ninth Squadron drives forward at full speed, aiming directly at the alien mother ship, Ulnar's hand flicks on the Fleetcomm microphone one last time. "All ships, this is Flag," he begins, studying the planning tank. Between the squadron and its target are a phalanx of Ka'slaq cruisers, poised for battle with the humans who dare to challenge them. Now is the time for David Ulnar to use everything he has learned about the alien fleet; if ever the Legion needed a victory, it needs one now.

"All ships will adopt Stealth mode," Ulnar continues. "Repeating—Stealth mode, all ships. Let's see how they like fighting blind." He pauses again, then continues with forced enthusiasm. "The honor of the Legion depends on you all."

He hears Sammis giving the last orders for Stealth mode and to open fire. *Valiant* gives a perceptible shudder as her vortex gun unleashes the first ball of atomic fire into the heart of the alien fleet. The eerie light of Ka'slaq annihilator beams flash back in response, and the final battle is under way.

Section 173

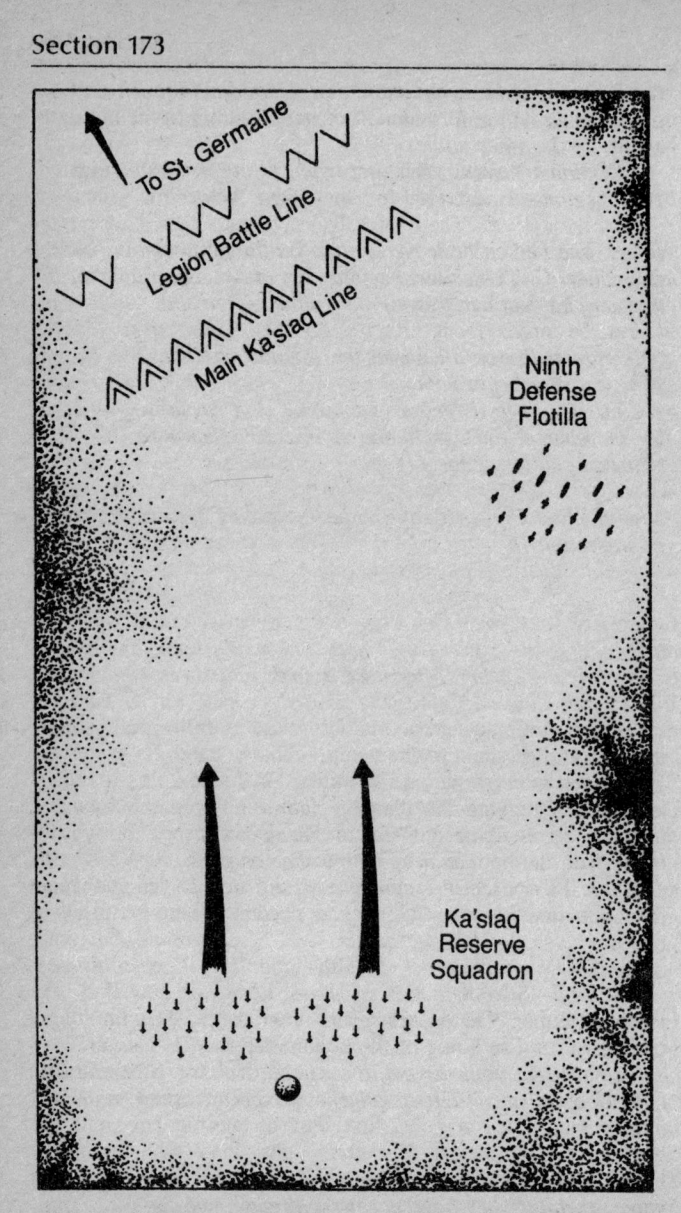

Section 173

Map 5 shows the basic situation at St. Germaine, though it plays no direct role in the formulation of battle tactics (as is the case in some of the other battles).

Resolution of combat varies according to the formation adopted by the Legion, as described in the sections that follow.

Wedge: *The Legion destroyers attack on the first combat round, using Chart C. Thereafter they may not attack again as long as there are battlecruisers available, although combat losses can always be taken from either wing. After the first round, battlecruisers fire on all subsequent rounds on Chart B.*

The Ka'slaq begin with 20 cruisers. They attack each round on Chart D. Keep a record of total Ka'slaq casualties suffered over the course of the battle; at the end of each round, if a roll of two dice is less than or equal to the accumulated number of Ka'slaq casualties, an additional 22 cruisers are added to the Ka'slaq force. After this second group appears, no more Ka'slaq reinforcements are available, so losses need not be tracked further or appearance die rolls made.

Cone: *Roll one die. The Legion battlecruisers fight for this number of rounds, firing on Chart C, and suffering any losses inflicted by the enemy. After these rounds have been completed, roll another die and fight using destroyers on Chart C for this number of combat rounds. Continue alternating in this fashion for the rest of the battle.*

The Ka'slaq begin with 25 cruisers. They fire each round on Chart D. Keep a record of total Ka'slaq losses accumulated over the course of the battle; at the end of each round, if a roll of two dice is less than or equal to the number of alien ships lost, an additional 17 cruisers are added to the Ka'slaq force. After this group appears, no more Ka'slaq reinforcements are available, so losses need not be tracked further or appearance die rolls made.

Destroyer Screen: *Legion destroyers enter the fighting first, using Chart C and suffering all losses inflicted by the enemy. They continue to fight until the battle ends, the Ka'slaq eliminate all of the destroyers, or Ulnar launches a special attack with his battle wing.*

The battlecruisers can launch a special attack once during the battle, providing they have not fired already and there are still

Section 173

destroyers in the screen. The special attack allows two rolls on Chart A during the first round (only) of battlecruiser attacks. Thereafter the battle wing continues to fight, firing once per subsequent round on Chart B. The same chart is used if the battlecruisers are drawn into the battle (through the loss of all the destroyers) before their attack can be launched. Surviving destroyers still in action when a special attack begins can only fight again if all the battlecruisers are destroyed.

Throughout the entire action the Ka'slaq fire once per round on Chart D. They begin with 15 cruisers. Keep a record of total Ka'slaq losses accumulated over the course of the battle; at the end of each round, if a roll of two dice is less than or equal to the number of alien ships lost since the battle began, an additional 27 cruisers are added to the Ka'slaq force. After this group appears, no more Ka'slaq reinforcements are available and there is no need to track losses further or make any other appearance die rolls.

Dispersed: *Legion destroyers attack on the first combat round, firing on Chart B. The battlecruisers fire on Chart A on the next round, and the two wings continue to alternate fire thereafter (until all ships in one wing are lost; then the survivors fire every round). Losses are taken from whichever wing fired in the current round.*

The Ka'slaq begin with 25 ships. They fire on Chart E. Keep a record of total Ka'slaq losses accumulated over the course of the battle; at the end of each round, if a roll of two dice is less than or equal to the total number of alien ships lost, an additional 17 cruisers are added to the Ka'slaq force. After this group appears, no more alien reinforcements are available, so losses need not be tracked further or appearance die rolls made.

Resolve the battle according to the game rules, within the framework provided above. Track the total number of rounds of combat as they pass, as this can be of crucial importance.

Voluntary withdrawal from the battle is possible only if the squadron's morale permits it; the do-or-die traditions of the Legion and the crucial nature of the battle make the squadron's captains unruly and difficult to control. At the end of a round Ulnar can retreat only if a two-die throw is less than or equal to the squadron's current Morale value. If the roll exceeds this value, no retreat is possible and the battle goes on as before. To retreat, go to section 162.

After 30 combat rounds the defeat of Admiral Merros releases over a hundred Ka'slaq ships from the main battle line. If this happens, go to section 182.

If Ulnar's squadron fights on until all Legion ships are destroyed, go to section 159.

If the Legion ships manage to eliminate all of the alien cruisers before 30 rounds are fired, go to section 158. This is the only way in which Ulnar can attack the Ka'slaq mother ship; it cannot be brought to battle until all the defending vessels have been wiped out.

Note that Ulnar is never required to retreat from the battle at St. Germaine.

— 174 —

Stealth mode is working; the squadron is eluding enemy pursuit. They have escaped from the ambush at Ulnar 118, but that still leaves the Ka'slaq fleet intact and in position to threaten the worlds of the Star League. In other words, the move to this system, the agony of decision and action—all were for naught. And the admiral is again faced with the problem of trying to cope with the aliens. Nothing seems to stop them, and Ulnar is growing as demoralized as everyone else in the squadron.

At least the battle here was not followed by the devastation of a League colony. But the next Ka'slaq advance will no doubt threaten an inhabited planet. All of Ulnar's decisions have gone astray so far; he cannot help but wonder now if he has any hope of changing his luck after all that has gone before. He has to turn it around; otherwise, the Legion and the Star League are surely doomed.

Reduce the squadron's Morale value by 1 point.

If Ulnar chooses to remain at Ulnar, go to section 103.

Section 175

If he decides to order the squadron to return to its base at St. Germaine, go to section 74.

If Ulnar instructs his ships to travel to S.C. 170, go to section 68.

If the admiral orders the squadron to go to the Baal system, go to section 58.

If Endymion is named as the squadron's next destination, go to section 53.

Should Admiral Ulnar issue orders to send the squadron to any other destination, go to section 73.

— 175 —

Captain Sammis is out of his chair, pacing back and forth behind the ultrawave and ultrapulse operators. "Set up generator feedback, maximum setting," he tells them, his voice deceptively soft and languid. Their replies are almost inaudible to Ulnar, but Sammis nods approvingly as the technicians lean forward to comply with his orders. He pauses in his restless movement to bend over the communications board, studying a reading. When he straightens, he turns toward Ulnar. "Stealth mode established, Admiral," is his report.

Green lights on Ulnar's console are signaling the obedience of the rest of the squadron. One by one the other ships check in, until none remain. The Ninth Defense Squadron, cloaked by ultrafrequency jamming, begins to alter course in its attempt to elude the alien ambushers. The dimly lit bridge falls silent as everyone waits, wondering if the maneuver will be successful. Failure means battle, at even worse odds than before if the escape attempt scatters the squadron too much to allow the ships to regroup and defend themselves. But the die is cast, and all anyone can do is wait and hope.

The aliens are spreading out, and not just to search for their fleeing quarry. Their fleet has lost much of its cohesion, although the disjointed maneuvers are still purposeful. Ulnar can see clearly, even before the ultrapulse operators verify it, that the squadron has not vanished from their scanners entirely. They are in pursuit, and their speed is still enough to catch the squadron fairly quickly.

He reaches quickly for the Fleetcomm microphone and the Flag computer keyboard. Battle orders have to be composed and issued at once, and without a preprogrammed computer file with a plan to cover the current deployments, Ulnar needs to improvise in haste. Even so, they could still be caught short without an effective formation.

Roll two dice and compare the result to the squadron's Stealth value. If the result is less than or equal to this value, go to section 156.

If the result exceeds the Stealth value, go to section 179 instead.

— 176 —

Ulnar barely hesitates. "Put me on Fleetcomm," he orders. There is a pause before the communications technician signals readiness. Then he switches on his microphone, thinking fast as he phrases his message. "Flag calling Ninth Defense Squadron," he begins. "Attention, all ships. Pursuant to discretionary orders given earlier this week by Admiral Merros, I am hereby activating the squadron for combat operations. Disregard previous battle orders and prepare to get under way."

He sees Sammis looking at him, a hint of a smile on his hawklike face. Probably most of the people listening to these words knew as well as Sammis that Merros had never issued "discretionary orders." But Ulnar was placing full responsibility squarely on his own shoulders and giving the rest of his officers an excuse for following him. He knew those men well enough to know how they felt about being left out of the action.

As expected, green lights on his console began to light up; the other captains are signaling their receipt of his message—and their compliance. It doesn't take long for every light that corresponded to one of his ships to glow green. The Ninth Squadron is ready to move.

"Take us out of orbit, Captain Sammis," Ulnar says formally. He begins keying instructions on the cruising order for the rest of

Section 176

the squadron while Sammis maneuvers *Valiant*. Soon the whole string of Legion ships still in orbit around St. Germaine boosts clear of the gravity well, their course an arc to take them out of the stellar ecliptic and in a wide arc that will avoid the main fleet and the lead elements of the Ka'slaq invasion armada. Ulnar knows that the only difference he can hope to make in this battle—particularly in view of the impossibility of coordinating with Merros—is to strike at the moon-sized mother ship, which the pickets have already reported behind the alien battle line.

"Command channel, Admiral," the communications tech reports.

Merros, calling to demand an explanation, Ulnar thinks. "Do not acknowledge or accept any signals on command channel, Mr. Dorlin. Not for the duration of this action, or until I order otherwise. Understood?"

The technician nods, but not without a nervous glance at his console. "Aye-aye, Admiral," he says. "No incoming messages on command channel." Ignoring an admiral's messages wasn't the best way to further a Legion career, but the unlucky Dorlin could always plead an even more immediate admiral's wrath to excuse himself at a court-martial, if it came to that. Ulnar smiled. "Relax, Mr. Dorlin. If we win this battle, *Valiant*'s crew will be too famous to charge with mutiny. And if we don't, neither you nor I are likely to care about what happens afterward."

The young technician gulps and nods nervously, turning back to his console.

"Strange way to encourage the men, Admiral," Sammis murmurs, stepping behind his chair.

"Everyone knows the score, Captain," Ulnar replies. "Let's go out and win some medals."

The flight into battle is far from quick; the squadron has a long way to go, by a curving, indirect route. Ulnar uses the time to run simulations of the coming action in the planning tank while Sammis prepares his ship for combat. The bridge crew is relieved so they can grab a meal and a few minutes to themselves, then relieved again to let their temporary replacements do the same. The ship's chaplain has the most to do. For the rest of the crew, once the ship is cleared for action, all they have to do is wait. Conditions on the other ships are the same.

The battle of St. Germaine is fought and refought a dozen times in Ulnar's planning tank as he seeks the perfect combination for success. The squadron monitors reports going to and fro among the main battle fleet; they learn a great deal about the

Section 176

tactical situation, even before they are close enough for a detailed analysis of their own. The Ka'slaq, despite losses suffered in previous engagements with human ships, now have a larger fleet than Larno reported from Endymion; at least 150 ships in their main fleet and forty-two more in reserve around the mother ship. Apparently they used the pause in their advance to replace losses and bring the fleet up to peak strength. Or perhaps they always had that number of ships, but held some back in the mother ship to have some extra strength ready for this crucial push.

With such a large fleet, the aliens can beat Merros easily—unless Ulnar is able to introduce an unexpected element into the equation. Every computer projection Ulnar runs agrees that a defensive battle would be worse than useless. If he is to have a prayer of taking the pressure off Merros, he will have to attack, drive through the enemy reserve, and threaten the mother ship. The computers have little advice to offer on the subject of how a handful of ships can threaten an artificial structure several hundred miles across, but Ulnar has a few ideas on that score himself.

So it is to be an attack. All Ulnar needs to do now is settle on the formation to use in driving that attack home. As the alien reserve grows close enough to scan in detail, Ulnar studies their phalanx formation carefully and runs through his options once more. When this battle begins, the Legion must be deployed in the best possible manner. Merros is already engaged, already taking heavy losses, and everything depends on what Ulnar does in these last few minutes before his ships plunge into the decisive battle of the war against the Ka'slaq.

If Ulnar decides to adopt a wedge formation, go to section 153.

If Ulnar chooses to order a cone formation, go to Section 155.

If Ulnar orders his destroyers to screen the battlecruisers, go to section 157.

If the admiral instructs his ships to scatter and fight dispersed, go to section 160.

— 177 —

As the Ka'slaq armada approaches, Ulnar has time to marshal his ships into a formation of sorts, ready to make a last stand on behalf of St. Germaine. His duty has led him into what he knows to be a final confrontation; he hopes the base on St. Germaine will use what time he can buy to put the geofractors to work to evacuate the population. When the Basilisk used the geofractor as his weapon against the Legion a century before, he rotated people and things from one point to another from a great distance and without sending or receiving stations. Though the technique was later declared unsafe, it was considerably safer for the people of St. Germaine than a Ka'slaq bombardment.

Ulnar sends his suggestions to the planetary authorities as the squadron prepares for action. They wait, knowing they face the end, but determined to the last to defend the proud traditions of the Legion of Space.

Then the Ka'slaq come, scores of cruisers closing in at high speed and in tight formation. The Ninth Defense Squadron stands fast against them, and their vortex guns take their toll against the aliens. But sheer weight of numbers is too much for them. One by one the Legion ships are blown apart by annihilator beams.

Valiant's death is a gallant one. The battlecruiser, hull scorched and pitted by near misses and scattered debris, rides serenely into the heart of the Ka'slaq fleet, the hellish fire of induced-antimatter explosions highlighting the name on her prow. She lashes out with her vortex gun; in return, she draws heavy fire from alien cruisers on every side. Her defensive fields glow as they absorb the energy of these powerful beams, but she is unable to radiate the energy off into space as quickly as it is poured against her. Finally, in a flare of light and intense radiation, the field fails.

Annihilator beams lick against her hull, setting up a matter-antimatter conversion wherever they touch. The coexistence of these opposites triggers a massive chain reaction that rips through the ship, the *Valiant* shudders under the impact as she is literally torn apart.

On the bridge the devastation comes quickly. Vice-Admiral David Ulnar is killed almost instantly at his station; as his body is caught in the full power of the explosion that destroys the entire forward end of the ship, his last thoughts are of honor, duty—and the glory of the Legion. Then he is gone.

Proceed to section 29.

— 178 —

The Ninth Defense Squadron is on the move again, accelerating outward from St. Germaine. Behind it the alien fleet is already closing on the sector capital, and everyone on board each ship knows what will happen now. Ulnar's decision to retreat has saved them from the holocaust . . . but to what purpose?

For Vice-Admiral David Ulnar, the hours spent boosting clear of the doomed system are the worst he has ever spent. Merros and his fleet are all lost; now St. Germaine and everyone left on the colony world will fall prey to the genocidal bombardment of the Ka'slaq armada. The geofractor complex worked to evacuate the populace as long as possible, but in the end the technicians in charge overloaded the power supplies and destroyed themselves and their machines to keep them out of Ka'slaq hands. The link with Earth was gone; Ulnar will receive no more reinforcements, and the squadron won't be traveling home any time soon. Someone else would have to be responsible for defending the inner worlds. David Ulnar had failed in his duty and was effectively out of the war.

Sitting on *Valiant*'s bridge, he is conscious of every eye, some stealing covert glances, others regarding him with open contempt. The great heroes of the Legion—John Star, Jay Kalam, Hal Samdu, even whining old Giles Habibula—would have stayed behind to triumph or die in defense of the Legion's honor. David Ulnar ran instead. What did he have to show for it? An intact squadron; against an enemy and without lines of supply or communications, it didn't count for much.

Vice-Admiral David Ulnar shakes his head sadly. They can't do much for the war effort now, but inwardly he vows that they will do everything they can to fight the invaders. He will harass them, attack them, keep fighting the alien Ka'slaq at every turn, until death catches up with him. Maybe that way, he tells

Section 179

himself, he can hope to redeem the Ulnar name and someday, somehow, win back the respect of these men whose contempt sears his soul more deeply than the Ka'slaq annihilators could burn a planet's surface.

Proceed to section 29.

— 179 —

"Alien ships still closing," an ultrapulse technician chants calmly. "Estimating contact in six minutes . . . mark."

Ulnar looks up from the Flag computer keyboard and scans the planning tank, absorbing the situation. There is no way his ships can assemble into a coherent formation in time, not even if he can get battle orders to them in the time remaining. Adapting a prepared program to unexpected conditions takes time, and he is nearly out. And the squadron, disorganized and demoralized, has virtually no chance of executing those orders anyway. If they were Ka'slaq cruisers, perfectly coordinated and able to make inhumanly tight maneuvers with hardly an effort, they could do it, but the Legion vessels are conned by humans, and humans have their limits.

Wiping the data on his monitor, Ulnar reaches for the Fleetcomm microphone switch once more. "All ships, this is Flag," he says resignedly. "Cancel previous orders. Prepare to engage the enemy. Ninth Squadron to scatter and fight the alien fleet dispersed." His left hand is moving across the keyboard, sending a computer confirmation of his verbal instructions, but already ships are beginning to acknowledge, and the yellow lights in the planning tank are slowly starting to draw apart.

Proceed to section 150.

— 180 —

Ulnar orders the squadron to get under way again, their course set for the world he believes to be endangered by the next Ka'slaq thrust. The ships of the Legion rise gracefully out of orbit around Baal, with messages wishing them good hunting and continued success. After their success at Baal, spirits are high. The Ninth Defense Squadron has turned the aliens back once. Now they set out to do it again.

Two days out from Baal, near the extreme limit at which ship-to-planet communications become virtually impossible to maintain, frantic messages begin to pour in from the colony. They are under attack; alien ships have appeared and renewed their assault on Baal. Garrison ships left behind were quickly overwhelmed and the planet itself is coming under bombardment. An hour after the first messages begin, they stop abruptly, but in the interim Ulnar has heard enough.

As before, there was only a small force of alien ships, with no sign of the moon-sized craft from Endymion. Once again their attack was mounted with singleminded determination and minimal attention to the defenders; only Commandant Rovin's orbital fortress was targeted for a major attack, while other ships were completely ignored unless they happened to get in the way of the invaders.

But there was one major parallel with the attack on Endymion: Baal was devastated without mercy and with a thoroughness that left not a single settlement intact. That was clear from the refugee reports picked up from ships fleeing the scene.

There is no chance of helping Baal now. The colony is gone, the Legion victory erased as if it had never been.

If Ulnar wants to turn the squadron around and return to Baal, add a total of four days (two out and two back) to the time consumed in the campaign and go to section 76.

If the ships are en route to St. Germaine, go to section 74.

If the squadron is traveling to Endymion, go to section 53.

Section 181

If they are on their way to S.C. 170, go to section 68.

If Ulnar's ships are heading for Ulnar 118, go to section 63.

If the admiral has ordered them to go to any other destination, go to Section 73.

— 181 —

Ulnar's eyes meet the Captain's in a level, challenging stare. "Don't be a fool, Sammis," he says softly. "Some other time, some other place, but not here and now. There are more than seventy ships out there. Do you honestly expect to beat them?"

"We intend to try," Sammis replies calmly. He seems more decisive now, and more determined. "You've had plenty of chances to outguess them, Admiral, and our record to date hasn't been very good. Withdrawing now will just give them another chance to slip away and attack a League planet. Now . . . what's your answer?"

"I don't intend to take orders from my own officers," Ulnar tells him coldly. "Whatever you do is on your head."

Sammis looks away. "I'm sorry it comes to this, then." He signals a guard at the hatch to the rear of the bridge. "Please leave your seat, sir. I am confining you to quarters for the duration."

"And afterward? If there is one?"

"We're ready to face charges, Admiral, if we're successful. Success counts heavily in these matters. If we fail . . . it isn't likely we'll be needing to justify ourselves. Not to temporal authority, at least."

In the face of the captain's determination—and Sammis plainly has the backing of the rest of the bridge crew, as well—there is no way Ulnar can fight them. He rises and allows the guard to escort him from the bridge. As the hatch closes behind him, he hears Sammis on the Fleetcomm net. "Sammis to all ships. The admiral is . . . indisposed, and I am taking authority as acting squadron commander. Prepare for battle. . . ."

Then Ulnar hears nothing more.

There is very little to do but wait. The mutineers cut off Ulnar's cabin computer terminal to prevent his interfering with them, so he waits in silence and darkness for the battle to begin. But even combat is hard to notice in his position. Now and then the ship is shaken by some external force, or the dimmed lights flicker under a power drain, but there is no measure by which the admiral can keep score. He has plenty of time, though, to reflect on the failures that brought them to this moment. If only the squadron had achieved something sooner! Frustrated at every turn, it was perhaps inevitable that the others would decide on a gambler's throw.

Perhaps, he tells himself bitterly, he should have bowed to their will. At least then he would be able to guide events, instead of lying on his bed and watching the blank overhead.

It is David Ulnar's last thought. The squadron, hopelessly outmatched and disorganized by mutiny and confusion, fights gallantly, but to no avail. As Ulnar is contemplating his mistakes, an annihilator beam penetrates *Valiant*'s defense fields and licks across the hull plating. The metal it touches is instantly transmuted to an antimatter state, and the juncture of matter and antimatter sets up a total, mutual annihilation that tears through the ship. The energy of the explosion consumes *Valiant* and everyone aboard her, and the flagship is gone. The other vessels of the Ninth Defense Squadron fare no better, and the Ka'slaq win the battle at Ulnar 118 with only the lightest losses. The defenses of the Star League stand open to the invaders.

Go to section 159.

— 182 —

As the battle rages, the Legion ships maintain their attack with determination and skill. Cruiser after Ka'slaq cruiser is engulfed in the atomic flames of Legion vortex guns, and although Ulnar's squadron suffers losses as well, it seems that victory is in their grasp.

Then a communications technician breaks the elation reigning on *Valiant*'s bridge. "*Pax* has been destroyed," he says somberly, looking up from the board where he has been monitoring the main battle. "The admiral is dead, and the rest of the fleet is breaking."

The words are hardly out before *Valiant*'s sensors pick up the

Section 182

approach of an overwhelming body of enemy ships. Released by the collapse of the main Legion fleet, the aliens converge on the Ninth Defense Squadron, just as they had done at Endymion when Larno advanced against the mother ship. There is no way Ulnar's weary crews and battle-scarred ships can win against so many.

If Ulnar decides to retreat, go to section 162. No Morale check is needed for this retreat, but neither is it required due to low morale.

If Ulnar orders the squadron to stand and fight despite the hopeless odds, go to section 177.

APPENDIX 1
TECHNOLOGY AND TACTICS OF THE LEGION OF SPACE

In the century that has passed since the retirement of Jay Kalam, the Legion's most famous commander, the forces of the Green Hall have adapted to a changing technology and the fast growth of the human sphere to remain Mankind's guardians. After the brief Social War, when Earth's colonies forced the Green Hall Council to reorganize into the Star League, the Legion fought no more wars but organized numerous minor police actions, and the dangers of exploration beyond the frontiers of the League kept them honed to the high standards of Kalam's day. They are the defenders and sentinels, the explorers, the elite who keep humanity safe and strong.

Technology

There was a time, following the Legion's clash with the Basilisk, when Dr. Max Eleroid's geofractor seemed likely to make conventional space travel obsolete. But the geofractor, which rotated objects and people across unimaginable interstellar distances in the blink of an eye, proved less safe than original estimates predicted. To be used as a practical means of transportation, it required both a sending and receiving complex; that meant that starships were still necessary. Along the frontiers geofractors were erected only slowly, so most trade and travel was limited to ships. The Legion established powerful frontier garrisons to handle the enforcement of law and order as well as the defense of the League's borders against any new race of Cometeers who might threaten man.

Ships: The bulk of the Legion's ships fall into two categories: destroyers and battlecruisers. Other vessels are available, from tiny couriers up to huge battleships, but most frontier garrisons rely on these two basic categories for virtually every Legion duty.

Fast destroyers are employed primarily for scouting. They are armed, but not heavily; their crews are small and their battle functions limited. Destroyers double as exploratory vessels. They are almost always grouped into a reconnaissance wing when serving with a squadron or fleet. Opinions differ on the best tactical uses of destroyers, but many officers point to the Social War, when colonial destroyers were able to defeat small battlecruiser wings in three different crucial battles, as proof that destroyers can indeed stand in a squadron's battle line.

Battlecruisers are larger, better-armed warships. In addition to their superior weaponry these vessels carry large contingents of trained Legion ground troops for the suppression of colonial disturbances. Employment outside League frontiers is rare. In combat the battlecruiser is considered the workhorse in the line of battle. A strong battle wing is maintained in every frontier sector, along with a central reserve in the inner worlds.

Engines: Legion ships still use the geodyne principles that first took man to the stars, though long since upgraded, and improved several times. The geodynes generate a local distortion in the space-time continuum in which normal physical laws simply do not apply. The Einsteinian light-speed barrier and the accepted principle of inertia cease to apply within the bounds of the geodyne fields, allowing ships to attain speeds and accelerations previously thought impossible. Indeed, in theory a geodyne could develop a hole in the fabric of space allowing instantaneous movement from one place to another—the basic concept of the geofractor—but limits of power, size, and safety keep the ships that use these drives to finite speeds.

Weaponry: Standard weaponry for all Legion ships, regardless of size or type, is the vortex gun first used by the Medusae in their unsuccessful invasion of the Solar system. Each ship mounts a single gun with a fixed-forward firing arc. The difference between a destroyer and a battlecruiser is strictly one of available power, not the number or type of guns used.

The vortex gun fires a ball of pure atomic energy at geodyne-induced speeds; thus, these miniature suns actually move faster than light-speed. Their range and destructive radius varies with the power of the ship firing the weapon. At whatever range is designated on opening fire, the fireball drops into normal space to create a nuclear explosion of incredible power.

Communications and Tracking: Ultrawaves, with faster-than-light speeds, are the basis for interstellar communications and a form of "space radar" called "ultrapulse tracking." Ultrawave physics was crucial to the discovery of the geodyne and the geofractor. Ultrawaves travel outside of our universe entirely, but can be heterodyned and used for a variety of purposes. They are limited to a finite speed, but an ultrawave message moves roughly ten times as fast as a ship under geodyne drive. They are easily transmitted from one planet to another, or across relatively short distances to or from ships. Across interstellar distances, ultrawave communication with a moving ship is problematical, at best.

Ultrapulse tracking detects disturbances created by physical objects in our own universe in the ultraspace where these waves propagate. The effect is very much like radar or sonar. Geodyne-powered ships cast a distinctive ultrapulse image in the other universe, which allows a fairly accurate reading of size, power fluctuations, and movement a competent computer can translate into a coherent picture of the ship in question.

Ultraspace is relatively free from distortion or static. However, it is possible to create a sort of ultrawave jamming by throwing out extremely powerful ultrawave and ultrapulse signals. Invented by a particularly successful colonial commodore during the Social War, this jamming, called "Stealth mode," confuses a computer's interpretation of ultrapulse readings. Under the right circumstances Stealth mode can so confuse a tracking system as to allow ships to elude their opponents entirely. The enemy knows something is out there but cannot fix size, position, or course with any accuracy except at very close range.

Command and Control: Squadron coordination is handled by a senior Legion officer, a commodore or an admiral. Each flagship is fitted out with squadron command facilities, including a special station on the ship's bridge. This console is adjacent to a holographic planning tank, a pit several meters in diameter in which computer projections translate current scanner data into a three-dimensional, multicolored display showing ship positions and various other bits of vital information needed to plan tactics.

The other major modification aboard a flagship is the addition of a "flag computer," a computer complex devoted entirely to the squadron commander's planning and coordination needs. The flag computer controls the tank and can be used to set up complex simulations. Battle orders creating a variety of tactical formations out of the ships available can be prepared and stored in the flag computer. In battle the admiral uses the computer and his fleet communications ultrawave network to transmit orders to the rest of the squadron. Some officers use computers to the exclusion of verbal orders, but no one is foolish enough to attempt to lead a squadron into combat without some kind of computer coordination.

Tactics

The Legion has evolved a number of specific tactical formations, each with its own strengths and weaknesses in battle. These are briefly described below.

Wedge: This is a formation used to attack an enemy, particularly an opponent with superior numbers. Destroyers (if any are present) form up at the leading edge of an arrow-shaped mass; the battlecruisers form behind them. In battle the wedge thrusts against a portion of the enemy force. After some initial firing, the destroyers drop back to work with their heavier consorts, but their offensive role is negligible. A wedge formation is considered ideal when the enemy has formed a battlecruiser or destroyer screen.

Cone: This is also an offensive formation, especially when the opponent has inferior numbers or widely scattered clusters of ships. Destroyers are not essential, but when they are available, they form the open mouth of the cone, while the battlecruisers form the tapering end. With its slight edge in speed, the recon wing attempts to engulf the enemy force while the battlecruisers keep it occupied. Once the globe is closed, the surrounded enemy is subjected to fire from all sides. A cone is considered best against an enemy globe, wedge, or cylinder.

Globe: A defensive formation, the globe is favored by those tacticians who regard destroyers as unsuited to battle operations. The battlecruisers take up a spherical formation while the destroyers wait inside the globe, out of harm's way. A globe is a good formation for a small force to adopt while under attack by a large opposing fleet. Only the battlecruisers fight.

Cylinder: The cylinder is a fairly recent defensive innovation, first proposed after the Social War. It is an adaptation of the globe, in which the battlecruisers form into an oblate spheroid with destroyers concentrated at each end. In theory the destroyers focus more firepower in their smaller area of coverage, making them as capable in battle as the more powerful battlecruisers. It is considered a poor compromise by most tradition-minded officers; it is more easily disrupted than a globe, but in a situation where every ship counts, a cylinder brings destroyer firepower into battle. A cylinder cannot be formed without destroyers.

Destroyer Screen: The most ambitious use of destroyers in a battle formation, the destroyer screen can be used either offensively or defensively. A destroyer screen deploys the recon wing in a loose, convex wall in the forefront of the battle. The light ships fight throughout the first phase of the battle. At a well-timed moment, a wedge of battlecruisers attacks through the screen and carries the battle from that point. This attack, which takes advantage of enemy weaknesses and distractions, is often decisive—if the destroyers hold long enough. The destroyer screen does poorly against a wedge but is a fairly effective formation in other situations.

Heavy Screen: Also called a "battle phalanx," the heavy screen is primarily defensive in nature, at least in Legion use. A wall of battlecruisers interposes itself between the enemy and his target, forcing combat over a broad front. No destroyers are used. As in a globe, any light ships present are relegated to the rear. The phalanx is particularly effective against an enemy cone, since it is hard to surround, but is vulnerable to a well-handled wedge.

Dispersed Operations: At once the oldest and the newest tactical form, this particular evolution has been suggested as a useful mode in a recent treatise by an unorthodox naval theoretician. Basically it calls for ships to scatter and fight on their own, stressing individual initiative over tight command control. The theory is that, offensively or defensively, a dispersed squadron will disrupt the enemy's formation; it is assumed that the enemy was not expecting to fight this way and will have trouble reacting to it. This formation is sometimes forced on a fleet if it is caught scattered, as after an unsuccessful retreat.

Destroyers can be used in dispersed combat, but they are not necessary. Most Legion commanders frown on the formation as overly unconventional, but several colonial successes in the Social War followed from such a scattered battle mode.

Stealth Mode in Battle: Another highly unorthodox tactic recently suggested for use in space combat involves the use of ultrawave Stealth mode jamming. This isn't a formation, but rather a ruse used in conjunction with any other formation. Basically, all ships in the squadron adopt Stealth mode as they go into combat, which distorts ultrapulse scanning and tracking systems and may interfere with ultrawave communications.

The drawback to this new tactic is that the jamming also interferes with friendly operations. In a tight formation, distorted tracking can lead to accidental fire on friendly ships, so Stealth mode reduces the effectiveness of most formations (except Dispersion). Many Legion officers are reluctant to use this extremely unorthodox mode of combat except when it seems obvious that disruption of an enemy will be more severe than the interference with friendly operations.

APPENDIX 1

TRAVEL TIME CHART

From ... \ To ...	St. Germaine	Ulnar 118	Derron's World	Baal	Trinidad	MacBeth	Thule	Endymion	Lochinvar	S.C. 170
St. Germaine	0	6	13	11	17	24	22	18	18	26
Ulnar 118	6	0	10	7	11	18	15	12	16	20
Derron's World	13	10	0	16	8	15	15	18	25	20
Baal	11	7	16	0	14	20	15	8	9	18
Trinidad	17	11	8	14	0	7	6	12	22	12
MacBeth	24	18	15	20	7	0	6	15	26	10
Thule	22	15	15	15	6	6	0	9	21	6
Endymion	18	12	18	8	12	15	9	0	12	10
Lochinvar	18	16	25	9	22	26	21	12	0	21
S.C. 170	26	20	20	18	12	10	6	10	21	0

APPENDIX 1

SHIP GAME STATISTICS

Legion battlecruisers
Manpower: 1 each
Ordnance: 6
Strength: 6
Stealth: 7
Morale: 9
[Melee: 8]

Legion destroyers
Manpower: 1 each
Ordnance: 3
Strength: 3
Stealth: 7
Morale: 9
[Melee: 4]

Legion orbital fort
Manpower: 1 each
Ordnance: 9
Strength: 9
Stealth: 0
Morale: 9
[Melee: 10]

Ka'slaq cruisers
Manpower: 1 each
Ordnance: 7
Strength: 8
Stealth: 8
Morale: 12
[Melee: 0]

Ka'slaq mother ship
Manpower: 1
Ordnance: 0
Strength: 0
Stealth: 4
Morale: 12
[Melee: 0]

APPENDIX 2
Legion Combat Formations

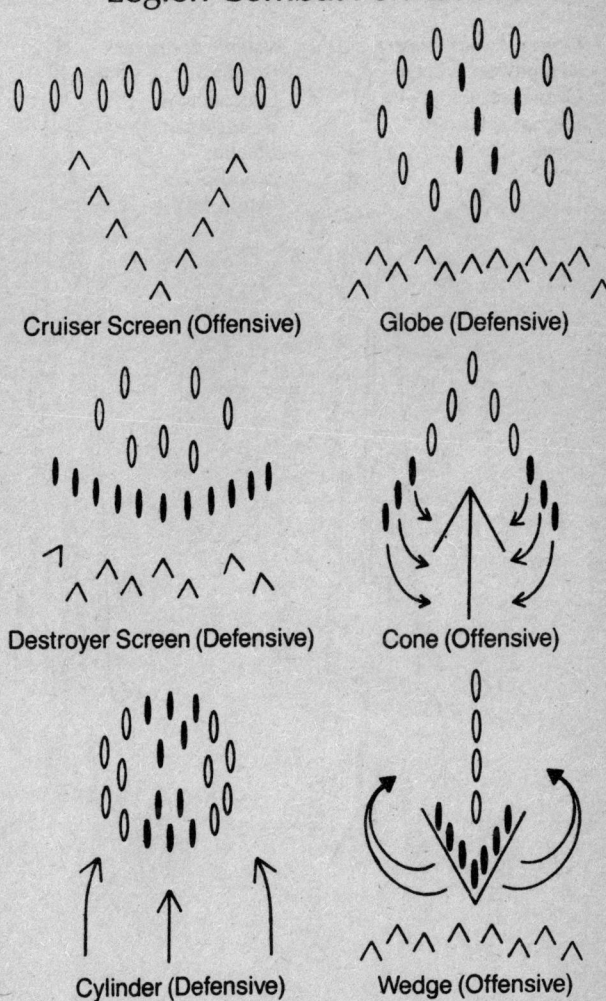

Cruiser Screen (Offensive)

Globe (Defensive)

Destroyer Screen (Defensive)

Cone (Offensive)

Cylinder (Defensive)

Wedge (Offensive)

◦ Battle Cruiser   ● Destroyer

APPENDIX 1

Legion Recon Ship

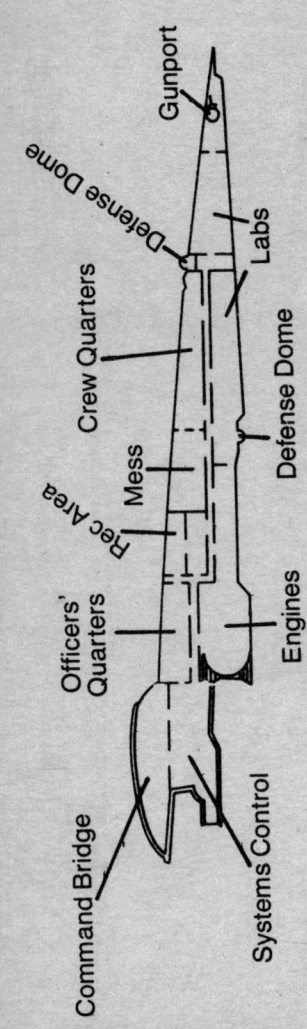

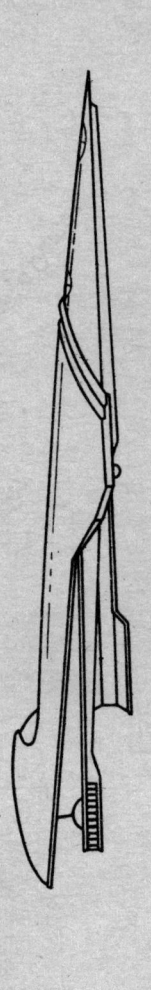

- Command Bridge
- Systems Control
- Officers' Quarters
- Rec Area
- Mess
- Crew Quarters
- Defense Dome
- Labs
- Defense Dome
- Gunport
- Engines

Appendix 1

Legion Battle Cruiser

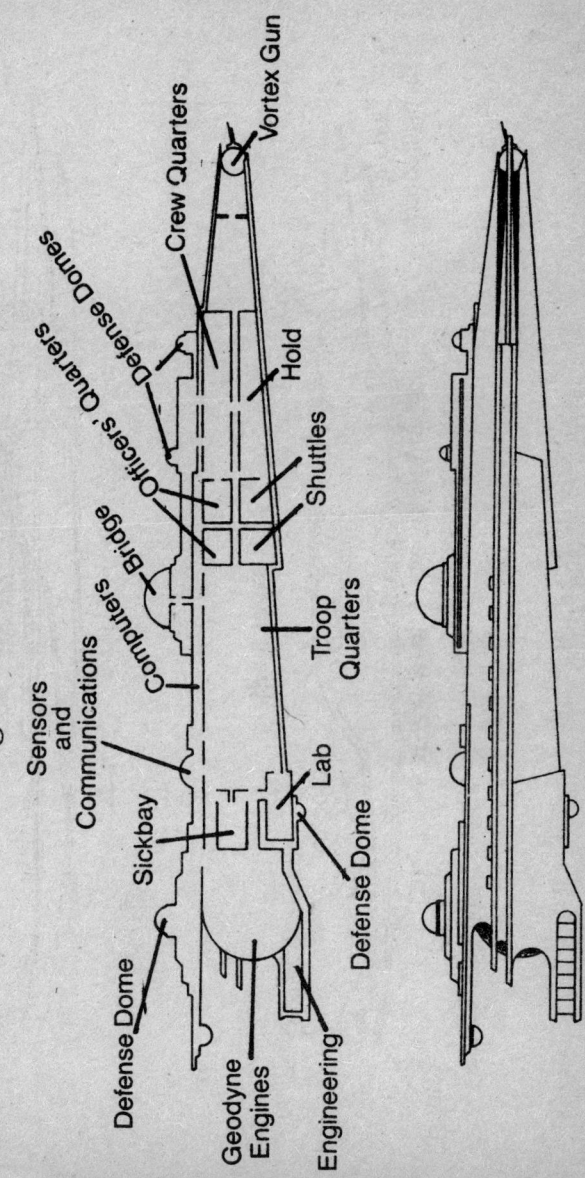

- Vortex Gun
- Crew Quarters
- Hold
- Defense Domes
- Officers' Quarters
- Shuttles
- Bridge
- Computers
- Troop Quarters
- Sensors and Communications
- Sickbay
- Lab
- Defense Dome
- Defense Dome
- Geodyne Engines
- Engineering

Ka'slaq Cruiser

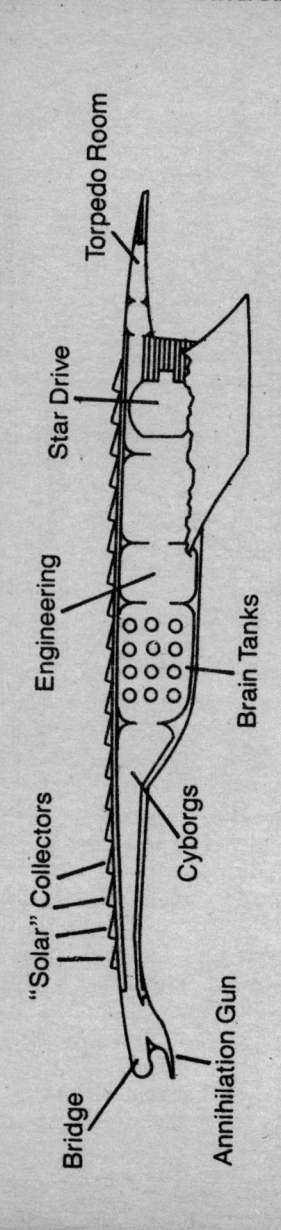

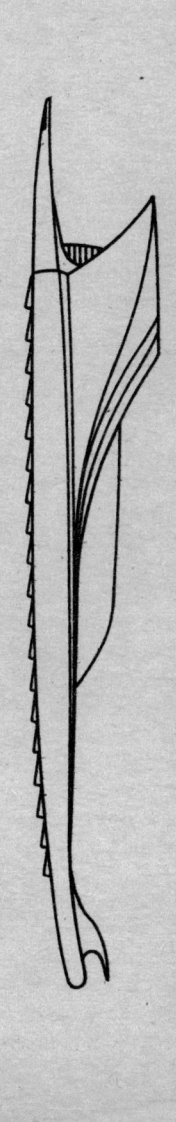

- Bridge
- "Solar" Collectors
- Annihilation Gun
- Cyborgs
- Engineering
- Brain Tanks
- Star Drive
- Torpedo Room